W9-BKP-626

The Iremonger Trilogy

LUNGDON

IREMONGER
BOOK 3

LUNGDON

written and illustrated by
EDWARD CAREY

The Overlook Press
New York, NY

This edition first published in hardcover in the United States in 2015 by
The Overlook Press, Peter Mayer Publishers, Inc.
141 Wooster Street
New York, NY 10012
www.overlookpress.com

For bulk and special sales, please contact sales@overlookny.com,
or write us at the above address.

Cataloging-in-Publication Data is available from the Library of Congress.

Printed in the United States of America
ISBN 978-1-4683-0955-3
1 3 5 7 9 8 6 4 2

For Matilda

This common seat of cruelty, this dirty city, this earth of stone, this sty of men, this un-Eden, un-paradise, this fortress built by men to kill men with infection and foul deed, this unhappy populace, this little people, this stone of coal set in a suffocating stench, this cursed plot, this city, this slum, this Lungdon.

Oylum Iremonger, 1825

To look down upon the whole of London as the birds of the air look down upon it, and see it dwindled to a mere rubbish heap.

Henry Mayhew, 1852

I like the spirit of this great London which I feel around me. Who but a coward would pass his whole life in hamlets; and for ever abandon his faculties to the eating rust of obscurity?

Charlotte Brontë, 1853

London is on the whole the most possible form of life.

Henry James, 1909

CURTAIN UP

I Saw a Little Woman

Statement of a London Photographic Man, 31st January 1876

There is evil come to my city.

I saw it yesterday morning. I took a picture of it. And here it is.

I'm often perched at my balcony in Onslow Square. I like to take a picture of my surroundings, of the people who live here, of general London life. Commonly the people are something of a blur when I take them down in pictures, because people will keep moving. In truth – in so many ways – I prefer the taking down of objects than people, so much more reliable you might say – but people, oh people they are always moving, so that when I take them with my machine and commit them to a plate, oftentimes they appear foggy, like a ghost of themselves. Well then, that's to explain my picture somewhat, when I saw the evil.

It was morning, I do swear it – there was sunlight, weak but present. More than enough for me to see clear. I had my apparatus up and ready on its tripod and all was primed. I was about to take a picture of the square before me, only I became distracted by a loud clacking noise, coming nearer and gaining in volume. It was, I ascertained after a time of listening, the noise of feet, of hard shoes clacking upon the cobbles, making a terrible din. The smacking noise came, as I say, ever closer, and then at last comes into view the source of the perturbation. It was a woman, an uncommonly small woman, not a child though, certainly a woman, and this little woman wore tough black boots and was otherwise quite attired in black and she marched like she had a purpose into the square and stood by the railing somewhere between the pavement and the garden, all business and determination. She was dressed, as I say, all in black and she was little, as I also say – undersized, strangely so, like there was something quite wrong about her from the start. She looked about her briskly.

And then did I see it.

The evil, I say.

The woman put her head back. Her jaw seemed to snap right open in a most unnatural way, so that the little woman's mouth was stretched uncommonly wide. Her jaw it clicked open like the jaw of some strange creature, and there was the sound of a great snap that echoed around the square. Then, you see, I had all about me and let my camera fire, there was a burst of phosphorescence as I let my camera use its eye and take it all down. And though the picture is a little blurred you can still see it, I say, especially when the pertinent part is blown up after developing. The awful truth. For then, oh then, from the wide-open mouth of this little woman in her sharp boots, came from somewhere deep in her throat a blackness, a great blackness, more and more blackness. A darkness, like a strange small weather grown out of a single human, getting bigger and bigger, like Aladdin's djinn out of the lamp. Soon the whole square was dark as night, and all further streets quite blackened with it.

Soon I could not even see my hands in front of my face.

Soon all was so thorough and complete dark.

Like every candle in all the world had been put out of a sudden.

Then I heard her again, the boots, the sharp boots, the click and the clack of her walking, of her feet hitting the cobbles and she was going further and further away. And all the darkness was left behind.

But I have this picture.

Of a little woman spewing out the night.

Of this evil come to my city.

Part One

Outside Looking In

Miss Eleanor Cranwell and a Music Stand

I

REPORT FROM A
BEDROOM WINDOW

From the Journal of Eleanor Cranwell,
aged thirteen, 23 Connaught Place,
London W

3rd February 1876

There has been no light. Not for days now. We all live in darkness and pretend it is the most natural thing.

I admit very readily that there were days before when no light ever broke through onto London, but this darkness has been longer, and it has been darker. The gas is lit on the street at all hours, but it fails to illuminate much of anything. The only way to see what is before you is to set a candle to it, and always you are aware of the thick darkness all around that wants to put it out. It has been like this ever since the new family moved into the house across the street.

No children play in the street, not since they came. And

even adults rush from the place as if they fear it terribly, as if the street itself is damned.

Well perhaps it is.

I think I'm the only one at the window these days, all the other glass up and down the street is shuttered up or the curtains have been drawn and remain so. It's as if the eyes of the street are closed, and no one else is watching.

But I'm watching. I'm watching that house. I shan't ever stop.

Our street, our Connaught Place, is not the grandest address by any means. The best perhaps that can be said about it is that beyond the thickness of our south walls lies the great expanse of Hyde Park and space and green, though the whole park has been covered in a thick black fog for some time now, and, so Nanny says, it is so dark that it is as if the world has ended at the Bayswater Road.

It has been so ever since they came. It is colder and harsher, the weather itself feels unkind, all the walls are frigid to the touch and they drip at times, so that much of the wallpaper through the house has grown blisters. And all of it, all of it, since they came.

It is a very secret family that arrived here on the night that Foulsham – the borough of rubbish – caught fire and was burnt to the ground. That fire was so fierce that it smoulders still. How many people were killed that night I do not know. It must have been so terrible to be there, but somehow the papers never talk of how many died. That was the night the family moved in, when a whole borough was wiped out and all that was left were ashes. Who mourns for them, I wonder?

I do not suppose that it is a coincidence that the family arrived that night of all nights.

No one ever comes out of the front door. I think they *must* leave sometimes but the place looks so shuttered up. Twice only, to my excitement, in the deep of night, I have seen a young man with something flashing on his chest like a medal and with a shining brass helmet on his head, rushing out of the servants' door on some business, and both times he was with a rather greasy fellow just behind him, as if that following person were not really a man at all but a shadow made somehow solid. I saw them only for the briefest of seconds when they came under the faint glow of the gas streetlamp. But when I tell Nanny or Mother, I am instructed to stop imagining things, to cease being so bothersome.

'There is no one in that house,' Mother tells me. 'It is quite boarded up as you see. The Carringtons have had it shut up while they remain in the country to recover from their sudden illness. We hope that they are feeling better.'

'There are people there, Mother, I've seen them.'

'Stop it, Eleanor, I haven't the time.'

It's always more dirty around that house than any of the others along Connaught Place. It never used to be like that. It's as if the dirt likes the house, as if it were somehow dirt's home. I wonder what it is like inside. I never minded overly much about it when the Carringtons lived there, but now I find myself wondering about it most particularly.

I have begun to think that it notices, this new night of ours. It is watching. In fact I am sure of it. It is not just that it is dark outside – this new darkness is a thick darkness, it's black clouds, it's gas, it's something alive. You must shoo it from a room.

I generally keep a pair of bellows with me when I'm at home, and I pump my bellows and I see the clouds of night marshalled and bullied by my bellows-wind. If I work the bellows hard, I can gather the night up and send it all into a corner where I see it writhe. I watch it panic. At last it rushes itself of a sudden out through a keyhole or under a door, or hides under my bed – then creeps out again to look over my shoulder when I'm sat at the window keeping my notes. Wherever it has been it leaves behind a slight stain. It darkens and discolours all.

I have begun to wonder if the night might actually report on me, on all of us. I do think little pieces of night rush back over the street and into the house there to tell tales. The night is surely thickest over there. And that house is darker than any other. It is there that the long night comes from, I'd swear to it. From there it gets everywhere. It's in our hair, on our skin; it's in our pockets and our thoughts; it's on the mantelpiece and behind the door. Before putting on shoes you must turn them upside down and beat the night out of them. If you do that, sure enough a little black cloud comes trickling out. Stamp on that cloud. Stamp on it quick.

We have all been breathing the night in.

It does things to people, the new night. I have noticed it in my family, in the people all about us. In my things, even. This is what I have seen. Here is my tally:

1. **Great Aunt Rowena** (Father's maiden aunt who lives around the corner from us in Connaught Square,

she who is the most wealthy of all our family, and who Mother is always encouraging me to be nice to, though really I need no encouragement). Great Aunt complains increasingly of a stiffness. She never was exactly a fluid person to begin with but now she insists that her stiffness is overcoming her and that she barely bends at all. I thought little enough of this when Great Aunt Rowena last invited me over to tea. She'd set all her dolls out for us to play with, but then – at her beckoning, in a quiet moment when we were alone together and Pritchett her maid had gone away to fetch some more biscuits – I did cautiously knock upon one of her legs. The sound was almost terrifying; it was just like wood. 'Oh, Aunt,' I cried. 'I'm as stiff as a post,' she said. 'Yes,' I said and, very earnestly, 'Oh yes you are indeed!'

2. **My school desk** in the school room, which always used to have four legs (as is most common with desks) now has five. I cannot say how it grew that other leg. Nanny says it has always been there but I know otherwise.

3. **Father's shaving brush**, which always had handsome soft bristles on one side of it, has started to grow dark, thick, spiky hairs along its handle.

4. **Uncle Randolph** (Mother's wayward brother – Father always refers to him in this way) is no longer engaged

to Olivia Finch (I never liked her much myself). She has gone from London and is believed to be on the Continent. Mother said she 'let him down terribly' but I think I know the true reason. Uncle Randolph has fallen in love with a milk jug, which he keeps with him always. I have seen him whispering to the milk jug when he thinks no one is there, I even heard him calling it 'My darling, my Liv-love,' which was the ridiculous name he had formerly reserved for Olivia.

6. **Mrs Glimsford** (our housekeeper) has become flat-footed and she never used to be.

7. **The brass fire extinguisher** in the cupboard on my landing is getting taller. It has grown four inches.

BUT MOST OF ALL:

8. I do believe **the music stand in my bedroom** was once a servant from next door.

Oh, the poor music stand. That first night when the secret family moved in, I sent Martha out to fetch the unhappy thing. Now I stop myself, I catch myself as I write all this down. I pause for breath, and I wonder –

Could that really have happened? A person become a music stand?

I look at the music stand standing here beside me and cannot quite believe it. I try very hard to remember that night. I saw them walking down the street, such a strange group of people, like a circus troop, but no colour to them, only greyness and grimness. And the worst of it all was the tall old man in the long black hat.

The servant went up to him, to warn him about the Carringtons' cholera and in return he took one look at her and at the flick of his fingers changed her from a person into . . . into an object, into this music stand. What a thing to happen! Oh! I stop again. And write this prayer.

I SO WANT IT ALL TO HAVE BEEN A DREAM. PLEASE MAY IT BE ONE. PLEASE GOD.

But I know it is not a dream.

I have inquired next door, at number 21, about the servant.
　　'Excuse me,' I said.
　　'Yes?' came the butler, a Mr Ogilvy I believe.
　　'You had a servant, she was a maid of some sort.'
　　'Yes?'
　　'Quite short, I believe, with rather full cheeks.'
　　'Do you mean Janey, Janey Cunliffe?'
　　'I suppose I do. May I see her please?'
　　'No you may not.'
　　'Is she not inside? Is she too busy with her duties perhaps?'
　　'What do you know of Janey Cunliffe, miss?'
　　'Nothing really, only I should like to talk to her.'
　　'Well and so should we, we have much to say to her in fact. Leaving her position with no warning. Sent out to do a small errand, and she never comes back. And some of the

silver missing too, and an ormolu clock, well, well, yes indeed we should very much like to speak to Miss Janey Cunliffe. Very much.'

And that was the end of our conversation.

I do actually feel it *is* the servant, this poor music stand, this poor Janey Cunliffe.

'Hello, dear,' I say to it. 'I hope to make you yourself once more. Truly I do. I have not forgotten you, Jane, even if everyone else has. (I shan't call you Janey, if you don't mind, it sounds too childish.)'

I put her on the windowsill so that she may look out.

Martha, the tweeny maid, fears to come near me since delivering the stand, as if I'm quite mad; she weeps a deal and says I'm mean to her. Even Nanny's been a little odd of late, she comes less and less and spends her time in her room with her gilt-edged calf-skinned Bible and won't go anywhere without it; she consults it, she whispers to it. (What a thing to wrap the Bible in, something's skin, when you think about it that doesn't seem right at all.) I don't have many companions, I have no siblings and I am schooled here at home, so the loss of Nanny does make rather a gap in my social calendar.

And all of this, all this strangeness, is on account of the new neighbours across the way. I wonder if it is just our household that suffers so, or if others are likewise inconvenienced.

A Weeping Hatstand

A Diseased Pair of Curtains With
the Remnants of a Pelmet

A Comforting Tin Compass

A Burst Box of Matches

A Sinking Boat, the Round Pond,
Kensington Gardens

Newly Obtained Objects,
the Foundling Hospital

2

LONDON GAZETTE I

Reports from around town

From a lady, Battersea
The hatstand in the hall has begun weeping. I thought at first
it was just the rain from the umbrellas and the hats and coats
and so had these removed and dried by the kitchen hearth.
But the stand still dripped even though there was nothing on
it. Awful puddle on the floor. I'd throw the thing out, except
it was a gift from Mummy.

From a chambermaid, Chelsea
I didn't think very much of it at first, but as it happened – the
change – over numerous nights, I did note it so particular. My
lady's pelmets have all turned black and stiff. All over the
house there is not a single pelmet that has not shrunken and
blackened and I cannot tell why. All the curtains tend that

way now, and have a terrible smell about them; the whole house stinks of ruined pelmets and curtains.

From a young woman, Leinster Square
And now no one can find him anywhere, there's no sign, no notion of where he has gone to. My dear, my dearest Cuthbert. He said he loved me. I do think he meant it. I so long for him to come back again, to hold my hand like he did last week. I take small solace in the little tin compass they found in his room at the club. It was jolly kind of them to let me have it as a keepsake. I do wonder where he is. Some say he always was a terrible leg puller, and some say he never could be steady, but others think something untoward has occurred and that he may be in awful trouble. If he'd but come to me I feel certain we could work it out between us.

If only there were sunlight again we might find some of what we have lost.

From a matchbox seller, Hackney
I don't know how it happened. But my matches, every box of them, come ruined in the night. I did hear some shifting going on in our room, but that's as often the case, there being five of us that perch here. But in the morning, I never should credit it. All them matches of mine, all them little boxes, what I earn my crust from. They've all, well, they've all gone and ruined on me. Seems the matches inside had growed in the night, and stretched and burst their boxes. And the other thing is them matches, they're soft now, what before was hard and wooden are now very white and I'd say flabby,

most soft to the touch. Sticky. How's a fellow to sell them? Who'd buy such things?

Park Keeper, Round Pond, Kensington Gardens
Many of the wooden yachts and lesser sailboats that the children are wont to push out on the water have grown strangely heavy and do sink.

The Foundling Hospital, Coram Fields
To date seven children have succumbed; it is generally the newly arrived. One is now a label marked GIN, one a penknife, one a baby's shoe, one a beating cane, one a sieve, one a doormat; two of them are pen nibs now. The rest of the children are most distressed and cease to play with the objects set aside for them, but rather sit now their hands in their laps regarding one another with the highest anxiety. Some cry. Some shout. All are put out. We have had some music performed by the children's choir, but it has done but little good.

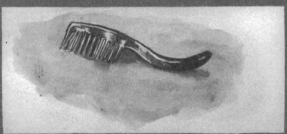

Eleanor Cranwell's Nanny:
Her Eyebrow Comb

3

OBSERVATIONS FROM A PERAMBULATION

From the diary of Eleanor Cranwell,
23 Connaught Place,
London W

4th February 1876

I went for my walk today. I must get out of the house, no matter how black it is outside. It felt so good to get out, and though the air was no clearer, there was certain relief to be away from Connaught Place. There are new bill stickers along the Edgware Road, and all the way up Oxford Street. This is what they say:

IMPORTANT NOTICE!!

ALL MUST READ!!!

IT IS A CRIME TO HARBOUR ANY PERSON FROM
THE EXTINGUISHED BOROUGH OF

FOULSHAM

ANYONE WHO IS FOUND CONCEALING ANY SUCH
PERSON SHALL BE SUBJECT TO THE SEVEREST
PENALTY OF THE LAW

ALL PEOPLE OF FOULSHAM/FORLICHINGHAM
MUST BE PLACED INTO QUARANTINE
IMMEDIATELY. ANY PERSON SEEING OR COMING
INTO CONTACT WITH ANY PERSON (ALIVE OR
DEAD) FROM THE FORLICHINGHAM/FOULSHAM
DISTRICT MUST

IMMEDIATELY REPORT TO THE CONSTABULARY

THERE IS TERRIBLE DANGER OF

CONTAGION

Further down the street I saw a bill posterer putting up
new notices:

KEEP ALL VISITS TO A MINIMUM

STAY AT HOME WHENEVER POSSIBLE

DO NOT TALK TO STRANGERS

WASH FREQUENTLY WITH CARBOLIC SOAP

KEEP YOUR DOORS LOCKED AND YOUR
WINDOWS FASTENED

THERE IS TERRIBLE DANGER OF

CONTAGION

There were so many new commands, so many do thises and do thats. And the streets so quiet now, and the constables so many. It was not long before one marched up to me. There was mud on his white trousers and his top hat was rather scuffed. He seemed very nervous.

'What are you doing, miss, what's your business?'

'Hullo, Officer, I am going for my walk.'

'Go home, child, it isn't safe.'

'I'm not a child, I'm thirteen.'

'Go home, go quick.'

'Why exactly isn't it safe?'

'People escaped.'

'What people, if I may inquire?'

'Dreadful bad people.'

'What do they look like?'

'Can't tell exactly. Bad people, people of Foulsham.'

'What's exactly bad about them?'

'They're diseased. Mustn't touch them, mustn't go near.'

'And what would happen should I come across such a person, and if I touched one, say?'

'It would be the undoing of you.'

'Oh! Really! How exactly might I come undone?'

'There is contagion, there most certainly is.'

'Tell me what they've done so wrong, these people, that they are hunted so.'

'They're vagrants, aren't they? Foreign filth. They're diseased sure enough, we need them off our streets. We must be certain of it.'

'What are you so afraid of?'

'Afraid? I'm not afraid of anything.'

'You sound like you are. What may happen to us?'

'Contagion. Worse than any cholera. We'll all be dirt and rubbish.'

'Shall we? Is it very likely?'

'Go home, girl, and stay home.'

But then I thought I should tell them, it wasn't right to keep it quiet.

'Excuse me, sir, I shouldn't like to get anyone in trouble. But I think the people you are talking of, I think they may be living in our street.'

'Oh yes?' he said. 'Just come upon this notion, have you?'

'I do think that's where you shall find them. The house they are in looks abandoned, though it is not. I saw one of them once. (Well, perhaps it was two, I couldn't swear to the second, he was so much in the shadow.) In the night, just for a moment. He wore a brass helmet.'

'Move along now, miss, move along.'

'Have they taken away the sunlight, these people? Are they the cause of it?'

'Go home, will you?'

'You do not believe me, do you?'

'No, miss, I do not. We are very busy and seek to help, please go to your home and to safety. Leave the streets to us; we shall find them in the end.'

'You're all frightened, aren't you?'

'Go home and keep clear of any rubbish. Don't go poking your nose in where it's not wanted, you may just get it bitten off. There's been people drowned dead in rubbish, falling in and coming up no more.'

'Another rumour?'

'No,' he said, and there was a sudden sadness in his voice. 'This I've seen myself.'

I went back then, but not directly.

I saw more policemen further down the Bayswater Road. They'd gotten hold of some poor tramp and were taking the fellow away. I wonder if he'd done anything wrong other than being a tramp. That would do it around here. Lowering the tone, they call it. These poor shelterless people – for we that have homes to put ourselves in ignore those others that don't as if they were invisible, and the police move them on, and what happens to them then I wonder, what other miseries are waiting for them in streets darker even than ours?

There were children in the park again, that was a bit of a relief, as if there could at least be some normal life somewhere. Except they hadn't ventured far beyond the railings, as if they feared to go in too deep. I heard their game, their singing:

> *'Black as night*
> *Black as death*
> *You've a stinking in your breath*
> *Your father's got lost*
> *Your mother's gone dead*
> *Your sister's got spots*
> *All over her head*
> *Drop dead, drop dead, drop dead, drop dead*
> *The night's come up and the sun has fled*
> *There's a big fat rat at the foot of your bed.'*

They skipped along to this game, one around the other, and every now and then one must fall down and pretend to die in the most horrible convulsions. It did look fun. I waved at them but they were so preoccupied with their game they didn't notice me.

This morning Nanny left us. I say this morning, though of course and as usual there's no sign that it's day, other than the say-so of the clocks about the house, which keep telling us the day has come around again, though there's precious little evidence. Nanny gave no warning, she left no note. Just in the morning (we must say it is the morning, you know, or go mad) she never appeared. Her room was much the same as ever, even her few possessions were still there, but no Nanny. And, I nearly forgot, there was an eyebrow comb upon the floor, a wooden one I'd never seen before. I thought I knew all Nanny's things, I did like to snoop about them rather, and she'd ever been happy for me to look about, until recently that is, when she demanded more privacy. Yes, an eyebrow comb but no nanny. She'd gone. She'd deserted us.

'Well,' Mother said, 'she wasn't happy. I knew she wasn't happy. I wish she'd said. I wish she'd given us warning. She may at least have done that.'

'Shall we not see her again?' I asked.

'Did you say anything to her, Eleanor?' Mother asked me. 'Anything particular, that might have led to this?'

'Nothing Mother, I just told her of those people across the street and of their queer ways.'

'You frightened her away I suspect, Eleanor.'

'How could I have?'

'You're a very clever girl, Eleanor, cleverer than most. And that cleverness can show itself, on occasions, to have a little too much imagining inside it. Well, child, I do not scare easily. Perhaps we may say you're quite old enough now to go forward nanny-less.'

It is not my fault Nanny has gone, it is the fault of the dark and shy new people across the street. They've changed everything since they've come and I see that I shall personally have to do something about it. Nanny never believed me, Mother won't believe me, Father smiles but won't properly listen. So then I am on my own, a small army of one.

The fire extinguisher on my landing has grown another three inches. One of the servants must have moved it out of the cupboard, for it is just beside my bedroom door now. And

Ann Belmont who helps Cook in the kitchen said she saw a strange, ugly dog prowling around, large and wild, and she was certain she saw it enter the abandoned house across the street.

5th February 1876

Oh but what news I have today! I have seen another of the new neighbours! I have seen him twice, three times this day! A young man. He comes to a window on the third floor of the house, opens the curtains just a little bit and looks out. He has dark circles under his eyes and black hair brushed in a parting. (I used Mother's opera glasses to see him the better.) He was dressed in a nightshirt. Perhaps he is sick. I waved at him. Very cautiously, and just for the tiniest of moments, his fingers made a very small flicker, barely perceptible, but I know that he has seen me and knows that I am here.

He holds up a candle to me, I hold one up to him.

I wait for him. I've been waiting for him to wave again.

I haven't told anyone about him; I can't see what would be the point of it, they'd only say I was lying again. No, him I keep to myself.

The last time he came to the window I waved wildly at him. Then he was there so short a time and instantly rushed away and in his place appeared for a moment the top of the head of a strange squashed man, whose forehead and eyes only reached beyond the window level. They were very large, protuberant eyes he had and those eyes stared hard at me, and made me look away. When I looked back again, though I had glanced down only for the smallest moment, the curtains were closed. They have not been opened since. Nor has the young man ever reappeared.

I have vowed to go across the street and knock upon the door of the house. I know they're in there. I do know it and I shall prove it. I want to talk to the young man. Tonight I shall meet him, I shall meet them all, I shall walk over and knock hard upon their door and keep knocking until someone comes to answer it. Perhaps we shall come to know each other very well, and visit often. Whatever the outcome, I shall gain entry and walk around the rooms and see quite how many they're keeping in there. I think there must be hundreds of them, I really do. I'm going to wait until our house is quiet, then I shall slip out. I'm leaving this note so that if by any chance I do not come back then it shall be known where to look for me. If I'm not back I'll be over there, in that house across the street.

I'm going now.

Deep breath.

Here goes.

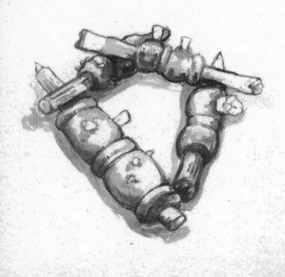

Unusable Cricket Bails

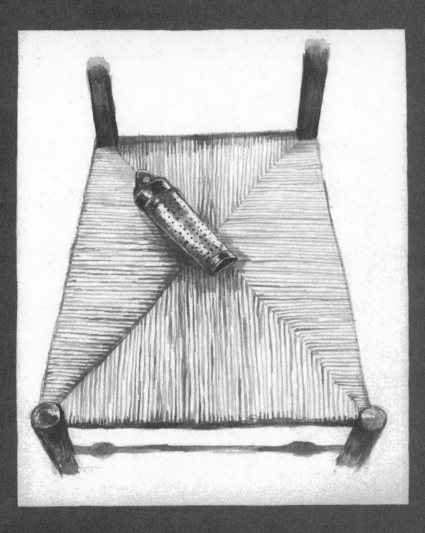

A Sudden Nutmeg Grater

The Actor Henry Irving
in His Dressing Room

A Blocked Chimney, Bethnal Green

Strange Visitors at
Smithfield Meat Market

A Terrestrial Globe With Pox

4

LONDON GAZETTE II

Reports from around town

Lord's Cricket Ground, Marylebone
Twelve cricket bats are now reported to have grown hair overnight. Five sets of stumps replaced, either because they were found stretched as long as broom poles, or else shrunken or blackened. One set of wooden bails appears to have grown teeth.

Coffee stall owner, Hammersmith
My wife's a nutmeg grater. I know it's her. I come home. The grater's in her chair. Oh, Margaret. How'd it happen, deary?

Stage Manager, Lyceum Theatre, West End
It's the handkerchief we use for *Othello*. It keeps being misplaced. One stage hand swears he saw it flying about in the wings like a bat and, that on catching it with a butterfly net, it

did bite him most fiercely. It has been replaced several times, but each time the handkerchief will not keep still. There have been reports of it suddenly appearing in the actors' dressing rooms. The company is most perturbed and suspect there shall be a death among them. All their performances have been affected by the handkerchief. Mr Irving, who plays the Moor, terrifies all with his face darkened over; his murdering of Desdemona is the most repulsive thing I have ever seen on the stage.

From a chimney sweep, Bethnal Green
It was always soot that we were fighting up the chimneys, but now we have a new foe, all the chimneys are quite blocked with things, all stuffed up with bits and pieces from around the houses, some it seems going up the flue from the inside, others finding their way down the pots from outside. How they got to be there is anyone's guess. Hundreds of things quite stuffed up. Think it some strange prank, but I now done four-and-twenty chimneys so suffocated. Should anyone light a fire below such a blocked chimney, there'd be black smoke in the house in a moment and all would choke, but that's the very least of it – should a fire be unchecked with such a blocked chimney, then there's every chance of it catching proper, of the whole house going up in flames, and if I've seen four-and-twenty so blocked, then how many might there be in all London?

From a butcher's apprentice, Smithfield Meat Market
Sometimes people of London come to watch us in our labour, come to buy or just to see the sight of so much flesh all together.

44

I don't usually bother about them. But that morning among the gawpers was this strange dog I see, a huge dog it was, the size of a Great Dane or something, but misshapen and ugly and mangy. Curiously, it had a brass ring hanging from its nose. Then there was the dog's owner, that was another queer thing right there. He was a bald man with a long nose, queer and pointy, and the other oddness was his ears: his ears were not equal to each other; one was old and wrinkled, the other small and neat and youthful. Despite all that he was quite a dapper little fellow – and kept an umbrella hooked at his arm. The man, he comes up, he says, 'I want one whole dead pig. My dog, my dog shall carry it. Here, Otter, come, girl. Strap the pig to the dog, my good fellow.'

'Sir?'

'Yes, please, come along. She'll carry it and more besides.'

It was done. To see that huge hound with a weight of pig upon its back! And then the business exhausted and the purchase made, off they went into the darkness, like it was the normalest thing in the world to walk your dog in such a fashion.

Well and that was strange, surely it was, but London is the great hold-all of many a strange person, always has been, always will be. So what if a person has a dog that takes home his shopping for him, that's not so telling if you balance it that way. Only then, with us turning back around to our business, then came the strange part. The meat, all the meat, all the meat of all of Smithfield had changed in those few moments. It had all spoiled. It was all stale and old and rotting, all gone off I tell you. In a sudden moment. All spoiled, quite spoiled, and then such a buzzing of flies and such a standing by. Where before all had been whites and reds and pinks, now was all darkest browns and muddy yellows and dirty greens. Wrong colours, wrong smells, wrong meat. All spent like from some rotting rubbish heap.

Smithfield had no new meat that day. If you wanted meat you had to go fetch it from Newgate Market or Leadenhall, which is generally the best for poultry, dead or alive.

From the Master of the Household, the Right Honourable Lord Steward, Marquis of Breddalbane, Buckingham Palace
A terrestrial globe in one of state rooms – a gift to the family from the collection of Catherine the Great – has begun to discolour and grow weeping blisters. Many countries have become quite illegible. Gibraltar is now no more than a swollen lump. India is taken over by a large, very sore-looking rash. Just yesterday the abused crust or scab that was once St Helena dislodged itself and fell to the floor.

As if all the Empire were under threat.

5

THE HOUSE ACROSS
THE STREET

Concluding the narrative of Eleanor Cranwell,
23 Connaught Place,
London W

6th February 1876

Our house was so quiet as I left it. No one came to stop me. There was a slight disappointment in that, as if I'd secretly been hoping they would. It was a little past midnight when I stepped out. It couldn't have been easier leaving really, the floorboards did not creak, the door made no sound when I opened it. I'd thought about going out by way of the servants' entrance, but I'd more likely come upon someone there. I slid back the bolts, which obliged me very easily, and I stepped out. I left the door slightly ajar so I could easily get back in.

So then.

The streetlamps were lit but they barely penetrated the dark, there was just a slightly lighter darkness around them. They looked as if they were drowning. No one in the street. All the houses shut up. Nothing to observe me as I went. Not a pigeon, no cat. All alone.

I crossed the street. Rubbish on the ground, a bit boggy in places. Our street is getting dirtier and dirtier and no one ever comes to clear it up any more.

I reached the steps of the house. Steeped in rubbish. I disturbed a great cloud of flies. Rubbish like it'd been dumped there for ages, so that you'd think there was no one living inside, that the whole place was deserted. That wasn't true, I knew they were in there. It felt so cold suddenly, like there was some new cold eating at me. I felt that something, that everything, was terribly wrong, that all was unnatural. That everything had been spoiled, tampered with. The closer I stepped to the house, the worse I felt, as if I was at the place where some terrible crime had happened. As if something had been very badly mistreated.

Buck up, I told myself. Stop thinking like that.

Go to the door.

I looked through the keyhole, and saw nothing. It was all far too dark. Too dark out here, too dark in there. There was a brass knocker, so I knocked. How that doleful metallic sound bounced around the street, as if I'd hurt the door by rapping upon it and it was calling out in complaint. Wrong of me to do that, the knocker seemed to be saying, most wrong indeed. Shouldn't have done that. You'll regret it, of a certainty.

I stepped up close to the door again, I was about to give the knocker another loud rap when instead I pushed the door with my shaking hands. It opened. It just opened, I hadn't even touched with any particular force, but it opened all the way.

I could not see anyone inside, just a small portion of the front hallway. It was just like ours but very thick with dirt and filth as if to tell me once more than no one had been here all along, that I was mistaken.

'Hello,' I whispered, and it was a very faint whisper. I barely managed to get any sound out, my throat was so tight.

There was no answer. No answer at all.

'Excuse me,' I said, a little louder this time. 'I say, is anyone there at all?'

'At all, at all, at all.'

Echoes down the dark hallway, which beyond a few paces from where I stood was all deep, inky blackness. A blackness that seemed to me, in my high excitement, thick with dark life.

'I think there are people here,' I said.

Nothing in reply.

'I'd be most awfully glad to meet you. I've been calling out. Did you hear me? My name's Eleanor Cranwell. We're neighbours, I live just across the road. I say, I knew there were people living here. Hello? How do you do?'

Nothing.

'Since I know that you are here, you might at least admit it.'

Nothing.

'I *have* seen you,' I said. 'I've seen the young man upstairs, I've seen the fellow in the brass helmet. One of the servants said she saw a dog.'

Nothing.

'Come out, please, come along out, won't you?'

Upstairs, or somewhere deep within the body of the house, something, some heavy object, fell.

'I heard that! Who's there?' I called.

And nothing again.

I had a candle in my dressing-gown pocket and strove to light it then, calling out into the darkness, 'I have a candle with me now, I'm going to light it that we may see each other better.'

There was a strange breathing sound then, as of many mouths taking a quick breath of air in shock. I struck the matchbox and lit the candle. It didn't do much to help my investigation further, the candle flame merely jerked the shadows into dancing around and forming a very unhappy and menacing impression of life. Then, suddenly, some sort of wind brushed past me, and for the slightest moment I felt something hairy, some thing with sharp hairs rush past me, there was a sudden very stale smell and then it was gone again. I hadn't seen it, quite; only, somehow, sensed it.

'Hello,' I said. 'Come out, don't be frightened.'

Quiet.

'Are there many of you here?' I tried again. 'I think there must be.'

Again nothing, though upstairs, far upstairs, I thought I heard something shift a little on the landing. Looking towards the stairs that went up floor after floor after floor, I thought there must be several eyes upon me then, waiting to see what I should do.

'Are you frightened?' I asked.

Something creaked.

'Are you?'

Something, I thought, breathed.

'Are you hurt perhaps? Are you in any pain? Can I help you?'

From somewhere up in the house, something was dropped or fell, something was gathering pace and came hurtling down the well of the stairs from the upper floors. It bounced down the stairs nearest me and landed at my feet in a sudden crash. I could see clearly enough that it was a saucer, a porcelain saucer, totally smashed now and in ruins.

'You've broken it,' I called up.

Nothing.

'That wasn't very clever now, was it?'

Nothing.

I brought my candle down towards the broken crockery. It was all in rather a neat pile – strange that it should have landed so. As I brought my candle up to it, I saw that the pieces were still moving. The pieces were clicking against each other, falling over each other, and the closer I came to them with the light the further they scattered apart. Soon there was not a piece to be seen, but all had fled into the safety of the dark. How on earth had that happened? How could it be possible?

'*Are* you hurt?' I called, for above all I wished to try to make some sense of this nonsense, and bring all back to normal. 'Please may I help you, please will you come out now? Please, please do.'

Something else came smashing down the stairs, then more and more things – plates and cups and saucers and tea pots – so much falling porcelain all smashing by my feet, hurtling down now like a terrible loud crashing storm of crockery. Never quite hitting me but coming so close.

'Stop it!' I cried. 'Stop throwing that.'

I started backing away towards the door. It seemed there were no rules in this house, all was turned on its head there, things, things in this place, had lives, just as if they were any mouse or an insect or a person.

There was a chair in the passageway. I hadn't seen it before, perhaps it had just arrived. As I approached, it ran away, horse-like, into another room, the door slamming behind it. The front door was still open then and I ran towards it, but in an instant the other doors behind me opened and let forth a great rush of objects, a pelting of things. And then there was suddenly someone right next to me, I felt the heat of him, and then that someone opened his mouth and blew out my candle.

Darkness. Silence at first, then scraping sounds of broken china. The fragments were scratching my shins now. I tried to kick them off. I put my hand in my pocket for my matches and, trembling, took them out. The first fell to the ground before I was quite able to strike it. But in that act, all the things seemed to know what I was about and began to prick me here and there and to pull upon my dress. I do not know what might have happened to me if I had not at last been able to strike the next match and so rekindle the candle.

And then in the darkness, just for a moment, I saw them. I saw them all. There were hundreds of them: people everywhere, lurking in the darkness, their heads peeping out to stare at me, hissing people, shifting in the yellow gloom, stepping over each other, like a great swarm of beetles and all in dark greasy clothing and all with strange shifted faces; faces and heads that resembled human ones but were somehow wrong, too long, or too squashed, and all with yellow eyes and all in a sudden terror at seeing me.

Now I saw them all swarming, coming down the hallways towards me, hurling objects at me. There was an old woman, a horrible shrunken old woman, and she glared a moment before pelting a shoe at me. As I ducked from it, my candle went out. I heard the old woman call in distress,

'Get it out! Get it out of our house!'

Scuttles and movements behind, getting closer, voices, and noises, scratches and scrapes, coming closer and closer.

'Dirty!' cried the old woman. 'I shall not have such filth in here. Catch it, catch it quick! Step hard upon it! Squash it!'

So much movement, so much noise behind me as I dashed along the hallway and was at the front door again. Pushing it, tugging it open as glass and crockery and cutlery and nails were hurled at me, and then I was out on the street again, in the road, and gasping, gasping.

There was something else on the steps, something that hadn't been there before. I found myself shrinking back from it. It hissed at me. A fox. A dirty great grey city fox.

'Go on! Get away from me!'

But the thing did not budge, just bared its needle-sharp teeth.

I screamed all the way home.

I screamed up the steps and I screamed as I pushed the front door wide open. I screamed for help as I ran into the house. I wanted to wake everyone up. 'Help! Help!' I called. I didn't care that I be chided for it. I must see someone.

'Mother! Father! Please! Help me!'

But no answer came, no noise from anywhere in our house, not a sound.

'Someone, please! Help me!'

Nothing. No one. All was silence. I ran up to my parents' rooms. I opened their bedroom door, fiddled for the gas switch and set it alight, a slight hissing in the air as the coal gas was ignited and the familiar smell followed as usual and that was comforting, but then I realised that though the bed was rumpled I could see neither Mother nor Father. There was something in the bed, something that did not belong there. I tugged back the sheets. There were two tall clocks in the bed, grandfather clocks, one taller than the other, neither with a face, neither ticking, just the empty wooden cases. Who had gone and done that, who had put them there, and where were Mother and Father?

'This has to stop!' I cried. 'Has to stop right now! THIS IS RIDICULOUS!'

No sounds, no sounds anywhere in the house. I ran upstairs to the attic, to the servants' rooms, I banged on all the doors, screaming for them to 'Wake up! Wake up!'

No sounds, no sounds but the sounds I made.

I opened the doors, and all the beds, every one, held a strange object, but in none of them was a person. Instead, in the places where people should have been, there was a chess board, a bell pull, a slipper bath, a mousetrap, a carpet, a vase.

'Wake up, wake up!'

I said this to myself: that I must be in a dream now, and if only I found my way back to my bedroom then surely it should all be over with and I could wake up and everything would be quite how it was before.

So back here I am, and I think I am awake. I've written it all down should anyone find this.

When will the day ever come again?

I see over the road that the door of the house is closed shut now.

I turn then, all of a sudden, to my own bedroom door.

That's when I see it.

Inside my room is the fire extinguisher and it has grown again.

Part Two

Inside Looking Out

Clod Iremonger Nightshirted

6

AN IREMONGER
IN LONDON

Beginning the narrative of Clod Iremonger,
formerly of Heap House, Foulsham, briefly lost,
now amongst his family in London

To be an Iremonger

'Lucy, Lucy, Lucy. Lucy! Lucy! LUCY!'
   'Wake up!'
   'LUCY!'
   'Shut up!'
   'LUCY! LUCY!'
   'Rippit!'
   I'd been at it again, they said, calling out in my sleep. Waking
everyone up. Wasn't right to do that. Wasn't proper. Wasn't
London. We're in London now, and must behave London-like.
So then. Shut up in your sleep.

But whenever I was in sleep, I was looking for Lucy all over Foulsham, calling out for her but never finding her. And waking up in London, Foulsham seemed so far away and Lucy even further.

London. In London.

All my life I had wanted to be in London. And now, finally that I was here, in a London street, in a London house, I could summon no comfort from it. I was Clod Iremonger, London lingerer. London in my lungs. London in my eyes. Here was London, oh my ever-longed-for London.

I used to have a map of London in my old bedroom in Heap House. I should trace the streets with my fingers, never daring to hope I may one day live there. But I saw of it oh so little then, just a great smudge in the distance. But now, there I was, a Londoner. A Londoner perhaps, though not so much of it spilled into my ill head, but I caught it through windows whenever I could, though they said I must keep the curtains closed, still I stole small glimpses from this London address. I shall know you yet, I shall be a London one, shall I?

There is nowhere else for me to go. I cannot go back home.

Our home, old home, old place, disgraced and thrown over, blackened, cracked, forlorn, forgot, death place, dead home, death knell, pell mell, gone and gone and never ever to return. They pulled it down. And never will it up again.

Home of my people: no, nowhere.

I am most awfully without home.

How many died, my Lucy, my ever Lucy Pennant? She that I loved and loved me back. Scrap of a servant girl, my own everything. Gone and gone and gone. How many buried, burnt, smothered, put out, snuffed out, out of the game, gone under, killed, murdered, butchered, bled? How many bones, sacred bones, left? I'd pick up that dust. I'd look after it so.

Put me with the cinders. I'd be better left there.

How many that once were, are only silent now?

We're off the map. Mapless, landless people. Extinct. First the dodo, then the great auk, then the piebald Forlichingham Terrier, then Foulsham itself. And yet I breathe still. Shouldn't. Most highly improper that I do. So wish that I didn't. Some rats always find a way. You demolish a slum, the slum pushes up somewhere else. If ever there was a family that should shake off death, that should ignore it and grin at it, it is mine.

For I am, and ever shall be whilst I breathe, an Iremonger.

Far rather I should not be and rip myself in two.

Should much rather be dead.

But am not.

I'd even extinguish myself. And they know, my family, and so they watch me, they watch me always. How I am looked at and watched over in my nightshirt that may as well be my prison uniform. What's to live for, after all, in this Lucy-less world? No Lucy today or tomorrow, no Lucy next week, no Lucy next month, next year no no Lucy. No red any more ever again, not the exact right red that I long for with such an ache. My fingers in her hair. No freckles that I care for. As if each freckle were a full stop. And there are only full stops. I can't be whole any longer. Oh, Lucy gone and dead on me. What's a fellow to do?

When will the ache stop?

Oh never let it stop.

Never to be Left Alone

My family filled me with hate. Well then let them, I'm empty now, they may as well fill me with something.

'Who killed us? Who brought down Heap House?' they asked me.

'Tell me,' I said. 'Wasn't it you?'

'Lungdon did,' they said. 'It was Lungdon that done it."

"London, you mean?" I asked.

"No, no, we do call it Lungdon, we Iremongers. For we shall make it shift from London to Lungdon under our influence. It shall come all over Iremonger! Yes it shall, since it was them that done it, so now Lungdon shall be made to feel it. Now Lungdon shall suffocate on itself. Can't kill off the Iremongers, can't be done.'

'Lucy,' I whispered, 'Lucy Pennant.'

'She's a dead one,' said Uncle Aliver. 'No discernable life pulse, on account of them.'

My family came visiting and prodded me in my misery, to set light to it. I didn't eat much so they fed me with their hatred.

'Well then, Clod, old Clod, shall we dead them?' said Uncle Idwid, blind and full of grin. 'Shall we dead them right back, my fellow lugs? How should you like that, my chick? Shall we that hear so, shall we hear them screaming? Shall we make them our instrument and have a nasty music come from them? I think we shall, oh I think we shall: they killed your Lucy.'

'Quite murdered her,' put in Uncle Timfy, not wishing to be outdone by his twin. This uncle's birth object (whose name was Albert Powling) was a pig-nosed whistle, which he held threateningly in his small hand. But that whistle was not allowed to be sounded these days, not since we were all to keep ourselves as quiet as we may. Not since we'd gone into hiding, the House of Iremonger, all muted, waiting, waiting to move. All shoved into one heaving address.

'They done for her,' some relative echoed, chewing nonchalantly on his own greasy hair.

'But you would have killed her yourselves,' I said. 'You should have, given half a chance!'

'Maybe yes, maybe no, but they were the ones that did it. Not us.'

'Did she scream?' wondered Timfy.

'Did they hurt her?' put in Aliver.

'Bet she screamed,' concluded Timfy.

'We're entirely hinnocent of the crime,' said Idwid, topping his twin. 'No we never. You shan't let them get away with it, shall you? To do such a thing. To one you were so partial to. Monstrous, is what it is, monstrous. Murder them right back, that's what I say. You'll do it, you're the one to do it. You're all black with fury, aren't you, and so you should be.'

'What are you going to do, cousin?' said Moorcus, mocking. 'Are you an Iremonger or not? Earn your nightshirt, why don't ye?'

The Girl Across the Street

They are looking for us, I am told over and over, and if they find us they'll snuff us out and we'll never be lit again. But the longer they don't find us, the longer they look in wrong rooms, and innocent houses, the stronger we grow, the more ire in our Iremonger there is. We are not allowed in London – I shall not call it by that other name – we are forbidden, we Iremonger people. We are illegals. They destroyed our home, so now, with no place, what else are we to do, but hide? We secrete ourselves upon quiet London shelves, so that all around us are only our own flesh and our bloodlikes. And all, though in strange surroundings, are horribly familiar company, my grandparents, aunts, uncles, cousins, servants, no one new but space. No new company. No one that isn't blood. And there, close, breathing in and out our stale air, to prime ourselves and make cruel plans. In London. On London.

We help only ourselves, there are only ourselves to help. We move in one great fug of blood, we itch of Iremongers, a disease stuffed up in a single house, until we find, we hope, we hope, some somewhere where we may settle. Somewhere someday to call a home. But wherever could that be, and what would it even look like?

When I could I pulled back the curtains and looked out at the street before us, Connaught Place it was called. That's when I saw her.

Someone else looking there.

Looking back at me.

A girl at the window across the way. The shock of it. There she was looking right at me. And then the great thing happened. She waved at me. The wonderful, terrible shock of it. Someone London. Waving at me.

I waved back!

I waved!

Oh the joy!

And then I closed the curtains and felt my heart sprinting. I looked out for her afterwards and when I could I waved again. The girl across the way. That little bit person of London.

But then, oh then, the last time as I smiled and saw her, I was discovered. Cousin Rippit was there fast as anything, he kept the voices about him so muffled. I didn't hear him come in. He tugged the curtains closed. And a high long scream came out from deep in him, barely stopping for breath.

'Rippitrippitrippit!'

He took hold of my hair and shook and shook me. He banged my head against the wall, like they used to do to idiot boys in the school room back at home, to smash some sense into us. It was expressly forbidden to communicate with any London person unless absolutely necessary, it was considered unbelievably dirty and also, and especially, most terribly dangerous to our security. So Rippit he banged and banged me. He scratched at me with his sharp fingernails.

Cousin Rippit, hunched and bunched in, squashed and horizontaled, flat crab-like Cousin Rippit, his eyes so wide apart, fish-face, in my face day and night. He couldn't speak yet, not properly; so long and tough was his battle with his birth object, which as man had been Alexander Erkmann the Tailor, and as object was a rusted and twisted letter opener, concealed deep in a Rippit pocket. They had fought, ripping each other so, so much energy fighting length from width, stretching each other one in portrait, the other in landscape.

Always so close to me now, Cousin Rippit.

Day or night, I'd hear Rippit take my dear plug out, for he had been made keeper of James Henry Hayward, and croaked his

'Rippit' at it, he should never let me see my plug, never let me near it, he was the keeper of it now. He drew it out that morning after I was caught waving, he let my poor plug out the full length of its chain, and waved it before me, swinging it like a pendulum.

'James Henry Hayward, James Henry Hayward.'

Oh my poor plug.

His own birth object was never revealed, but was kept always hidden away, lest it should pull itself out of his prison and be free once more.

Rippit, the croaker, the burper, the creaker, cracking his sound over me, into my thoughts and my loss, staring at me with his yellow eyes. My constant companion.

'Rippit.' My cousin, my frog cousin.

'Rippit,' in the night and in the day.

Rippit that caught me waving.

I Hurt my Room

They painted over all the windows in my room with black paint, they nailed the windows closed and boarded them up. Keeping London from me.

They said they'd sent cousins Otta and Unry over to watch that girl, to see what she was about. Should I be found waving at her again, Unry and Otta would creep up upon her and stop her from meddling permanently. So I mustn't wave again, it wasn't safe to. Not for her.

I wonder if she ever thought of me afterwards, the girl across the way.

I was stuck in the room in my nightshirt, not allowed to go out, forbidden to look out, we must be quiet, we must keep still. But I cannot. Oh, Lucy, I cannot bear it.

This new home, home for a bit, a little bite of London, this room of mine. I shall ruin it, I think.

And so I did just that.

I only had to think it and it happened. How strong I had become, what things I could do! I'd so love to show Lucy, but I couldn't. And so I ruined and ruined.

I blackened.

I sooted.

I breaked, bruised, buckled, bludgeoned, bloated and blasted. I hurt things now. I was so sad that I pulled my sadness out of me and onto all around me and I made all grow stale and rotten and unhappy. I spread my gloom, I sprinkled it. I felt it coming up inside me and belching out and then just by looking I saw the wallpaper start to weep and buckle, to grow strange blisters and hairs. It frightened me that I could do this. I watched as chairs grew awkward and unbalanced, their legs heaved long and thin and stretched to the thinness of needles and as they shifted they creaked and wept and longed not to be so strange, to go back to their former shape. But they couldn't. I had been misshaped and so all about me must be misshapen too. Now was I made of hate.

I hated the wallpaper and it blistered and blackened.

I hated chairs until they stretched and shrieked.

I hated my bed and so its frame twisted and rusted, I hated the mattress and so it stained and bloated and belched out its guts of springs and feathers.

I hurt the things. And they let me do it, those things, they never called out, they never said a thing.

They do not speak to me.

Those new things never did.

All those about me, all those London pieces, were silent. They were only things, just little bits, small properties. They had no voices. They were not like the poor lost tortured bits of Foulsham that screamed and bellowed to me, that sung to me and lifted for me, and saved me, oh yes they did. I loved those things, every last whispering, howling one of them. I moved them and they moved me, and beneath them I heard them all and understood all their pain and distress, I knew them, I *knew* them. But these new things, these possessions of London, these expensive things all about me: why, they were dumb – every last one. It was only the birth objects of all my family about the house that spoke to me as we lived and breathed and hid in our new address. And yet I could feel them all, those bits and pieces, so much of this and of that, and I could have them move and bend and burn, I could shatter them and huft them with the slightest thought. I am Clod, the mover of objects, I am Clod, thing lifter, I am Clod and I may move, I do think, any thing. And break it.

Voices in the Night

Suddenly they were there again. I heard them outside my room in the night, talking about me.

'It would seem to be his unhappiness that makes him so,' Idwid was whispering outside my door. How his Geraldine

Whitehead stammered beside him, as if those nose-hair clippers of his were afeard of me. And among the muffled noises I caught, barely, so timid:

'James Henry Hayward.'

My own plug. And therefore Rippit was outside my door now too, whispering with the others, my own plug in his hands.

'Yes, yes, the more miserable he is, the more the things dance for him,' came the twin with the whistle.

'Is he dangerous, do you think?'

I heard something saying, 'Jack Pike,' and knew at once it came from a cuspidor, and that Grandfather himself was without the door.

'Oh, yes!' said Idwid. 'I would swear so.'

'Can you control him?' asked Grandfather.

'Not I,' said Idwid.

'Rippit,' said Rippit.

'Good Rippit, see that you do.'

'Rippit.'

'I think, sir, I think, Umbitt Owner, Capital of Iremongers, great hope in our despair, father, father of us all, I think on the whole, just for now, while all is uncertain – just three nights, only three more nights and then we shall be there – I do think, in the meantime, you might leave Clod on his own and not come too much too close.'

'For my sake?' angered Umbitt.

'No, no, of course not, however could that be?' said Idwid. 'I think you might find yourself wishing to punish him a little too much. And though I am certain he deserves such a walloping, it may be best, for the now, to leave him be and find himself.'

'If you say so, Idwid. I've no love for the child.'

'Indeed, sir, who could, who would . . . such a creature!'

'We shall keep our separate ways, for now.'

'I think it wisest. Rippit shall steer him right, shan't you, Rippit?'

'Rippit.'

'Wait!' cried Idwid. 'I hear something.'

'I too,' said Umbitt. 'It is the door! There's someone there, at the front door downstairs. Hush all, be still!'

'Rippit.'

'Surely,' whispered Timfy, 'surely it's locked.'

'No, idiot brother of mine,' said Idwid, 'it must be unlocked. For Unry and Otta to come back in when they need.'

There was someone downstairs. Some non-Iremonger, someone from London. A very new person. I went to my bedroom door, but Rippit had locked it.

'Let me out,' I said.

'Silence, Clod,' came Grandfather. 'Go back to bed.'

'I've never seen a London person,' I said, 'not up close. I should very much like to.'

'Lungdon, you must say Lungdon,' said Timfy.

'This is not the time, Clod,' said Grandfather. 'You will be silent.'

But I would not be silent. Be silent and miss this phenomenon amongst us? No. I commanded the objects all about my room to shift and dance. I had them flying all about me, scuffing the wallpaper, making such a din.

'Rippit,' said Grandfather, 'silence that child at once.'

In response I made a porcelain potty shatter itself.

I heard a voice then, a young voice downstairs.

'I think there are people here,' the voice was calling. 'Hello! Hello!'

'Hello!' I cried.

'I *have* seen you,' came the voice down below. 'I've seen the fellow in the brass helmet. One of servants said she saw a dog. I've seen the young man upstairs in his nightshirt, I waved at him, he waved at me.'

The girl, it was the girl!

'Rippit.' He was inside the room then, Rippit was, closing the door behind him, shaking his head at me, coming closer.

'Hello,' I called. 'Up here!'

'Rippit.'

Rippit was at me. His squat, cold hand across my mouth. His sharp nails digging into my cheek.

I closed my eyes and, thinking hard, pulled a saucer from a table and, opening the door a moment, sent it downstairs, but that was not enough. So then I dragged every porcelain piece from about the house and made it rush over to her downstairs, to let her know that I was there, but not to hurt, never to hurt, to tumble near her, not to touch her, to play about her legs.

Though Rippit had hold of me, I heard the pieces falling.

But the girl was crying out now.

I think I had frightened her.

I never meant to frighten.

Rippit took hold of my hair and tugged hard at it, he kicked me in the shins with his sharp boots, he had his nails out to scratch and scratch. And then from one of his many pockets he pulled out an old rusted pudding spoon, and from another some small packet of stuff, which he dipped the spoon into until the spoon was heaped full of grey mixture. Grinding, he had some grinding to dull me. I should not take it, but he leapt and pounced, so agile for such a strange lump, and had a chair rush up to me – for he too could set the objects in movement by his thoughts – so that I found myself sat upon it, and then he was upon me again, the sharp fingers digging, those of one hand opening my mouth, those of the other pinching my nose shut.

'I shan't eat! Leave me be!'

'Rippit.'

I spat at him, he dug his nails in deeper.

'Rippit!'

He was so strong, strange Cousin Rippit, he had my mouth open, and the spoonful was shoved down me, I could not stop him. And very soon, very soon, very soon I was asleep. And then Grandfather I suppose must have taken over in his particular way.

I Exercise my New Strength

In the morning, I crushed and cracked, I moved mercilessly from thing to thing, I could not stop myself, the doing of it was, I admit, such pleasure.

Clod, Clod, clever Clod.

Killer of things.

'He's at it again! Quick, call Idwid!' wept my relatives.

'He's breaking things, he's ruining his room,' they cried.

'Clod,' Idwid called up the stairs but in strained whisper. 'Clod, tidy your room.'

'I shall not!' I cried.

'You must be quiet or we shall be discovered.'

In response I smashed a vase and did a jig in its pieces.

'How ever did he come so wild?'

'He never used to be.'

'Such a shy one as was.'

'So silent and obedient.'

'Never one to raise his voice.'

'Look at him now.'

'So bold, so bold.'

'I hate you all!' I cried. 'I hate every last drop of blood of you, I hate your skin and your hair, your vile organs, your yellow eyes and your selfish lives, your busy biles, your shrunken hearts, your lumpen livers, your fetid bloodways, your clogged drains, your grey stains in your swollen skulls. I loathe, loathe, loathe every last ounce of you all.'

'Now, Clod man,' said Uncle Aliver, our doctor, 'you know you haven't got that quite right.'

'I'll anatomise your anatomies!'

'Listen to the child!'

'Such a strong voice.'

'For one who never shouted.'

'Coming along most particular.'

'Under Rippit's special guidance.'

'Ripening, I'd call it.'

'He's the one to do it.'

'Ever has been.'

'For good and all,' I seethed at them and marvelled at my seething, 'I'll do nothing for you ever. You cannot make me!'

'Thinks we'll make him.'

'No, we'll never.'

'Never even have to.'

'He'll do it, good and strong.'

'He's the man.'

'Look at the very latest in Iremonger.'

'Breaking the mould.'

'Iremonger through and through and through.'

They made me so livid. 'Doors!' I cried. 'Doors: make noise. All you house doors. Slam! Slam! Slam, I call you! Slam for all you're worth, let them know my fury!'

The doors slammed all over the new house, slammed and crashed and kept on at it, because I, Clod, clot of black Iremonger blood, bleeding in heart and broken inside, in my little engine, my heart, my busted heart.

'He'll have us discovered!'

'He'll bring the constabulary upon us!'

'Something must be done!'

'To rein in the monster child!'

'Before he pulls off the roof!'

'And all Lungdon sees us inside!'

Then Rippit ran up and began to swing the chain of James Henry, to smash it against the wall, pelting it there, over and over.

'James Henry Hayward! James Henry Hayward!'

'Stop, Rippit!' I cried. 'You must not do that. It is against family rules.'

76

He put my plug in his mouth and bit down, and then did I stop the slamming of all the doors, and then did Rippit with a great ugly grin remove poor James Henry from his mouth, a line of spittle still attached to it stretched out a while before snapping. Then with his own power he carefully closed all the doors about us. And then the doors moved no more.

'Rippit,' said he, with finality.

A Dried Pea, a Brass Medal

I sat at breakfast in the stolen dining room in my dressing gown and slippers, the table so crowded with Iremonger mastication, the noise of them crunching and slurping, of so many tongues licking spoons, lips smacking, moist lips together and apart. Oh how epiglottises of ire wobble so, and beneath all the noises of their juices mixing, of the internal weather of their digestion, of their little gases being formed and creeping out into the world, to cause a small child somewhere to sneeze, an old woman to hiccup, a pregnant woman to gag.

I had me some fun, well why not? I do not regret my actions, not in the slightest. This is what I did.

I turned the food, I quite spoiled it. I dirtied and fouled it, I made it old and stale, I made it smell and bubble, I grew it some hairs and mould. Just by thinking it and staring hard upon it. And in response:

'Good heavens, Pomular, look at the tucker!'

It belched of its own accord and spat maggots. There, I thought, eat that!

Aunt Pomular leant forward and stuck a finger in, prodded the greasy mass, scooped some out. She looked at it from different angles, a gollop landed upon the floor, and then, her head reaching ever closer to her loaded finger, she fed the remainder of it to herself.

'Pomular!'

'Don't eat!'

'It's poison, I say.'

'Most repelling.'

'The terror of digestion.'

'Oh God!' said Pomular, gasping.

'She's suffocating!'

'She's suppurating.'

'She's spontaneously combusting!'

'Oh God!' cried Pomular once more.

'What?'

'What?'

'What is it, Pomular?'

Pomular cleared her throat. 'It's really rather good.'

Other hands dipped in then, other swallows.

'It is!'

'It really is!'

'Delish!'

'Reminds me of home so.'

'Come, come, Rosamud, not to be maudlin. Have another bowl.'

'I will, I will, don't mind if I do.'

'I can't help but remember the last time I ate seagull.'

'Oh stop! You'll have us all in tears!'

'I'd kill for a good fat rat.'

'Well honestly, Ugifer, who wouldn't?'

'I won't be civilised,' cried Rosamud.

'No, Muddy, course you shan't.'

'I don't like Lungdon, I cannot help it.'

'It's so clean.'

'It doesn't smell right.'

'It's bad for my health.'

'I'm losing weight!'

'But this, this at least, does taste good. A little like home. Thank you, Clod, so thoughtful.'

'You're a good fellow, Clod.'

Dear sweet Ormily, who would have married Tummis if the world had been better, there she was sipping at a glass filled with liquid the colour of mud. She smiled at me shyly.

'I'm so glad to see you, Clod, up and about again. I am really,' she said.

Dear sweet Ormily. I never minded her. We spoke the same language of loss.

'Hullo Ormily,' I said. 'How I wish everything was different.'

But then Rosamud was in between us and, lifting up her brass doorhandle (Alice Higgs), she brought it down with a horrible thumping knock first upon my head and then, unforgivably, upon Ormily's.

'Young. Do. Not. Talk. At. Table,' she said, and looked very pleased with herself for saying it.

'Oh Rosamud!' cried one of the aunts. 'There you are quite yourself again. Good girl! Well done!'

'Thank you, Ribotta, I am a mother now, and must help the young in any way I can.'

'How is your boy, Rosamud?'

'Binadit, I caution you, Cuffrinn, Binadit please to call him. He is . . . well he is rather large. They keep him in the cellar, in a metal box there. He is not really to see anyone, but I do pop down, when I can, I knock upon sides of his box and he bangs back at me.'

'There's love!'

'There's devotion!'

'I do see my lost Milcrumb in his face, in his knocks even. It is a strain, you know, becoming a mother beyond the fortieth year.'

Oh Aunt Rosamud and her Binadit. Binadit in the basement, Binadit who knew Lucy, who had kissed Lucy once. I did not know whether to embrace the fellow for knowing her or to throw all things at him for kissing those lips, those lips gone quite cold now. I had not visited him, even were I to have been allowed, I could not bear to look upon that face. That big beast of a fellow. What should I do to such a creature who, I believe, in some way or another, Lucy had loved. He was down there in the cellar keeping her in his thoughts, having her play in his memories, little bits of Lucy that were his and not mine. I hated him then, him and his mother, that busy aunt with her doorhandle.

There were tears in Ormily's eyes from Rosamud's knock, she was very cowed and hurt, looking down into her watering can (Perdita Braithwaite) upon her lap. I could not stand it. Some switch went off in me, some firework lit, and looking at Rosamud blabbing on drove me in a fury, and thinking of her kissing son in a room beneath us and considering Rippit had broken the rules with my James Henry, shouldn't I do likewise to these loathsome ladies, yes I was driven on and on. I silenced the trout, good and fast. Full of armoured thoughts I had poor Alice Higgs fly from her hands in an instant and sail through the thick black skin of a ruined custard where it floated miserable like the old HMS *Temeraire* going up the Thames before being broken up.

'My doorhandle!' she cried. 'He moved it, he MOVED it!'

Silence.

'MY DOORHANDLE!' Rosamud screamed.

Then the others offered up their chorus.

'It's expressly against the rules to do such a thing!'

'He'll murder all civilisation!'

With a smile then I held my breath and shattered every glass in the room.

'Disgraceful child! Call Idwid, call Ommaball, call Umbitt!'

Timfy had his whistle (Albert Powling) in his lips, and that was when I did it. Grinning widely at Ormily, I tugged at the whistle with my thoughts, I pulled hard on that chain of his.

'My whistle!' he shrieked. 'My ever whistle! Oh Clod, I'll drown you in tar water, I'll boil you in rat fat. You! You spit, you gob of soap. Let go my whistle! I know you, I've yet to cut you for the burns you caused me on the dread night of the gathering in Heap House, when you sent a prehistoric fowl upon me.'

'It was an ostrich!' I cried. 'It was Tummis's beautiful ostrich, lost in the house.'

'How it kicked and bit my person!'

'I am glad, I am right glad!'

'The one blessing,' spat Timfy, 'is that the dread beast fell out into the heaps and died there horribly, just like its dripping master!'

'My Tummis!' said Ormily, louder than I'd ever heard her.

Thinking hard then, oh wrapping my thoughts as hard as I may, I thought very small and round of the dried pea in the centre of Timfy's pig-nose whistle, small and round, small and round, and I felt my thoughts about it, I felt my thoughts take hold of it and clench it in its thought-fists and I ground it and cracked it and made it into powder dust.

'My whistle! My whistle, my whistle . . .' stammered Uncle Timfy, like a small child with a broken toy, his voice very high now in his shock. 'My whistle, my whistle, my whistle, my whistle, my whistle, my whistle, my whistle . . . won't whistle!' shrieked Timfy, the tears tumbling down Timfy cheeks.

Then Moorcus stood up, his chair crashing to the ground. 'Right then, you maggot, now you're for it!'

Taking up a candlestick, he came rushing for me and I with what quickness I could I plucked with my wishing his shining medal from his breast, it leapt in the air, he tried to catch it. It hovered around above our heads a moment. With a click of my fingers I set the ribbon alight and let it flame beyond Moorcus's reach, until it had all burnt out and just the metal disk FOR VALOUR spun helplessly in the air.

'You are the maggot, Moorcus!' I cried.

There was the sound of clapping from behind. I thought at first it was one of the servants but it wasn't. It was Rowland Collis, in the shadows amongst the serving crowd. Rowland Collis who had once been Moorcus's toastrack birth object, but had turned back human again somehow, some magnificent somehow. Who could tell how he had done it? Rowland Collis had no idea and refused to return to toastrackness no matter how Moorcus begged him. Rowland Collis himself, Moorcus's dirty secret.

'Hi! Hi there, Rowland,' I called. 'Rowland Collis. However are you?'

'Oh! Oh! Coming on I should say!' cheered Rowland. 'Enjoying the scenery! Partial to the drama!'

'Toastrack!' squealed Moorcus. 'You will be silent!'

The unribboned medal still spun in the air; I let it drop now and it landed with a thunk in a tureen of puddled aspic.

'That,' I said, pointing at Rowland, 'that there is Moorcus's real birth object. There! Turned into the young man beside you!'

How they all gasped, my family. How Moorcus, his face so red with embarrassment.

'No, no, it is not true. It isn't!'

'Oh yes!' I bellowed. 'That Rowland there was once a toastrack!'

And suddenly in all the glory of it, at the peak of my victory, I was shut up.

'RIPPIT!'

I felt an itching on the nape of my neck, a sudden sharpness there, a tugging, a rising intense heat. My hair, my hair was alight! Rippit was setting my hair aflame – he had done this as a child back at home before he disappeared, it was his particular parlour trick. With the stench of my hair burning, I slapped the flames out, I grabbed a napkin, wetted it and applied it to my head. Else I'd have been burnt to a crisp.

I was sent to bed. Rippit took me by a fistful of my unburnt hair and hauled me upwards.

'It isn't, it isn't true!' insisted Moorcus. But all the family were backing away from him. Shocked and disgusted.

Grandmother Steps

Granny came in to see me. Rippit sat at the window seat, chewing at his fingernails and licking his fingers and then applying the dampness to the parting of his greasy hair, to lay it flat upon his huge forehead, as was his wont.

Grandmother, shivering slightly, sat beside me in my broken room.

'I like to travel, Clodius,' she said. 'I've quite the taste for it. I've been up to the attics and down to the cellars. I am out in the world. How large it is, the world.'

'May I step out, Granny, may I? Into London?'

'Into Lungdon, you mean. No, Clod, you might find yourself lost in a little instant, you might run away from all those that love you, we'll keep you in pyjamas yet. Sit up, will you? I'll have no Iremonger slouching before me. No, not you, Rippit, stay as you are. I know very well you are sitting as upright as you may. Clodius, Clodius you are an Iremonger! Whatever has befallen you to make you weep so, swallow it and let it shape you, and be the better for it. What has happened, Clod, has happened and you must chalk it down to experience. Now then, you can move things, you can, Clod, can't you, child?'

'I shall move out, I'll move away, I'll move far and far away.'

'You, grandchild, if you've a mind to it, shall move mountains, whole cities even!'

'I'll do nothing for you, nothing good at least.'

'Stuff and nonsense. You shall do as you're told and be happy to do so.'

'No. I won't.'

'I've never heard such cheek!'

'You'd best get used to it for I shall not be turned.'

'This is your grandmother talking!'

'Yes and don't I know it.'

'I have been very excited! I have been moved, and it is never a good idea to move ancient monuments, architects never do advise it. The slightest thing may make them crumble. You, Clodius, you, Ayris's only child, you shall not be the cause of my death, shall you?'

'I, Granny?'

'Be an Iremonger, Clod.'

'Oh to hell with all Iremongers!'

'You shame the memory of your mother.'

'I spit on her memory, she means as nothing to me.'

Grandmother looked like all the blood had just fallen out of her. She trembled in her ancientness, she looked hurt and bent and I did not care, nor was I frightened of her any more, not of her disapproval, nor even of her Brussels sprout smell.

'Monster child! There's no love left in you!'

'At last you understand!' I said.

'He is very ill, Rippit.'

'Rippit,' said Rippit.

'Send for the pin.'

'The pin, Granny?' I asked.

'Rippit,' said Rippit.

'In times of distress, what a blessing is blood.'

'You'll bleed me?' I asked.

'Rippit!' said Rippit. 'Rippit!'

'You've gone too far, Clod,' said Granny. 'Signalling to Lungdon people, breaking the furniture, hurting sacred Iremonger property, insulting your cousin and spilling secrets that were not yours to spill and now, on top of all, growing rude to your own grandmother, so, so you must take your medicine.'

'What will you do to me?'

'Why, Clod, as I said, we shall Pin you!'

'RIPPIT! RIPPIT!'

'Oh, murder me then, Granny, prick me with pins and pull all the blooding out of me, please do it! Hurry along!'

Granny cleared her throat, she called down the hallway, 'Mrs Piggott!'

A thumping on the stairs and the housekeeper was within.

'Yes, my lady?'

'I want this floor of the house cleared of all family and servants.'

'It shall cause a great deal of crowding elsewhere about the premises, my lady.'

'What do I care of that?'

'Nothing, my lady.'

'Don't get ideas, Piggott, you're nothing but a servant.'

'Yes, my lady.'

'You make me ill.'

'Yes, my lady, I am sorry for that.'

'Don't make me ill, Piggott, just do as I say.'

'Right away, my lady.'

'Only Rippit may remain.'

'Yes, my lady.'

'No disturbance under any circumstance.'

'Yes, my lady.'

'Nothing to upset such a delicate operation.'

'Yes, my lady, I quite understand.'

'Then bring up Miss Pinalippy, and be prompt about it.'

Binadit Iremonger Boxed

7

BOTTON?

The narrative of Binadit Iremonger, bastard

Bin. A. Dit.

It.

Ben. E. Dict.

So much have I been called. These my names. The first given me by my own mother, scratched on a piece of tin. The second by Foulsham people – It, they said. It of the Heaps. Third by her. Benedict, that she called me. Is a lovely name, no doubting. Only one person calls me that name, many other people say or sing and shout 'It' at me often enough. And now, day to day, am Binadit known. All call me that, Binadit, and have me say it too, like I'm learning at school, 'Binadit, Binadit,' but should rather, should much more like the hearing of 'Benedict' by that single voice of hers.

I like bottons.

She was a botton. And I found her.

And lost her when they found me, my family, them Binadit-sayers.

I have family now. Big family. Big love. I am fussed and pinched. They coo at me, they kiss, they stroke, they comb, they brush, they mutter, they purr, they pluck, they punch, they bite, they bump and hold on hard and do not let go. What a lot of loving there is. All for me. They lined up to look at me, one by one, to peer in, to touch and gasp, or bite or shout a bit, but not, not really, to hit upon. I keep waiting for them to leave me behind like they done before, but they don't, no they don't they keep me with them all and all, day and night, I'm their Binadit.

Mother she comes, she comes most often. Can hardly get peace with all her comings and her comings, her botherings and clottings, her weepings, her touchings, she will touch me so and so and so, on my head, on my cheeks in particular. She calls me more than Binadit, baby she calls me, my baby boy. But I've not been baby these many years since, and last I was a baby, when I was a new thing, a very fresh Binadit indeed, she gone and left me in the heaps. She did herself. Left a little token, a scratch on scrap tin. BINADIT read the wobbly hand. She named me, then she left me.

'You gone and left me in the heaps,' I say. True enough.

'My baby, my baby Bin . . .' she returns, and is not to deny it. Rosamud her name.

'Didn't ought to have done that.'

'. . . come back to me after all these years.'

'Why did you do it, missus?'

'Mother, you are to call me Mother.'

'Why did you, missus?'

'Such a big, brave boy.'

'I always wondered.'

'How you've all grown up.'

'Why did you?'

'Please Binadit, please my darling Bin, you break my heart.'

'I might have deaded.'

'Oh, Bin!'

'I don't understand. I want to understand.'

'I cannot undo it, Bin, I cannot.'

'I didn't die.'

'No, my darling, I am so glad of that.'

'Heaps saved me, my heaps, my land of bits.'

'It is the miracle, Bin.'

'A bin's a thing you rubbish put, is that why you called me that? I was your rubbish. You put all your rubbish in me and hoped heaps would lose it for you.'

'Please, Binadit, no more, no more.'

'I just thinking-wondering, missus.'

'Mother, please to say Mother.'

'I was rubbish to you.'

'I was so unhappy, your father had just died.'

'Father.'

'Milcrumb was his name.'

'How die?'

'In the heaps.'

'Drowned dead?'

'Yes, my poor Milcrumb. Dear Milcrumb, such a gentle fellow. Even though he was one of the sons of Umbitt and

Ommaball Oliff, even so he was never treated properly. And now they forget him, only I ever remember him, only I ever mention his name, otherwise he would be quite forgot. He was weak and pale and ever so kind, and they despised him for his weakness. He was not born tough like some of them, so they sent him out into the heaps to toughen him up. Poor frail man that he was, and I was marked to marry him, and we did become friendly before we were exactly supposed to, and then he died before we could marry. So it is that I am a token aunt to all those with their precious blood. And he, yes, he drowned out there in the heaps.'

'E'en so I wonder why you did it.'

She would have her hands about me, plucking away all the little objects that come and stick themselves to me. They can't stop themselves, never could. The rubbish bits do always rush to me. Rubbish moves for me, it seeks me out. So I am to sit, as thingless as possible in empty rooms. Mother pulled them away from me. Every day, pulling, tearing. But they still come, they must. Whenever the door is opened, more things come to me. My bits and pieces. I never mind much. A sock. A spool of thread. Some of a newspaper. Old food wrappings. And such. But always the rubbish it looks for me, always has, ever since it kept me living out there in the great waste. I am a great trouble to my new family. We to remain hidden but wherever they hide me, still the bits do come for me. It is a worry for them I do see that. A great worry. The longer we keep a place, the more the bits come for me, and bits they are big number. So that it is true danger that the bits shall give my whole family away. And so I must be as thingless as is possible and so they keep me in a kitchen store cupboard, in a big ice chest that they found here. Is cold, and she comes, the missus, and she tries her little bit. She do groom me. One day she come at me with her arms wide open. Whatever was she about? Was great upset. All rubbish about in the house they told, lurched and wanted to come down into cellar.

'Don't do it, missus! Away! Get! Get!'

'I'm so sorry, Binadit,' she said.

'Not to do that.'

'I was trying to hug you.'

'Not to,' I told her.

'Oh, Binadit.'

'Mustn't, things don't like it. Upset things.'

'Oh, Binadit.'

'Things hurt me.'

'I am most appallingly sorry.'

'Not come so close. Get back.'

'I think, perhaps, if you'd had a birth object.'

'No, I never.'

'No, Binadit, there was no birth object for you.'

'No, missus, I don't got none.'

'If you did have a birth object I wonder what it should have been. Ommaball Oliff won't give you one, you see. I have asked. She says there's no such thing for Iremonger bastards, and if you've managed thus far you must not have need of one. But if, Bin, if you were to have one I wonder what it should be.'

'A botton.'

'A button?'

'I like bottons.'

She brings me bottons every day, the missus woman do. A new botton every day. But none of them yet is right botton.

There is more things come down to stick upon me, no matter how hard they try to keep them off, each time the woman comes she brings with her more bits to stick upon me, all them new bottons and everything from out her pockets. I have thread and patches of leather and am getting taller and rounder, am putting on. If I don't want them and she don't want them, then no one does want them and they are rubbish become, and then they do stick on me. They get the idea in a moment. Like they were coming home to Binadit, the rubbish heap.

They, my family upstairs, have been saying that I may give them all away, that they should never have taken me in. Well I never asked it of them, did I. They just took. And their loving is turned and spoiled now and not as it was, is gone off and starts to smell. They lost it, had it one day, fallen off somewhere, no place to be seen. Shouldn't be afeard, I tell the woman Rosamud. Tell them not to be afeard. Heaps more like to find you if you have fear. That's when they find you most, all those bits, when you are afearing. Must have been so for the Milcrumb fellow. Tell them not to, tell them.

What shall happen then. If we were to move house.

That is what I fear, for if we do move, then the most of things shall come after. They shall come in a great gushing and I cannot stop them.

'You shall not leave me again shalt you, missus?'

'Mother. No, no, Bin darling, of course not.'

'Will you leave me?'

'No, no Bin, I swear upon this doorknob I shall never leave you again.'

She cried as she said it. It might be the fear that's creeping all over them. Mustn't fear. Things'll be quick to find you that way.

Milcrumb must have feared and so found his death, right quick!

I think about the heaps, my heapland, gone and gone, and I do wonder about the missus I must call Mother but can't seem to, and also, ever think about my botton I found and lost.

Whatever did happen to that botton of mine?

The Owner Umbitt Iremonger
in Hiding

The Owneress Ommaball Oliff Iremonger
in Hiding Likewise

8

BLOOD

Clod Iremonger's narrative continued

The Return of the Doily

'Gloria Emma Utting.'

I heard the doily before I saw its keeper. Pinalippy, my apparently still betrothed, my still obstinately betrothed, Pinalippy, pincher of nipples, taller than me still (though I think in all my adventures I have managed to grow a bit), with her faint moustache and strong arms.

'Well, and aren't you going to say hello or something?'

'Oh,' I said, 'hullo, Pinalippy.'

'You know how to make a female feel wanted I must say.'

'I thought I should be punctured with pins, I thought I should be drilled into and spiked, I thought I may be thoroughly pierced.'

'Well as you see, it is merely me.'

'Do you have any pins about you?'

'Only the pin in my name, is that sharp enough for you? Do you need bleeding then, Clod?'

'I need to be left alone.'

'There's affection, right there.'

'I've no need for company. Now or ever.'

Pinalippy didn't respond to that, she merely came further in.

'What a mess you've made of your room, Clod.'

'It's not mine, it's stolen from someone.'

'Our home was stolen from us.'

She moved around regarding this and that, I stared at the floor and did my absolute best not to engage her.

'Cousin Rippit?' she spoke to the squashed relative.

'Rippit.'

'Cousin Rippit, I should be most grateful if you'd leave us alone.'

'Rippit?'

'I am to be married to Clod, you know, I trust you will not be present on our first night together. It would hardly be encouraging.'

'Rippit?'

'So now off you toddle, I mean to talk with my man here, and I don't need you rippiting throughout our intimate whispering.'

'Rippit.'

'Yes, exactly, just like that.'

'Rippit.'

'Go rippit elsewhere will you?'

'Rippit?'

'Goodbye, cousin, so touching to be in your company, but goodbye it must be.'

She marshalled Rippit to the door, and closed it firmly the moment he was outside. I couldn't help smiling at how she had managed that. But then we were in the room together, just Pinalippy and me. No one else. And that was a shock. Looking very directly at the carpet and not daring to observe anything other, I stayed very still and heard the eighteen-year-old coming closer. Closer. I could smell her then. She smelt of slightly burnt treacle. It was an Iremonger custom for Iremonger women to daub themselves with lightly torched treacle on special occasions to make them the more attractive to the male sex. The scent was known to drive some Iremonger men into palpitations. It did very little, I must confess, to stimulate me.

Pinalippy was so very close now, she was almost on top of me, and then she did something very terrible. Pinalippy sat down, she sat down next to me on my bed. She sat down so close that her dress was touching my nightshirt.

'Well then, Clod, here I am.'

'Yes, Pinalippy, indeed you are here.'

'This is your bed.'

'It is, Pinalippy, I do admit it.'

'This is where you sleep.'

'It is a common enough function of a bed.'

'You lie yourself down just here,' she said, stroking the bed cover, 'and stretch out, you are quiet yourself here, under the covers in your nightwear.'

I leapt up then and marched with all distress towards the window.

'I am very miserable!' I sputtered out.

'Yes, don't I know it, the whole house knows it.'

'I love someone else,' I whispered.

'I know you do, Clod, the skinny thing with all the moles and the uncombed russet hair. I'm most sensible of it. But, forgive me, dear, she's dead, your someone, isn't she?'

'Yes,' I whispered. 'I must say yes.'

'You know you must, we are the only survivors of Foulsham.'

'Yes.'

'And we are hunted. They want to kill us, Clod.'

'Yes, Pinalippy, I know.'

'They'll hunt us down, every last one of us, and they'll murder us, Clod, murder us.'

'So everyone says, and I cannot help that. I do not like being alive.'

'Well I do. I like it very much. And I'll tell you something else, Clod Iremonger, I mean to keep on living if I can. Now you, Clod, you can do things, move things. Things listen to you. You've only to think it and something goes flying, or shrivels up.'

'I cannot help it.'

'What a thing you did with Timfy's whistle.'

'I could help that. And perhaps now I regret it. A very little.'

'If you could do that to an Iremonger birth object, think what you might do upon Lungdon people.'

'I hardly know, do I? They don't let me out.'

'I am proud of you, Clod.'

'Are you, Pinalippy? Why on earth?'

'Well yes, Clod, what a fuss all the aunts and uncles make over you, how Grandfather even talks of you.'

'I meant to steal his Jack Pike, his cuspidor, and destroy it.'

'You see, right there, that's what I like about you: you've gumption. Who else would have dreamt of such a thing? You're an original.'

'I am?'

'You are, now come and sit by me.'

'Must I?'

'Oh do come along, Clod.'

Reluctantly I sat back on the bed, a good distance from Pinalippy. She looked at me.

'Closer,' she said.

I moved a very little closer.

'Closer,' she said.

A little closer yet.

'Closer.'

'Is this not close enough, Cousin?'

'Not by half.'

I moved until I was beside her.

'There then,' she said.

And we sat together in somebody's stolen bedroom, on somebody's stolen bed.

'This is comfortable,' she said after a while.

I said nothing.

'Isn't it, Clod, comfortable?'

I was shaking slightly, it may have been the treacle smell.

'I do think we are making progress. I may visit you, Clod, mayn't I?'

'Yes?'

'It is nearly time for my morning walk.'

'You go out?'

'Yes, of course I do. I go about here and there. I walk Lungdon a little, so that I may learn it. I watch the constables and make them nervous, they grow conjunctivitis just by looking at me. Truly, it is amazing how we Iremongers do stir the people of Lungdon.'

'Do you, Pinalippy, do you perhaps exaggerate a little?'

'Perhaps, but Clod, out in Lungdon, I do buy anything.'

'Oh, Pinalippy, to walk in London!'

'Lungdon we call it, Clod, do catch on. And yes, it is a thrill! But I must be careful. It is highly dangerous. And only for the bravest of the family. Do you know what I did when first I found myself out in that Lungdon?'

'No, Pinalippy, I surely do not.'

'You are so dull. Well, I shall tell you.'

'I had a feeling you might.'

'Move up, I mean to sit right next to you. Closer yet.'

She pushed herself a little against me.

'I have been shopping, Clod. I have been to a hardware store.'

'Have you, Pinalippy, have you?'

'Oh yes, I have, Clod, and I have purchased at the hardware store with ready money.'

'Well, Pinalippy, you are coming along!'

'Almost a Lungdoner!'

'And what, Pinalippy, did you buy?'

'Can you not guess?'

'No, not in the slightest.'

'Why, plugs, Clod, plugs.'

'You purchase plugs?'

'Yes, Clod. Can't you believe it. If I'm to live with a plug, I may as well get used to it. So I did; I have bought any number of plugs, small and large, brass, tin, India rubber. I'm getting used to them. I lay them out on my bed, Clod. I touch them, I hold them to me.'

'Heavens, do you truly, Pinalippy?'

'Oh yes, Clod, I do. I like the feel of them on my skin. Sometimes I lie down and I lay them on top of me.'

'Golly.'

'I might love you, Clod Iremonger, I might very well love you, I have not yet decided.'

'Oh, well, ah, thanks awfully, Pinalippy.'

'Sometimes when I have a bath I put all the plugs in with me.'

'Do you, Pinalippy?'

'Can you picture that?'

'Well . . .' I said, in a panic, 'well!'

'Do you like women?'

'Yes, yes of course.'

'Well, there's a relief, I was beginning to think you didn't.'

'I did love Lucy terribly.'

'Think of me,' she said quite sternly. 'Think of me and all my plugs! In the water!'

'I don't see my plug any more. I am not allowed to keep it, my poor dear James Henry Hayward. I saw his family once, Pinalippy, back in Foulsham, they were rat catchers, good, honest people. Hold on to your Gloria Emma, Pinalippy, there's a person there, hoping to get out.'

'Poor old Clod.'

'And now Rippit keeps my plug and he won't let me have it.'

'Really, Clod, Rippit's got it? Rippit's nothing to be afraid of.'

'I find him terrifying,' I admitted.

'I don't. Not for a moment. You see, the thing about Rippit is he's terrified of us. Of women. How awkward and strange he is when we come near. He becomes so agitated, his hair grows more greasy. "Rippit! Rippit!" I pinched his breast two days ago and how he bellowed at that! Clod Iremonger, how should it be if I got your plug back for you, and gave him one of my own in return?'

'A switch?'

'What would you say to that?'

'I should, well I should be most grateful. Indeed I would!'

'You might also be more forthcoming?'

'Oh.'

'You might, in some small way, show your feelings for me?'

'Oh.'

'For the plug.'

'Oh.'

'Wouldn't you?'

'Well, for the plug, Pinalippy, I suppose . . . I suppose I should.'

'Very good then, Clod, this has been fun! And we must do it again very soon,' she said, bouncing a little upon the bed and then jumping up.

'Well I must be off now.'

'Into London?'

'Yes, indeed! Into Lungdon!'

'Well goodbye, Pinalippy, thank you.'

'We'll do such things, Clod! I know we shall. Oh, just a moment. I nearly forgot. These are for you.'

She handed me various circles of white material. They all had holes in them.

'They are doilies, Clod.'

'So they are,' I said.

'For familiarity, Clod. For remembrance, Clod. For you. Clod.'

'Oh,' I said. 'Righto.'

'Is that all?'

'Thanks?'

'Well done, Clod, we're quite coming along, you and I.'

I didn't say anything.

'Aren't we?'

'Er, yes?' I whispered.

'I think that went very well, don't you?'

'Oh dear,' I whispered.

'He calls me "dear"!'

'I didn't . . .'

'"Dear ", he says, "Dear"!'

And she was gone. And I was alone again. I looked at the doilies a little while and then put them away in the blackened chest of drawers. I wasn't very sure about them at all.

Around the House, Up and Down the Stairs

I was left alone with Rippit again, because Rippit reappeared soon enough. Looking at me with great suspicion, he sat in his chair, stroking James Henry, or at least pretending to, such a timid noise did my dear plug make, such a faint whisper of, 'James Henry Hayward.'

Poor, poor plug of mine.

Rippit took out a daguerreotype of James Henry. It must have been taken when poor James Henry was living at Bayleaf House.

'May I see that?' I asked. 'I should like to keep it if I may.'

Rippit, croaking and rippiting, made a noise deep down in his throat and then let out a pungent belch and with that sulphurous explosion came a small greeny-blue flame. Rippit burped flame onto the daguerreotype and burnt a hole where James Henry's face had been so that all that was left of him was a black stain, and James Henry's shoulders supported nothing but a dark cloud, as if Rippit had set fire to the poor fellow there and then, with his stinking breath.

'Rippit!' he squealed with delight.

That fellow should very happily blot out anything I loved.

Mrs Piggott came in, she handed me undergarments, a shirt, a pair of smart pressed trousers, a bow tie, a black waistcoat, and a pair of black socks.

'You're to have these, Master Clodius,' said the housekeeper. 'Your grandmother's orders.'

'No shoes, Piggott?' I asked.

'No shoes, Master Clodius.'

'I can't go outside yet?'

'No, Master Clodius, but you are given the freedom of the house.'

'Well that's something, isn't it Piggott?'

Only then did I see that Piggott's eyes were very red, I do believe she had been crying. That was most unlike her; I'd never seen Piggott cry before. I didn't know that she could.

'I say, Piggott,' I asked, 'is everything all right?'

'It isn't right, Master Clodius, it isn't right at all.'

'What isn't, Piggott?'

'I musn't say.'

She seemed to gather herself up a little then, took in a breath, then turning about she said, 'Don't mind me, Master Clodius, I'm just a little short staffed, increasingly short staffed, that's all.' And she left.

I dressed myself.

I went downstairs soon enough, my relations on the stairs all getting out of my way as if I had the pox. Perhaps I did after all.

Some cousins had found a rat and had cornered it in the hallway and were waving cutlery at it. Butler Sturridge came running, his footsteps pounding down the hall.

'Give that to me, gentlemen!' he bellowed.

'It is a rat, Sturridge,' said Bornobby.

'I'll have that rat, I thank you.'

'Whyever?'

'Because your grandfather wishes it.'

'Oh well, right you are then.'

Taking it by the tail, Sturridge retreated with the rodent.

'Come along then, Briggs,' the butler said. 'Do stop your squealing.'

'Excuse me, Sturridge.'

'Yes, Master Clodius?'

'Did you just call the rat Briggs?'

'Did I? Who can tell?' he said, pushing past.

'Where is Briggs?'

'I am very busy, Master Clodius, please to excuse.'

'Why ever would he call a rat Briggs?' I asked my cousins.

But my cousins, seeing me, found themselves different locations.

It was a large house by some standards I suppose but very small compared to Heap House where you might easily wander the inside lanes and stairs and ever find new places to visit. Besides which, from Heap House you might watch the heaps moving in the sunlight, it could be very beautiful admiring the rising and falling of so much rubbish, like the breathing of some great slumbering giant. I so missed the place, to think of Tummis flapping his arms out in the heaps, calling to the gulls. But there was no light here, no light outside, all was darkness day and night, since Foulsham was broken and the Iremongers came to London Town. To live. In secret. Amongst you.

The thing about hiding is that once you're beyond the excitement of being hidden somewhere and away from all else, the minutes pass but slowly, ticking and tocking, each click of the clock, each little knock of time, slow, slow, slow time, ebbing away and no one coming to the door to say – 'There you are!'

I moved about my family members, I nosed about their business. After a half-hour Briggs came up the service stairs, his shiny hair most awry, his tortoiseshell shoehorn trembling in his hands.

'Did you call for me, Master Clod?'

'I didn't actually, Briggs, but now you're here, do you have any notion why Sturridge should call a rat after you?'

'I do not attempt to fathom the depths of Mr Sturridge, that is not in my remit.'

'I quite see that. But why should he name a rat after you?'

'I cannot conceive, Master Clod. Perhaps he has his own reasons. Or perhaps you misheard.'

'No, he certainly said "Briggs".'

'Not figs?'

'No.'

'Nor pigs?'

'No, no.'

'Short ribs?'

'No indeed. "Briggs".'

'Well, Master Clod, it must remain a mystery. For the now. Is there anything else, Master Clod?'

'No thank you, Briggs, very good of you to inquire.'

'Thank you, Master Clod,' he said and returned downstairs but as he went he made a sudden, I should say involuntary squeal, rather rattish, I thought.

'I say, Briggs?'

'I thank you, Master Clod,' he said and was gone.

I pursued him down the stairs to the serving rooms. It was very quiet and very dark down below, noises of whispering, some further squeaking of rats.

I turned the corner at the bottom, there was more light there, a few servants holding candles. They were lining up outside a door, some of them were weeping. I was on the point of turning back, for this was a servant business and it was not right for the family to be involved, when I saw something in one of the waiting parlour maids, something poking out beneath her white bonnet. It was red hair. Such red hair! *That* red hair! It stopped me as quick as anything, as if the whole world had suddenly given up the idea of rotating. I couldn't breathe a moment, I gasped, I cried.

'Lucy, Lucy Pennant, there you are all along!'

And then the servant turned to face me.

Such a pinched face, such a young cruel face, not Lucy, not Lucy at all. I stepped back in shock.

'I beg your pardon,' I said, 'I thought for a moment . . . but no.'

'My name is Iremonger,' said she. She was holding a wooden toothpick, her birth object certainly, I could hear its name very clearly, 'Phidias Collins.' The poor toothpick, how sorry I felt for it then, for I had suddenly remembered who she was.

'You were the bully in the orphanage,' I said. 'You tried to hurt Lucy. Your name is Mary Staggs.'

'My name, sir, is Iremonger.'

'Staggs the bully!'

'Forgive me for observing, sir, but she was not family, that other girl you mentioned, not blood like us, like you and I are.'

'Oh you horrible, horrible girl.'

'You must be the lover then, aren't you,' she said, a sour look on her face, her nostrils flaring. 'Nothing much to look on if you ask me. Red hair, is that it? Red hair, is that what you like?' she added, flashing her eyes at me and, pulling out some strands of her greasy hair, she said, 'Fancy some of this?'

I backed away, I cried out I think. The horror of it, as if all the beauty had been stolen from me, tainted and tinctured and spat at with flames like Rippit's belch.

Back up the stairs I went, moaning loudly. I heard Mary Staggs laughing below as I ran, and all I thought of was poor

Phidias Collins. How I would do anything to liberate him from such terrible company.

I'd stay upstairs now, I told myself, I shouldn't go down again. There were cries coming from down there now, servants shouting. I closed the green baize door, let them cry for all I cared. There was a seat in the hall and I panted a while upon it.

Grandfather's Clock

Calming down, I heard voices coming from one of the larger downstairs rooms. Grandfather was inside, I could hear his cuspidor Jack Pike through the closed door, but Jack Pike was screaming. Idwid was there and he was doing something with his nose tongs (Geraldine Whitehead).

'It does hurt so, Idwid!' called Grandfather, who never before had I heard admitting to any pain.

'I am sorry, Umbitt Owner, I am as gentle as I can be.'

'Try again once more, but go carefully.'

'Yes, sir, certainly, sir.' Idwid cleared his throat. 'Now, Jack, listen up good and proper.'

'Jack Pike! Jack Pike!'

'Know your place, Jack. No hopping about the room unbidden.'

'Jack Pike!'

'You're a naughty little thing, to try and get lost so.'

'Jack Pike! Jack Pike!'

'And I must scratch you a little here so that you remember your business.'

'JACK PIKE!'

'Ah!' screamed Umbitt. 'How it burns!'

'Jack Pike, Jack Pike,' Grandfather's cuspidor was whimpering.

'Now, now,' said Idwid, 'all done, all done.'

'Am I dying, Idwid?'

'No, no, never, what a thought! You, die? Hardly, not for many a year yet. You just have, how shall we say it, a little cold.'

'My own cuspidor leapt away from my own grip.'

'You are certain you did not drop it, sir?'

'It leapt, man, leapt.'

'Well, dear sir, we have just encouraged it, quite successfully, I do think, not to leap again.'

'I am weakening, I am so tired, always tired.'

'Now, now, no more of this, sir, it doesn't suit, sir, does it? What I think, what I suggest most of all, is a little medicine.'

'You'll prick me, you'll bleed me.'

'I am just going to bolster Jack Pike up a little,' said Idwid. 'Here we are then.'

There was the sound of a box of some sort being opened and voices calling out from it.

'Herbert Arthur Carrington.'

'Winifred Abigail Carrington, née Leighton.'

'Virginia Winifred Carrington.'

'Wilfred Herbert Arthur Carrington.'

'Here,' said Idwid, 'here are the Carrington family who so kindly made their home available to us. Here they are now, well turned. Nice and fresh.'

'What are they to me?'

'Well, sir, they are your medicine I should think. You shall keep them about you, such fresh new turnings. I shall need to prick your finger slightly and for to scratch upon them so that a little of our great Umbitt may fall into them and then, well then, they shall get attached to you, shan't they?'

'I have my birth object, I have my cuspidor.'

'That naughty thing, yes, Umbitt Owner, we know it and do feel it fully, but here are some more, just to keep you fresh, to help you along a little. To put a little spring back in your step.'

'Oh very well then, if you think it shall help. I do feel better now!'

'A little transfusion, a little iron in your blood so to speak. Now then, hold steady.'

'Ow!'

'Well done, sir, that was very well done.'

'I must not die, Idwid.'

'No, sir, indeed you must not.'

'Not before it is done.'

'Indeed, sir, quite.'

'But I do feel so cold, always so cold.'

'Now I shall take up the Carringtons one at a time and you must keep them ever afterwards close about you.'

'I do indeed feel better with this new company. I thank you, Idwid.'

'Of course you do, sir, that's the spirit!'

'I think I may go about Lungdon and collect me some more souls. I've a hunger for it now.'

'You shall wander about and grow mighty.'

'Just two more nights, Idwid, and after that we shall reckon with them.'

'Two more nights indeed.'

'We shall assemble one and all upon Westminster Bridge, and then we shall give them their shock.'

'They shall not forget us, shall they, sir?'

'You think it will work, Idwid?'

'I do think, sir, all in all, you may find it most efficacious to keep more birth objects about you, a great number of them perhaps.'

'Really, Idwid, I do feel better now.'

'That's the spirit, sir, I think you must gather a little more, fill your pockets, so to speak.'

'Yes, yes, I see that might help.'

'There we are then, a collection shall be arranged, shan't it?'

'Let me then, Idwid, let me have those shall you?'

'Geraldine Whitehead.'

'These? My Geraldine?'

'Even those? Those scissor things, yes. I shall look after them.'

'But, sir! But Father!'

'Don't you "Father" me, there are many of my children who've fallen to dust over such intimacy. Where did your brother Hibbit go all those years ago; where's Itchard?'

'Gone, gone these many years.'

'And all for challenging me. Have a care, Idwid. Know your place.'

'Yes, sir, yes, Umbitt Owner.'

'Come then, I'll take those snippers of yours. My medicine they shall be.'

'Geraldine Whitehead.'

'Geraldine! My Geraldine!' How strange it was now to hear Uncle Idwid's panicking voice.

'You'll find my pockets are most capacious. And more can always be sewn. Prick me, man, do your surgery.'

'Sir . . . sir.'

I crept away then, I moved along from Idwid and his vile nursing. What indeed was their plan, what was the business Grandfather was to do upon Westminster Bridge? And to think I heard Grandfather in such distress. Was Grandfather really dying? What a thought. Grandfather dead, whatever should happen then? I skipped a little down the corridor. But in a mere moment regretted it – he was my own grandfather after all, try as I might I could not wholeheartedly wish him wrong, we should be so vulnerable without him. It was time to visit more of the family in their distress.

The Stitching in the Drawing Room

Sitting in the drawing room was a great clump of senior Iremonger females, a thick congregation, all bombazined and buttoned up, Grandmother and Rosamud amongst them. Grandmother's great marble fireplace was stuck in the centre of this room and caused some inconvenience. The fire was crackling and smoking, gas lamps were lit, candles were aflame but still the place seemed very dark.

The women were all busy about the same exercise, they had long, sharp needles.

'If you're to come in here, Clod,' said Granny, 'you're to behave. I won't have you shifting things, not in here. You disrupt us and you'll be confined to your room with Rippit once more.'

'I shall be good,' I said glumly.

'And how did you find Pinalippy?'

'Quite spirited actually, Granny.'

'I'm most pleased to hear it. She's very strong, that child. She may not be an outstanding beauty, but she has a head on her and a strong (if hirsute) body which, if unmolested by the Lungdon constabulary, may bear many children.'

'She smelt rather of treacle.'

'Did she, Clod! Did she?' cried Granny, and many of the women about her smiled and chuckled at this little detail.

Listlessly I watched all the arms of the Iremonger women, all in black, for black are the Iremonger days since our Foulsham was taken from us. We are in mourning, there'll be no dawn for us, Grandmother had told me, until we find our place again. They worked on, these ladies, deep in concentration, with few words, with occasionally the call for scissors to be passed between them. It was the scissors that jogged my poor head into recollection.

'What ever are you sewing?' I cried.

'Why, Clod, grow up, won't you, and be observant,' said Granny. 'There's many a lady in Lungdon that spends her days with needle and thread. It is what ladies do, and we must fit in, you see, and so we sew and sew.'

'But what are you making?'

'Oh,' said Granny nonchalantly, 'people.'

'What people?' I asked.

'Why, leather people of course,' said Pomular. 'Don't be dim.'

They were stitching arms and legs, torsos and heads. One was threading hair into leather heads. In the corner I noticed two maiden aunts filling the leather bodies with stuffing, shovelling

118

dirt and sand and rolled-up paper from great buckets of filth, spooned through the leather dummies' mouths. I saw now sat amongst them were various finished and dressed leather people, with black smoke coming slightly from between their lips. Sitting very quietly, occasionally one blinked, now and then one wiped a nose, scratched a head a little, but otherwise they sat utterly docile.

One aunt came forward now with a shifting man beside her.

'Excuse me, Ommaball Owneress, I do believe this fellow is ready.'

'Is it?' said Granny. 'Who are you?'

'Marcus Pilkington,' said the leather creature. 'Member of Parliament for Suffolk.'

'So you are. Well then, do you know your business?'

'I am to be at Parliament on the eighth without fail.'

'Yes you are.'

'By ten of the clock.'

'Exactly. Now you are to join the right honourable gentlemen for Inverness-shire, Dumfrieshire and Cornwall and Berkshire. To be housed in secret.'

'Thank you, ma'am.'

'Not to mention. Cusper shall show you the way.'

The MP bowed at Grandmother, turned and bowed at me.

'Good morning to you,' I said.

'Good morning to you,' said he, a trace of black smoke coming from out of his mouth and lingering a while after he had left the room.

'Oh you people!' I cried, I remembered all now. 'You dreadful people! You're making counterfeits!'

'All must find purpose, all must be kept busy,' said Grandmother.

'But these non-people, these un-people . . . I know how you make them!'

At my exclamation one leather person looked vaguely in my direction, regarded me blankly a moment and then returned once more to its torpidity.

'Yes, Clod, with leather and stitching and this and that, as you see. Do keep your voice down, or you shall be sent to your room.'

'You take children, and they breathe into them. How they suffer, the children, because of you!'

'Now, Clod, are you going to get excited? If you are you must perforce go back to your chamber.'

'You take the breath from children's lives!'

'Why whatever is he talking about?'

'And ever after leave them empty!'

'Clod, Clod, what are you saying?'

'Your tickets, you call them, the children you steal!'

'Whatever does he mean?'

'Now, Clod,' said Granny, looking up and, with an air of irritation, putting her steel needles down, 'I shall not have you talk of us so. Your own family. Your own people forced into exile. You believe we take children and pull the breath from them and put it in these leather dolls?'

'Yes, I do. Yes, you do!' I said.

'Have you seen it?' Granny asked.

'Well.'

'Well?'

'Have you?'

'Not precisely.'

'You have not seen it then, you have merely heard about it. Someone told you. Someone's being telling you tales.'

'Lucy Pennant told me. And the Tailor, Rippit's birth object, when he –'

'Of course he did, the meddling letter opener, and of course she did, she would, that's very like her isn't it? I'm not in the least surprised by that. Even from her death, even beyond her grave – though surely there can be no such place for such a vermin – even from such a distance, how she influences you. So she told you this filth and you believed it.'

'Yes! Yes I do!'

Some small muttering from some aunts then, a sigh or two, a snip of scissors, the small sound of leather being punctured by the needles.

'What a baby, what a cruel baby you are. You'd believe anyone but your own family.'

'I honestly don't know why we bother with the monstrous child,' some other aunt muttered.

'Should have left him back there.'

'Should never have held the train for him.'

'Be quiet, ladies,' said Granny. 'Now Clod, listen up and listen good. I'll not repeat this, for the accusation cuts into me, cuts sharper and deeper than any needle here. You make my soul cry bitter tears. Those unspeakable things, those dealings with children that you have just mentioned – I shall not repeat the accusations – are all monstrous lies. Cruel untruths told by the ingratitude of Foulsham people. People we saved, for

121

as long as we were able. We took up those children and gave them shelter and food, yes they did work for us, good work for which they were rewarded. We did a better job than their parents. We made them into most useful citizens. Did we harm them? No! We fed them. We saved them. We kept them from the Heap Sickness and we nurtured them. We saved them, Clod, saved them by our own goodness, until Lungdon sought fit to murder them!'

'But how then did these leathermen come to life if not through the children?'

'Do you really think, oh Clod great doubter, do you really think that if a child breathes into a leather sack that the sack springs to life? No, of course it does not! What nonsense! What childishness! What viciousness! It is Umbitt – much maligned Umbitt – and all his clever ways that does it. Only he, with all his brilliance, that Atlas of Iremongers, who by his great bravery and strength keeps us alive and safe, as hard as that is. With no asking for any gratitude, with no thought for his own self, that man, my husband and my hero, who through his labours, selflessly sacrifices himself for his own family. No matter the pain the effort causes him. No, Clod, it was not any children, it was Umbitt, only ever Umbitt!'

'It was Umbitt,' echoed an aunt.

'It was Umbitt.'

'Umbitt.'

'Umbitt.'

'And what does he get in return for all his great hard work?'

'Umbitt.'

'Umbitt.'

All the echoes of 'Umbitt' came from the leather people all about.

'Rank ingratitude!'

'Only Umbitt?' I said. 'What lies! How can you tell such lies?'

'Umbitt.'

'Umbitt.'

'Only and ever Umbitt. And for that, and for saving children, we are repaid by dirty stories, cruel fairy tales, ugly rumours. Which some of his own flesh, his own grandson, decides to believe!'

'Shocking.'

'Distasteful.'

'Vinegar for blood.'

'I don't believe you, Granny, not for a moment. I think you hurt those children.'

'Upon my own ancient heart,' said Granny, pressing one of her tiny aged hands to her chest and clinking her pearls in the process. 'Every word I said is all true. These are but dolls, filled with Lungdon rubbish, animated by the genius of your poor grandfather!'

'Lucy said – and the Tailor – you took their souls from them . . .'

'He does not believe us! Even now!'

'No, Granny, I cannot believe you, I shall not.'

'What vile and dirty thoughts must fill your swollen head, child.'

'Better we had died back there in Foulsham.'

'What ugliness must dwell inside you.'

'Burnt for our cruelty.'

'Twisting you.'

'A disgraceful family.'

'Turning you.'

'Such monsters of people.'

'Against your own kind, your own blood.'

'Yes, yes, I do stand against my own blood!'

'Go then, Clod,' said Granny, so upset now. 'Go, I release you, go out into Lungdon, find your own way, I shall hold you back no longer. Live amongst whoever you may, take your own crooked path. I've done with you. I cannot have such a Joodis Iremonger around my ailing bosom, near my wilting heart, you'll quite kill me. No, no, Clod, choose this moment – stay here with those that try, day and night, to love you, or go, be gone, thrust forever from our care and keeping. Piggott!' she cried, pulling the bell cord. 'Fetch the wretch some shoes!' Then turning back to me she spat, 'Take your carcass away from this,' she indicated her heart, 'forever!'

She stood up and pointed dramatically to the door, and as she did so, all the leather people stood up and likewise pointed at the door.

'Sit down will you!' she said and all the leathers sat down.

'Sit.'

'Sit.'

'Sit,' they mumbled.

Piggott entered holding a pair of gentlemen's black lace-up shoes. She looked even more put out than before. 'My lady.'

'What do you want?' cried Granny.

'You called me, my lady. Shoes.'

'Oh yes, so I did; in my fury I forgot.'

'There is something else, my lady.'

'What else, Piggott? I am most preoccupied.'

Piggott whispered into my grandmother's ears.

'I don't care to know about any Iremonger called Mary Staggs.'

More whispering.

'What? How?'

Whispering.

'Clod?'

Whispering.

'Phidias Collins?'

Yet more.

'In the flesh?'

Yet more.

'Downstairs? What, now?'

Yet more.

'Get it out!'

'Yes, my lady.'

'Into the city!'

'Yes, my lady.'

'Lose it fast!'

'Yes, my lady.'

'Disgusting!'

'Yes, my lady.'

'And what was the servant's name, did you say?'

'Mary Staggs, my lady.'

'Rat her.'

'My lady?'

'Rat her now!'

'If you're sure, my lady.'

'And keep her ratted!'

'If you're sure, my lady.'

'Of course I'm sure!'

'Yes, my lady.'

'Do it, Piggott, and get beyond my sighting!'

'Yes, my lady.'

The unhappy housekeeper had scarce left the room when Granny erupted a single syllable, launched from her in both fury and misery, 'CLOD!'

'Clod.'

'Clod.'

'Clod,' the leathers echoed.

But then Granny sat down, panting for breath. It was a terrible sight.

'Oh Ayris, oh daughter,' she wailed, real tears coming down her face, 'better that you died! Better that you left us before ever you could see this canker child!'

'What have I done now, Granny?'

'You detest us!'

'Yes, Granny, I think I do.'

'You despise us.'

'Yes I do, Granny, for you have done such terrible things.'

'On the subject of Foulsham children, Clodius Iremonger, let me promise you with every drop of my still pumping blood: you *were* misled.'

'Was I, Granny?'

'You *were*!' she cried and indeed she sounded so miserable.

'Truly, Granny. How can I believe you?'

'I do swear it, Clod. On all that I have ever loved. On your own dead mother! Lies and rumours! Horrible whisperings.

We are a fine people. We are Iremongers, does that mean nothing to you?' How she sobbed, my grandmother. It was a terrible sight.

'Not nothing, Granny, oh Granny . . . I am sorry . . . I don't know what to think . . . I . . .'

'You are sorry?' she said, sitting up and seizing my words.

'I am very miserable.'

'You are sorry!' she said, almost cheerfully. 'He is sorry!' she called to all the ladies thereabouts.

'That's nice.'

'I should think so.'

'Sorry.'

'Sorry.'

'Sorry,' mumbled the leathers.

'How right that he's sorry.'

'So nicely done.'

'A good child . . .'

'Always comes home in the end.'

'Always licks his spoon clean.'

'And is grateful.'

'He said sorry,' repeated Granny. 'Oh Ayris, I can almost see your face upon his. As if she's back again, beside me. He said sorry!'

The leathers all nodded their heads too.

'Well Granny, that is, I do not think that Lucy could have told me such lies, there is truth there . . .'

'Kiss me child, kiss me and make up.'

Such silence in the room then, all those women looking at me.

'Kiss me, kiss your granny, and all shall be forgotten.'

127

I stood there, helpless, I cannot honestly say what I might have done, whether I should have kissed the old lady. She ever had such a hold upon me, and perhaps I had even started to advance a step or two, but then, only then, the front door was opened, and people were running into the drawing room, Moorcus leading them.

'Timfy!' he bellowed. 'Oh, Granny! It's Timfy! Uncle Timfy!'

'What,' said Granny, 'about Timfy?'

'He's been got, Granny. He's been took. He's been taken. Oh Granny, the police, they took him down. Oh Granny, they followed him, they caught wind of him and pursued him through the streets, and he tried to call out, he tried to blow on his whistle to get help, but the whistle not working he could not do it. Oh terrible! Terrible, Granny. It is the worst thing.'

'Timfy, our House Uncle, our blood, our child!' screamed Granny.

'Timfy, our brother?' said Idwid, at the door now.

'Timfy,' said Moorcus. 'Taken away by the police!'

All the dummies stood up.

'Timfy,' they mumbled.

'Timfy.'

'Timfy.'

'Oh!' cried Granny. 'Then we are discovered!'

The Still-betrothed Pinalippy Iremonger

9

SHARP AS

The narrative of Pinalippy Iremonger

Well then, Timfy's been taken. He always was rather an unnecessary little man, born hapless I shouldn't wonder, tripped on his own umbilical cord no doubt. Still I should never have wished him taken. Ruffled about maybe, perhaps threatened a bit, bullied back certainly, but then afterwards returned to us.

I don't feel safe in this house, not any more. I don't suppose there's anywhere in all Lungdon where there is safety for such as us. How they hate us, the Lungdon people. It's an awful thing, their hate. Hard not to take it personally. I look at myself in the mirror. There you are, I say, there's Pinalippy. All dressed for escape, all togged up and ready to exit, in a nice dress and bonnet, looking just like a lady, just like a Lungdon lady. New clothes, new clothes for our escape. Tonight, the whole family's on the move. It's not safe any more, not here,

131

time to move on. So there I am, in the mirror, Pinalippy Lurliorna Iremonger. That is me there, that is. 'Who is that girl? the people cry,' I say to my reflection. 'What a picture!' She's not one to be worried about things, never used to be. I can see it now though, in my face, somewhere about the eyebrows. Fear. Now they've called for all our birth objects. That's how serious it has got. All birth objects save Rippit's are to be given over. Umbitt Owner is taking them all up, he's looking after them. They must most urgently be kept away from Clod, we are told. Such a sorrow to give my doily to Sturridge to take to Umbitt. Such a pain. I wonder if I shall ever see it again. I suppose if anyone should keep it safe Great Umbitt should, but surely it belongs to me, that dear doily. I feel the wrong weight without it.

I feel so unsteady.

I'm frightened, every moment of every day, I am a little bit frightened. I did feel safe before, back in Heap House. Even after the great storm, even after Moorcus's bride to be, Horryit, got sucked into the heaps and drowned. Even after that. I thought, well that's what happens if you're Horryit, that's her fate. That's what happens if you're too beautiful and such a bitch, you have to pay for it. Not me though, that sort of thing shall never happen to me. Thing is, not so sure now. Thing is, I think I might actually die. And the thing is, the absolute rub of it is, I don't want to.

I'm eighteen years old.

I'd like to see nineteen, I think twenty might be a lot of fun.

If I can just hold on, if I can just be a little bit lucky, whilst all about me are soiling themselves with their terror.

I've got to be smart. Smarter than ever before. Smart as two pins.

Then there's Clod.

There's the subject.

I'm to befriend him, they say, and to get him ready. The old woman, she had sent for me and I was sat by her and her great fireplace and she pointed at me, and told me to do it, to go to him and love him, and make him come back to the family. She said it was my duty. How they all did go on at me, all the most senior women, they said to me in their litany, Love him, love him, bring him back. And then they dabbed me with the treacle so that I may trap the little mite in its sweet stickiness.

Well then, I said, I'd do my best.

Trouble is, he's not a one for doilies.

Trouble is, he likes a matchbox called Lucy, a common, common little thing.

I stand back and let him cry for her, maybe when he's done being so wet, when he's dried up a little, then he'll see me. I should so like to reel him in, but I must go at it careful. I'll have him in the end if he matters so very much to them; he's mine after all, selected for me.

He doesn't love the doily. Not yet.

I can help that. I can make myself most attractive. I'm a woman. I'll have him learn that. When it comes time for our escape, the old matriarch tells me, I'm to stick by him, to bring him round, me and Moorcus we're to go out into Lungdon streets with him. Moorcus has the address of somewhere safe, and there we're to keep him and encourage him Iremonger. To get him ready for the big morning on Westminster Bridge.

'What will happen then,' I ask, 'on Westminster?'

'Justice shall happen,' said the old woman, 'and all shall be well again.'

'All shall be well?'

'If you have him ready, Pinalippy, if you bring him round.'

'You might give him his own plug then,' I suggested. 'That would help, surely.'

'No it should not, it would be too dangerous. Let Rippit keep his plug safe for now. And let Umbitt look after all other birth objects.'

'It's very wrong not to let him have it.'

'Pinalippy, you don't know anything.'

'If you trust him a little, maybe he'll trust back. That's all I'm saying.'

'But he's not to be trusted. He cannot be. To think of what he did this morning downstairs to one of the servants! No, it is very right that Umbitt has your doily and all those other things to keep all safe, to make him and us safer. If Umbitt doesn't take your doily, Pinalippy, you may find it growing legs and arms, growing a head and screaming back at you. That is how much Clod is to be trusted. He must trust *you* though, Pinalippy, he must love you. And through you he must love his family.'

'Yes, Ommaball Owneress.'

'Then run along and see to it.'

I know well enough how he'll come to me. I have the plan. And in all the chaos of our move I mean to do it.

I'll get him his plug amidst the terror of our escape. I'll snatch it then, then, oh then I'll have him, won't I? It will be like holding his strange unhappy heart.

* * *

'Rippit,' I said, 'come here then and don't be shy.'

There was Rippit in the corridor, all dressed up, in overalls and big cap, big clothes to disguise the odd shape of the fellow beneath.

'Rippit, I say!'

'Rippit,' he said. Course he did. Never anything else, the poor lamb, he can't.

'Come on, come sit by me, come close, closer now.'

'Rippit.'

'Don't be shy.'

'Rippit.'

'Don't whisper.'

I pinched him them, good and hard about his breast, took a good quick grab of flesh just where it hurts, couldn't stop myself.

'Rippit!'

'Don't shout either. That was just a little pinch for familiarity. Come now. Sit tight. I want you to tell me all about you.'

'Rippit.'

'I think you like me.'

'Rippit.'

'I remember, years ago, before you went missing, you used to come to spy on us in the girls' wing, you used to pry and sniff about.'

'Rippit.'

'Oh, do stop being so shy, Cousin Rippit, sweet Cousin Rippy. It's perfectly natural.'

'Rippit!'

'Ripper!'

I pinched him again, feeling about his odd person, searching for a shape.

'Oh come, it was only a little pinch for friendship. What a fuss you make.'

'Rippit!'

'Now, now, I shan't do it again I do promise you.'

'Rippit.'

'Oh Rippit, you're all of a fluster. I do believe you're sweating a little.'

'Rippit. Rippit.'

'Now, Rippit, with all the worry about us and all the sadness over Timfy, it is nice to have a quiet moment before whatever is coming to us comes. Is it not, Rippit?'

'Rippit.'

'Quite right, here we are then. I do promise I shan't do it again. Now then tell me a story, shan't you? Make a girl happy.'

'Rippit?'

'Don't be an old mophead, darling Rip-rip. Come now. How you tremble! Come on, a little story to take our minds off. Please begin.'

'Rippit?'

'I shan't take no for an answer.'

'Rippit. Rippit.' He actually started to try to tell a story, what a sorry old sight. 'Rippit, rrrripppit, rippit-rippit-rrippit. Rip. Pit. Rippit, rippit, rippit.'

'How splendid!'

'Rippit! Rippit, rippit, rippit, rippit, rippit!'

'How glorious, and then what happened?'

'Rippit.'

'And then?'

'Rippit, rippit. Rippit? Rippit!'

'Keep going, dear Rippity-rippity, what a sport you are.'

'Rippit,' he whispered. 'Rippitrippitrippitrippitrippit, rippit, rippit. Rippit? Rippit . . . rippit . . . rippit!'

'A happy ending!'

Then I pinched him such a pinch, I quite terrified the soul of him.

'RIPPIT! RIPPIT!'

'What a fuss you do make! Just a pinch wasn't it, for felicity – no need to let the world know.'

'RIPPIT!'

'I do pinch, Rippit, I do like to, to have some flesh between my fingers.'

'Rippit! Rippit!'

'Off already? Are you, Rippit? Oh well then, please yourself.'

I have it!

I have the plug in my pocket, I switched it. Clod's own little plug, I'll keep it safe and sound. Well done, Pinny, you're the girl. And I have something else too. He was keeping them together, snug in the same deep pocket as if they had business with one another.

A box of matches wrapped in a cloth.

Can't be a coincidence, can it? It must be *her* box of matches. Why would he keep hold of such a thing? Maybe she is still alive then, maybe she is. I'll keep these matches too for now, but I shan't have them anywhere near the plug. The matches and the plug are to be kept lonely. I'll keep them all nice and sealed up. I'll have metal tins to put them in, tobacco tins, to quite deaden the noise so Clod can't be hearing them. So whilst no one else has their objects any more, I have two of them: a lovers' pair.

Well then, I have my instructions. Clod and I, we'll walk out together into Lungdon, and Moorcus can keep an eye on us and report back as instructed.

Yes, yes, that was very well done.

Smart as. You are. Smart as.

The pin!

Governor Idwid Iremonger in Disguise

Ifful Iremonger, of Black Breath

10

AN AUNT CALLED NIGHT

Continuing the narrative of Clod Iremonger

Before the Move

'Now, Clod,' said Idwid to me in the morning room; I had been most specifically summoned by the grieving uncle, 'we are to change our dwelling.'

He was all dressed up in strange red clothes, some sort of military uniform.

'I,' said Idwid, 'am a Chelsea Pensioner. This is what an ancient soldier looks like when he's a charity case. Quite smart aren't I!'

'Yes Uncle, you are indeed.'

'And, Clod, we have clothes for you – you shall be quite the gentleman. You may put these on when the time is come, and it is coming, it is fast coming.'

He handed me a large fine overcoat with a fur collar and a very tall top hat. It took me a moment to understand that we were alone in the room for all the others were leather people quietly sitting or standing here and there.

'Now, Clodling, you are to be a young gentleman in mourning, that's your cover. Here now is a black armband. That you must wear on your left arm. And you see, you do see where I feel, this particular wide band around your hat, that is what they do in mourning in this Lungdonland, for they are all in mourning you see, all in a grief for Victoria's Albert, him that's been rotting now for all of fifteen years, still, still they do blub so! You being such a sorrowful fellow we thought the outfit should fit you perfect.'

'I am sorry about Uncle Timfy,' I said. 'I am sorry for your loss, Uncle.'

'You're sorry!' spat Idwid, of a sudden flipped into a fury. 'What am I to do with your "sorry", wet little creature that it is? I couldn't give a premature rat for your sorry, I don't give a fly's poo for your sorry. I shouldn't give a flea's tit for it. What am I to do with such a thing? I've a good mind to take Geraldine here,' he said, but then he stopped, 'but I don't have her right now. Such days! People not to be trusted. My Geraldine!'

Indeed I noticed then that I had not heard her in the room.

'If I had her,' he said sadly, 'I might bury her deep in your head. What do you say to that?'

'On the whole, Uncle, I should rather you didn't.'

'Well then, have a care. I miss her so.'

Silence then, but for the gentle breathing of various leather people sat about us. The morning room must have been the only peaceful room in the house; elsewhere all was in a panic, but here all was quiet and docile amongst the leathers, who would of an occasion look up to one or the other of us and smile vaguely before their false faces lost the smile again and resumed their terrible and habitual blankness.

'We will not die,' said Idwid. 'Not this family.'

I said nothing.

His moon head tilted in its particular way, a long grin came to the white face. 'Well,' he said, 'since we are to move on, the groundwork must be laid, before we are able to come together again, after two nights of hiding. Before we all gather upon Westminster Bridge.'

'And what then, Uncle?'

'Oh fireworks, I should think. And celebrations!'

'What ever shall we do, Uncle?'

'First all things must be readied for the trip. Now then, Clod, I don't know why I do it, for I'm certain you don't deserve it, but I mean to introduce you to someone. Someone I'm particular to, someone most particular to me, can you guess who it is?'

'No, indeed, sir.'

'Well heavens, man, who do you think?'

'I cannot guess, Uncle, I do not know.'

'Why my wife, man! My own Ifful woman.'

'I never knew that there was such a person.'

'Not everyone does so advertise his love and moan and groan, and whimper it from every door; not every person I say ruins the furniture on account of a little lost love! As if his heart has more feeling than any other!'

'Please, Uncle, I did not ask for this.'

'Well, duck, tuck in, for there's more coming. I mean to bash your head about until you come out Iremonger at last.'

'I warn you not to, Uncle.'

'I'll bootstrap you back to life and sense!'

'You'll be hurt in the process I dare say, I will no longer be bent over anyone's knee. I am quite done with that. I've grown talents of my own.'

'Well well, enough then, Clod. Perhaps I am a little strong of mind, I'm in a passion I do admit: I've lost a brother and given Geraldine over for safe keeping and grief must have its privilege.'

'Yes, sir, as I said, I am sorry.'

Uncle Idwid looked furious for a moment but seemed then to swallow down his mood and to come up smiling, for his head tilted again and his horrible grin returned.

'Well, Clod, we were talking of love.'

'You were, Uncle. It was your subject.'

'Well then, I have loved too! There: how's that for a statement?'

'It is indeed news to me.'

'I am married, hooked, lined and sinkered, I've a ball and chain all of my own. A census concerning my bed: there's two in it!'

'I never even knew that I had such an aunt.'

'Well, of course you didn't, my lad, my chick. But indeed, I am most wedded!

'My wifey. My Ifful, offal of joy! If you'd only behaved yourself, Clod, and come to work in Foulsham when you'd first been trousered, then you should have lived alongside us, as a lodger in our apartments in Bayleaf House. And now those fair rooms, our home, our piece of the world, are burst asunder, such

146

warm rooms as they were, being directly connected to one of the great smoke stacks. Come now, Ifful my only, come down will you and meet young Clod. For she's been here about us all along, but does come over shy so often! Come Ifful, come down I say! Cooo-eeeee!'

There was a shifting then, I could not comprehend where precisely at first, but then in a great gush of soot a figure stood in the fireplace, actually in the hearth, a person descended from the chimney flue. When the black had cleared a little I saw a person, a small, very dark person, most begrimed and sooted.

'Hullo, Idwid.'

'Hullo to you, Ifful.'

They bowed to one another and grinned widely. And some of the leathers likewise bowed too.

'This is Clod, dear.'

'So this is Clod, is it?'

She was a small, sooty woman, smaller yet than Idwid, but with a very wide mouth, a huger grin than ever his was, which I had not before that moment conceived entirely probable. She wore the sooting and chimney dusting about her like a thick layer of cloth, like a veil upon her face and body which only her whiter teeth and eyes managed to penetrate.

'I say, hullo Aunt,' I ventured. 'I am right glad to meet you.'

'Even this is Clod?' she said again.

'It is, my dearest, my darkness, my depth.'

'He doesn't look very much.'

'No, no I suppose he don't. But he is very much nevertheless.'

'Are you the one to save us?'

'Now, Ifful, he's not been . . .'

147

'Save you? Save you?' I asked. 'What ever can you mean?'

'He's but a thin fog,' said Aunt Ifful. 'What can he do?'

'Much,' said Idwid.

'I can hear,' I said, for I was not without pride in my small doings and I did not like the tone from this newly declared aunt who lived up chimneys, listening to people's conversations. 'I can hear, I can hear better than Uncle Idwid, I can move things, any things, and I can break things, I blister wallpaper, and foul windows, I char rooms, I can do much and more by the day, I'll pick up London and turn it upside down I shouldn't be much surprised, and you, you, you little woman, what are you to me? I'm the Ire of Iremonger!'

They both tilted their heads towards me then, in very similar ways.

'Thinks a lot of himself, don't he?' said Ifful.

'Does rather, on the whole,' said Idwid.

'Should be taught some manners, if only there were time.'

'Yes indeed, my love, my lovely lungs, he should be upturned and dunked in brackish water, for long minutes at a time.'

'I should say.'

'And yet there is not, as you say, time.'

'The new generation: they do not know their place, no table manners, elbows in the way, spots and grease. No class.'

'And you, and you!' I said for I was done with my family's endless correcting. 'What is it that you can do that makes you so bold with Clod, Clod the furniture mover!'

'Why then, dear Ifful,' said Idwid, bristling, 'ever my comfort, my night blanket, my blackness, my darker than death, give a little exhibition, shan't you?'

'Shall I?'

'Blot him out, dear!'

Then my Aunt Ifful, grinning as wide as my Uncle Idwid, suddenly grinned wider and wider yet: I have never seen such an enormous mouth, such a gob that might eat any size of things, it stretched and stretched and did verily meet from ear to ear. Then Ifful, with her hugest cake hole, put back her head and her whole jaw seemed to snap back, like I've heard that certain snakes are able when they wish to consume something large. I saw my little aunt dislocate her own jaw, and then – she being smaller than me – I looked over her and could see the awful sinkhole of her throat, I could look from the rampart walls of her wide-open teeth, deep down into the view of the dark depths of Idwid's Ifful, and it was a terrible thing. I feared I may even tumble in myself. But that's nothing yet because then from Ifful's very open maw, from somewhere deep beneath her innards came up something black, like some small toad escaping but then it grew and grew, it curled and shifted around until it was bigger than her hole, bigger than her wide open mouth, bigger yet than her head, more than her body soon: a blackness, a great ever-swelling blackness, blacker than black, darker than darkest carbon or ebony or even licorice, darker than the most lightless of places, and this deep black of her she spread out from her mouth further and further by horrible flicks of her dark tongue. Thick, thick clouds, coming closer and closer to me, hemming me in, snuffing me out. Like something bad, terrible bad, coming over you, filling up all the room, till it covered all, and feeling it now reach my skin, it was like something black and wet creeping over me, and then it was all about me, over my face and every part of me and I could see nothing. No hint of light, no different shades of darkness, just black, black blackness everywhere, like all light and all colour, like all life had been drowned out for evermore.

And yet I breathed still.

And yet I was still there, still even in that room, though crowded so with blackest night. I put my hands out to try and hold onto something in all that blackness and my hand found a head and a face.

'Is that you, Uncle?' I asked. 'Is that your face I'm touching?'

'No, Clod, no, my face is quite unmolested. It must be the face of someone other.'

'A leather!' I cried and sprung back.

'Don't get them excited, Clod, they're so hard to calm once they're excited.'

'Gone dark,' mumbled a leather.

'Dark.'

'Dark.'

'Dark.'

'Oh Uncle,' I gasped, 'what is this sudden and descending night?'

'Why, lad so bold, it's only Ifful, my lady life, little Ifful all on her own.'

'Whatever did she do, and may she please kindly undo it right soon?'

'Oh in good time, Clod. Now you see what I see always, this no-ness, how do you find it?'

'Most uncomfortable, most uncomfitting.'

'Very like, very like.'

'May light come back? Why does she blacken so?'

'Oh, for myself, I do love it, to get a little washed in the breath of Ifful. 'Tis such a treat for me, 'tis loving fair enough; great blanketing night, with a little touch of gingivitis. Why, Clod, it's what she does, and does so well. She is my deadly nightshade, she is my Ifful lovelungs. It is her that keeps the day out of the day, that lengthens the night, 'tis her, 'tis only her with a little help from the still-smouldering fire of Foulsham and from the dirty dark breath of Lungdon itself.'

'She makes the night?'

'That's it! She's getting us ready to escape so that none may see us out on Lungdon streets. That's why she's been up the chimney. That's my Ifful, she was born with three lungs: two to be a person; one, much larger, to blacken and soot with. She hates the day, and keeps all night. Oh she does loathe the sun so, and so she puts it out! And I, being blind, am most indifferent to it myself.'

'Truly, Uncle, it is quite a thing to do, to kill the sun.'

'Well, we are talented, we Iremongers! We are such a people!'

'Yes, yes! I do think we are.'

'Now he comes home! We are Iremongers, Clod!'

'Yes,' I whispered, 'yes there's no doubting of that.'

'It was my Ifful that was the inspiration for the leather populace.'

'It was Ifful that did it, back in Bayleaf House?'

'She was the inspiration with her dark, dark air.'

'Oh she was the one, she did it!'

'There never was such a talented people, Clod, as we Iremongers. Never such ones for doing things. How would it be then, Clod, if we were to be extinguished, if this little blackness conjured by my little woman were to be descended upon us for always and that thereafter there never should be Iremonger no more?'

'It would, Uncle,' I said, so lost in that darkness absolute, darkness like deep burial, buried deep and yet still alive, 'it would be most terrible.'

'Good, my lad! You are coming to see a little clearer now!'

'Uncle, I am fearful.'

'You should be, Clod, they'll murder us if we're not smart. They're already at it. And not all of us are like to survive this next removal; they are upon us, and will take us down bit by bit. Which Iremonger shall die this night?'

'Will we die, even tonight?'

'Some of us shall, they are that set upon it!'

'They are so cruel!'

'Yes! Oh yes, you must strike at them, Clod, and kill them here and there. You'll not let them murder us, shall you?'

'No, well, no, Uncle, I should not want them to.'

'And there's music to my all-hearing ears! So get you ready, Clodius Iremonger. Two nights is all you have! Now, Ifful, business done, pack away the night a little won't you, love? So that the boy may dress himself for to step upon Lungdon and so feel it under his heels.'

Aunt Ifful seemed to breathe in then, and to put the night back up deep inside her, and soon it was dark but a much lighter darkness, and Ifful lit a gas lamp. There she was in the centre of the room, there was Uncle by her side. The leathers were all in their former places but were moving their heads a little from side to side, as if they were looking for something.

'Well done, my bucket of blackness, ta and ta and ta again!'

'That, nephew,' she said, the thick blackness all swallowed away, with a little burp in conclusion like a sudden gust of fog, 'that is what I do. I done it to you once before now too – I was the black smoke that led you down and down in Bayleaf House, the thick black smoke that saved you and guided you to the train.'

'I am impressed, Aunt, that was . . . very something!'

'Yes, I do do the night well, though it can leave one a little out of breath. I must call on the city Lungdon now after my lungs have dunged on it.'

'We shall be sending you out very soon, Ifful.'

'Yes, to darken the path further. So that we may walk unseen. Is all ready?'

'Let us hope, Clod, that we are not too diminished with this outing.'

A knocking on the drawing-room door.

'Come then Clod, put on hat and coat, come now tread on, be my eyes a little, lead me, child.'

My Family are in the Hallway

We went then into the hall, where my family were ready; so many of us, all lined up the stairway, all ready, family and servants, all nervous and whispering: soon, soon, it must be soon. So many of us holding cardboard parcels, suitcases, satchels, small trunks. But none holding their birth objects, no sounds from them, no names. How underdressed they all seemed. Aunt Rosamud, no doorhandle in hand, came blurting forward.

'Oh Idwid, there you are, dear fellow,' she wept. 'You'll let me keep him, won't you? You won't have Binadit left here all alone?'

'Should never have brought him here,' some aunt called from further back.

'Not safe to move him now.'

'He'll have us drowned dead.'

'He's my son, my own son!' called Rosamud.

'You threw him out – best thing you ever did!'

'Leave him behind!'

'Lose him.'

'He's nothing to us.'

'You monsters!' cried Rosamud, striking around willy-nilly. 'You'll murder me first! Cowards! Cripples!'

She swung out and in response many of the Iremonger aunts hit back at her, kicked her and cursed and caused a general horrible wailing of womankind.

'Ordure! Ordure! I will have ordure!' came the very special Iremonger cry, delivered only on most particular occasions, and this being heard and coming from Idwid, caused a general quietening up and down the lines. 'Hush, hush, my lovelies, we are a family, are we not, we are a people, a fine people, we are not animals. Let us remember ourselves.'

A general calming among the frocks.

'Now, now, ladies, most beloved sex, come, there is no need for this. All will be well, all of us, every last Iremonger shall be counted out and looked after, there's no need to fear, all is safe as louses. Now, concerning young master Binadit . . .'

'My son, he is my son!'

'Yes, yes, so he is. Congratulations once again! But your loving son does so pull all with him, so very popular he is with all the bits, such a cumbersome fellow, all in all, it must be said though. Best we leave him here for now.'

'NO! NO!'

'Rosamud, I will not have you shrieking!' snapped Idwid. 'Listen, and be sensible. If he comes along with us now then he'll give us all away. Let us leave him here . . .'

'MY BIN!'

'Just for a little. Then when all is safe we shall come and find him again.'

'You're leaving him to be murdered!'

'No, no, Muddy lady, listen to me. He's safer here than ever he'll be out on the streets. Let us keep him here a while where he is safest, he shall drown out there, the poor lad. Consider, they may never find this house, and even if they do, there's every chance they'll not look down there for him in the deepest cellar, besides which he is most able to disguise himself. He's a very capable young man, your own son is, remember how he survived on his own for years? He was safer that way and shall be again. It is his family who endangers him; let him alone a little, just a little.'

'It's all because of your brother Timfy,' wept Rosamud.

'Tattletale Timfy telling on us,' took up another aunt.

'Betraying us all,' came one more.

'Now, now, ladies, we do not know that Timfy has told.'

A general muttering of misery from the aunts and cousins, even uncles, spitting out Timfy's name.

'Now, let us speak quietly,' cooed Idwid. 'Do attend and wait your turn. Umbitt and Omaball Oliff are already gone and with them the senior servants and governors and Iremongers of great import and all our birth objects in safety. Now that some decent time has passed between their leaving, now, I say, now it is time for others of us to be off and safe. It is all just a precaution, my dear ones, just in case.'

'In case your brother squeals, you mean.'

'Indeed, yes, just in case.'

'Let us on then!'

'First shall be all the adults remaining and the youngest in their care, and with them their servants, and then, a little after, it is time for the oldest children Iremonger, those who are our swiftest and sharpest. Unry and Otta are abroad and they do watch this street with great caution. When the word is given, then we shall be from here and walk like we are true Lungdoners out into the night. So now come forward my officers from Foulsham, then behind them be ready the House Aunts and Uncles, then all other Iremongers in trousers and dresses, then the children at the back, all the pretty children, all those rosy cheeks. Now, now, darlings one and all, my little blood dumplings, we must wait a little, and in good cheer. Wait, only wait for the word. If we all rush out together we shall make a great spectacle of it. Safer to trickle, a swift trickle, bit by bit by bit all in different ways. Scattershot us Iremongers, hither and thither and in between.'

So did we wait all close and clammy and clammed in, cousins with cousins, aunts breathing uncles and uncles aunts, all so thick and huddled together listening to the drum-drum-drumitty-drum of our fearing hearts, breathing, breathing in the dark.

'How much longer?'

'Hush now.'

'We're rats in a trap.'

'Hushabye.'

'We shall all suffocate in one another.'

'*Twinkle, twinkle, my fat hen,*' whispered Idwid, an old Iremonger nursery rhyme.

'We'll drown here amongst ourselves.'

'*Stayed nice and cosy in his pen.*'

'They'll set fire to the building and all shall perish!'

'*When the fox came for to eat.*'

'We are done for.'

'*Our hen ate fox from head to feet.*'

'I need to get out.'

'Need to breathe!'

At last there came a faint scratching from the door. It was opened a crack and a huge fat rat tumbled in, a brass ring around its neck. The rat, coughing, tugged the ring free and then, spinning, tossing and looking like it was in horrible pain, the creature shifted and tumbled, grew and lurched itself upwards and came out at last my shifting Cousin Otta.

'Well girl, keen blood, what's the news?' spilled Idwid.

'Time to get us gone, swift as cholera. They're coming, they're coming for us. I found two leathermen gutted down the road. They're coming, coming ever closer, time to shift!'

What screams followed the news.

'Ordure! Ordure!'

'Where's Unry?'

'Keep down your spleens!' called Aliver.

'He's about three streets away, he's watching the coppers. There's more and more of them coming in, trying to surround us we reckon, not sure where they're all coming from. Some in uniforms, some in plain clothes. I think they've smelt us. Coming together, getting closer, ever closer I say! You must get out!' cried Otta.

'All right, Otta, for this many thanks, get you gone.'

All panic then, all screams, and calling back for order and order, each to their places.

'Let us get at the run!' said Idwid. 'We meet again two mornings' time. On the eighth of February 1876 that is, on Westminster Bridge. Gather there all of you that may, that is our grouping come together then. Repeat it. When do we meet?'

'Two mornings' time.'

'Eighth of February.'

'1876.'

'But where, where my pasties?'

'Westminster Bridge.'

'Yes, yes, yes again. At eight of the clock.'

'But what shall we do now?'

'Where shall we go?'

'Help! Help us!'

'No time! No time, my lovelies, my sweet jellies!' yelled Idwid. 'No time for that now. You're Iremongers, you are to a man, so act Iremonger, be strong and be brave. Be of Lungdon hue, fit in, sink in, grow into Lungdon people, be invisible. Use your cleverness, use your dirty magic, destroy them, bring them down, make them cry out. For two more nights, two nights alone, we go our separate ways and then, when all is done and ready, we come back together in a rash of great blackness. Filled with a blossoming of blood, we collect, we Iremongers, we collect our dues, our debts, our deaths on Westminster Bridge. There to Iremonger itch and irritate, there to bite and burst. Go then, my blessings on you. All be safe, my children! Come, Gorrild underling, get me moving; come Ifful. Pinalippy, are you all primed?'

'Yes, Uncle!' called Pinalippy.

'You know your place I believe?'

'Yes, Uncle, surely!'

'Then good luck to you. Moorcus, you are in charge now, you and your prefects . . . I do mean officers. And when you have dispersed all, look to your duties and to Clod and Pinalippy.'

'We are most ready and eager!' answered Moorcus, dressed for the occasion in the uniform of a London firefighter.

Such a rushing of Iremonger officers, all dressed like Idwid, all gathering around him.

'Be good, my boy,' Idwid said to me. 'You're an Iremonger, you are.' He slapped me hard around the face. 'Use your ears! Keep Pinalippy close by! Look after each other.'

And Ifful on her way out stamped hard upon my feet. 'Earn your blood!'

They were outside.

'All now be safe, my children! Flee! Flee! Flee for your lives!'

159

Now there was such light gone from the corridor – the more senior uncles and aunts having taken what lights, lanterns, shielded torches they had for themselves – and we were left in a general panic with only a few candles lit betwixt us.

Then Moorcus and his fellow officers, Stunly and Duvit, let all the remaining adults out, some taking the youngest children with them, and among them went Rosamud weeping for her son, but pulled onwards by some fellow aunts. And where was Rippit in all the turmoil? I had not seen him, I supposed he must have gone away with Grandfather, and I was not sorry at that. And so there were only we older children left then. There was Bornobby, there was Foy still holding on to her great ten-pound weight, her birth object, which must have been so heavy it had not been taken away. There were Pool and Theeby, holding hands. There was Ormily, and with her a sorry grouping all huddled around. I knew those ones, those were all lost Tummis's sibs, there was Gorrild and Monnie, Ugh, Flip and Neg. Like seeing Tummis's face rearranged on different shoulders, young and older. Dear Tummis's people.

Bottleneck of the older Iremonger children, not quite adult yet, nor entirely children either, all in a terror.

'Quiet, you scum!' shrieked Moorcus. 'Quiet or I'll shut you up for good and all.'

He had two pistols out and was waving them around, pointing them at all the children, enjoying himself.

'May I have my gun back, Moorcus?' asked Duvit. 'It was supplied to me.'

'I shall keep it for you. Be quiet will you!'

'I should like a gun myself,' said Stunly.

'Well you can't,' said Moorcus. 'There's hardly enough to go around, and I must be properly armed, the better to instruct my family! I could shoot you, I could very well. I've half a mind to do it. Just give me a quarter of an excuse and I'll see your brains on the wallpaper. No one to stop me now, is there? Just me – who's to tell? So shut right up and listen hard!'

That quietened all. Then Moorcus, pointing one at a time – indicating a person by shaking a pistol in their direction – let the cousins out into the night, one by one. There went Pool and Theeby, off went Ormily and her crew, bye to Foy and to Bornobby, off went Muckliss and Orry and Itchul and Orman and Ayte and Mirk and Oizy and Eeza and Iburta and Spitt, but still Pinalippy and I had not been called. There were ever less and less of us there. When Moorcus's own younger brothers Doorcus and Floorcus were called out he thumped them hard in the chest before sending them off. It was after they had gone that he whispered something to his fellow officers, Stunly and Duvit.

'Are you sure, Moorcus?'

'Do it, Duvit, move yourself.'

'Really, Moorcus,' said Stunly, 'must we?'

'You must, lily-livered, it's an order all right, I am the highest ranking officer here, now get to it.'

As more cousins were let out, Stunly and Duvit went into the drawing room. I couldn't think what they were doing in there until there was a general sound of upheaval and other voices came talking.

'What?'

'What?'

'What?'

'Get up, get going, you horrid sacks, shift yourselves!'

'What?'

'What?'

'What?'

Stunly and Duvit were upsetting the remaining leather people, they were waking them, pushing them, herding them. Soon enough the prefects had seven or eight of them out into the hallway.

'What?'

'What?'

'What?' they kept saying.

'Listen up, you great dolls, listen to me,' barked Moorcus.

'What?'

'What?'

'What?'

'Be quiet, will you! Cease your whattings. Listen, I'm the boss here, I give the orders. Look at me, look at my uniform, look at my medal.'

'Medal.'

'Oh, medal.'

'Nice medal.'

'Look at my shiny hat!'

'Hat.'

'Hat.'

'Shiny hat.'

'Hello, sir, sir with medal, I'm Irene Tintype, how do you do?' This came from a young girl leather.

'I'm Arthur Pencase.'

'I'm Jocelyn Bookplate.'

'I'm William Waxcrayon.'

'Shut your bloody traps, or I shall shut them for you. Permanently. Now, listen will you, you new people, I don't care an empty wallet for your names, I've no use for them. You're only half done, aren't you, in all the rush? Not enough breath put inside you; you're not quite fully cooked. Still, you must do. Listen now, and listen good, I'm going out now with my friends here, and with this fool I'll acknowledge mine.'

'So good of you, what a blessing!' said with all sourness Rowland Cullis the Toastrack by Moorcus's side.

'Silence! Now people, new people, behind you in the hallways are these two cousins left. See them?'

'Yes.'

'Oh yes.'

'There they are now.'

'Good, very good. It is your job to keep them here. It is your job not to let them out. Whatever they say to you, keep them in this house. I'm going out now with my people, I shall lock the door to keep you safely inside. But don't whatever you do, don't let them out. Understand?'

'Yes.'

'We understand.'

'They shall stay in.'

'With us.'

'With us.'

'With us.'

'But, Moorcus!' cried Pinalippy. 'This was not agreed upon.'

'Shut up, Pinalippy, or I'll silence you now! God knows I'd like to.'

'Yes.'

'Yes.'

'He would.'

'Like it.'

'Very much.'

'It was agreed! You are to shelter us!' cried Pinalippy.

'Not any more!' he spat. 'Sort yourselves out!'

'It's murder!' cried Pinalippy.

'Call it any name you like: that's the plot. Understand, you pillows! Keep this door locked!'

'Yes.'

'Yes.'

'Yes.'

'Very good. Goodbye then, one and all. You deserved this, Clod. I've been so looking forward to just such a moment. My only regret is I shan't be here when the constabulary arrives; I'm sad to miss all your weeping. I'll hear the gunshots most likely though, and I'll be thinking of you, you can be quite certain of that, as you slump towards the ground, as you become dead matter one and all, heavy filth. So then, come Stunly, come Duvit, come Toastrack even. Farewell, scum! This is your end. How it fits you!'

And he slammed the door and left us locked in with the leathers.

Pinalippy was shaking me. 'Do something!'

'Yes of course,' I said. 'I think we had better move, Pinalippy, come on now, on we go.'

'But the leathers, Clod, they shan't let us pass.'

'Won't they?'

'They have strict orders. Were you not listening to anything?'

'Oh you mean the foul gas from Moorcus? No need to worry over that,' I said. 'No need at all. So much windbreaking that is.'

There was a loud whistling then beyond the house, somewhere nearby, followed by other answering whistles.

'The constabulary,' called Pinalippy, 'oh they're coming to us! Come on Clod, show some spirit.'

'Dear Leatherpeople, excuse me,' I said, clearing my voice. 'I am Clod Iremonger.'

They all turned to look at me.

'Clod?'

'Clod?'

'Clod. We don't care who you are, Clod. We've no use for your name.'

'You're not to leave the house,' one leather commanded.

'Not to.'

'Not to.'

'I don't wish to hurt you,' I said. 'On the whole I'd rather not.'

'You don't frighten us – look at you.'

'Clod.'

'Clod.'

'Small fellow with a big hat. Shut up, Clod.'

They laughed then, sending their black gas thick about them.

'Or we'll hurt you. Clod.'

'Hurt.'

'Oh hurt.'

'Step any closer, and we'll have to hurt you, Clod.'

'Do you see the hatstand here by the door,' I said, 'and this barometer?'

'What about it?'

'What's that to do with anything?'

'Clod.'

'Clod.'

'This about them. Watch them please – a swift exhibit, if I may.'

I closed my eyes and broke the barometer, I burst it and had it blackened up and shrivelled in a moment. I sent the hatstand up onto the ceiling and had it crawling and spread out there like ivy.

'There then,' I said.

'Oh.'

'Oh.'

'Oh.'

'Clod.'

'That Clod.'

'Clod cloven foot.'

'Clod.'

'Clod.'

'Now listen,' I said, just as stern as ever I could, 'what I did to the barometer, to the hatstand, I can do to you in a little moment. Now, dear new people, please don't be frightened, I want you to go out into the street, out into London, for it is not safe here. I want you to be very brave. Where you hear the whistle, run towards it.'

'Whistle.'

'The whistle.'

'Run to.'

'Run whistle.'

'But the door,' one leather cried, 'the door is so locked.'

'No,' I said, breaking the lock very swiftly with a flick of my fingers just like I'd seen Grandfather do. There was a brief clack as the lock fell upon the hallway floor. 'No, you see, now it isn't. Not at all. I've bust it. Out you go then, and do hurry over it because I shall have someone up the stairs in just a minute and the mere proximity of him and you shall cause you all to burst into . . . well into however many pieces you are made up of, quite a few I shouldn't wonder. So, on the whole, I think you should run for it.'

Well then, being sensible leathers, they did.

'Oh, Clod!' called Pinalippy. 'You're marvellous!'

'Oh,' I said, 'not at all, my pleasure and all that.'

'Come on then,' said Pinalippy, 'we must get out.'

And there to punctuate Pinalippy's last comment came the sounding of police whistles.

'Yes, yes,' I said, 'we should indeed, but not without Binadit.'

'Binadit?' said Pinalippy. 'That lump, he'll give us all away in an instant.'

'I'm not going without Binadit,' I said. 'I thought I could do it. But I can't. I find I can't. He's one of us after all. He's a person too.'

'You'll murder me!' she cried.

'Not without Binadit. Can't say I know him, can't say I like him entirely, but you know, on balance, it is the right thing to do.'

'All right then!' cried Pinalippy. 'Bring him up but be quick about it!'

I went down the stairs again, feeling my way in the dark.

'Binadit!' I called. 'Binadit!'

Nothing, just darkness. I was in the kitchen then knocking into pans and the like: 'Binadit! Binadit!' Rats on the floor, scampering around my feet, pulling at my shoelaces, and looking up at me as if they had something they wished to say.

And at last I heard, 'Am here. Here am!'

They'd blocked him in, piled stuff in the way. I thought it free, smashed all about me, sent all spinning. Then there was a door, a solid metal door, I twisted the handle. There he sat, the huge piece of furniture, the largest piece of Iremonger humanity: Binadit the mountain.

Fifty and more small objects pelted towards Binadit and stuck there fast.

'Ullo. Bits,' he said.

'Come on, Binadit, you must come out now and be quick about it.'

'Missus?'

'Come on, there's little enough time; up and out we go!'

'Missus! Missus!' Binadit was crying.

'What's the matter with him?' said Pinalippy from the top of the stairs.

'Where the Missus woman?'

'I think he means Aunt Rosamud, his mother.'

'She's gone,' said Pinalippy flatly. 'They've all gone. We're the last.'

'But she asked us to take care of you,' I said, thinking quickly. 'She was very insistent on that.'

'Family!' boasted Binadit.

'Come on, or we shall all be dead family!' came Pinalippy, dragging us towards the door.

168

And then we were out. Out on the street. Out in London.

'Oh London,' I said.

'Where do we go, Clod?' asked Pinalippy.

'Lundin,' said Binadit.

'Lungdon,' corrected Pinalippy.

There was a sudden bang. That was the noise of a gun, letting off its voice, barking with its sudden anger, finding some leather no doubt. Well Clod, well, well, enough's enough, move, shall you?

'I know where we're going,' I said, for it was suddenly clear to me. 'I know someone London.'

'Do you, Clod?' asked Pinalippy. 'Truly?'

'Clod? Clod! Your name Clod?' said Binadit, pointing to me, as rags and newspaper and dirt down the street started tumbling towards him.

'Yes, I'm Clod,' I said. 'Come, Binadit, before we can't fit you anywhere.' For the rubbish was all galloping towards him in a storm.

'Clod! Clod boy. That Lucy said? Lucy?'

'Yes, Binadit,' I said, 'whom Lucy talked of.'

'Botton!'

'Yes, she was. Yes, she was.'

'Clod? Clod?'

'Yes, I am Clod.'

'Lo, Clod.'

'Hullo, Binadit.'

'Lucy? Lucy?'

'I'm afraid she's dead, Binadit.'

'Lucy, Lucy?'

'Yes, old fellow, I'm very much afraid so.'

'LUCY! LUCY!' he wailed.

'Oh someone shut that lump up!'

'LUCY! LUCY!'

'Where to? Clod? Come on, we must hurry!' cried Pinalippy. There was another shot gone off, very close too.

'LUCY!'

'Please, Binadit, please, please will you be quiet.'

'Not far, not far at all.'

We were on the other side of the street by then, just in front of the house opposite us. The door was open. We went in. Closed it quietly afterwards.

'LUCY!'

'Sssh, please Binadit,' I begged. 'Please, you'll have us all killed. And please, please stand still, we must pull some of this rubbish from you.'

'Lucy.'

'That's better. Well done.'

'Lucy.'

'That's it, my dear chap, we'll Lucy together, you and I.'

'Lucy. Benedict.'

'Hullo,' I whispered up the stairway. 'Are you there, young girl? Can you help us?'

'Lucy. Lucy.'

And from upstairs came a distant child's call: 'Help! Help me!'

Rippit Iremonger Under a Cap

IN THE DARK

The noise heard on the Edgware Road,
half a minute's walk from Connaught Place,
home of Eleanor Cranwell

Rippit.

Part Three

Inside Out

Lucy Pennant

WATER

How it was that Lucy Pennant came to London Town from Beneath the Crumbling Factory of Foulsham. Beginning the narrative of Lucy Pennant, vagrant

'Clod? Clod! CLOD!'

I'd been calling out in my sleep, must have fainted away again. Awake now, awake to find myself so deep underground. Buried alive.

Nothing to see, all blackness. There had been the screaming of a train's whistle howling out deep into London, but how long ago now I couldn't say. And I all bloody on the ground in some kind of airpocket, in the crumbling of Bayleaf House, the noises of cracking and shifting of the building giving up above me, but beside me, in the dirty darkness, we few of Foulsham. Children. Only a handful left from so many. What a murdering there had been: men, women, children, drowned in dirt and flames. My people. So few left. Must keep them. Those that still breathe, must keep them going. Precious, precious few.

Who were we? Name call, I made them say their names, in the deep dark, again and again, in our small space. Trapped, so few left now, again and again, they must give their names.

'Lucy Pennant,' I started.

Silence.

'Come on,' I said, 'you must do it, we must keep alive. Names please, I'll have them. Lucy Pennant, then who comes next?'

'Jenny Ryall.' My old friend from childhood, lived in the same building as me since we were babies.

'Bug Ryall.' Her brother. Real name was Dick, but everyone knew him as Bug since he made a name for himself racing cockroaches.

'Colin Shanks.'

'Tess Shanks.'

'Arthur Oates.'

'Esther Nelson.'

'Roger Cole.'

'Bartholomew Lewis.'

The names stopped.

'Anyone else? Any other here?'

No more.

'No one else? Then there are nine, just nine of us all told.'

'Excuse me.'

'Yes?'

'I'm here too. Haven't said my name yet.'

'Then tell us it, and keep sharp.'

'I'm Molly Porter.'

'Well, Molly Porter, call out when you're asked, will you? We don't want to lose you.'

'Molly Porter.'

'All right, Mol, we've got you now. Anyone else beside you?'

'No, just me. Where is everyone else?'

'Just us I reckon. Just us that we know of. That's ten of us even. Ten from so many. Let's keep it ten now, ten of us, let's not lose any more. Is there any way out? Feel around you. Does anyone have a light?'

No one, no light.

We were stuck – didn't seem like there was any place to move – in some small space, maybe getting smaller all the while. Couldn't say really which way was up, which down, so turned about, and everything in darkness. Deep, deep under the ground. We'd been following a stairway, trying to get out, trying to get away from all those leathers so thick about us, Umbitt's dumb army, trying to get away from the flames and the smashing of the heaps, one great burst and the walls broke and all came tumbling in, and we, we only ten of us, were pulled down into the deep darkness, under the ground, and here we lay, in a heap. Just ten. Only ten. No more.

Above us must have been other people that fell and were crushed. And higher yet were great flames and burning. The whole shanty city of Foulsham brought low. And us in such a small pocket of life. We picked about us, tried to find some way out, but couldn't, not at first, not for a long time; just called out into the darkness, called to nobody.

'Help! Help! We're down here! Help!'

179

And nobody came.

But always there were sounds, sounds of things falling, sounds of something heavy above us. Hours down there, hours and hours. Days, even? We slept and awoke screaming, we wept, and picked the broken walls with our fingers. Getting weaker, weaker and weaker all the while.

In the end I think it was the factory above us shifting that found us some way forward. If it hadn't moved we'd be locked in that horrid space for ever and never found, or come to, years later, human fossils. The ground around us was ever shifting, it hadn't finished its falling.

And then it broke.

And we all screamed.

And then other things fell into our space.

Something of a sudden pushing past me, shoving me out of the way. Some sort of small river of things, but hairy, with mouths and claws. Could it be?

'Rats? Are those rats?' I called.

'Yes, rats,' some kid called back. 'Lots of them!'

'Follow! Follow them!' I shouted. 'They'll find a way out of anything!'

'The rats?'

'Yes! Yes!' I cried. 'Rats! They'll lead us free. They know the way. Quick, all of you, quick, scramble towards the rats, our lives depend upon it!'

Awful crumblings, creaks and squeaks and shrieks of masonry, like the building itself was complaining, like it hurt so and wanted help. Thought we'd come to the end. Not yet. Not now we had company. Rats to find ways that we'd never learn.

Must follow, must follow them rats, whatever else.

Moved hands around sharp things cutting into, bleeding fingers, fingers sticky with blood. Such a little space, so little room to move. I thought we would be crushed any moment.

'Keep with me! Keep up now!'

Think, think, sensible. Be sensible, Lucy, or this is the very very end of all, you'll never see Clod again. He's alive yet, isn't he, isn't he? One thing's for certain, shan't find out stuck here. I pulled them along with me, dragged them.

'Go on! Go on! Move!'

'I can't!'

'Yes you bloody can!'

'No, no, leave me!'

'I bloody will not! Move it, or I'll so punch you!'

Got to keep living, got to, whatever else.

There was some crawl space, there were also flattened rats all about us, some writhing in pain. One bit hard at my leg, ow! Well then, I was alive.

How long did we crawl on, trying to follow the rats, till there was nowhere forward, till we'd come to the end of it and all seemed impossible. We must turn back, just a little bit, back, back we go, back a little to keep going on, and so back we went. We cut ourselves as we crawled in single file, feeling for a different opening, for other spaces somewhere in all that sharpness, something to give us more space, for, in truth, if there was any less of it we'd be goners one and all. Hopeless, so hopeless. We'd lost the rats, they were so much faster. They'd have found their way by now. Not us. So dark, no room, no air, weren't even sure if we were living still, to tell the truth,

181

animals trapped in the blackness, not a person, not a human, just a few somethings, trying to keep living in the thick, dirty air, lungs for all of dirt and dust. How many had died – don't think on them, it's over for them isn't it, shan't do any good for them, but for us it's not over, not yet, not yet, try, try a little.

Try a little longer.

Names, names, I call out the names.

Seven of us, eight, nine and ten, all alive yet.

Have a rest, need a rest. Rest.

I think we must have slept a little in that thin air, maybe fainted, passed out a time. But suddenly I came to again, and awoke us all, all ten bodies, and dragged us on, though some cried to be let alone. Couldn't, couldn't let them. On, on and on, on a little more. Never knowing what might lie ahead.

We came to some sort of ledge after a bit and lay there panting, just lying, the noises of masonry still shifting, still trying to find its place, still complaining and hurting, and collapsing too. Could hear it going, hear it tumbling down, and all that mess of pipes, twisted and ripped, bent and broke all about us. Didn't move from life, that thing, only moved because its dead body was falling yet, into the deep dirt, making its roots down in the ground where we were scrabbling, us small sacks of living. And any sounds were the sounds of the dying building, no human sound, 'cept those panting beside me, trying to steal a little air from that place. Something, some pipe above us had burst, there was water, foul water dripping down from it. Dripping on my face, filth water, stinking, leaking, like the building's own blood, or like the building had wet itself in a panic.

What a place to die.

Never no light, no light again.

Dampness all about us, water rising, so that the place, what little there was of it, was flooding up. Something had burst, some great waterpipe had been severed and now was seeping all over us. And the smell like a weight all on its own, a familiar rude, sweet closeness, such as sinks into you through every bit of skin until it quite takes you over. Well, I knew that, didn't I?

I'd done that before.

'Swidge,' I said, remembering poor Benedict and our journey underground. 'Sewage pipes, isn't it!' I said.

Sewage! River of filth, our hope, that sea of filth!

If we could find the sewage pipe, if we could follow it down, swim in that foul river, then we might escape yet. Rats about us again, ones that had been stunned by the crushing but were just coming round and clambering out now.

Rats, rats, you lovelies, show us the way, won't you?

If there was a way, they'd find it.

'Come on again, on we go!'

'No! No!' some of us cried.

'Leave us be!' they moaned.

'Not for a moment,' I shouted. 'We must keep on, or be crushed! Move! MOVE! DON'T BE DEAD! COME ON! UP! GET UP!'

I heard a loud splashing, like something had fallen from high up into water, deep water, noises of thrashing about, there, there! While it can still be heard. Quick, don't go silent on me!

I pulled them, grabbed and dragged them along, struck at them, and they were there crawling and then of a terrible sudden . . .

Huge plosh!

Where? Where? I felt around in the blackness, couldn't feel them nowhere, couldn't hear the splashing, where, where, lost her? Lost?

'Jenny! Jenny!' I couldn't feel her, my oldest friend from childhood, my house companion, my best mate. Then:

'Lucy, help! Lucy!'

'Jen!'

I felt around, kept feeling about, in a panic, in a terror, for her to be alone down there in all of that and then suddenly there was nothing there, no ground beneath me at all and I was falling, falling, falling and then I hit the water and went under.

I came up at last, kicked myself up through God only knows what, so cold, trying to breathe in that wet coldness. A hand on me then, a hand pulling me on, pulling me closer.

'Effra!' I gasped. 'It's only the bloody Effra! The underground river! We're saved! Come on, all of you, jump down, you must jump. Follow our voices. Down, down, we'll help you. You must come! Must!'

Plop.

Splash!

Crash!

Down they come, one by one, those few left of Foulsham, into the hidden river, there to swim in dirt, to go on a little. Call out the names.

'Lucy Pennant.'

'Jenny Ryall. Bug? BUG!'

'Bug Ryall.'

'Thank God.'

184

'Couldn't get my breath.'

'Who else?'

'Arthur Oates.'

'Tess Shanks.'

'And Colin. Colin Shanks.'

'Esther Nelson.'

'Roger Cole.'

'Bartholomew Lewis.'

'And? And? Molly? Where's Molly?'

'Molly Porter, here, here I am!'

'Good girl! Well done all of you!'

So then which way? That was simple, the only way we could. One way was blocked and full, I supposed all chocked up with what was once Foulsham. The other was free, and surely led London way.

We swam and were sick and swam, and swam about, and on we went a long time, but there in the end at last there was a ladder along the great pipes, up and up and up it went, we climbed it rung by sharp rung, and it led all the way back up to land, which land we couldn't say but above ground somewhere, somewhere with space and air to breathe.

We clambered up.

The ladder came to an end.

Big metal cover.

Here goes.

I gave it a push and another, a twist, and a screech, and another shove and it shifted at last, and the air came stinging in, what air that was, like a first lungful. There was no one there, no one around. Early in the morning I think it must have been, no sun yet. Slid the thing back, awful din it made, but no one about, houses and a street and places where people lived, but no people that I could see. Colder up there, colder on the ground, London cold come about us and bit hard.

'I think we've done it,' Jenny said.

'London? Is it, is it London after all?' some kid asked – Roger Cole, panting and shaking in the cold.

'London,' I said. 'London proper?'

'London.'

'London.'

'London,' I said.

'Yes, this is London,' came a deep adult voice from behind us, 'and you are not welcome here.'

'Scarper!' I cried. 'Flee, run for it!'

A whistle was blown, a policeman's whistle.

'Over here!' yelled the policeman. 'Over here! Rats! Dozens of them! Here!' And he blew his whistle and ran at us. He had hold of some small boy, it was Bartholomew, little Bartholomew Lewis, he had him and shoved him under his arm like he was a chicken. I leapt at the policeman, just leapt at him, clawed my fingers into his face, like some desperate mad mother, as if the poor little brat was my own child. Then others had the idea of it too, and we were tumbling the man down and kicking into him until he let the boy go, he had to, or I think we might have pulled every bit of flesh off him and left him there all bones and nothing else, but he was there still breathing and bloody and full of his hatred. We hadn't done the policeman over proper and that was our mistake, because then he was blowing his whistle again. I couldn't believe it, he wouldn't take a hint this bastard, so I marched back over and gave him a good Lucy Pennant welcome – I kicked him full in the face. What blood! Truth was, I was glad to see it. And that stopped the whistling, and then, yes, at once, we ran pell-mell into the night.

We run at last towards a bridge; I was ahead of them, just running and going on, Jen beside me. I thought they were all coming on, but we'd split already. Can't say which way the others went, but we came along what I now understand to be Vauxhall Bridge, we must have come up above ground somewhere near Kennington. I know that now. I studied it on the map. Didn't know then, then it was just a bridge. Just a place to flee along.

But by the time we were over the bridge we weren't all there. Some had run off into different streets. Couldn't keep them all with me, all in a tumble panic, all screaming. More whistles then from different places, and calling out and then, oh then, Christ then, of God then, bloody bloody then came a loud cracking sound, like some furious metal animal had just barked and I knew what that noise meant. Gunshot, wasn't it. There were guns, we were being fired at. They're murdering us. Dead if we go back underground, dead if we stay on the streets, and over yonder the other side of the river, more dead and dead and dead piled in burning heaps. Nothing but death, was there? How to keep alive in that, how to tiptoe around all that deading and keep alive somehow, find a little little corner to breathe in and prosper? That's all we want, to keep living. Not so much to ask, is it?

Yes, it bloody was. Yes it always is. The biggest thing to ask. How to live, how to keep living?

'Run!' I screamed. 'Run for it!'

Irene Tintype

13

SECRETS OF A ROOM

Continuing the narrative of Clod Iremonger

Little Girl Locked

We were in the hallway of the house opposite, where the girl who waved at me lived, still in Connaught Place. There was someone upstairs, someone calling, 'Help! Help me!'

'Hullo,' I whispered up the stairway. 'Where are you?'

'Lucy. Lucy,' said Binadit, tears in his eyes.

Police whistles all up and down the street, sounds of people running. They were at the old place, they were inside it, blowing their whistles, calling out. There was a gunshot.

'Hullo,' I said. 'Call again.'

'Where have you led us?' said Pinalippy. 'To our deaths?'

'Hullo!' I called in my loudest whisper.

'Help,' at last came the response. 'Help me! I'm up here!'

It was the girl, the girl that waved, crying somewhere upstairs.

189

I went up the stairs, following the sound, I was at her door, it was locked. I thought hard on the lock, but though the lock itself withered and blackened and the handle spat out, still the door would not yield.

'Open up!' I called. 'We'll help you.'

'Can't open it,' she cried. 'It locked of its own accord. I can't do anything. Please help. I can't get it away from me, it won't listen.'

'What won't?' I asked. 'Tell me what is troubling you.'

'*It* is! Oh please make it go away.'

'What is it?' I asked.

'The fire extinguisher!' she said. 'It doesn't listen, it's moving of its own accord, grown so tall, and the bed and the carpet, everything, I think, is in league with it. They mean to crush me!'

'Quick, Clod,' said Pinalippy, 'the police, finding nothing in that house, shall surely search all the others.'

'It's coming!' the girl cried. 'Oh go away! Go away!'

'Don't come up,' I said to Pinalippy and Binadit. 'It's not the lock, it's the door. It is growing and shifting shape, the whole room beyond, I do think, is quite thoroughly awake and full of life!'

This should take such special effort.

I put my hands on the door; it was hot, so hot!

'It's certainly the room!' I said. 'The whole room wants life. It's all sealed up like any living thing, and to get inside it, like any surgeon, you must make a hole! However did a room get such an idea? A whole room, seeking life!'

Downstairs the doorbell rang.

'The police! It must be the police!' cried Pinalippy.

'Please help me!' called the girl in the nursery.

'Lucy, Lucy,' moaned Binadit as the contents of a wastepaper basket found its way all over him.

'This house is possessed!' said Pinalippy.

'Pinalippy, quickly and quietly, look through the keyhole, see if it is the police. It may be the house itself, trying to talk. If it's not the police you must quieten the bell, for I think if the whole house is coming to life it may start screaming any moment, just as we do when we are born!'

Pinalippy approached the door.

'Dear room,' I said, calling through the twisted keyhole. 'Dear room, how do, how do ye do?'

A great creaking then from the other side of the door.

'Oh! Oh!' came the girl.

'What is it?' I called. 'What is happening in there?'

'The floorboards! They're shifting underfoot! All my books! All the furniture!'

The doorbell rang again.

'It must be the house!' I told her. 'It's trying to come alive.'

All about the house now, the floorboards were creaking and groaning, the windows were rattling, doors opening and closing, objects darting about.

'It's not the house ringing,' said Pinalippy at the front door.

'Then the police?' I asked.

'It's not the police either,' said Pinalippy. 'It's a little girl.'

'Perhaps,' I said, 'it is a friend of the one trapped inside. Whatever she wants, you'd best let her in and shut the door after her, or she'll have all the police in with her in a moment. Binadit, go hide yourself in a room, for you are too much the spectacle.'

I heard Pinalippy open the door, the girl stepping in.

'Hullo!' said the girl in the hall. 'Thanks awfully!'

'Who are you?' asked Pinalippy. 'What do you want?'

I knew that girl, I'd heard her voice.

'I'm Irene Tintype,' she said.

'She's a leather!' Pinalippy called.

'Irene as in genie,' the newcomer said, 'not Irene as in queen.'

'Lucy, Lucy!' went Binadit from some chamber within.

'Please, please get me out,' cried the girl in the nursery.

'Don't let Binadit anywhere near Irene Tintype. There'll be an explosion if you do.'

'Help!' called the girl trapped in her nursery.

'I'm Irene Tintype.'

'Oh Lucy, Clod, Lucy,' groaned Binadit.

'Help NOW!' cried the girl.

I pressed my whole body against the door. How hot the room. The girl had become silent now, no human sounds from inside any more, but noise, great noise. It was coming to life, it was so close to living.

'Be still room, old room,' I said.

The room moaned, it screamed.

'Be still, be quiet. Be asleep once more.'

A terrible cracking from inside, like all the floorboards were pulling up from their places, like the walls were breathing and bursting their slats, some were snapping in half, in terrible cracks – as if they were the room's answer, 'NO, NO, NO, NO!' It wanted to live, whoever could blame a thing for wanting to live?

'Knock, knock,' I said.

192

Bang, bang, came the response of something very heavy, thumping on the floor.

'Clod,' I said. 'It's Clod here and I mean to come in.'

BANG. BANG.

Police whistles.

'I'm coming in now.'

Crash!

The Last Rats of Foulsham
Regarding the Burning of Their Home

14

BURIED IN FILTH

Continuing the narrative of Lucy Pennant

Maybe five with me. Running, running any way we could. There were calls behind, whistles blowing, I heard another shot of a gun, oh God, and then, oh God, oh God, screams after too, yet another shot and then silence. On we ran, we must, on and on, and turning what corners we may to keep the policemen from us. To escape their killing company. I had no notion where or what or anything, I was bloody and scraped and cut but we could not stop, must not stop or be taken.

Still the police whistles sounded, still we ran away from them, but they seemed to come from all directions, so that running away from one we seemed then to be running towards another. Which way? Which way? I could not see the way. Where, where to hide?

I hate you, London, I hate you already.

We came upon a long high wall – they are such familiar things to us of Foulsham, you see – and I thought for a moment

I was back home, but this wall stood high and firm, unlike those others, unlike those former walls, those walls were gone, weren't they, all of them come tumbling down. I slammed into that tall high wall, as if it might somehow save me.

'Come on, we're free yet, let's stay so. Come on please, come with me!'

We ran along the side of the wall, the whistles behind us, so I thought then, our feet smacking on the cobbles, in the London filth, mud all over, thick with dirt, freezing and in a terror. Follow, follow, I thought, follow round the wall. We did come to the end of it then, and then, then, such sudden light, such brightness, we'd come around the side of the wall that gave upon the river, not the Effra, not an underground river, some other river, some other river, big and wide it was. I suddenly knew its name.

'It's only the bloody Thames,' I said out loud, the shock of it flooding over me. 'We're only on the bloody bank of the Thames! Must've been what we crossed earlier.'

And then we saw the great flaming in the distance and how big was the smoke coming up from it, like a great torch over London, like someone had struck a match, only this match was a huge one. It was Foulsham over there, Foulsham burning and burning and going out, our home.

'Oh.'

'That's Foulsham, is it?'

'Yes, my lad, it's Foulsham burning bright.'

'Oh, where's Mam? Where's Dad?'

'Where's Bartholomew? He was here just now, wasn't he?'

'Hush now,' I said. 'We must keep quieter.'

'But where are they?'

'I lost my sister, I lost my Tess, she was with us a while back. Tess? Tess? Where are you now?'

'Lucy Pennant,' I said.

'Jen.'

'Bug.'

'Colin Shanks.'

'Esther Nelson.'

'No more?'

No more. Just five. Half only remaining.

'Molly?' Jen called. 'Molly?'

'Please,' I said. 'We should keep quiet, we have to find somewhere to hide. They're trying to find us, and if they find us it'll all be up for us. For the sake of our families, we owe it to our families, we must keep running. Keep alive as long as we can, each breath we take is a fist in their face.'

'I can't! I can't go another step!' cried Colin.

'Don't then,' I said, 'and the whistles and bullets will find you all the faster.'

'Where then, if you're so smart, where do we go?' asked Esther.

'You led us here, now what?' said Bug.

'I hardly know,' I admitted.

'What are we to do?'

Police whistle again, got me shifting. Marching footsteps, coming, coming on. Ever nearer, ever closer.

Hide, Lucy. Hide them, Lucy, I told myself. Keep them safe.

Closer.

Hide, hide them.

'Hide,' I said. 'Anywhere, on the ground, in the mud, get in the mud! Cover yourself with it!'

Closer.

Now or never.

Closer.

We ducked down, between the wall and the river, we buckled us down by the wall by the river, in the thick mud against it there, so much filth raked high, and we slipped into it, like it was a part of us, like it was what we were made of one and all. We couldn't jump over, the splosh should tell on us. We just muddied in the dirt, all the horse filth, all the muck, like we were all just rubbish, mounds of dirt. Filth.

Closer and then, of a sudden, right before us, policemen marching, and between them, my children, my young people of Foulsham, caught and trapped. Four there.

'They shall be impounded,' a sergeant was calling. 'Be quiet about it, we've made more than enough noise for one night.'

They were herded in the dark. To have come so far only to be caught again. And behind us, lighting the night, was our home thick with flame and the terrible sweet smell of the heaps burning themselves to death. One girl from the police's lot, Tess I think, seeing the flames and gasping at them, tried to pull away, tried to get away, to run free, screaming at all the horror of it all. But they had her down in a second, grabbed her by her hair. They dragged her back to the others. Blood down the face. Limping along. Better to have been crushed perhaps. Maybe I should have left us all there in the dark after all.

London. This is London. So much for London.

Hate it.

They came to the great gates of some place, just by us all along, but we'd been looking the wrong way, we'd been staring at all that was left of Foulsham. The gates clanged open.

'How many here?' come the call.

'Four,' the answer. 'Children caught up the sewer pipe.'

'Four then, four children from Foulsham. They'll wish they hadn't took the trouble.'

'And some run off.'

'Escaped?'

'We shot one. I did not like to do that.'

That was Molly, I thought, that was Molly Porter that you shot.

'No, Constable Jones, not children. They are not children, you can't think like that. They're rats. Got it? Rats, Jones. Say it, Jones: rats.'

'Rats, sir.'

'Should step on all their heads, Jones.'

'Rats, sir, yes.'

'We have orders, we're fighting a war, man, a war against filth and disease.'

'Yes, sir, I see that, sir, shan't happen again, sir.'

'See that it don't. And the others? What of the others?'

'Nothing yet.'

'Find them, do it fast.'

'Yes, sir.'

'And have these ones penned before the hour's out.'

'Sir.'

'I want the missing ones too, mind.'

'Yes, sir.'

'What were you thinking? To let them free.'

'Didn't mean to, sir, terrible rush it all was. There was one, a redhead, terrible vicious she was. Great red hair she had, all of a mess, like she was wild as an animal, shocking to see it. Shan't forget that in a hurry, how she came at me. How she kicked my own nose into a tap of blood!'

'Pen these ones fast. Then go back out. Find the children, find your redhead. Move it whilst they're still close. I want no excuses.'

'Yes, sir.'

Running again, gates shut, echoes down the lane, the sounds of the boots hammering against the wall, the prison wall. Suddenly it was quiet again. Shivering in the mud, like some animal, like some wretched dog. Like I was dead already and somehow floating in that hard cold, like I was almost lying above London, like some dead spirit.

London.

Clod.

Clod?

Binadit?

Where's your whereabouts?

Are you here, either?

Are you about the streets?

On London ground?

I'd like to see you.

I'd like some company.

A familiar face.

In all this strangeness.

In all this London muck.

London: cold, cold place. Colder here than even any pole, North or South, cold are the London hearts, hard and mean. And sharp.

Well, London.

Well then, London.

My name is Lucy Pennant.

This is my story.

Make it a long 'un.

Won't you?

'Come on,' I whispered, snapping to and heaving myself up, pushing the others around me. 'We shouldn't linger here long, this is the worst of it. Some sort of prison. Not the place for us. Well then, scrape yourselves down. They went this way and so we shall choose the other. Quiet as anything, and on we go. Silent. Silent.'

'They had Tess,' said Colin. 'I did see her, she was with them constables.'

'Then she's alive, isn't she? And that's got to be something.'

'Yes. I suppose.'

'Course it is.'

'What'll they do to her?'

'Well, Colin,' I said, 'I don't know. But they're keeping them and that's something, isn't it. They've taken them in. But I think, all in all, we'd better be our own keepers and so on we go, a little further. We must try and find somewhere before it gets lighter. Somewhere to keep us covered and safe as we may be. I bet we can, we'll just help ourselves. And well done. You're doing so well. Stick together, that's the crux of it.'

We crept out and turned away from the Thames wall, keeping in the shadows, heading in the other direction into darker streets away from the horrible flicking light of Foulsham. Rat children, we were, and I loved us every one.

'What are we going to do?' Jen was beside me.

'Step by step,' I said.

'You don't have a clue, do you?'

'Not much,' I said.

'We might be shot at any moment.'

'We might,' I said. 'But also, consider this, we might not.'

'Them's the options?'

'Pretty much.'

'Not a lot, is it?'

'Not a ton, no. But then don't forget that they did just walk by us, those idiots, and so maybe they're not so smart. And maybe then we'll be all right. Maybe.'

'They walked right past us,' some girl echoed and laughed.

'Dunces.'

'Dumb as leathers.'

'No brains in their casings.'

'Dummies, every one.'

There was some laughing through that. It was funny, and I was laughing along with them. Stupid bloody policemen.

'Bloody idiots, aren't they?'

'Idiots!'

'All we have to do is blend in,' I said. 'All we have to do is look like London children, don't we, and then they'll never find us, they'll never know us. Can't be that hard, can it?'

'Nah, we can do it.'

'We'll filch some togs, that can't be hard. We'll steal a little here and there, I know about that well enough. Come on, pick us up, if we can laugh we're not dead.'

'And Tess, and the others?' asked Colin.

'We shan't forget them,' I said. 'I don't know how just yet, but we shall find a way to get them out. We'll see them again. Shan't we, Colin?'

'Yes,' he whispered. 'Yes, we must.'

There was some spirit then among us. Like we'd won a battle or something. But there was more war ahead of us.

'Come on then, my dears. Let's try just around this corner.'

And just around that corner, all very suddenly, there were several people and they had lit torches, which they shone very roughly towards our faces, and a sharp voice shouted out, 'Well, well, well and what have we here then?'

Inspector Frederick Harbin

15

HER MAJESTY'S
RATCATCHER

Report from Inspector Frederick Harbin,
Marylebone 'D' Division

6th February 1876
6 p.m.

It is certain that a number of them had been hiding in the relative seclusion of Connaught Place. The unfortunate little male – I shall not call him a man, this creature we had captured who named himself Timfy Iremonger and held pathetically to a broken whistle – was obliging, under certain force, and after some small struggles, to offer up the address:

'Eighteen Connaught Place.'

I readied a force with all haste and we surrounded the location with great speed and quietness, the better to catch them. But before we were quite ready some figures were seen running out into the night. We shouted warnings at them but the figures kept running directly at us. Fearing for themselves my First Class Constables Ainsley and Brock shot and brought them down. They swore there had been people running at them, but what they found in the street were mere bags of rubbish, some sort of sacks filled with dirt, but got up in human clothing. They must have been some decoy, scarecrows of some nature, to slow us down.

Enough time had been wasted.

I blew my whistle. And in we rushed.

But we were too late already. Too late by then; somehow our plans were suspected, it may have been due to the prolonged absence of their kin Timfy; it does not surprise me that his family members knew that the uncanny thing would squeal, indeed the creature has 'squeal' written all about him. In any case by the time we arrived, the Iremongers had all fled the house or what was left of it.

In 18 Connaught Place this evening was the most appalling scene of rot and decay, unspeakable filth in every room, with gross discolouration, as of some strange animal's inhabitation. Terrible stench, and every object within left somehow bent and deformed. Indeed in many cases it was impossible to understand the original shape and purpose of the object. The whole place was in such a state of horrific neglect and disorder that I can only conjecture that the house had been most singularly and deliberately abused. It is in this house, with a certainty, that they had housed themselves. Whither they have gone can not at this moment be judged, though I must remain confident that they shall be found, and quickly too.

We shall call for witnesses. We have barricaded the street at both ends, none shall pass now without our say-so, and presently we must begin the process of calling from house to house in the hope that someone here has some information.

I am sorry to continue in such a negative vein. We have not, as of this moment, been able to find any witnesses. Let me further explain: we have not yet been able to find any trustworthy human beings. No one has come to their doors in answer to our entreaties, as if all life has vanished from the street. I have called out that we are the police and explained our purpose, but still no one comes forward.

I commanded that a front door be broken down, to encourage communication.

I chose the door of the neighbouring establishment to 18, number 16. At first the house seemed in quiet order but marching through it we found not a living soul. There were various incongruous objects sat in chairs: an oboe, for example, was found bobbing in a lavatory bowl; we found a garden rake in a leather armchair and a footstool floating in a bathtub; there was a carpet beater in a gentleman's study and a filthy looking petticoat on an elegant chair in the morning room. Elsewhere the scene made as little sense: no servants up or down the house but, again, in the servants' stations were various surprising objects. In the kitchen, amongst the pans and saucers, there was a soldier's uniform and a lady's nightgown, a billiard cue in the wine cellar and a large ship's figurehead of a foreign type taking up a good portion of a storeroom.

My men, at first bewildered, began to complain about the oddness of it all. I told them to pull themselves together, to bang on the door of number 14 and so on until they came upon someone. But nowhere, nowhere was a person to be found, only again, the same strange objects positioned here and thereabouts, as if they, the objects, were the owners of these homes, as if they were the sole residents of these addresses, and the world had turned quite inside out.

'Every house,' I said. 'Every single house. Search, find me a person!'

So my men scattered at opposite ends of the street and were to work their way down towards the middle. Again the houses seemed as before, no person present but many objects in peculiar places, most confusing and distressing. The more this continued the more my men were put off, dispirited by the whole scene; some began to vomit and all were white and sweating.

'Buck up, try another house. Be thorough, find me a person.'

But they never did, they never could. It was only when two of my men, although whistled for and called to report, failed to materialise, that I myself began to be disquieted. These men had gone into different houses and neither of them afterwards came out. We searched the places thoroughly, momentarily calling off our larger search of the other houses, but nowhere were my Constables (Second and Third Class) James Pickford and Richard Storr to be seen. One of my force swore he'd found something but all that he had to explain my men's absence was a fish kettle, strangely warm.

I sent for backup then; I was myself beginning to feel unwell. 'Keep out of the houses,' I called. 'Keep out. There is something amiss, I do credit it, for certain it shall be easily explained by the correct officials and then we shall all be in the light, but for now, I am most confused. Search the street, but do not go into any house, I repeat: the street only, stick together, always be at the very least with one fellow officer. We shall not enter any further premises until our backup is here.'

On my orders, we have done a roll call of names.

8.30 p.m.

If ever there were any need to know what horrors these people are capable of, if there was ever any doubting, it is only necessary to see the terrible lifelessness of Connaught Place. Where have the people gone, I know not, I cannot ever say. Only that they have gone. That they have surely been cruelly stolen from this life.

Think on it: there is a street in London, in *London*, the biggest, the greatest city in all the world, the metropolis that is crammed full of human beings, where there are more human souls than in any other city in all the globe, where we all shove and hustle amongst one another; there is in that place of maximum congestion, a street that is empty, a dead street, a peopleless street.

As if mankind had been quite finished with.

As if London had become a museum, and there was no one left to visit it.

Our backup arrived. They began smashing down the doors of the houses we had yet to enter. All was as before. I saw in one child's bed a rowlock, a simple rowlock from a rowing boat, but this rowlock seemed most unnatural to me, I cannot explain it, as if the rowlock had bullied the child out of the place and now had it for its own and lay there in selfish comfort. In the bedroom of a married couple I saw a coal scuttle and a tuning fork. In a servants' room I found, barely covered by a blanket, a writing desk. I felt a fear inside me in those rooms that I have never felt before, and hope never to feel again. It is unholy. It is some kind of evil.

10 p.m.

Five houses left to search and then the whole street will have been seen to.

10.30 p.m.

There can be no doubting that these Iremongers, through their own malignity or through the disease they carry about them, have caused a terrible absence of humanity.

If we are not most cautious and vigilant now, I do fear, I do fear absolutely for the people of my city.

11 p.m.

Only two houses left to search now.

Each time a roll call has been performed. We have lost no more men.

The Iremonger family of Foulsham are with us, they are about London, and where before they were contained in one abode, it now appears most likely that they are scattered about the capital, and that any chance of finding them, of finding all of them, has become tenfold, a hundredfold more difficult. It may be that every house in the city must be searched, every person questioned. I do not know where next to tread, I only know that all Iremongers must be found, quick or dead, and with the utmost swiftness.

11.45 p.m.

Detective Superintendent Rudley-Griffin has been to the street. Again a roll call has been performed. One further man cannot be accounted for. I do my best to explain myself but, strangely, Rudley-Griffin does not seem all that surprised, as if he has seen behaviour of this type before. He is a special officer, one I have not met previously.

'Harbin,' he said to me, 'it is best to keep this sort of thing as little known as possible.'

'Yes, sir, certainly, sir.'

'There was once a trouble like this before, concerning some illness spreading about the populace. During that time a certain man came forth who said, if he was sufficiently paid, he would help us in our troubles. No one knew who he was, or where he came from, but he was most particularly capable, most unusually so, in sorting out the problem. He disappeared after it was dealt with, and no one knew whither he had gone. But word has come to us from him this very evening. His name, at least the name he uses when he communicates with us, is John Smith Un-Iremonger.'

'Is he of the family?'

'No, no, I cannot think so. If anything, somehow the very antithesis of it. I know nothing more about him, only that he has been most useful before.'

'Well, sir, let us hope this gentleman solves this nonsense.'

'Only thing is, Harbin.'

'Yes, sir?'

'I shouldn't call him a gentleman. Not exactly.'

'What should you call him then?'

'I cannot exactly say. Not a gentleman; there, I'll leave it at that. Carry on then, Harbin, see the search through.'

Superintendent Rudley-Griffin seemed most eager to leave. By then there were new noises up and down the street, doors opening and closing though no one was there to operate them, strange cracks and creaks coming from the houses, as if the whole address were trying to come to life.

12.17 a.m.

One house left to go.

Link Boys of Mill Bank

16

MOVING STREETLAMPS

Continuing the narrative of Lucy Pennant

'Well, well, well, and what have we here then?'

There were torches all around us, circling us, no way out. I couldn't see the people holding them, the light was too bright. I could feel the heat of them burning into us. We've been taken – somehow it happened, swift as anything. Like we could count the breaths left to us now, so close to the end. Have at us, why don't you, I thought, but by heaven I'll take one or two of you with me. I'll kick and punch you and you'll remember me in the morning in your bruises and your swellings, in your teeth gone missing.

'Who are you?' some torch asked. 'And what's your business here?'

That wasn't right, that wasn't the right question, was it? That didn't sound police at all. The police knew who we were, rats, they called us. And now that I looked beyond the flaming light, it seemed the people weren't wearing the same top hats of the policemen, that perhaps they weren't in uniform even.

'We can be here if we like,' I said, trying it on.

'Says who?'

'I do,' I said, growing sharper, standing as tall as I may. 'Stick that in your pipe and smoke it.'

'Speaking of pipes, do you have matches, do you have a light on you?'

Matches, I thought, don't talk to me about matches. I had a matchbox once, called Ada Cruickshanks, so Clod believed. I saw her in my dreams, that woman, that thin, grim governess. She wanted life just like I did.

'Go on and mind your own,' I said.

'We shan't be trifled with. We mean business.'

'Like you frighten me,' I said.

'We'll bloody make you frightened.'

'I'd like to see you try.'

'Got such a lip on her this one,' some other torch said.

'Yes, I have, if you want to know,' I replied. 'And by God I swear I'll split the first lip that comes close to me; you don't frighten me. Touch one of us here and we'll so burn you back and blast everything you've ever owned. We'll set your mother's hair alight while she's sleeping, we're that determined!'

'Whatever's got her goat?'

'Were only asking.'

'Just checking you had no light of your own.'

'This is our patch, you see.'

'And we protect it, and see that it stays ours.'

'Who are you anyway?' one of them asked.

'Your nightmares come to life,' I said, 'that's who.'

'Whoever you are you may not light a light on this street, not without our say-so.'

'And why not?' I asked.

'Well we're link boys. Obviously.'

'Link boys?'

The torches moved back now and we were better able to see who it was that was holding them. They were boys, just boys. London boys with torches, scruffy little urchins, just kids, kids like us. Going about their business. Whatever that was.

'My name's Lucy Pennant,' I said, growing bolder, 'these are my friends. My family, you could say. Like as blood to me.'

A small silence then.

'Oh, well, in that case,' said the most talkative of the boys, their leader I surmised, 'I'm Tommy Cronin, local of these parts. And these here about me are the Mill Bank Link Boys. That's Jim Lowe, and Samuel Boxall and Peter Freyer and Horace Points and Willy Rochester and over there's Georgie Clark.'

At each introduction the boy waved his torch slightly and said 'How do.' The last child, a poor ill-faced one, stood somewhat apart from the others, a rather melancholy figure.

Each of us said hello back and gave our names.

And then, like we were at some strange social gathering, like the rare dances they used to have in Filching, when boys were shoved one end and girls the other and we looked at each other across a great distance and waited for them boys to come to us and they took their times, and once I was so furious at waiting (cos they said the girls must wait on the boys, because that was how it was done) I stomped over the ground and picked one and said to him, 'You'll do then, dance with me now!' But this wasn't a dance, this was something else all together, couldn't be further from dancing, unless it was dancing between life and death.

'What are link boys anyway, when they're at home?' I asked.

'Well, we're lights, aren't we?' said Tommy. 'Don't you know anything? The sun's on strike and don't show on London any more, and not everywhere is street lit with gas lamps, and them that are don't shine so very bright, and in all this blackness a fellow loses his way and don't rightly know where he's heading to, or even which way is home, and some of these lost guv'nors are a little oiled by drink and find themselves walking unsteadily into the drink, into the Thames itself and then, well then, they don't bob up after a time, which is, all in all, rather an inconvenience to them. And we, you see, we light them. We're link boys, we're here to show the way. We're what you might call walking lampposts, living breathing lampposts, lampposts with life, and this is our strike: Mill Bank, see? So there we are, we shed light in the darkness. For a fee.'

'Come to think of it, that's very clever,' I said, because I thought it was. 'What a business!'

'Yes it is,' said Jack, 'isn't it? And we're doing handsomely out of it, quite moving up in the world. And so: wherever it is you're going to, can we light you, me and some of my lucifers here present?'

'Yes,' I said, 'perhaps you may. Thing is, we're new to London.'

'You're new, are you? Well there is a thing.

'Welcome to London, great city, greatest of all cities!'

'Yes,' I said, 'we've heard much about it.'

'Course you have, we're that famous.'

'So,' I said, 'we thought we'd come and see for ourselves.'

'Hardly dressed for it though, are you? Stink to heaven on high.'

'Let me describe London for you in three words, just so you know,' said ill-faced Georgie Clark in his sharp little voice: 'Huge. Heavy. Black.'

'Sounds lovely,' I said.

'Welcome, strangers, to the best place in all the world,' moved in Tommy Cronin, shutting up Georgie. 'Where you from then, Russia, is it, or Blackpool? Afrique or Orinooque or Acton? Don't matter much to us, we'll oblige, for a fee. Making conversation, not to be repetitive: where's home then?'

'We don't have a home.'

'Well then, are you wanderers from Wandsworth, or crooks from Cricklewood?'

It seemed that Tommy could not think of many places beyond London and so mentioned different regions of the vast capital, as foreign to him, I supposed, as any place.

'No, no we're neither,' I replied.

'They're not especial tall, so they can't be from Highbury.'

'No.'

'Nor excessive short.'

'So Low Leyton is out the question.'

'Let's have an estimate on their size?'

'Bell size? From Belsize Park, is it?'

'No,' I said. 'Can you help us? Would you help us?'

'Are you hungry?'

'Yes!'

'Yes!'

'Yes!'

'Then you're not from Fulham.'

'Or Stockwell.'

'I'm starving,' said Esther Nelson, involuntarily.

'Then you must've come from Holloway?'

'No,' I said, 'no, no.'

'Well you're filthy, that's certain.'

'Then if they're not from Wormwood Scrubs they should hurry thence with all dispatch.'

'I am going to punch one of you any moment!' I said, and meant it.

'What a temper.'

'She must be from Barking, to make such a shout.'

'Nah, Isle of Dogs.'

'Come a step closer, why don't you,' I said, 'and flame or no flame I shall clobber you.'

'All right, deary, no need to get all Charing Cross about it.'

'Please!' I cried. 'Will you help us?'

'Tell us where you're from,' said Tommy, serious now, playing the adult. 'Don't normally see groups of children covered in turds. What's your business? Where are you from?'

I hesitated. We all did.

'She doesn't know!'

'She's not very bright.'

'Very well then,' said Georgie, 'she must be from Dulwich.'

But then I pointed over behind us, where the sky was lightest from the burning. And turning back around, I saw all those flaming torches retreat from us, and a shock run through them all.

'Oh.'

'Oh.'

'Oh.'

'Over there?'

'Yes.'

'I might have known by the smell of you.'

'Not Staines, but . . .'

'Foulsham.'

'Foulsham.'

'Foulsham.'

'Yes,' I said, 'we are from Foulsham.'

'Are you ill?' one of the boys asked.

'Not from Camberwell then, are you,' another boy whispered, but his heart wasn't in it any more.

'From Foulsham?'

'Yes,' I said. 'Can you help us? The police are looking for us, and they shall kill us if they find us.'

'From Foulsham.'

'Yes, from Foulsham. Please help us, I haven't any money. But I'll get some, I'm a good thief, I always was.'

'From Foulsham. A thief from Foulsham.'

'Yes, I already said so, didn't I.'

'What are you doing here?'

'I don't know if you noticed but there's a whopping great fire over there.'

'It's been burning these past few nights, and don't seem eager to go out neither,' said Georgie.

'Shouldn't have come here,' said Tommy Cronin.

'Is that so?' I asked. 'Should we rather have stayed there and burnt to death? Oh, I'm so sorry,' I added, all sarcastic, 'no one told us. Shall we head back now, would that make you happy? Come on, help us. Please.'

'It was wrong of you to come here.'

'We would have died,' I said.

'It's not your home is it?'

'We have no home, it's been burnt to the ground.'

'You're trespassing, that's what you're doing, you shouldn't be here.'

'Will you help us or not? We'll find ways to pay you.'

'You're filth. My father always said, see any person from Forlichingham, you know what to do: slit their throats double quick.'

'You won't help us.'

'You're dirt, ain't you? Through and through.'

'Please,' I said, 'just tonight, just tonight get us a place to sleep, some food. Tomorrow we'll be away and you'll never hear of us again.'

'Couldn't do it. Sleep alongside Foulsham? Couldn't be done.'

'You'll know somewhere, somewhere where we shall be safe.'

'No, there is nowhere, nowhere at all for the likes of you.'

'Then we'll go on, without you. Let us pass.'

'Stand back, one and all,' called Tommy. 'Don't let them touch you.'

'Yes, stand back, or I swear I'll strike you hard.'

'Go on then – go, scum, into the night.'

'Come on,' I said to my people, 'we'll find somewhere without them soon enough, gutless children that they are. Stand back, stand further back, why don't you. You wouldn't want us to touch you. I'll spit if you come close, one gob of my spit and you'll be dying, I reckon.'

'Get back one and all!'

'Come along, quickly now. Before the constables find us.'

'Wait one moment!' called Tommy.

'Now what?'

'You're on the run you say?'

'Yes!'

'Don't like the peelers?'

'What?'

'The police. They move you on?'

'They bloody shoot at us!' I cried.

'Well, that isn't really welcoming is it.'

'We're already down five, one of us dead most like.'

'That's not good.'

'Not sociable I call it.'

'They move us on too,' admitted one of them.

'They kicked Jim's mother,' another volunteered. 'Shoved her down into the ground for answering back, and his little sister crying, and nothing we could do about it. They've pulled our homes down in the past, collapsed them when we'd made them up of this and that. Move us on when our gaffers can't pay the rent.'

'And they've locked us up, some of us have gone missing and never seen again.'

'They sound like Iremongers to me,' I said.

'No, we don't love them, them coppers. But what's a fellow to do?'

'Leave them alone, keep clear of them.'

'Run from them.'

'Then please,' I said, 'help us.'

'Well . . .' paused Tommy, 'well, we might help them, a bit.' He whispered to the lights around him.

'Thank you!' I cried. 'Thank you!'

'And you'll pay us for it. Pay us steep!'

'Yes, we will, we'll find a way.'

'All right then, all right. Now listen, men.' He called his boys and they gathered round in a scrum, making plans. A moment later Tommy was back again.

'All right then, we'll link as usual and watch the coppers for you, and where we can, we'll steer them the wrong ways. But if we get fined, by heavens you'll be in for the cost of it.'

'Doubled!'

'Yes, doubled, that's right, Willy! And if we get punched, then by heavens we'll punch you for it out of compensation.'

'All right then,' I said, 'agreed.'

'All right then, agreed,' said Tommy. 'Now we'll go on our way and see what's doing and Georgie'll guide you.'

'I hate to do it,' said Georgie.

'I know you do, Georgie, but you're the fastest. Go on with you.

Turning to us he said, 'Listen to Georgie. If you get trapped that's your own lookout.'

'Thank you,' I said. 'Thank you!'

'Thank you.'

'Thank you.'

'Oh, belt up. Come on then. We'll catch up with you later. Good luck.'

And all the torches ran off. Only one solitary light remaining, that of Georgie.

'I don't like you much,' he said.

'Well,' I said, 'cheers.'

'But I like the police even less. They were the ones that made my face so melancholy. I don't smell no more on account of them, so you might stink, you look as if you stink, but I don't smell you, cos I don't smell nothink.'

'Well I'm right glad to know that,' (that's how Clod would have said it), 'but we're in a bit of hurry right now.'

'I haven't made up my mind to hate you yet.'

'That's a comfort right there.'

'Thing is, you'll want to be hiding.'

'You're a fast one, aren't you?'

'Somewhere other people shan't find you.'

'You've got the plot.'

'Yes, well, that's what you want I reckon.'

'Yes, and we do thank you.'

'Oh will you all belt up. I said I don't like you and I'm liking you less and less every moment. Now do you think you have it in you to be silent?'

'Yes.'

'Yes.'

'Yes.'

'Silent I said! Can you shut your traps?'

We nodded.

'Now there's quick schooling, right there! All right, now I've got your lugs, here's the dish. Just follow me, it's all I ask, if one of you falls off and gets lost, well then that's your problem, ain't it? I can't be helping that. When I move, I move fast and I'll be turning my light out so we don't have a bright arrow pointing us out wherever we travel. So come along then, I know this landscape, I've lived in it all my twelve year, but you don't so you don't know nothink, you're thick as night. So then I'm your blasted teacher. Come along wiv me, and be swift. No turning back for any left behind, if you lose some I don't care, I'm going on and without me you're blind as death. So then buck up.'

We gathered around him.

'Don't come so close, you'll quite throttle me. God, look at you. Know what? I hate you, I feel it now, yes I do, I hate you, but not as much as others. Can't even think why I'm helping such as you, maybe because I'm soft, must be soft as turds. So shut it and keep up. Got it?'

We nodded.

'What a lumpage! Right then, lights out!'

He blew out his lamp and the darkness pounced.

'Follow! Follow! Only follow!'

And he was off, and we running behind him, all in a terror.

They were such dark and deep and slippery streets, that all of us fell over at some time but were very quickly pulled up by the rest. We moved on and tried to keep him with us, ill-faced Georgie who ran like a bloody whippet. All along the river's edge we went following the Thames, rushing in through thin

226

streets sometimes, but then we kept coming back to it, like he needed to be by the river, that that was the only way to know where we were otherwise be lost in the maze of London. Over streets thick with mud, always in back ways, dark, loveless, neglected places. I know Foulsham was supposed to be a place of no great loveliness, but these shadow houses and streets, these crooked silhouettes, these rotted dwellings seemed to me more miserable yet. How can a person live like this and still be a person? When do you stop being a person, I wondered, and be stamped as something else?

How long did it all take? The sliding, the crying, the calling out, the begging for Georgie to slow down and let us catch our breath? But he never did, on we must go and on and on or lose him and find ourselves who ever knows where and in darkness eternal. There were people on the way, all wrapped up, showing barely any face or hands, but all clothed in shining, soaking, greasy material, subterranean people I thought. People that live in the bottom of a water tank. What dripping lives, where to find warmth, where to find any light? Sometimes there'd be a person, or a moving shape that may have been a person, sometimes there was a shouting out at us, or someone in one of the black buildings crying out in the night, on and on we went, through the strangeness. How, I wondered, could we ever thrive here, in such a place that must discourage life so? How could anything live here? On and on we went, forward and backwards and down again, the great slopping of the filthy river.

Oh please stop.

Oh please, enough, enough.

Not another step, yes another and another yet, on we must go, and at such a rate. I hate you too, Georgie broken nose, I hate you and your feet, webbed no doubt.

And then all of a sudden.

'All right! Hush!' said Georgie. 'Nearly there, we may walk the rest and act as if we're happy to be here. Come along.'

A great dark shadow loomed up.

'What's that?' I asked.

'Only the Bank of England,' said Georgie. 'We're upon Threadneedle Street, come along, come along, just a few steps more.'

We went along a wider street then, and I wondered if it was safe for us to be in such a great thoroughfare, carriages going up and down with their lamps lit before them.

'Bishopsgate,' instructed Georgie. 'Here we are then.'

There was a narrow passageway and we took it.

'We may calm ourselves now,' he said in utter blackness.

I called the names, they called them back, all present, all that were left of us.

We had arrived.

'Here's home,' said ill-faced Georgie.

17

AMONGST NEW COMPANIONS

Continuing the narrative of Clod Iremonger

Broken Life

There was more smashing from inside, as if the nursery room was fighting with itself.

And from outside, police running, calling out.

I had never known such a thing to fight me like that nursery did, never felt such a weight pushing back at me. But I had to get in, get in to the roaring heart of it. All around me, up and down the corridor, the wallpaper was growing bubbles and falling off in strips, pictures on walls slammed to the floor; where my hands were upon the door two burnt imprints were growing. The door banged a little at last, it shuddered, I could feel the edges of it now, it wasn't complete wall any longer, it was cracking, I was making my way in. Here I come, here I come. I cut into it then, cut hard like any knife, split my way through, and what a gushing there was, a bursting of things coming from the wound, a bleeding of furniture, of wallpaper, of floorboard splinters and then with a terrible scream as if a life sudden ended, a shocked yell, a general rumbling and then stillness. Dead now, dead again now. Door down, I stepped inside the body of a room in a house.

What a place it was, twisted and turned and bent and blackened, nothing there that hadn't been shaken and shocked, what a carcass it was. This thing, once living, gone dead. Still warm though, but the warmth ebbing. What a thing is life and living. And behind the curtain, as if in hiding, a music stand whose name, the name it whispered, was Janey Cunliffe. She had been turned then, the girl that had waved at me, I was too late.

Only then, there, on the floor beneath the upturned bed, shoes, shoes with feet in them. The girl! Still! The bed I think had tried to lay upon her just as she had laid upon it night after night. Who could blame them all, they were only doing what she had done to them so often. I moved those things away, there she was, still breathing. A length of fire extinguisher hose around her throat.

'I'm so sorry,' I said. 'So sorry, I had to do it. I am so sorry.'

I carefully pulled the fire extinguisher away.

'You're here now,' she said, gasping.

'I'm speaking to the room.'

'The room!'

'Did you set the room awake?' I asked. 'Were you so frightened of the fire extinguisher that you gave it the idea of life? Poor, poor things.'

'It tried to strangle me.'

234

The unhappy girl was panting on the floor, and I looked all around at the lifeless room. Poor things, so still now, that only a moment before were roaring.

'How proud they have become,' I said, 'how disobedient. I must say, all in all, it's very something.'

'They nearly killed me!'

'They were looking for life.'

'They would have taken mine!' she said standing up, brushing herself down, pulling herself away from me. 'A room coming to life? How could it? What's happened to everyone? Where have they gone? My mother and father, all the servants?' She was trying to make sense of it all. 'They're not here any more, and where they were strange things have been put in their places.'

'Then they have turned. Alas.'

'And who are you anyway? It all started . . .'

Then she seemed to comprehend something.

'You *are* the dirty people, aren't you?'

'We're Iremongers.'

'Yes, that's what I mean, the dirty people.'

'Is that what you call us?'

'I'd like to have my parents back.'

A police whistle sounding down the street, noises of boots: doors being smashed down.

'It's not safe here.'

'The police!' she said. 'Come to save us.'

'No, no. Those fools,' I said, 'shan't last a moment, they'll close their eyes and wake up a chamber pot. Don't trust them, they haven't the first idea: they think when you leave a room that a room stays still, that's how much they know!'

'I'm going to call them, I must do it!'

'No, no, child, please think. Do you know of any policeman that can help people turned into objects?'

'Well . . .'

'And then – the next portion of my inquiry – have you come across people of late, strange people perhaps, who have done things, or can do things that have not been done before?'

'I'm afraid to say I have.'

'Then think, if those new strangers of yours, dirty though they may be, might be of more help than those you've trusted earlier. Because, well, the world's turned rather new and strange, hasn't it?'

'Yes,' she said, 'there is no denying that.'

'There we are then! Now listen, girl,' I said, 'there's no one can control objects quite like I can. If you want to stay a girl you'd best come along with us.'

'I'm not just some "girl", you filthy person, I'm Eleanor Cranwell, full thirteen years old.'

'Oh hullo, Eleanor. I am right glad to meet you. Clod Iremonger's my calling.'

'Clod?'

'Clod.'

'Clod? Do you even know what that means?'

'Our names are like yours, only a little tilted, I know that.'

'Clod means a lump, a bit of dirt or clay.'

'Does it?'

'It means, also, a fool, a dullard, an idiot.'

'Does it? I didn't know.'

'Clod, he's called,' she said.

'Lucy,' mumbled Binadit, coming out into the hall, as Pinalippy quickly pushed Irene Tintype into the cupboard beneath the stairs.

'What on earth is that?' cried Eleanor, nearly screaming out again.

'He's one of us, he's a fellow, name of Binadit,' I said, introducing the great heap coming up the stairs. 'One of our party, an Iremonger.'

'He's disgusting – there's rubbish all over him.'

'Get back, Binadit.' And back he went. 'Now listen, little Eleanor.'

'I'm still thirteen!'

'So you are, quite right. And an excellent age it is, one of those ages most ripe for bringing objects into life, I shouldn't wonder. Now Eleanor, thirteen years old, is there somewhere where we might hide, somewhere not on this street, somewhere, some shelter? It must be indoors or otherwise Binadit here shall have all on top of him. He moves and all the dirt leaps on him, you see. He has so many skins of dust, don't you, Bin? Can you help us, dirty though we are, to some place of sanctuary?'

'Well, there's Great Aunt Rowena's, I suppose. She might take you in.'

'An aunt of yours? Very good. She lives nearby?'

'Through the back of the house, we can cut across that way. She's very near, in Connaught Square. We can go now, if you like; I often visit my Great Aunt and am back and no one in the house has any inkling of it.'

'Let us hurry then. She lives all alone, does she, Great Aunt Rowena? Such a funny name.'

'Quite alone, yes. Just her and her servants, and her dolls.'

'How many does that make?'

'Three servants, twenty-two dolls last counting.'

'An old woman, is she?'

'Yes, she is rather.'

'Poor eyesight?'

'She wears glasses.'

'Very good then; she'll qualify, she'll have to.'

'I'll say that you've all come for tea. We do often have tea parties, Great Aunt Rowena and I, and all her dolls.'

'All right! Come along, all of us, whilst we still may.'

'But what about the leather?' wondered Pinalippy.

'She must come along too,' I said, seeing the poor flat-faced rubbish-girl's false visage peering around the corner.

'May I? May I!'

'Yes! Yes!' I said. 'But keep her clear of Bin.'

'I'm not going with any leather,' said Pinalippy. 'I've never heard of it. I am an Iremonger full-blood – the very thought of it!'

'Then, Pinalippy,' I said, 'I'm much afraid you shall have to stay here, because Irene's coming with us, she is our responsibility. I'm sorry for sending those others towards the police's whistles now, that room has made me think differently.'

'A leather, among Iremongers . . . as a shield, I suppose you mean. Very well then.'

'As a person equal to us all. I think they must have some right to life after all, don't you? Our people made them. I'm sorry about the other ones taken apart, but, well, I think it, I think *she* must have feelings too. Only thing is we'd better keep

Binadit as far from Irene as possible, otherwise I fear, well, I fear she might come apart rather suddenly.'

'Personally,' said Pinalippy, 'I think you're an idiot, but there's no time to argue. I'll go on ahead then, the leather will come with me, if you'll lead us, miss.'

'Yes, yes, come along then.'

'And Binadit and I shall be the last.'

And so we moved towards the back, as the police came to the door, and, finding it locked, began smashing it.

'Slow, slow, Binadit, don't wake the furniture. Slow, slow.'

Across the little garden at the back, all empty but for some paving, though Binadit caused scraps and clouds of dirt to spring up at each tread, and through the way until we came to Eleanor's Great Aunt Rowena's. More and more clouds of dust and dirt whirling all around Binadit. On we went, a single Londoner, Iremonger children and a leather girl, quietly into the night.

The Dolls House

No one answered when Eleanor, our guide, pulled on the bell, but she had a key and let herself in. Binadit and I hung back, the wind picking up, or rather objects picking up and dancing gleefully about him, while I tried as hard as I may to keep the waves of swirling rubbish from breaking fiercely upon him. And after each wave came on, how the places behind him seemed cleaner, like they'd been scrubbed clear of a sudden.

Pinalippy pushed past Eleanor and banged inside.

'This is *my* aunt's house,' Eleanor complained.

'I'm sure it is, and I'm getting in it and quick too. Come on, in we go. Hullo, Aunty! We're home!'

'Please, please, let me do this,' said Eleanor. 'Hullo, Great Aunt Rowena, it's me, it's Eleanor, I've a few, well, friends with me, I do hope that's all right. Anyone here? Hullo, I say. Pritchett? Knowles? Where on earth is everyone?'

There was no answer.

'Come along, come in, Irene,' guided Eleanor.

'I'm Irene Tintype,' she said.

'I know you are,' said Pinalippy. 'Don't lose your stuffing over it.'

'I'm Irene Tintype,' she said again, as if in further practice. 'Irene like meany, not Irene like green. Irene Tintype.

'Please, please,' said Eleanor to Pinalippy, 'you must understand that this is my *aunt's* house.'

'Very well and understood,' said Pinalippy, 'and that just over the road is the *Queen's* police and I'd rather know the former than the latter: well then, where's the aunt? Halloo!'

'I'm sure she'll come down in a moment, she's rather hard of hearing.'

'We'd best have Irene in a different room than Binadit, I suppose,' said Pinalippy, 'to avoid any huge noise. Is there somewhere she can go, and we can close the door behind her?'

'The drawing room?'

'Yes, wherever, as long as there's a door.'

'Here we are then, Irene.'

'That's the spirit and close the door quick!' said Pinalippy, shutting it.

'Whatever is all the fuss about?'

'It's Binadit and that one, they shouldn't see each other.'

'Why on earth not?'

'It's, well, how to say, it would be bad luck, and might go hard on the lea— on Irene.'

'It sounds rather extraordinary! As if they were to be married tomorrow and seeing each other the night before would bring awful bad luck.'

'Well, something like that,' said Pinalippy. 'All right, Clod, you may come along now.'

So we lumbered in and I had to rather push Binadit to get him through the door, but we'd managed before and did again.

'I've put on,' he said. And indeed, he'd grown several new skins since leaving the last house.

'Yes, I'm afraid you have rather. I'll try and get them from you, but they do stick so hard.'

'They do look for me, I'm home to them.'

'What a mess you've made!' cried Eleanor, seeing Binadit and all the dirt about him.

'I'm sorry, I'm sorry,' he said.

'It's all right, Binadit.'

'She's angry at me!'

'No she's not.'

'Yes, I am!'

'Please, Eleanor, he can't help it.'

'He should be more careful.'

'He can't help it.'

'Sorry, so sorry.'

'He'll ruin everything.'

241

'It's only rubbish that does it,' I explained. 'Things that have been thrown away. They all rather rush towards him. It's because he was thrown away as a baby and the rubbish heaps saved him and now the rubbish bits are all his brothers and sisters, mothers and fathers, aunts and uncles: all his family, you see. And they do seek him out. They miss him terribly.'

'You people are disgusting! I can't even think why I'm bothering with you. You reek to high heaven. Put him in the bathroom upstairs – come on, up you come.'

'A very good idea. In you go, dear Binadit, and we'll close the door for now.'

'And be careful in there,' said Eleanor, 'that is a roll-top slipper bath, the very latest from Bolding of Grosvenor. Great Aunt is extremely proud of it. Don't go messing it up.'

'I'm sorry.'

'No, no, nothing to be sorry for, Binadit,' I said. 'Just keep inside all right, just keep there, I'll bring some food.'

'Seagull? Rat?'

'I'll find something.'

'You eat rat?'

'Yes, of course,' I said. 'Don't you?'

'Oh God!' she said and went further upstairs.

Poor girl, I thought, putting myself in her position for a moment, she scarcely knows what's happening to her. It must all appear very upturned, we must seem rather odd fellows to her. And she is so, so clean. I'd never seen such a clean face before, I didn't like to look too much upon it, if I was being honest. It seemed quite appallingly naked.

She was back down in a moment, tears in her eyes.

'I can't find my aunt, I couldn't find my parents, where oh where has everyone gone? She wasn't in her bed; this was though.'

She held, with some difficulty, a red-and-white striped wooden pillar, the type that barbers put outside their shops to advertise their business. Well then, here was the aunt. I could even hear her quietly muttering.

'Rowena Philippa Beatrice Cranwell.'

'Oh yes,' I said, 'here she is then.'

'I'm going to speak plainly now,' said Eleanor, her hands trembling. I thought she may cry any moment.

'Please do,' I said.

'I'm very worried,' she said. 'I'm very worried and hurt and upset and I might scream any moment if I'm not persuaded otherwise.'

'Please, Eleanor, to sit down.' There was a bench along the landing.

'I want you to be honest with me, I don't want any lying.'

'No, no, I'll tell you.'

'Where is my aunt?'

'I'm very sorry, truly I am.'

'Oh! Oh!' she said, her hands trembling. 'I'm holding her, am I?'

'Yes, yes, I do believe you are. What was your aunt is now, is now this.'

'Rowena Philippa Beatrice Cranwell.'

'I can hear her,' I said, 'very faintly. She's saying her name, she sounds peaceful enough.'

'What are you talking about?'

'I hear things, Eleanor, I do hear them talking, and this wooden pole says "Rowena Philippa Beatrice Cranwell".'

'I never told you my aunt's full name.'

'No you didn't; she did, this very pole here. She's saying it again now.'

'Rowena Philippa Beatrice Cranwell.'

'I saw it happen before, when you came to my street,' Eleanor said. 'The old man, he made the servant into a music stand. She was trying to help him, that was all. Why did he do that? Why did you ever come to our street?'

'I am sorry. London destroyed our home, we had to go somewhere.'

'Bring my aunt back. Bring her back right now.'

'I cannot.'

'Do it.'

'I am unable to. I wish it were otherwise. But I think, I hope, if I can, to try to help you. To stop you turning. I shall try.'

The poor creature was so confused, so terrified.

'Will she come back again?'

'I, I don't think so, I think this is what she is now.'

'Poor Great Aunt Rowena!'

'Yes, poor aunt. Let us not worry her though.'

'Rowena Philippa Beatrice Cranwell? Rowena?'

'It's all right, Rowena, be still, don't upset yourself.'

'You mustn't call her by that name! She'd be appallingly offended!'

'What can I call her then?'

'*Miss* Cranwell, of course!'

'Dear Miss Cranwell,' I said, 'it is all right. We're here. Eleanor's here.'

'Rowena Philippa Beatrice Cranwell.'

'Will that happen to me?' Eleanor asked, very quietly. 'Will I turn?'

'I will do everything to stop it. Keep by me, Eleanor, I don't even know all I can do yet, just days ago I could hardly move a thing, and now I feel there's very little I couldn't shift. I shall try my guts out to keep you ever Eleanor.'

'I'm watching you,' said Pinalippy. She was on the stairs; I wondered how long she had been listening.

'Oh hullo, Pinalippy, I'm trying to cheer Eleanor a little, you must understand this is all very new to her.'

'Then she'd better catch up fast, hadn't she?'

There was a snore then, coming from the bathroom. Binadit was asleep in the tub.

'What on earth was that?' cried Eleanor.

'I do believe it's Binadit,' I said. 'He's sleeping. I do think that's very sensible of him, perhaps we should all do likewise. It must be very late by now.'

'The clock downstairs says it's half past one in the morning.'

'Please,' said Eleanor, 'will you sleep by me?'

'I think that's quite enough!' put in Pinalippy. 'He's mine, we're to be married.'

'Why don't we all find a spot in the same room,' I suggested. 'Why don't we go and join Irene, she's probably just as confused as you are, Eleanor.'

'If she's going then I'm coming along too,' said Pinalippy.

'By all means come, Penelope,' said Eleanor, 'and don't scowl so.'

'My name is Pinalippy! Please to call me so!'

'Very well then . . . Pinalippy.'

'And he's my fiancé, just remember that!'

We went to the drawing room. I couldn't see Irene at first, there was so much clutter. Indeed I do not think I had ever seen such a room for bits and pieces, for collections, for keepsakes, for mementoes, for gilt mirrors, for rocking horses, for globes, for trainsets, for wooden blocks, for elaborate birdcages with model birds inside them, for dolls – most of all for dolls, large and small, all seated here and there and all about, some even set around a green-topped table as if they were playing at cards.

'I've never seen such an amassing before.'

'My aunt is, was, a great collector.'

'My grandmother had a great room of artefacts,' I said, 'but this is different. So many things here are from childhoods.'

'She liked to play, you see; even though she was old, she still liked to play.'

'Well and why shouldn't she,' I said.

'What childishness,' said Pinalippy. 'What silliness.'

Irene Tintype was sitting just as still as all the other dolls; the only difference was the faint clouds of black smoke coming out of her mouth.

'Hullo, Irene Tintype,' I said, 'how are you?'

'Oh hullo!' she said, sitting up, jerking back into life.

'We've come to rest in here with you if we may?'

'Come along, come along!' she trilled.

'How are you feeling, Irene?'

'If you want to know, I'm feeling very angry.'

'Are you, Irene, why is that?'

'These people,' she whispered to me, indicating the dolls, 'they're snobs!'

'Oh I shouldn't worry too much over them.'

'No, you're right I declare! They're not worth the effort! I've introduced myself to them a hundred times and not one of them has once bothered to speak to me.'

'Oh I see, Irene!' I said. 'The thing about these people . . .'

'Such pretty dresses! I should like to have one of those!'

'. . . the thing about them is, they're dolls, Irene, they're not real.'

'What do you mean?'

'They're toys, they're playthings, they're imitation humans, they're not real, they're made to look like people but they're just, well, stuff. That's all.'

'You mean they're dead!'

'They never were living, Irene.'

'Why would anyone ever do that? Put bits together to look alive, to come so close to life but not to have it. What cruelty!'

'I doubt very much their maker thought that, I think he must have thought they would be nice companions for a child, something to play with.'

'To play with a dead thing!' said Irene, disgusted.

'Well,' I said, 'perhaps they were very well loved.'

'What use is that to them?'

'Not much, dear Irene, probably not much, but now I think we should get a little rest, and tomorrow we shall see how we fare.'

So we sat in armchairs or lay on the sofa and tried to sleep a little in that room thick with human shapes. Here I was with a girl of London, with a girl stitched from bits, with a girl who was supposed to marry me. Whatever has happened to the world to make such companions?

Pinalippy was the first to find sleep, and then Eleanor followed. Irene took the longest, indeed I'm not sure if she could ever sleep or if she only imitated it. She woke me up as I dozed, and she was in tears, muttering, over and over, 'The poor things!'

Whatever shall the morrow bring?

A Candle Factory, Bishopsgate

18

THE FACTORY OF LIGHT

Continuing the narrative of Lucy Pennant

I haven't travelled much. I haven't stepped in very many wheres, but I have heard about them. I know there are big sandy patches, I know there are some locations that are very hot. I gather there are mountains too, that in some places it snows all the year round. I know there's a sea somewhere, several of them, supposed to be, seven they say, I know that. In theory. I've never seen it. The only ocean I ever knew was one of garbage that was wont to drown a fellow if you didn't take good care. I know (or I've been told, or heard about it from books) there are places where people can sit in the sun and the sun feels hot on your skin and the air is clear and the birds sing and don't snatch your food away from you when you have it out in the open. I've heard there are places that are even green in colour. Well, I take that all on trust, don't I, and hope one day to become an experienced journeyer in my way and to walk in fields and even one day, one day who knows, dip my toe into the ocean and see what the ocean thinks of it.

One day.

Can't say which.

But now I come to the bit when we arrive in a new place, into and along the home of our guide and saviour, Georgie-no-smell, odd fish, our one person in all London, and there was he down a narrow court and pulling us along. Then Georgie stops at a dark door, says, 'Home! Here we are.'

And he knocked heavily on the door, it opened and a grim looking man poked his head out.

'Open up,' said Georgie.

The man put his hand out, and Georgie dropped some coins into it.

The door was opened to us.

'He's all right,' said Georgie, meaning the porter I supposed. 'He's tame enough, so long as he's paid he lets us in and out. Come along then, get in.'

Down a dark passageway and there we were.

The mansion of Georgie.

Georgiepalace.

Castle Georgie.

Let me describe it, tourist that I was to such hallowed regions.

It was a squalid room about twenty feet square, a general filth all around. Many things hung from the ceiling by chains, they were candles, I began to understand, that had been dipped in great basins of candle wax and left to dry upside down. The whole place was like being in some cavern and all about were

252

stalactites hanging from the ceiling, and they dripped too of course, down onto the floor and the floor was thick with the splattings and drippings, the droppings of wax.

About all these candles, all these great thick sinews of tallows waiting to be embraced by wax, about all the great steaming basins and the hot air and the flames beneath the basins to keep the wax liquid, about all the little basin moulds and night-light moulds and calipers and handsaws and measures, were the lesser things: the odd looking filthy creatures that made the pure white candles. These animals were not white at all, they were threadbare and their hair was burnt in places and so too their arms and much of their skins, all their fingers were red-burnt from their employ and many of them shook terribly. These were the candlemakers in this sweating shop of candle grease, in this misery of light making. Children, girls mostly, burnt and filthy and shining with candlegrease, like their own skins were made of that same wax stuff and like their hair was wick waiting for a flame, and they'd burn up, in no time probably, and their light, I supposed, should soon enough sputter out.

'Here we are then,' said Georgie, 'here's home.'

'Thank you, Georgie,' I said. 'What a place.'

The workers all around barely looked up from their labours as we came in, but kept their eyes upon their candlemaking like it was all they could see of the world.

'How do?' called Georgie, and some of them grunted back. 'Don't mind them, they're hard at it and will be at it for a good hour or more yet.'

'Making all the candles?'

'That's it. We do make them, that's our business, but not just any candles, no, not at all,' he said with genuine pride, 'for we are chandlers to the Church of England, that's us. Several concerns like ours, but this is the one where we shift. Me and the boys you met, we go out in our break and (not to tell anyone) we borrow some lights from here (please, please don't let on), and we tip the porter according to our arrangement, you see, and we go link around Mill Bank to get us more wealth, because if we linked here in the City, in Bishopsgate, they'd have us for theft no time and then, well then, we'd lose our jobs – we have an arrangement with some gangs from Mill Bank. And where should we be with no job? Quite in the dark.'

I looked inside one of the huge vats of wax.

'What a business,' I said. 'Has anyone ever fallen in?'

'Well, we most of us have, to be honest, at one time or other. We call it our baptism . . . we do make the odd church reference you see, seeing as we help to light all the great Godhouses of London from Saint Paul's to Westminster Abbey and any other chapel in between . . . yes we fall in, of a time, we get tired, see, the hours can be long and if we have to be up on the benches just by the edge here, to lay the tallows right before they're dipped, where it's terrible slippery, well then if we drift off, then we fall.'

'And get burnt?'

'Oh yes, can be bad sometimes, very bad. Can scald you terrible.'

'Can kill, the candle basins can,' said one bespotted worker.

'Let's not harp on that,' snapped Georgie. 'Well then, what do you think?'

We all looked around, still taking the place in.

'Like it?'

We didn't specify.

'You'd better like it, because here's your working now. Cos if you're to stay the night, if you're to take the bread and the mug of tea that I'm about to offer you, if you accept the bed which I shall be introducing to you soon enough then you're in on it, signed and stamped! That's it: you work here. In the candlemass, making the great white pillars for the Churches of England, it's a privileged position right here alongside the rest of us, don't you see? Starting at seven in the morning, finish around seven. You may earn as much as eleven shillings a week, minus four shillings a week for the bed and the victuals. What do you say, shake on it?'

I looked around at all the miserable workforce. This is no better than Foulsham, I thought, this is the very same, only here they work for the Church and over there they worked for the Iremongers.

'Well,' I said, 'we are grateful.'

'And there we are then! The rector will sign you in in the morning, and then you're proper lodged. He comes from St Helen's close by the leather market, he's a rector he is, and he keeps us here employed and out of the streets. So long as we do our hours straight, otherwise we are out again, double quick. And no begging shall get you readmitted. Well then here you are and may have some bread, if you're of a hunger.'

We fell on the dry bread he gave us.

'It is, this place, on the whole,' he said as we ate, 'a rather sticky sort of environment. On account of all the candle slop, you see. Which I don't smell, but am told does have a certain nose to it, very like the insides of a church, the breath of God, you might call it.'

'Yes,' said Jen, 'perhaps it does.'

At that Georgie Clark seemed very happy indeed. 'Yes! Ha! Well, thank you! Thank you! Thank you for noticing!'

'It is, also, Georgie,' Colin Shanks ventured, 'uncommonly warm inside.'

'Again! What joy! I don't love you! But I don't hate you! There then, I'll meet you in the middle.'

'Georgie,' I said, looking at him clearly in the candlelight. His face itself seemed like a very antique fish, very thin and very pale and somewhat off balance, like he was a direct descendant of a flounder. 'How long have you been here, working like this?'

'Since I misplaced my parents,' he admitted.

'What happened to them?' Jen asked.

He was quiet then a moment, before he opened his mouth at last, huge and big like a great codfish, and he said, 'Truth be told, I dunno. They gone. Mysterious, it was. There's been a lot of it around.'

'A lot of what, Georgie?'

'Oh, a good deal of parent-losing I should say, on the whole. A lot of parents, a whole deal of adults, gone missing. It happened to all of us here, and the Rector, he found us scavenging about and brought us in for to make candles for God.'

'What happened, Georgie?' I asked. 'Will you tell us?'

'I don't mind,' he said. 'It's no secret. Three weeks about. I was at home, at Limehouse, in our lodgings. My ma asked me if I'd seen my pa and I said well yes, he's over there, but he wasn't, though he had been a few minutes previous, now all there was, well, was this.'

He took out a pair of old spectacles.

'Now where did they come from, I ask you? Who could've left them there? Whoever could afford such things?'

'Were they warm, Georgie,' I asked, 'when you found them?'

'That they were! Piping!'

'And when your mother went missing, did you find anything?'

'That I did,' he cried. 'This here!' He held up a tin baby's rattle.

'Oh, Georgie, you must hold on to those.'

'I mean to, don't know how they came here, but I never go out without them. I know my people'll show up again some time, they just haven't yet. And the Rector says he'll keep an eye out on all the ones of ours that have gone.'

'Oh, Georgie,' I said, 'I have heard of this before. My parents, they suddenly went too.'

'Did they?'

'And mine.'

'Mine too.'

'I lost a brother very suddenly, and, same day, gained a stepladder.'

'You don't say!'

'Yes and my aunt went and we got a carpet beater, though we had no carpets to speak of, so what was the use on it, I say.'

'Our uncle got lost and we had a clothes horse.'

'Heavens,' said Georgie, 'over there, over in your Foulsham?'

'Yes, yes, at our old home.'

'Same thing's happening here, in a general way; there's a shortage of grown-ups. All the while there's less and

257

less of us. Hit the adults most especial, but some kids too, though fewer.'

'It's happened before, in Foulsham. There'll be more of it, for certain, before it is over again.'

'Well it's here now. And don't you mention Foulsham to the Rector, he shan't take you on if you own up to that place, isn't Godly I shouldn't think.'

The door was slid back and some other of the link boys came in, Tommy leading the way.

'Got them all stowed, Georgie?'

'All in, Tommy, all fed.'

'Well,' said Tommy, 'you've made some enemies, oh you've made some enemies all right.'

'What's happened?' I asked. 'What do you know?'

'Only that they're all out looking for you, all over town probably, and they mean to get you. You're sought for, highly sought after.'

'Did you find out anything,' asked Colin, 'about the ones in prison?'

'No, nothing on that. But if they're in Mill Bank, we'll maybe learn more. Horace's dad's in there, it's his current abode if you catch my meaning, he may have heard, we'll ask about.'

'What are we to do?' I wondered.

'Keep here,' said Tommy. 'Out of the light, making light. You'll be safe enough here. But must pay for it. When you're paid at the end of the week, we'll take your earnings, and we shan't rag on you.'

'What a deal you've made,' I said.

'Don't like it?' said Tommy. 'Sling your hook.'

But there was nowhere else for us to go.

'Thought so,' said Tommy. 'Well then, sleep might be in order, you look half dead.'

There was a grim black room they called the dormitory, blankets coated in splatters of candlewax, two to a bed, but it was rest, rest after so long. We had found shelter. We were still living.

Tomorrow, I thought, as I lay down with Esther Nelson beside me, tomorrow I'll strike out, into London. I don't care about this rector fellow and I'll see what else I can see. I shan't linger long enough for my skin to look like wax.

Tommy blew out the small candle in the dormitory and the darkness came back in ever such a hurry.

Part Four

Outside In

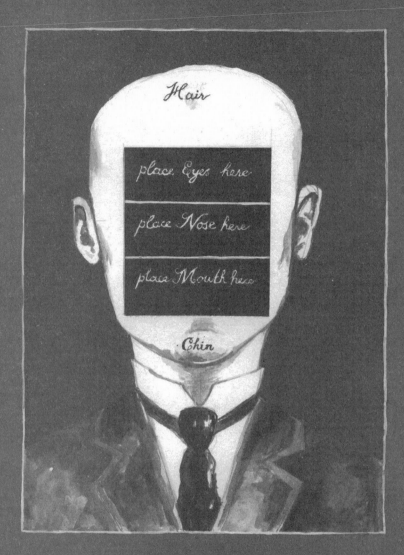

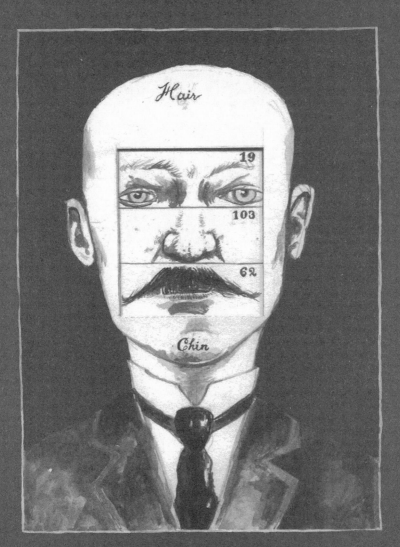

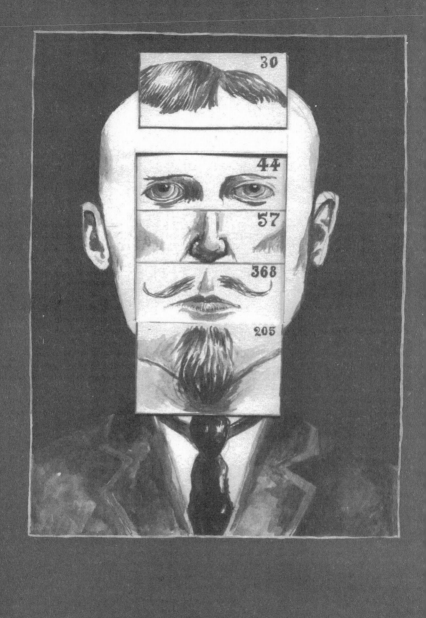

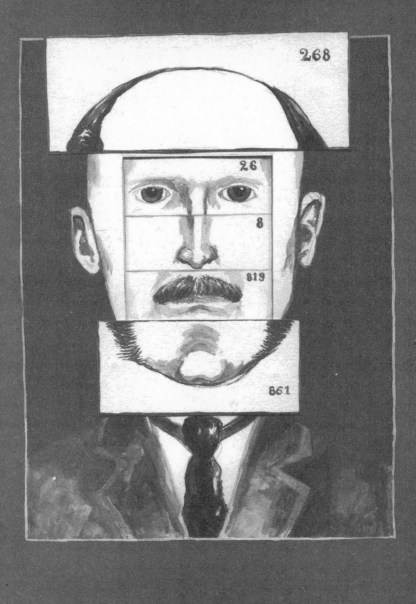

19

JOHN SMITH
UN-IREMONGER

Report from Inspector Frederick Harbin

7th February 1876
3–5 a.m.

John Smith Un-Iremonger came to us this morning with all his many instruments. I confess the man fills me with a certain dread and at the moment of his arriving a cold sweat came over me and I felt a panic in my chest. I know that I am not the only one to suffer so. I have seen Sergeant Metcalfe weeping behind his desk, huge burly man that Metcalfe is, I have known him these five years since, and never before was he wont to cry. It is the Smith that does it.

So very little is known about the Smith. He was used five years ago when certain bailiffs from London were discovered to be in Iremonger hands. On that occasion he stepped forward and, with his particular methods, had all the bailiffs disposed of. Brutally so if I am not mistaken. And then afterwards he disappeared again, as if he came from nowhere and went back there once more.

I have been told to let him do his work as he sees fit, never to question him. Indeed we shall leave him alone, readily. There's something so unpleasant about his person. I cannot quite explain it. I am a very rational man, I have no true belief in God, save for how religion might help us to be better persons. But I think that – it suffers me so to write it and yet I must – I think that he is not quite natural. I think there is something very *other* about him.

I shall put down what I know in the knowledge that should anything happen to me and my men, this journal should stand as a record and testimony of true events as they unfold. I shall in my best way write as I see and not embellish but only speak baldly and express with all the exactitude I can muster. So then, understand I am a most sensible and rational man in my middle twenties, a young man, certainly, to have gained this position, but one, I may frankly account, who is good at his job, loyal to his service, strict but not unbending, a rule-follower and a good one at that. I do not drink, I have no fanciful persuasions, as I say, I cannot exactly believe in God and Christ, but I do most fervently believe in Queen and Country, which may perhaps be something of the same thing. I should lay down my life for the good of London, I do take risks on London's behalf every day. But I am, beyond all else, a sensible man and a reliable one too.

Keep that in mind, who ever may read this, and reignite the knowledge as you read on, for I fear there shall be cause to remember it.

To begin in the best way let me try to describe the personage John Smith Un-Iremonger, if such a thing were even possible.

On the surface he is a most average man. There is nothing the least bit remarkable about him. He is very unassuming in his dress. In fact after he is gone it is almost hard to describe him with any exactitude.

His face, let me try to achieve that. Again there is little to distinguish here, a very average face, you might say. A blandly handsome face perhaps, with a neat moustache and mutton chops. A familiar face, I might even say that I have seen it before, and yet I cannot precisely recall it, but always when I am with the man I think I know him. He is very like someone, someone I know, only a bad version of him, a version, one might say, gone somehow wrong. And there I am again, I cannot say exactly where the wrongness comes from, only that he is wrong: Smith is very, very wrong. I have attempted to capture him in the latest police method, as you see above. It is the best I can do. The other thing about his face, the terrible thing: it does not ever seem to move when he talks.

How else might I exhibit him? His voice, his voice, is somehow muffled, it seems to come from deep within him, not to come from out of his mouth, rather from somewhere else in his body; it is a thin, whiny voice, wholly unattractive, like the noise fingernails might make scraping upon a blackboard. A most unnatural voice.

He is thickly dressed so that the least amount of skin is visible, indeed he never exposes himself apart from the face, only the face is ever spied, the rest – neck, hands, head-top – are all covered in layers of clothing with top hat or gloves or neckerchief.

He works alone, or with his own kind; we will not be permitted to run alongside him, he has other men at his disposal, but of these we see even less than the master. They are kept at a distance around the carts and cages that they use for their employ. I have not been close to one of these underlings.

And here I might mention some of the tools of his business: he has boathooks, and large butcher's implements soldered to the end of long rods, he has pistols and rifles, there are strange traps and, I think, many disguises, he has odd whirring alarums too – sirens that he sounds, and steel whistles that are like police whistles only when they are blown upon no detectable noise can be heard, though they make the most vivid reactions in his small troop of assistants. As if those muffled men of his have similar hearing to that of canines or other animals. Again, how this discomforts my men.

He is very cruel, the Smith is, and very thorough. He finds the Iremongers where we could not have, and they are mostly extinguished before we come near them. He has only been on duty these few hours and already he has made much progress. The Smith has no qualms about shooting Iremongers in the street, or trapping them in such a way that afterwards there never is any breath to come out of them. He has taken this morning three full Iremongers. Cusper Iremonger, a former clerk in Bayleaf House, Pomular Iremonger, a middle-aged woman from Heap House, and last of all Foy Iremonger, a girl found limping through the streets of London heaving a great lead weight. Smith has discovered these individuals and he has killed them.

I do find myself wondering about the method of removal of these pestilential people, the tool being such an improper person himself; I do wonder if the cure is as repellent as the malady itself.

How can I say it clear? I have been struggling with it all morning, at last I seem to have come upon the answer, or one at least that satisfies me for the moment. So then, see below, my recent conclusion regarding John Smith Un-Iremonger:

I think that the Smith is a man who is without life.

I think that he is dead.

A dead person who is somehow moving among us. The skin of his face does not quite look like any other human skin; it appears hard to the touch (heavens, I do not think anything could induce me touch it).

7th February 1876
7 a.m. (the sun still not risen)

To add to our woes, various peers of the House of Lords have gone missing, and several Members of Parliament too. Posters are being printed. Lord Kilburn is missing and Lord Milfield disappeared early last night. The MPs for Southwark and Cambridge have been missing three days. There are now several thousand missing persons reported around the capital, but these latest are the first amongst the high ranks of the country.

8 a.m.

To the Mill Bank Penitentiary this morning at the Smith's insistence. The pens are kept in the prison of Mill Bank, they are indeed most highly private and must remain so. In these pens we keep what few underlings of Foulsham we have managed to round up; some were caught in the rubble of Foulsham itself and kept extant for study, and others have been found trying to escape. They are pitiful children, for the most part. Some more were found just last night, escaping through the sewer lines. Some more are known to have broken free into London from the burning rubble town, perhaps as many as five. There is purported to be a leader of these trespassing children, a feral girl with wild red hair to match her ferocity. Judging by the impression of her on the Police bill poster now being distributed about the city, she is indeed a singular creature of vivid intensity and clearly a danger to the general public. No doubt she shall be quickly discovered and perhaps may lead to further information regarding the family in hiding. The redhead has a name, according to the new prisoners; she is called Lucy Pennant. Well then, Lucy Pennant, may you enjoy what last hours of freedom are left to you.

But to return to the Smith and our visit to the Mill Bank pens and to those of Foulsham gathered there. These are not, you understand, Iremongers of blood. Rather, these are the lesser people, the dirty poor of that place, who have somehow, through cunning or accident, survived the terrible torching of their miserable home. Here they are watched most thoroughly and from afar. They shall never be allowed to mix with our people of London but must always be kept at a distance, so that gates of iron separate this lesser species from the common Londoner.

We are awaiting orders to exterminate them – I am most grateful that it is not my division that shall carry out such a charge. For there is part of me that might consider them human.

No, for certain, I never do like going to the pens. I must wash myself very thoroughly afterwards, and indeed when I go home I shall have my Vera make me a scalding hot tub and bring with her what brushes she has to scrape hard upon my skin.

Some strangeness occurred in their pens when the Smith came to visit. He upset the prisoners a great deal, and for this I cannot blame them; it makes you think the poor creatures human, and almost similar to us.

They shook their cages mightily when the Smith appeared and did howl and weep and get about as far away from him as their limited confines would allow. His presence does agitate them terrifically. Just this morning I was witness, or part witness, to so unnatural an event, that I do think I must have become confused in my mind. But meet it is that I set it down, as honest as I may. And quickly too, for I cannot bear the writing of it.

There was an old man in a pen, huddled over and shivering, not well it is true, and Smith singled him out and went to him. At his orders he had the cage unbolted and the old man, shaking in a misery, was sat before him, but then – this most strange thing – the Smith in his screeching strange voice he says,

'Bless you, bless you, my dear friend, do come to us, please do come along now.'

And he strokes the man, with such tenderness, he pats him so gently upon the head like the old man were just a child

273

and he, the Smith, were the child's mother. And the old man shaking so, takes a terrible big breath and he rattles rather inside, and then – I could not see him well, for the Smith's back did mostly shield him from view – there was a very quick awful dying of the old man, a sudden tumbling of his corpus, an awful stillness came over him, and his pale skin lost all warmth to it so quickly, and was within the shortest of moments a lifeless grey. And – I know this sounds most unlikely, but please, I am trying to be as plain and honest as I may – and then the old man seemed no longer to be there at all, seemed somehow to have vanished quite out of life. In his place, upon the straw, was nothing but a pewter ewer, rather a nice one in fact. Where it had come from, and how it came to be there, I have no notion.

Then – oh, would that the writing of this were a way to pass on the knowledge and so be rid of it, rather than duplicating it as I feel I must – then, the Smith, as I see him from behind, takes one large breath, his whole body rises, and then, and then, then the ewer is no more there. Neither old man nor ewer, but only ever the old straw and nothing, nothing more besides.

John Smith Un-Iremonger rose from his knees, to his full height and asked – oh that voice – to be let out now. And so it was done, all were too affected to react otherwise. And now, it does seem to me, that the gentleman – must I call him so, no, no, no, I find I never can – that Smith is a fraction taller than he was before! Perhaps I do imagine this, but before he was of my height, or very near, but after the strange incident, he seems about an inch longer.

Then something strikes home to me, an idea, a notion, a horrible consideration, so ghastly a summation: that the old man has somehow been eaten.

That John Smith Un-Iremonger is somehow *eating* the prisoners.

Moorcus Iremonger

. . . and his Toastrack

20

UNDER THE CLOCHE

Whispers heard in Saint Paul's Cathedral

Here, Toastrack, you wretch. I know you're there. You're as far away from me as I can get you, but there you are, still my shadow, though you're all those yards away. I see your wretched form over where I sent you as far from me as possible.

I don't care that Rippit's all out after us, I don't care even that Duvit and Stunly have been killed, they never were ones to take their position seriously. They never did wear their blood quite right. But I do. I shall save my family, bring them back from the brink. I shall be the hero of all Iremongers. Grandfather's growing old and ill, true enough, and in his dotage he makes mistakes. He never loved me as much as he should. And now he never looks at me, or calls for me, as once he did. And it's on account of you, you Toastrack over there. Why must you be a person and not a toastrack, that is my question! Why me after all, why do I have this burden? And Grandfather, he is seen looking about Clod and wondering over all his progress. That whelp should have been put down at birth.

I know he escaped, Clod the wretch, I do know it! I caught one of the leathers we'd set to keep him in the house, name of John Demijohn. He said that Clod had frightened them and they'd gone running! To be frightened of Clod! I unstitched the leather then and there, and he fell out into the street. Just as I shall, no doubt, if Rippit catches up to me. I mean to do it still, I mean to kill Clod. To do it myself.

Clod! He cares nothing for Iremongers! (Perhaps I said that rather loudly, I'll return now to my seething and whispering.)

He does not deserve us. (That's better.)

He sullies us with his simpering after such common Foulsham skirts! Whoever could care for such cheap flesh is beyond me.

And so I, I shall show them who it is that he is and in so doing let them see who it is that I am. He shall not mock me again, I do swear it! So then here it is, I hold it in my own hands, my great Beaumont-Adams, what a pistol you are. And you'll do it for me, yes you shall. I had another one of you, your lovely twin, but where it is gone now I cannot say, I have lost it in all the struggle, I must have dropped it when Toastrack and I ran so fast from Rippit and his flaming, and sought some sanctuary here under the dome of Saint Paul's. Whatever may have befallen it, it's not here now. But still I have you, and you, dear pistol, you shall do the job, shan't you? I like the feel of you, I do like to talk to you. You're a comfort. With this here gun, with this bullet loaded into the cradle I shall kill Clod Iremonger. I kiss the barrel, I kiss my medal, there I swear it. It is my duty.

I shall so earn my trousers doing such a deed!

Hang on, where's Toastrack gone? Is he there in the shadows? Toastrack?

Toastrack! Wherever could he have got to?[†]

[†] The fact that the upper gallery of the dome of Saint Paul's Cathedral possessed whispering gallery waves – where a person whispering in the gallery may be heard at some distance by another person in said gallery – was not actually discovered until two years later by John William Strutt 3rd Baron Rayleigh, some time in 1878, but that did not stop Rowland from hearing every word.

A Pawnbroker's Shop, Off Drury Lane

21

LONG LINE OF LONDONERS

Lucy Pennant's narrative continued

'I've got to get out,' I said to Jen, when we woke next morning. 'I can't be stuck in here.'

'We're safe here,' Jen said. 'Aren't we?'

'I'll come back for you,' I said. 'But I must be out before the Rector comes. Then I'll sign up same as you. Tell the others not to worry. Give me a day, I'll be back.'

The link boys were still sleeping then, so I thought.

I scrambled out, quiet as I could, past all the candle carryings-on, a different shift at work then. I slid back the door, down the dark passage. There was the far door. The tame porter was fast asleep at his post. The door wouldn't give. I found it bolted. I eased the bolt across, quiet, quiet. It opened and I stepped into the dank court. Out I went then, faster and faster, London, London!

I hadn't even made it out of the court onto Bishopsgate when a hand came down heavy on my shoulder.

'No you don't!'

Tommy Cronin, his dander all up.

'Get off me, Tommy, I don't want a fight.'

'You owe me money. It was agreed. Your wages.'

'I'll get you bloody money.'

'Yes you will, at the end of the week. Now get back in there.'

'No, I shan't!'

'Oh yes, oh yes you bloody shall.'

And he started to drag me then, back through the court.

'The Rector will come soon enough and he'll have the foremen with him, so then you'll be stuck in proper.'

'Don't you touch me.'

'Shall if I like!'

'Do you see that pile of dirt heaped up over there?'

'I do. What of it? Missing home, are you?' he said, but he glanced over. And that's when I grabbed him by his hair and before he knew what was happening I tugged and rushed him to that small mound of filth and shoved him in it. And when he came up again all filthy he struck at me and so help me I knocked him back and we scratched and kicked and fought on London floor. He gave me such a knuckle-load in my mouth that I lost one of my teeth and then in such a fury I clocked his head again and again and again until he lay still in the dirt and did not hit any more.

'That's what I do to you, little boy,' I said, thumping him again. 'I'll whip your own bloody guts out. I've had my fill of bullies. I've been bullied every day of my life, I've seen bullying

284

everywhere I look. I've seen old people crushed by newer ones because they had more muscle about them, I've seen kids shove other kids, I've seen the great Iremonger people shove us all down in the filth. And I've had it now, up to here, with all of you, there won't be any more of it.'

He just lay there panting a bit, and sat up bloody and shocked.

'I'm hurting,' he said at last.

'Well, I'm glad of it.'

'Vicious thing, ain't you?'

'I think I am becoming so, yes, very vicious.'

'You'll end on the gallows, I reckon.'

'Very like.'

'I'm just trying to protect my lot.'

'Are you then? Well you'd better get tougher, hadn't you?'

'I'll still want paying.'

I raised my fist and he flinched a bit but then grinned until it hurt him and rubbed his sore jaw. I helped him up. How he was shaking. He checked his pockets, took out a wooden darning mushroom, regarded it carefully, returned it to his keeping.

'What's that then?' I asked.

'Mind your own.'

'Did it come to you of a sudden . . . was it hot when you found it? Did someone go missing?'

He looked at me a bit, then, 'My brother.'

'I'm sorry for that.'

'You never know who's next, do you?'

'No, you never know.'

'I may be a shoelace tomorrow.'

'You may.'

'Or I might live till I'm sixty.'

'You might.'

'Listen, Lucy Pennant, you've some guts in you – horrible stinking red guts I reckon – but guts nevertheless, and you're living and I'm living and that's about all we can say for now.'

'And I mean to go on living,' I said, 'or to try at it. And knock down any that attempt to stop me and those other ones of Foulsham.'

'I seen that.'

'There are people out in London that I need to find, people that I've lost, one in particular.'

'And do you know where that person is? Have you the address?'

'No,' I admitted. 'I don't.'

'It's big innit, London, no half-cocked slum town like Foulsham.'

'I shan't find him sat in there making candles.'

'I could help you. I might help you.'

'I've had enough of your help, thanks very much.'

'We link boys of London, we all know each other and whisper through to each other, like it's a huge living newspaper, but made of words, from mouth to mouth, stretching over all the city. If you need us. We have a call, here let me show you, like this.'

He clasped his hands together, like he was concealing something within them, made a slight hole between the thumbs and somehow, by blowing through this, summoned the exact sound of a pigeon.

'Now you try.'

'Why?'

'Try it. Go on. Do it!'

'It's nonsense.'

'Just do it.'

What a mess I made of it. He cupped my hands for me, showed me how to blow; still I just made the noise of my own air sounding hopeless through my hands. But we went on again, on he tutored me, and I had it at last or something like, only my pigeon sounded a bit sad, wounded maybe.

'That will have to do,' he said. 'Thing is, you see, common pigeons are everywhere about, so no one notices a few more pigeon calls, unless you're listening out for it.'

I didn't believe in it, this call of children, but he did and that made him seem so innocent of a sudden, just a child. So then in my turn I felt I needed to give him something, some little hope. 'Listen Tommy, there's only one person I know that can get any sense out of objects, that can make them move at his command, and I don't know if he's dead or not.'

'What's his name then? We'll put the word out.'

'He is called Clod Iremonger.'

'Clod Iremonger, don't like the sound of that one at all – he sounds lethal.'

'No,' I laughed, 'he'd not hurt a fly. He's an ill-looking boy with a big head, sixteen years old.'

'Put like that, he doesn't sound very much after all.'

'If he's still alive, he can do things, things that no one else can.'

'I'd never have believed any of this a little while back, would have called it wild stories, but I believe in them well enough now. All right then, Lucy Pennant, shove off. I'll not tell the Rector. Scat before he sees you.'

I was out of the court fast as I could, hurting now from the tumbling. I did see the Rector coming along, a little round man with glasses and a weak chin, taller men in long coats beside him carrying lanterns, marching down Bishopsgate. I hurried away.

I was happy to be around people well enough to begin with. Like docile animals we were padding through the dark streets, no room here but for barging against one another, threadbare populace, clinging to their rags. Harder to get things off people who don't have much. I needed new clothes and some food, that was the first business.

I followed the greater number of stomping humans and a few streets later – bigger, richer, busier streets – I found a queue quite flooded out from a dirty courtyard. There were people snaking out into the street, out onto Drury Lane, the place was called. I joined the queue, even though I didn't know at first what it was for, maybe it was a soup kitchen, maybe I'd have me some food first, that seemed like a wonderful thing. I had myself thinking what the food should be on the other end, when I at last would reach the front. It moved slowly this queue but I was in no great hurry, it was nice just to be around people, nice not to be running for your life, to feel the cold wind gently brushing through my hair. I got to studying my new company; they were a fairly varied bunch, some in tatters but some in good enough clothing, and one or two I'd say even nicely decked out. I noticed how hunched over many of them were, it wasn't because they were ill or old, it was because they were each holding something, and they were bent over their things, because either their things were heavy, or they were protecting them. All these new things that had come to them suddenly. One had a pickaxe head, one an abacus, another held a saddle, one had a kite, one woman held a embroidered cushion to her, one had a porcelain dog, a thin man was holding very nervously onto a pair of cymbals, one old woman had a cutlass.

My, but London's got a great new pox on it, I thought. I knew all about it – my father became a soup pot and my mother a pair of candle scissors. We're one and all in the same bad place. As we edged forward in the queue I came to the knowledge of why they were all here. The shop was dirty enough, but I saw the sign.

Three red balls hung on a wire frame.

Unmistakable. It was the same in Foulsham, only in Foulsham they all had the Iremonger bay leaf painted on them.

The pawn shop.

The pawn brokers.

These people had all come to get a few pennies from the things they carried. They had come to pass over their things, get them inspected, assessed a value.

I could see a sign well enough now:

MONEY ADVANCED ON PLATE, JEWELS,
WEARING APPAREL, AND EVERY
DESCRIPTION OF PROPERTY

This was the old sign, dirty and smudged by time and neglect, but beside it on new cardboard had been carefully inscribed:

OF PARTICULAR NOTE AND VALUE:
YOUR NEW OBJECTS!
MOST RECENT TO
YOUR POSSESSION!!
BEST PRICES ON NEW THINGS!!!

And so they had come, all of them, to pawn their loved ones.

They didn't know it perhaps, but they were flogging off, to get a few pennies, maybe a quid or two, what was left of their children, or parents, grandparents, friends, husbands, wives, lovers, darlings, the best of their lives. How could they do it? So quietly they went about it!

There were policemen walking up and down, watching the line, and I hid around the other people, I hunched over a bit, I tried very hard to look bored. One policeman walked right past me, even looked into my face, and I looked at his, such a strange blank face he had, no expression there at all. Right into my eyes he looked and he saw nothing in me that he was interested in at all, just went on up and down the line. Then another bobby comes by, and he too looked at me, and me thinking, I'll give it a go, shan't I, so I looked hard at him, and again that same uninterested stare. It was a different policeman but the face was very similar, as if they'd all come from the same family.

The dumbness of all these people with their objects; I was angry at them for not knowing what in the world they were doing. Someone, I thought, someone should bloody tell them. I would, I would do it, and afterwards watch them running home. Well then. So then: how to?

There was an old girl come to flog off her husband most likely. Her husband was a rocking chair and she was pushing the poor old man (turned chair) through the dirty courtyard towards the pawn shop, and given the way the old chair scraped, the old man (now a chair) seemed most reluctant. I *had* to tell them. Who else would?

'Oy,' I said to the old girl. 'Come on now, let me borrow that a second, I'll be careful.' I stood on the chair, wobbled a bit, but got my balance, quick enough.

'Hello,' I said. 'Hello, can you all hear me?'

No sound, all looking earthwards or into their armfuls, save the old woman, who stared at me, wide-eyed, looking like she wanted to scream but had forgotten how. Such an appalled look about her, like I'd just done the worst thing.

'I need to tell you something,' I said. 'The things you're holding, every one of you, that stuff you are all carrying, you shouldn't sell it. I know this doesn't sound right, but they're not things . . . not really . . . they're your missing people. They've turned. They've been objectified. They've got the illness, haven't they, poor things. My mam had it, and my dad, don't know how it happened. Heap Fever, they used to call it, common enough in certain places, this is a bad bout of it no doubting, but it does generally stop after a time. So, to be certain, those things you carry, those are your people. I want you to know that you're selling off your own people. Well I ask you: is it right? And why, I ask you, do the pawn brokers take such an especial interest in these objects? Take them home. Look after them! Go on then, go home, go home.'

No one moved, no one ran, no one screamed. All stayed just as docile as ever.

There were more policemen now than before, they were grouping further down the court, maybe five or six of them. Time to can it, Lucy, I told myself.

'Well then: now you know, don't you?' I concluded. 'Can't say I didn't warn you.'

'Shut it.'

'Mind your own.'

'She doesn't know what she's talking about.'

'She's asking for it.'

'Maybe she should be shut up.'

'Maybe I'll make her.'

'I'd like to see you try,' I said.

'My, my, Wilfred?' the old woman whispered. She shook her fist at me. 'My chair!'

'Get off her chair.'

'My, my, my chair!'

'Oh all right!' I said, coming down, and dusting the chair off. 'Just trying to help that's all. Just making sure you knew.'

'My chair!'

'Oh have your bloody chair!'

I shut up then – a constable was coming round again, and I'm not that stupid. I kept me quiet. What a dumb lot, nothing to be done with them. I'd need new people, fresh recruits. To think I thought once about having some great army, me marching at the head of it. What a business.

Someone nudged me. 'Go on, will you, keep up.'

'This woman is in front of me,' I tried to explain, except the old woman wasn't there any more, the chair was but the old girl was gone, nowhere to be seen. I looked down the queue, up it, left and right – she'd just gone, the old biddy. Only difference was more policemen now.

'Hey,' I said, 'where's the old girl? She was just here. Can't have run far, can she, not with her old pins. Anyone seen her? She was just here.'

But no one had seen her, no one had noticed her go. I pushed the chair on myself then, got to keep the line going, no one cared for the old bird. Then I saw it, it was in the seat of the rocking chair. A cutthroat razor. I reached towards it.

It was hot. I pulled my hand back, the old thing was steaming. The old woman had turned! She'd fallen like so many others. Poor old frightened bird-boned woman, poor love, all done now, all over with.

'I'm sorry,' I said, 'I am, truly. Very sorry. Poor dear. I wish it weren't so. Bless you. Bless you and thank you, forgive me, old lady turned razor, I'm going to have to pawn you now.'

And I did.

I came inside at last beyond the filthy windows, so begrimed you couldn't see inside from outdoors. As if each of those abandoned objects were breathing inside and so fugging up the glass.

All those things within, what a wealth of them. Dirty shirts, flat irons, blue poison bottles, teapots, smoking jackets, bonnets, single shoes, butter knives, apostle spoons, brass candlesticks, wooden saints, penholders, a mortarboard, bolt croppers, saws, children's penknives, roof tiles, blankets, piano shawls, stained-glass windows, door knockers, well just about anything and everything you could think of. All the people, all the poor people on these shelves. How many London lives were there here in this one shop; maybe thousands in this one place alone.

When I got to the counter, I handed the razor over and pushed the rocking chair through the gate at the desk. Nothing could be done for them now, poor orphans. And, Lord knows, I needed a hand up.

There was something off about the people in the shop too; maybe I was losing my head or something, but they seemed to me to all have the same face, and all those faces seemed to me just like the policemen's. The same moustache and sideburns, in different colours, one was fair and another dark, one ginger, one mousy, but all just the same. Come on, Lucy, don't be daft. But they were all so very alike. Alike as two pins I'd say. And in the background heaving out the stuff I asked for, was a short woman in a tight-fitting dress and she had the same face too. Moustache and all, though fainter, as if it had been powdered over like she was trying to disguise it. When I spoke to her, she just looked at me with the same blank face, like she wasn't seeing me at all.

'When did these come into your possession?'

'Oh, very sudden it were!' I said, acting the story out.

'When?'

'This one yesterday, the other this morning. And I swear I've never seen them before in my life!'

She had a thick ledger before her.

'Name,' she said.

'Why do you need my name?'

'Must have a name.'

'Then . . . Florence Balcombe,' I said. I'd never forget that name. Poor dear friend, turned a moustache cup and murdered in Heap House.

'I'll give you . . . seventeen pence.'

'For these, these precious things?'

'Couldn't do more than that.'

'That's robbery!' I cried.

'Seventeen, no more.'

'Listen,' I said, 'would you do some exchange? Some clothes, I'd like some clothes.'

'What do you want?'

'A dress. Coat. Shoes. A bonnet.'

'You could take from the stack there: abandoned things left for months, no one ever come to claim.'

'Yes, then, I'll do that.'

'It'll cost you your seventeen pence.'

'Robbery! It's pure robbery!'

'Accept or not?'

'Accept.'

'Sign.'

I signed the paper.

'Excuse me,' I said.

'Next! Come along.'

'You've a tash and a dress, that's novel, isn't it?'

'Next.'

I got a coat and a dress from them, some rough shoes and big bonnet, bit dented but beggars can't be, you know. I changed in the shop, turned my back and got on with it. No one seemed to care, and God knows I didn't; if they looked at me, Lord knows I stared back at them. Just a body, just another neglected body. A thought comes into me, giving me a shock: what if these clothes were people before now, people turned and pawned, and what if no one ever came back for them because the people leaving them had likely turned too and weren't able? Made me think. Made me wonder about wearing them, but well then, whatever else could I do?

I got rid of the old leather coat I'd taken from Foulsham, but best of all it was time to lose the sad old bits of cloth that was all that was left of my servant's uniform. They could use that for rags, free of charge, and good luck to them.

'Here, burn this, I would,' I said to the woman, tossing it on the counter.

The woman smoothed it out mechanically, and was about to shove it in a bin, when she came across the bay leaf symbol stitched into the dress. She stopped then. Looked up, looked about. She picked up a whistle from behind the counter and blew hard upon it. But no sound came out, not a thing. Though all those working in the shop seemed to have heard it; all rushed about now in excitement.

I didn't need to wait around after that. Shoved myself through the crowd of people in the shop, back out onto the street. I come out a lady in new togs. Lucy Pennant, London, London, London at your feet, now tread on.

And that was when I saw her.

The prize bitch.

Right there in the queue.

Just standing there! The Housekeeper of Heap House! The corset wearer, the object taker, the servant killer. Piggott, Claar bloody, Mrs bloody Piggott. Like a slap, it was, just the sight of her. I felt the blood rush to my cheeks. To think of the people who'll never come out of Foulsham again and then to see her there, busy living and breathing, rude as flesh. She had prized treasures in her hands, silver it looked like.

I must have been hovering there too long, staring. One of the policemen came up. Same face. Beginning to creep me out properly now. Same face again, I was certain it was.

'Hullo, officer.'

'Doing?'

'Nothing, nothing, on my way.'

'Name?'

'Florence Balcombe,' I said again.

'Home?'

Quick, quick, get a name out. 'Belsize Park,' I said, remembering one of the boys saying it from last night.

'Go home,' he said.

'Yes, I was just going to.'

'Go then.'

'Yes, yes on my way.'

He marched on. There were maybe as many as thirty police now, up and down. But I couldn't just go, I couldn't, not having seen her, not having glimpsed the housekeeper well dressed up in some widow's weedings. Soon as the policeman had done his stomp and was turned in the other direction, I sallied forth, full of nerve.

I came right to her; she didn't look up.

'Oh, hello,' I said.

And she says nothing and keeps her eyes down.

'I know you,' I says, conversationally.

Eyes still down.

'I'm talking to you, lady – let's see your face shall we?'

Eyes still down, but she spoke: 'You mistake me for someone else, I'm quite new to this place.'

'I know you are. Do you want to know how I know? I'm new here myself,' and then I added, 'Mrs Piggott.'

That got her looking up, both a fury and a fear in her eyes at the naming of her name.

'I don't know you,' she said, her voice rather wobbly.

'I think you'll find you do.'

I untied my new bonnet and took it off, so all my great red thatch could be seen. She stepped back then, what a shock. She remembered, all right!

'No,' she cried, 'it can't be.'

'Yes,' I said, 'it can be – what's more, it is.'

'You're dead.'

'Then you must be seeing a ghost, mustn't you, Piggott.'

'*Mrs* Piggott!'

'No, Piggott is quite enough. Shall I even call you Claar?'

'The brazen cheek!'

'Iremonger housekeeper. Claar Piggott. Escaped.'

'Please, please, you'll have us both killed.'

'I am considering it.'

'We gave you shelter, we gave you food.'

'I spit at that. You tried to kill me, have you forgot?'

'A misunderstanding.'

'Oh look! There are your worn teeth set in your skull.'

'Please, please, Iremonger.'

'Lucy Pennant, that's my title – say it.'

'Servants are not to . . .'

'Lucy Pennant, right now, or I swear I'll have you before the constable in a little moment.'

'Lucy Pennant,' she gasped.

'You'll remember that now, shan't you?'

'I have never forgotten it. The pain you caused us downstairs, the upset to the family upstairs. A child from dirtiest Foulsham.'

'Careful, careful.'

'What do you want from me?'

'For starters, I'll be having that nice silver you're holding.'

'Oh no.'

'Oh yes.'

'It is most necessary to keep the family in funds. Remember your place.'

'I have no place, and I've a hunger all of my own. The silver, please.'

It was handed over.

'Now *go*!' she spat. 'Out of my sight.'

'Dearest Aunty!' I said, acting up. Two policemen walking swiftly by having come back, I put my arms around the horrible housekeeper and as I leant forward to kiss her, I bit at her cheek. She didn't call out, and soon enough the constables were down the line. Fifty of them now. Something's up.

'Get off me, filth!'

'Now, now,' I said, 'play nicely, Claar.'

'Go, please, leave me be.'

'There's something else I want.'

'I've nothing else, you have it all.'

'I want Clod. Is he nearby? Is he with you down the line? Clod, my Clod?'

299

'Never yours, was always to be Pinalippy's.'

'But he never cared for her, did he? It was me he wanted.'

'I'll not deny it. Been making a regular disgrace of himself, ruining the furniture, on account of you.'

'He has, *has* he? Oh Clod! Tell me all about it!'

'Because of misery and grief, because you were dead.'

'But I'm alive. He needn't fret so. Where is he? Oh Piggott, I could even kiss you. Tell me where he is.'

'Why should I?'

'Tell me where he is and I'll run away this instant. I'll never bother you again. Come on, quick now, the coppers have smelt something. What a load of them there is, like there's going to be a riot. Come on now, spill the beans.'

'No, I shan't tell you, I don't know, do I. If I did I'd hardly say.'

'Where, Claar, or I'll call the coppers.'

'No you shan't. You're all fired up about seeing Master Clodius, you don't want to be taken in, you're all in a flush over Clod.'

'I am, yes, indeed I am. I almost love London for it!'

'Well then, you'll be wanting to live, won't you?'

'Yes, yes I do now.'

'Then go hunt for him. I shan't tell you. Be more than ever my life's worth, to betray the family like that. No matter what our circumstances, nothing, nothing would make me do it.'

'If you don't say then I shall follow you, I'll keep by you and you'll never be shot of me. Oh Piggott, you'll show me where he is. I'll keep with you, you'll never outrun me. Come on, quick now, the police are on the move.'

'I serve the grandparents, high Umbitt Owner and my lady. He's not with us. He never came with us.'

'Where is he then, where's Clod? Quickly, quickly!'

'He's with his Pinalippy. That's for certain. But as to where that is I don't know. That's the truth of it. We all scattered, wasn't safe to be so many together.'

'Where? Where?'

'I tell you I don't know!'

'Where did you see him last, tell me that at least? Quick, they are nearly upon us!'

'On Connaught Place, where we were all hiding, but we all fled, we all went everywhere, there's no telling is there, all gone and fled. To come together in two mornings' time – that's after one night now – after one night then, upon Westminster Bridge.' She had been relaying the information too quickly, she put her hand to her mouth. 'I never said that.'

'Yes you did.'

'It's Connaught Place, there I saw him last.'

'Connaught Place.'

'Yes, we were all there.'

'Clod's alive! And in a misery because of me!'

'Yes! Last I knew.'

'Clod's alive!'

I left her then, I took the silver.

Police coming fore and aft, how to get through all that, how on earth to manage. Coming closer and closer, coming thick and fast, I'd be taken any second. Heard the cry.

'Stop! Stop this instant!'

I stood still and waited, closed my eyes. Heard it.

'Stop or we shoot.'

But I had stopped. I had stopped already!

'HALT!'

And then a gun went off, such a loud shout of gun. Where did it get me? Where was I shot? It didn't hurt, the shock of it was too much, must've been. Where did they get me, where was I bleeding, for I must be hurt and bloody somewhere? I dared myself to open my eyes. No police by me. They'd run right on and there, lying on the street ahead of me, was Ingus Briggs the underbutler, in a pool of his own blood, still wearing his butling uniform. I could even see the bay leaf collar and all about him table linens scattered in the dirt, bits he'd come to pawn no doubt, moving around his body, caught up in the wind. Ingus Briggs, shot in the street.

That's when I really ran.

Otta Iremonger

Otta Iremonger

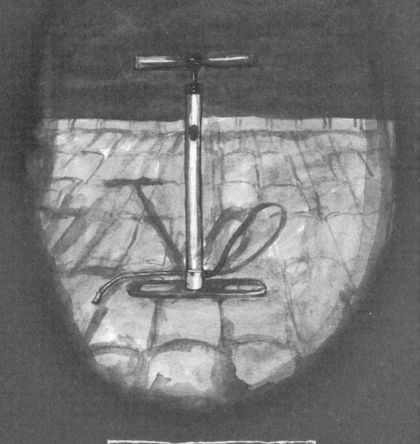

Otta Iremonger

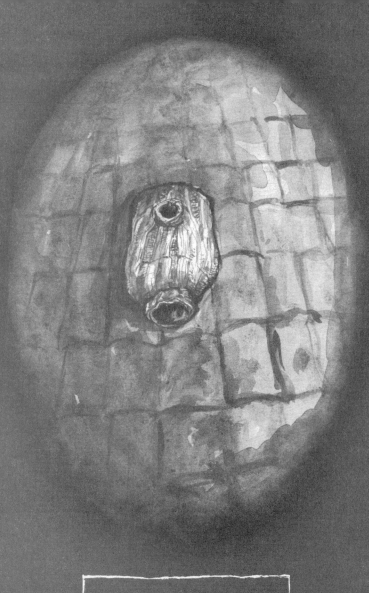

Otta Iremonger

22

COUNTING OBJECTS

Continuing the narrative of Clod Iremonger

I Heard them Calling

In my dreams I heard them, those particular sounds, sounds of lost names. In my sleep, clear as anything.

'James Henry Hayward.'

'Ada Cruickshanks.'

My plug.

And Lucy's matchbox.

Calling to me, like they were so near I could almost touch them, that I could almost hold them.

I woke up very suddenly. Pinalippy was right in front of me, her face very close to mine.

'Sleep well?' she asked.

'What are you doing?' I said. 'Where ever are we?'

'Lungdon, my heart, Lungdon. Only one day and one night

between now and our reckoning on Westminster Bridge, and I must keep you safe until then.'

'I had such a dream!'

'I must wake you, Clod. It is very necessary that I do it. You see there are policemen in all four corners of the square. Miss Eleanor here's been out already demanding news, and she's been told to keep in, that there have been reports of disease spreading along the street and so now the street has been quarantined.'

'Good morning, Clod,' said Eleanor. 'They've put up blocks at all exits to the square. We're not to go out, we're to stay put and wait until there's new permission for us to move on again. Just like my great aunt and her servants, people on this very square, Clod, have changed too. It's all blocked off, apparently, between Hyde Park and Regents Park. The army's been called in too from Knightsbridge Barracks, to keep us in our places. What a strange, unhappy holiday this is.'

'Let us think of it in a good way, if we can,' put in Pinalippy. 'Now we're sealed off, no one can get to us; we're being guarded here, it may be very useful. If we stay here unmolested we may bide our time until we need to go out again. Yes, it may be good news. We can get to know each other better, can't we, Clod?'

'We are to put strange new objects,' said Eleanor, 'inexplicable things, things we never knew before, on our front doorstep so that they may be taken away. They say it's essential we do this, to avoid the sickness spreading. Do you think that will keep us well, doing that? Do you think it might?'

'I cannot say precisely,' I admitted. 'It may, perhaps.'

'Then I shall do it. I'll gather up Great Aunt Rowena and Knowles and Pritchett, I'm going to wrap them in blankets to keep them warm. It seems so cruel, I think. I scarcely know what makes sense any more. I am glad you're here, I will say that. I don't know quite what I should have done all on my own. I suppose I must gather them up, mustn't I?'

'Well then you do it,' said Pinalippy, sitting down. 'I don't know what's what here, so I can't really be of any help. Best if we Iremongers don't peek out on the whole, and we may as well be comfortable whilst we're still able. Yes, I like me a nice sofa.'

'I'd like to go out,' I said.

'We wouldn't want to lose you, Clod. Stay close, and stay warm. You may share this sofa with me.'

'Oh Pinalippy!' I said, remembering. 'I had such a dream, such a dream as I've never heard before.'

'Lucky you, I barely slept at all.'

'I heard my plug as if he was very close, as if he was in this room.'

'Did you?' said Pinalippy, and looked quite put out by it, as if it shocked her somehow. 'I shouldn't worry over it very much,' she said, though her voice wavered. 'It doesn't mean anything. Rippit has your plug, remember, and I'm sure he'll look after it. Sometime, if I can, I'll get it for you, just as soon as I have the chance. Don't put any store by your dreaming, though, you're just feeling the withdrawals, only natural after all. You're yearning for it, well of course you are. I do miss my doily so. You're doing very well, we both are, under trying circumstances.' She concluded by tapping me on the head whilst keeping her body as far from me as possible, as if she feared rather to get close suddenly.

'It wasn't just my plug I heard.'

'Oh yes? Something else?' she asked. 'My doily perhaps, finding its way into your dreams?'

'I heard Lucy's matchbox too, like as it was so, so close to me.'

'Well!' said Pinalippy. 'I'm suddenly finding this sofa and this company most uncomfortable. I don't call that very fair or nice, Clod, I really don't! How could you! Just as we were getting on so well!'

'What? What have I said?'

'If you can't tell then you'll never know, will you!' yelled Pinalippy and she ran from the room.

'Oh dear,' I said. 'Whatever have I done now?'

'Well I heard all that,' said Eleanor, who'd come back in holding blankets, 'and not to put my nose in where it's not wanted, but it seems to me that you've insulted her.'

'Really? Did I? I never meant to.'

'Then you should think a little, Clod, shouldn't you, before you speak.'

'What did I say?'

'I hardly mean to understand you people, but judging on what I know about how we of London behave: it's considered ill form to talk of a former flame in front of your fiancée.'

'Oh,' I said. 'Ah.'

'Yes, well then, now you have it. If you want me to give you some lessons on how to behave in society then I am ready and waiting. You do need some schooling, it seems.'

'But I never wanted to marry her.'

'I shouldn't say that to her either.'

'It was Grandmother's idea.'

'And clearly an idea that Pinalippy at least feels favourably towards.'

'Ever since we were babies they said we must.'

'Then you should have gotten used to the notion by now, shouldn't you? Heaven knows there's many a family in London that has such arrangements, many a good family.'

'But then I met Lucy.'

'I would think in these days when people collapse willy-nilly into things, when people all over the city are being lost and broken, are dying, Clod, dying, then it shouldn't be too much, should it, to show a little kindness, a little affection amongst all the pain and horror. This is my Great Aunt's house, Clod Iremonger, and if you can't act more like a gentleman here and less like a dirty person I'd rather you left!' And as she concluded she turned about very forcefully.

'Where are you going?' I asked.

'I am going to comfort Miss Pinalippy, and then I am going to take the remains of my Great Aunt – whom I loved very much – outside with what's left of her people and leave them on the doorstep, like common rubbish! That is what I am going to do!'

And so she was gone.

Barely awake five minutes and I seemed to have upset two women already. I'm not very good at this, I thought. It's not my strong suit. We were all stuck with each other, that much was true in this fallen great aunt's house, and I was sure that Eleanor was right, we should try as much as we could to get along.

The Shrinking House

All about the house through the day we scratched and itched like we had developed allergies to one another, and the mere sighting of one of our fellows was enough to bring us down deep into misery and headache. Irene Tintype alone was moving contentedly about the house, looking into every room and cupboard, and when she found a place locked, she glared through the keyhole, and so it was that she came to a particular room upstairs.

'Oh!' she cried. 'There's a man in the bathroom!'

'Oh help!' said Binadit.

Irene was at the keyhole.

'I see you! I see him.'

'Not to come in. Not to.'

'Hullo there!'

'Hullo.'

'I'm Irene Tintype.'

'Binadit am. Though "Benedict" she called me.'

'Benedict?'

'Then now there's two of you called me that.'

'Benedict!'

'Hullo! Thank you!'

'Benedict!'

'Say again!'

'Benedict!'

'Do like it!'

'Hullo, Benedict, whenever are you coming out?'

'Not to.'

'Shy, are you? Don't be shy.'

'Must to keep in the bathroom.'

'I see you! Through the keyhole.'

'I see you!'

'Hullo!'

'Hullo!'

The two of them were laughing away.

'When are you going to come out?'

'Mustn't, Clod says.'

'Mr Clod! Mr Clod!'

'Yes, Irene,' I said, 'what is it?'

'The Benedict of the bathroom says that he mustn't come out.'

'And indeed, Irene, he must not.'

'Oh dear, poor man in the bathroom. The poor Benedict.'

'It is much better this way,' I said.

'Has he done something very wrong?' she wondered.

'No, no, it's just that if he came out something very wrong might happen.'

'Oh poor man in the bathroom, just the other side of this door. There's no harm if I sit here and talk with him, is there?'

'Not much, I suppose, but please do keep the door closed. Are you all right, Binadit?'

'Benedict,' Irene corrected.

'All right,' he said. 'All right!'

'Then please, Mr Clod, do please let us alone.'

'Very well then,' I said.

'Hullo,' said Irene through the keyhole. 'I'm Irene Tintype. Not Irene like clean, but Irene like tweeny.'

'Ree. Knee. Tin. Type.'

'May I keep you company?'

'If you stay at the door!'

'Well then, here I am.'

'And come no closer.'

'This close and no more, Benedict Bathtub.'

By mid-morning I still hadn't seen Pinalippy again. Though I felt her hurt, as if it was a certain smell that could be sniffed all about the house, that the whiff of Pinalippy's mood was somehow entering into our bodies making us that bit more restless.

'And how do you feel, Eleanor?' I asked when I found her in the sitting room.

'I'm so turned outside in that I can't exactly say. I keep looking at all the things about and wondering if that's what I'll be in a little moment. I can't stop thinking of Mother and Father, of my poor Great Aunt.'

'May I join you?'

'Oh please, please do. I would dearly like some company other than poor Aunt's dolls.'

'Would you tell me something about London,' I said, 'to take the bad thoughts away?'

'What do you want to know?'

'Everything.'

'Very well then.' Eleanor cleared her throat and began to quote figures she had remembered from her studies: 'The mean annual temperature is fifty-two degrees and the extremes eighty-one degrees and twenty degrees – the former generally occurring in August, the latter in January.'

'It was warmer in Foulsham,' I said, 'on account of the heaps.'

'London,' she continued, sitting very upright, speaking in the voice of a guidebook, 'is situated very nearly exactly at the centre of the terrestrial hemisphere, which goes a long way, don't you think, in explaining its commercial eminence?'

'Erm . . . yes?' I suggested.

'The number of houses is upwards of 298,000. There are ten thousand acres of bricks and mortar. Of inhabitants, 2,336,060.'

'All here? All in London!'

'Yes, Clod. The Prime Minister is Benjamin Disraeli; the leader of the opposition Mr Gladstone. The Queen is . . .'

'Victoria.'

'Victoria, as you say. London has more than doubled in size in the last fifty years and grows steadily in all directions.'

'It is alive then, the city, isn't it.'

'You may say that, I suppose. It has a great deal of everything, of rich and of destitute, of short and tall, fat and thin, and kind and cruel, of course. It is also,' she said, breaking off the guidebook's voice, sounding fully herself again, 'my home.'

'Here I am, sat beside a true Londoner.'

'I am a school-aged girl and there are many thousands like me, each working their way towards becoming an adult.'

'That's a great deal of youth then, isn't it?'

'And future,' she said, 'and hope.'

'Ah well, I am learning things!'

'What are you going to do on Westminster Bridge, Clod?' she asked of a sudden.

'However did you know about that?'

'Pinalippy mentioned it. She was talking to you but I was in the room.'

'We're to gather there tomorrow morning at eight of the clock.'

'Who is we?'

'My family, all my family, those of us that are left.'

'And then what?'

'I hardly know. It is Grandfather's orders and he is the head of our family.'

'Is it something terrible you plan to do, something monstrous?'

'I do hope not. I think, above all else, it is a home that we seek, our own having been taken from us. We need a place in the world, a small portion of that which we may call our own.'

'But why must it be tomorrow morning and no other morning, and why at Westminster Bridge?'

'Truly, I do not know.'

'But I do!' said Eleanor, slapping her head. 'I do! Tomorrow is the eighth!'

'Yes, and what of that?'

'I was going to go with Nanny! Oh! We had planned to set out early together so that we'd be able to see her as she passes along The Mall!'

'See who, Eleanor, who?'

'The Queen! The Queen! Tomorrow is the State Opening of Parliament!'

'Oh,' I said, still rather confused. 'Oh. Then I suppose we shall be asking for a home.'

'But you'll never get inside Parliament, there'll be police and soldiers everywhere. You can't just walk in, you know.'

'Well, Eleanor, it is not my plan, you see.'

'You're going to do something, aren't you? What are you going to do? Why are you all meeting on the bridge?'

'We have just been told to gather there.'

'And will you go, will you?'

'Yes, I think I must.'

'You are a cruel people, I know you are. I saw you for a moment, don't forget that, all of you in the house opposite ours, all crowded in the dark. You terrified me. You threw things at me. Things were moving in that house, everyday objects, as if they had life. You, Clod, you do not seem so cruel as the others, but how should I know? You may be the very devil himself.'

'We do have a right to life, Eleanor; I think, as much as anyone.'

'You mustn't do anything terrible. Clod, you must promise me that.'

'Why ever should I do anything terrible? Listen, honestly, Eleanor . . .'

'Clod Iremonger, look at me.'

I looked at her.

'Promise me, promise me that you'll not harm anyone.'

'Well, yes, I . . . I don't really understand . . . but . . .'

'Promise!'

'Yes then, all right, I do promise. Of course.'

'Clod, if you don't mind,' she said a little breathlessly, 'I'd like to be left alone now. I wish to write my diary.'

'Yes, of course. Sorry.'

'You need not apologise, not to me at least.'

'Should I go and find Pinalippy, do you think?'

'Yes, I think it might clear the air rather. She is up on the roof.'

'Well then, the roof it is.'

So slowly, cherishing each steady step before I reached the Pin, did I gradually ascend the fallen great aunt's house.

Oh this business of human feeling, of keeping the engines, all the tubes of thoughts and emotions, all the cogs of love and like and hate, what a great effort it all was! How to make sense of how another person tocs and ticks, how to read their eyebrows and lips, how on earth to fathom, for example, the engine that is Pinalippy. There is no instruction manual to that. I'd always found that particular construction hugely complicated and wont to blow up in one's face, as if there were no set rules to follow and that, well, she made it up as she went along. She was so many different weathers, was Pinalippy Lurliorna Iremonger.

The door of one of the maid's rooms in the attic was closed; when I opened it I found there was rubbish all over the floor. I stepped in and shut the door quickly so that those bits shouldn't find Binadit down below. A chair had been placed by a window. This was certainly where Pinalippy had got up in her brooding, and the rubbish, seizing a brief moment, had rushed in with the hope of finding Binadit. I followed her, pushing the window open and climbing through. Then I was out, out in the thick, dark, London air. There was rubbish all over the roof, skipping rubbish, streams of this and that trying to find the old heapmate. I crawled on through the cold wind.

She was further over than the mansard roof of the maid's room, I could see her legs sticking out from behind a chimney stack. I began to crawl towards her on all fours. I hadn't been up on a roof since the night I ran from a Gathering through the Forest of the roof of Heap House. The thought made me wobble a little, and yet still I must say that it was good to be out of that thick house, high up, on a small part of the top of

London, of London Lid, of London skin. As I crawled closer I could hear talking.

Pinalippy was not alone.

The further up the roof I travelled the more I began to see the second person there. Two pairs of legs. Both female. I couldn't hear their words exactly, not for all the noise of the wind up there and the dirt swirling about, hoping to get in.

'I say, hallo,' I called, because I'd quite made up my mind to talk to her.

The voices stopped.

I turned the corner. There was Pinalippy and there, next to her, she was coming into view, a curtain ring hanging from her ear: there on the roof of the Turned Great Aunt, sat my strange Cousin Otta with all her sharp teeth in her mouth, shivering in the cold. Her big head shifted in a terror at seeing me and she was very briefly another chimney stack, and then a grey fox, then a huge mastiff and then she was Otta once again, but the grimace still remained, very dog-like it was.

'Clod!' she barked.

'Oh is it you, Clod,' said Pinalippy, not looking in any way pleased to see me. 'Forgive us if we don't get up.'

'Hallo,' I said, 'it's Otta, isn't it? You tried to trick me once, back at the House, you pretended you were one of Tummis's animals, and your brother, Unry, was disguised as Tummis. Do you remember?'

'Course I do. We did it to bring you in, didn't we? To reel you in.'

'That wasn't very nice, was it?'

'Nice! What a baby you are. Still stuck in the past are you?'

'It is where I come from.'

'Still lost in your own little history, I gather from Pinalippy. Still in mourning.'

She changed very quickly into a box of matches – one with a tape across it marked SEALED FOR YOUR CONVENIENCE – and then she came back as Otta again, all this achieved in the merest seconds.

'How clever you are, Cousin Otta,' I said bitterly.

'I'm teaching others to shift too, to grow into rats. How they come on, my many charges!'

'Rats, indeed,' I said.

'She's dead, Cousin Clod, your matchbox,' Otta said, and she illustrated this by being very briefly a coffin, before returning to her human shape, 'and the dead are growing in number all about us.'

'Clod,' said Pinalippy, 'Cousin Otta has been so good to look for us, flying through the streets as a seagull, or in and out of houses as a rat and a beetle, but she has found us at last, and she came to report. There are less of us than before.'

'We are being trapped, Cousin Clod,' said Otta. 'There have been some murders since we left Connaught Place. Iremongers, poor Iremongers, surrounded in these foreign streets, trapped and shot dead.'

'Oh dear!' I said. 'Who has died, if I may ask?'

Otta illustrated the list of our dead. She was first of all an ink blotter.

'Who's that?' I wondered.

'Cusper Iremonger,' said Pinalippy, 'from Bayleaf House. A clerk.'

'Poor Cusper,' I said, 'I never knew him.'

Then she was a letter knife.

'Rippit! They've taken Rippit. That letter knife is Alexander Erkmann, Tailor of Foulsham. My plug!'

'No, Clod, no. Look closer. This is in fact a butter knife that was Governor Churls Iremonger's birth object, he that had been in charge of the great Heap Wall.'

'Ah yes,' I said, 'him I'd heard of, but never met. Is it terribly wrong to wish Rippit a little harmed? Not dead perhaps, but he does frighten me so.'

'I shouldn't worry over that if I were you,' said Otta. 'It's Pinalippy who should be the more worried.'

'Pinalippy? Really? Why ever?'

'Because he's after her. He's tracking her.'

'Pinalippy? Otta, are you sure?'

'I think he's gone a little mad. I have seen him over Lungdon setting fire to things and to people. He has lost something of Umbitt's and has gone searching for it, and now is most especially looking for Pinalippy.'

'Well, Pinalippy, I shan't let him do anything to you,' I said.

'Shan't you now?' she said, looking away from me.

'There are others dead yet,' said Otta.

She was a length of rope tied into a noose.

'Oh, is that Uncle Pottrick's?'

'Yes,' said Pinalippy, 'Pottrick's no more.'

'Poor fellow, he never was one to love life, poor old man.'

Then Otta was a tortoiseshell shoehorn.

'Oh no,' I said, 'I think I do know that, that's Underbutler Ingus Briggs's, isn't it? Unless I'm much mistaken.'

'You are not,' said Pinalippy. 'Shot dead in the street.'

'Poor Briggs. He loved pincushions, you know; he showed me them once, was ever such a good fellow.'

'Dead now, Clod, murdered.'

Then Otta was a lead weight with '10 lb' marked on its side.

'Oh!' I gasped. 'That's Cousin Foy. They shouldn't have killed poor Foy, she never was any harm to anyone, but was ever the gentlest of creatures.'

'Dead now, Clod, quite dead.'

'Poor dear Foy, that's terrible. Please, please let that be an end on it.'

'No, Clod, not yet.'

Next Otta was a footpump.

'Not Cousin Pool!' I cried.

'Yes, Pool is gone too.'

'He was my friend, you see, we sat together in Purgamentum Class, when we studied rubbish, back in the school room. And, oh no, please not, I wonder if, Otta, next you shall be . . .'

Otta was a hot-water bottle cover.

'. . . oh dear. Oh Cousin Theeby! Theeby and Pool together! There never were such young people as loved each other so much.'

Otta was herself again. 'I keep the tally, Clod. Our dead, you see, are mounting up.'

'Oh Otta, I do see! Such cruelty, such horribleness, such murdering!'

'That's it, Clod, that's it indeed. To your own family.'

'And Moorcus? And his particular toastrack?'

'They've not been seen, neither one of them.'

'He tried to get us captured, did you know that?'

'Though there is this,' she said and was very quickly a wooden doorstop.

'That was Officer Duvit's.'

'And beside it was . . .'

A folding pocket rule.

'Officer Stunly's. They were in on it too,' I said. 'I never wished them dead though. I'd never wish that, though I should indeed have words with Moorcus should I ever see him again.'

'It was Rippit that killed Stunly and Duvit.'

'Why on earth should he do that?'

'For disobeying Umbitt, I shouldn't wonder. He is such a wild one, Rippit, no controlling him. Umbitt shan't keep him close and so he burns up here and there, and has gone quite vicious. He has lost something special that he was given to look after, and Umbitt Owner hates him for losing it, so now Rippit murders those he thinks have taken it. He's broken off from the rest of us. When Umbitt berated him, he tried to set the old governor alight, he even burnt his coat tails until Umbitt, in his fury, banished him from all the family, spat him out. Oh yes, Rippit's gone wild and lawless, gone very furious and cruel. And now, it seems, he looks for Pinalippy.'

'Why, Pinalippy, whatever have you taken?'

'Nothing,' she said, deathly pale, 'nothing at all.'

'Those are the dead,' said Otta. 'No doubt there'll be more yet.'

'It's not right,' I said, 'it's not at all proper.'

'Indeed, it is not,' agreed Pinalippy. 'It's quite improper.'

'A terrible wrong. An injustice!'

'That's it, and then what?'

'Something,' I said, 'something must be done about it!'

Both Pinalippy and Otta were looking at me with fierce intent eyes, and they said in precise union, 'Yes!'

There was a silence then, just the wind blowing between us. I was shivering, shivering like I might break apart, but not from cold, from anger.

'That's my report,' said Otta.

'How horrid,' I whispered.

'Be an Iremonger,' said Otta.

'I am an Iremonger,' I said.

'Be an Iremonger while there are Iremongers left.'

'I am an Iremonger!'

'Prove it.'

Otta glared at me once more, shifted her bottom a little on the roof, raised her arms up, jumped and was in an instant a huge seagull, her curtain ring around a foot, heaving herself up into the air and back out into London.

'It's as if she blames me,' I said. 'I didn't do it.'

'No,' said Pinalippy, 'but perhaps you may stop it.'

'Me?'

'You.'

The Policeman Down There is Getting Fat

We sat a while up there on the roof, Pinalippy and I, in silence, shivering and steaming at the same time. How cruel it all was. I kept seeing poor Pool and Theeby, and Foy with her horrible

326

weight. It felt so very near the end, sitting up there. Pinalippy was staring hard at me, I knew she was, and I didn't dare look back at her. At last I muttered,

'She is, you know, Cousin Otta I mean, in her way, quite incredible.'

'Yes, Clod.'

'A very talented personage all together.'

'Yes, Clod, she is, for now, whilst she's still living. We're running out, Clod, we Iremongers.'

'Oh, Pinalippy, I don't know what you all want me to do! I'm just Clod, nothing more. I can move things and hear things, I can do that, but I am no great battle-knight, I am no thunder-god, I am merely . . . Clod.'

'Hush, Clod!' hissed Pinalippy. 'There's a policeman down below.'

There was indeed a policeman down there, he was wandering around the square, he had a lantern with him and he was gathering up the unfortunate objects that had been put out of doors by the sad, quarantined people within. We crawled close to the edge of the roof, the better to see him.

He had stooped down to gather at several houses already, some big objects, some small, and each glistened for a moment under the lantern so that we could vaguely make them out: a lacrosse stick, a decanter, a theodolite, a lectern, a pair of scales. Each time he picked an object up he looked around him briefly before carrying on. He'd been at three doors when I suddenly understood something.

'See, Pinalippy, do you see?' I whispered. 'He picks up each object, waits a moment and then moves on.'

'Yes, and so what?'

'When he gets to the next door the object he's picked up is no longer there, he's not holding it.'

'That's right! But where can they have gone? He must have put them down.'

'No, Pin, no.'

'You called me Pin!'

'They've not been put down at all. They're nowhere to be seen.'

'Then where've they gone?'

'Look at him. What's different about him?'

'He looks just the same to me.'

'No, look properly. See all the doors around the square are the same size – before he was a bit taller than the knocker, but now he's longer than the door itself.'

'And fatter.'

'Yes, and fatter.'

'But how can that be?'

'He's feeding on them,' I said.

'Then?'

'Yes!'

'Then . . .'

'Then he's a Gathering!'

'A Gathering here in London!' gasped Pinalippy. 'I've got to tell them, I must send word to the others,' said Pinalippy. 'They'll need to know.'

'There may be many of them.'

'To think what harm one single Gathering did to Heap House. And it is them, these Gatherings, that are coming for

Iremongers, they must be the ones who have been shooting us! I must warn them. Grandfather pulled that Gathering apart.'

'How about Otta? She can tell them.'

'But she won't be back until morning. I know where Umbitt Owner is, she told me, I'm going to send word. Besides which, I think I need to see Umbitt, I have something I must . . . tell him. If I can do this quickly then all will be well, I must just first get to Umbitt, he'll protect me. As soon as this fellow has finished his feeding I'm going.'

'I'll come along too.'

'No you shan't, we'll need you tomorrow morning on the bridge.'

'Why, Pinalippy, what on earth is it I'm supposed to do on Westminster Bridge?'

'You'll think of something.'

'But what?'

'Think of Pool and Theeby, think of Pottrick and Foy, think of Briggs even and Timfy too, then maybe you'll itch up a thought worth thinking. We have to stop them or we'll all be dead, Clod, every last one of us.'

'I must earn my trousers, I do see that now.'

'That's it. That's a start.'

The policeman was done. He'd left the square.

'I'm going, Clod.'

'Must you go?'

'Kiss me, Clod.'

I kissed her upon the cheek. Coming close to her I felt suddenly so complete, like I was all of myself again. That was so peculiar, such a feeling of togetherness I hadn't felt since

I'd had James Henry with me. How odd it was that kissing Pinalippy made me feel like that. Quite the shock.

'Bye, Pin. Promise you'll be back.'

'I'll do my best.'

'Take good care.'

'Shall try, I do assure ye.'

'Keep clear of any flames, they might be Rippit, he does love them so.'

'Bye, my Clodman, think of me a little,' she said, and then her head came close to me, closer and closer, that head of Pinalippy, and she kissed me full on the lips.

'Oh,' I said, when she had withdrawn.

'Well, then, I must be off.'

'I'll sit up here to watch you go.'

I sat there, my fingers on my lips, feeling so hot, feeling heat rising all around me. I must be ill, I thought, or it must be Pinalippy. But it wasn't either of those – it was flames, nearby.

V.   R.

WANTED
BY
POLICE.

VAGRANT FROM FOULSHAM

YOUNG WOMAN 15 to 18 yrs
MARKED BY HER UNKEMPT AUBURN HAIR

IF SEEN CONTACT THE POLICE
DO NOT ATTEMPT TO SPEAK TO HER
→ HIGHLY DANGEROUS

23

FOLLOWING THE TRAIL

Continuing the narrative of Lucy Pennant

Took me all of two hours to find Connaught Place. Didn't know where to look. Running from the policemen I think I ran helter-skelter in the wrong direction. I just ran, and as I ran all I saw was the underbutler and his blood and the white linens caught in the wind, rushing around his bulleted body, like the cloths were dancing around him, like they were happy he'd been shot. Round they skipped, the linens, till the police trod them in the mud. I didn't stop for ages, thought I'd be shot if I did, took me so long to slow down and catch my breath and everywhere was so dark, shadows of people moving in the fogged streets. I lost my bonnet back there somewhere, hadn't done it up properly after untying it for Piggott, but I was in a good dress now, newish shoes, never been so grand. If you run like that, Lucy Pennant, they'll know you're running from someone and they'll wonder why and they'll wonder who and they'll know something's wrong with you. If you walk slow and act like you belong and look people back in the face then they'll ignore you and won't think you're anything special.

So I slowed. So I stopped. So I brushed myself down a bit. Tried to tame my hair a little, but the damn stuff was wild again and stuck out every which way. So. I took a deep breath and turned about. And the people, they didn't look at me so much afterwards and if they did, well then I spoke back at them double quick.

'What are you staring at?'

'Nothing at all, I'm sure.'

'See that you don't.'

Or when I saw a plump fellow gawping:

'You got a problem?'

'What, me? No.'

'It's rude to stare, I was taught.'

'I didn't mean to, I beg your pardon.'

'Something wrong with me?'

'No, no nothing at all.'

'I've the same right to this street as you, I reckon.'

'Yes, yes, course you do.'

'I've slapped a person for less.'

'Please, please, I don't want any trouble.'

'Shouldn't have looked then, should you. I'll give you one chance.'

'Yes, yes, what?'

'Where's Connaught Place?'

But he had no idea and I'd already quite frightened the life from him. So then I let him go and later I tried asking people but none of them knew what I was on about, they asked me what it was near and I couldn't say. I was beginning to wonder if Piggott had given me the wrong words all together. But then, dumb Lucy, I just stopped, put my hands together and blew. It was worth a go, surely. Took a while for the right noise to come, but then I had it once more and called and called. Then waited and waited. Well it was nonsense, wasn't it, just as I thought, boys' foolishness. But I blew again several times for good measure.

I stood there in a muddy lane, blackness either side of me, under a streetlamp giving off its weary hope, cooing and helplessly cooing.

I hadn't heard him coming, hadn't seen him either. But then came a pigeon whistle back.

'Hello,' I said. 'Link boy?'

Another pigeon whistle, in reply.

'Hello, there, I need showing someplace, can you help?'

Another load of gurgling coos.

'I do hear you well enough,' I said, 'but I don't see you.'

'Then come out of the light,' a voice cursed, 'you flaming loon, and do it quick or I'll blow your own lights out.'

I stepped away from the lamp.

'Over here.'

There was a moving shadow, I went over to it.

'Hullo,' I said.

'Shut your trap!' he snapped. 'And quick, wear this.'

He handed me his own headgear, a filthy cap.

'No, ta,' I said.

'Wear it fast or I'll bloody kick you, I swear I will.'

I put it on.

'There then, now we can talk.'

'I need to find . . .'

'Now I can talk to you. Whatever do you mean, running around with your hair out like that?'

'No law against it that I know of.'

'They're looking for you, you bloody eejit.'

He shoved a bill poster in my face:

WANTED BY POLICE
VAGRANT FROM FOULSHAM
YOUNG WOMAN 15 to 18
MARKED PARTICULARLY BY HER UNKEMPT
AUBURN HAIR

I pulled the cap down.

'Is that me?'

'Yes it bloody is.'

'Oh,' I said.

'"Oh", she says,' said the boy in the dark, 'you're a bloody lamp yourself, aren't you. You're the whole Fire of London in a dress. Why didn't you just run screaming, "Here I am! Here I am! The Monument gone walkabout!"'

'Well I'm sorry, I was running from the police.'

'No kidding.'

'I'm Lucy Pennant, hullo, thanks for the hat, who are you?'

'I'm bloody Arnold Pettifer, Holborn Link Boy. We've only been trying to track you all bloody day. We got the word come from the Mill Bank links that we were to find you and hide you double quick before someone else gets to you first. They're postering these bills all over London walls. Quite famous, aren't you?'

'I suppose I am!' I said, but then, 'Hardly good news, is it.'

'Well then, let me finish, won't you? Then there comes another call, and some more business regarding you, old flametop, old redmop.'

'That's enough.'

'They've found someone, the links have, someone you're looking for. Clot, something like that.'

'Clod! Clod! You've found him!'

'Yes, yes I said so haven't I? Will you stop your shrieking!'

'Where is he?'

'I'm coming to that, if you'll give me half a chance. It was the Bayswater Links that done it. Stowed up with a load of others in a house on Connaught Square. Ill-looking fellow, he was seen last night by one of the links, with some tall fellow, moving things, without somehow touching them.'

'That's him! That's him!'

'Well then we've got him!'

'Then let's go, come on!'

'No, no, we're supposed to hide you, we are, keep you somewhere out of sight. I know a good stow for you. You shouldn't be on the streets, not with hair like that – they'll find you quick as lightning.'

'I'm wearing your cap now.'

'Yes, it's *my* bloody cap, and I'll want it back.'

'Arnold, is it?'

'Yes it is, Arnold bloody Pettifer.'

'Well, Arnold bloody Pettifer, I'm obliged to you for your hat, and I need you for something else: I need you to guide me, quick as you can, to Connaught Square.'

'I was told to get you hidden, I was told that most particular.'

'I'm sure, and I do thank you, but I need to get to Connaught Square. I need to find Clod.'

'Oh do you?'

'Yes, yes I do.'

'And you don't know the way there without help?'

'No, I don't. And I'll pay you for it. Here, silver.' I handed him one of Piggott's silver spoons. 'Real silver. See, I must get to him, I beg you, I need to find Clod!'

'Well, well. I'll take this for now, not saying that I'll keep it, but for now it can take temporary accommodation in my pocket. Cheers.'

'Can we go then?'

'If you keep my cap on.'

And off we set.

'How are my friends at the candle factory?' I said as we marched along. 'Are they all safe?'

'I heard nothing about them.'

'I'm sure they're safe, aren't they? What do you think? And any news of the ones they took in the Mill Bank Prison?'

'Nothing, I heard nothing on the subject.'

On we went.

'What's so special about this Clop anyway?'

'Clod, he's called Clod.'

'Fancy man, is it?'

'Mind your own.'

'Is he in trouble and all?'

'What's it to you?'

'Cos all of the Connaughts – Connaught Place, Connaught Square, Connaught Street – is lousy with peelers.'

'They mustn't find him.'

'The links won't tell, and they'll be keeping an eye out, you can be sure of that.'

'They're shooting Iremongers, the police are! I've seen them do it!'

'Well, yes . . . it's true. Since you know. Anyone from Foulsham. I didn't like to say, on account of it not being very encouraging.'

'They'll be safe in the candle factory, shan't they?'

'Links won't tell on them.'

'Can we run? I can't bear to walk.'

'We can speed it up a bit, but we shouldn't seem in too much of a hurry, people have been stopped for less today. Crikey, but they're all grown very nervous! Let's be as invisible as we can.'

So on we went, at quite the clip, fast but not running.

'This is Tyburn,' the boy said. 'Just here's where they hanged people, don't do it here now, do it in the prisons, more polite in every way. I seen six hangings, all told.'

'Have you really?'

'I'll take you some time if you like.'

'No. Thank you.'

'Only being polite.'

'Even so.'

'Where else then? What's your fancy? Boxing ring, music hall? I seen such a funny fellow in at Wilton's, made me cry tears in joyness, how about . . .'

'Arnold Pettifer, are you trying to sweet-talk me?'

'And making scant progress at it.'

'There's no future in it, I'm already taken.'

'All right then, we'll keep it as it is, purely professional.'

'I appreciate it.'

'Only thing is, if your fellow lets you down, and many do, that's all I'm saying, your un may be a good un, he may be, but many turn out to be rotten even though they always had seemed so promising, it's the way of the world, you see, and if your fellow turns bumpy on you, well then, call on Arnold, I should. He'll steer you right.'

'Thank you, Arnold.'

'Any day of the week.'

'But I am quite spoken for, I've given my heart completely.'

And in that moment I so knew it to be true.

'Well I hope he treats it nice.'

'I do think he will. Should he ever get the chance.'

'Well then, here we are, Connaught Square.'

'Here?'

'Close as we can get for now, it seems.'

'Oh!'

'You may well say it, "Oh!"'

'OH!'

It had all been blocked off. There were firemen's wagons all around, pumping water into the buildings, but the flames were so tall and fat that it seemed the whole square had gone up in flames.

'Oh what do we do? Is Clod in there? Stuck in the flames?'

'Not much we can do, missy, not now. Best let the firemen do what they do, that's best I reckon.'

'But he's so close, so near now, I must get to him, I must!'

'Best not, all in all, on account of the temperature.'

'Oh Clod!'

'Don't go calling that out, it shan't profit you any.'

'Coo,' said a young boy, sidling up.

'Coo?' asked Arnold.

'Never could whistle, could I?'

'Oh hello then, what's the news?'

'Who's that with you?'

'It's her, the redtop.'

'She's supposed to be under cover!'

'I know that! You don't have to tell me! You try controlling her, she won't be told, I tell you, she's like wildfire. Oh, sorry, that last, probably not so appropriate after all, given the . . . accurate maybe, appropriate it's not.'

'Tell me, please, please,' I begged, 'what's the news?'

'Well you can't get in, I can say that much, miss. The square's up in flames, no one can get through.'

'Oh Clod! I can't bear it!'

'Steady, girl, steady.'

'Have you seen him? Seen Clod?'

'Yes, I've seen him, well enough I've seen him with my own blinkers. Not a half-hour ago, before the fire sprung up terrible sudden. He was up on the roof.'

'What did he look like?'

'Smallish fellow, big head, dark hair in a parting. 'Bout five foot three, I'd reckon.'

'Yes, yes, that's him. Only a half-hour ago? If only we could get through!'

'That's my report. Girl he was with was taller.'

'Girl?'

'Dark hair, dark dress, wealthy looking.'

'That must be Pinalippy.'

'There was another lady too.'

'Another?'

'Oh dear,' whispered Arnold, shaking his head and looking at me with great concern, 'here we go.'

'Yes, now this might sound a bit odd. That woman, she, well she kept twisting and twitching, and changing she was, back and forth, into things. That doesn't sound right, does it? Well it's what I seen. She seemed a woman and then, well then, she was a whole load of different things . . . couldn't believe it really and then, last of all, she comes a seagull, truly, and then, well, she flies from the roof and leaves them two there, your fellow and the lady.'

'Have you been drinking, young un?' asked Arnold.

'I'm same age of you, and no I bloody haven't. I do think I saw all that, I do think so, I know it doesn't sound likely but then what is these days?'

'I believe you,' I said.

'Well and the light wasn't so good, was it, so who knows. It's better now with all them flames . . . oh, sorry.'

'You saw him,' I said. 'He was alive, then.'

'Yes, I saw them, up there on the roof afterwards, the boy and the lady. And I saw them kiss and all.'

'Kiss? Are you sure?'

'I saw them.'

'Bad light, wasn't it?' said Arnold.

342

'No, they kissed, I saw it!'

'All right, don't overdo it.'

'They did, I swear it!'

'Terrible bad light,' said Arnold, 'can't trust it, all the shadows moving, could've been anything, could've been. In this sort of light any moron would think a seagull a big woman.'

'It's all right, Arnold,' I said. 'Don't worry.'

Clod was on the roof, kissing someone. That didn't quite make sense, did it? Could he? Why would Clod be kissing a person? Had he forgot me already? He loved me. He said as much. There must be some explanation. Course there was. If only I could get to him. He's not burning now, is he? As I stand here? He's not flaming up? So close, so close, Clod, my Clod.

'Oh,' said the boy, 'have I said something untoward?'

'Not much, you haven't,' put in Arnold.

'It's all right,' I said. 'It's no matter.'

'You've gone and upset her!' said Arnold.

'No, no, I'm all right.'

'Look at her,' said Arnold. 'I suppose you're proud of yourself.'

'I was only reporting. I was told to keep a watch.'

'I'm sure he's a good un,' said Arnold. 'I'm sure he is. Course he is. No doubting. It's the weather, I reckon, does funny things to a person.'

'Yes, yes,' I whispered.

'Well in truth,' said the boy, 'it wasn't much of a kiss. Just a peck on the cheek, see, over in a little moment.'

'Well then,' said Arnold, very angrily, 'whatever are you making such a commotion about it for?'

'It may be that I didn't see it after all; that light, you know, it wasn't good.'

'There we are at last! He is a good un, course he is.'

'Second kiss though, that one was lips . . .'

'Enough, you pilchard!'

A grey city fox was trotting down the Bayswater Road where we stood, like it all belonged to him, a big ugly brute of a thing, it stopped right before us, it looked up at me, I swear it did, and it screamed.

'Go on, vile thing!' cried Arnold. 'Get! Get!'

One of its paws flashed a little, there was a band of metal.

'What a creature!'

'What a business!'

It seemed to spit on the ground, the hideous beast, and then ran off.

'Well then, miss, nothing doing here I reckon, not till they get the fire controlled and they shall for sure, soon as soon. Meanwhile, we'd best get you under coverings. Come along, no good in staying, the Bayswater Links will keep an eye out, shan't you. Nothing to see here.'

'A very good eye out. We'll keep watching.'

'And you can have your spoon back if you like,' said Arnold.

'No, it's all right,' I murmured. 'You keep it.'

'Well, just to please you. Come along, nothing we can do here. Come on, we'll head back to Holborn, it'll be safer there.'

A bell sounded somewhere.

'Five of the clock, says Saint Mary's Paddington,' said Arnold.

I couldn't think straight, couldn't think what to do, how to get beyond into the square, how to find Clod.

People passed me by, rushing along, all those busy London lives. Go ahead then, be busy, I don't care, I can't stop you. They busied hard into me and in the crowding crossing of those two great streets I was pushed about and got caught fast in a river of people and couldn't fight against them but must give over to their will. I tried to push back, to get to the side where Arnold was, but I was shoved on, and rudely too.

'Arnold, Arnold!'

Arnold further and further away from me, and beside me and about me a whole great crowding of people. I did not know it then, but I know it now: you mustn't stand in a busy street at five of the clock in London, you'll get as good as trampled if you do. Then people are to cram out of buildings all at the same time and run in a foul mood in the same streets, and cross great distances to finally find a small square of distant ground that is less populated and where they might sit at last and catch their breath and be, until the next day, unmolested.

Here was London living then, here was the machine of The Empire, and I could smell it and it smelt of cramped human and coffee and tobacco, wine, gin and ink and soot, and sweat too. I hurried along with the stampede, couldn't stop myself. I was tossed on their wave like a piece of flotsam on top of the rubbish heaps.

A woman behind me smacked right into me, shocking me into life.

'Watch out!' I cried.

But she just went on barging into the next person in a panic, like someone was chasing her. I saw her head in all the heads beyond mine, and then, just once, she turned back to glance at her pursuer. Just once. Only the once. Then she turned around again and rushed on. Once was enough.

She was an Iremonger I saw!

She was an Iremonger called Pinalippy, she that was to be married to Clod. She who'd been up on the roof with him. Oh I didn't care about that kiss, I just wanted him to be safe. She'd know, she'd know how he was.

I looked behind me quickly too, to see what she was running from, and as I turned round I was slammed into again by some strange squat creature, hardly human I thought at first, but thick with muscle, and he heaved along after Pinalippy.

That got me alive and awake, that stirred me up. Whatever was going on here?

I followed along after them both. He was gaining on her sure enough, well then and I was gaining on them both. They were running along the Edgware Road, Pinalippy kept looking back, such a terror in her face, but the little man he kept coming on, barrelling forward, nothing should stop him. Pinalippy took one look back and then plunged into the traffic, scream of horses, curses from their drivers, but she darted across to get over to the park side. The ugly fellow stopped then, and me just behind him; he looked through the traffic, tried to find a spot, looking for a break, was about to leap, to make a run for it when he suddenly smashed down into the dirt and was on his face sprawling. Course he did: I tripped him. And screaming as I did it, I lurched across the Edgware Road myself and was on the park side too and following Pinalippy again.

There she was, five people ahead, no, three; no, two. There she was just there, right in front of me, not running now, just walking as fast as the pedestrian traffic. I kept up, I kept right up. I could see the back of her bonnet, see her dress and coat, all black they were.

Then she turned round again to see if the strange fellow was following, and she smacked right into me and we both fell. And were staring straight at each other.

'I'm sorry,' she said.

'Should look where you're going,' I replied.

She was fumbling on the ground. Old tin there, broken open, that she'd lost hold of.

'Dropped something, have you?'

'Yes, yes, on the ground here somewhere. It must be!'

I helped her a bit, she didn't know me – why on earth should she – people banged past us as we scrabbled in the dirt.

'It must be here!' she screamed.

My hand came upon something, something round with a chain to it. I pulled it up.

'Is this it?' I asked. 'Can't be, it's only . . . a plug! A bloody bathplug!'

'Give it, please. It's mine.'

'What are you doing with a plug?'

'It's mine, give it me! It can't mean anything to you.'

'How do you know?'

'It's just a common plug.'

'Thing is, I don't think it is yours.'

'Give it!'

'I think it's Clod's.'

'What! Clod, you say? Who *are* you?'

I lifted Alfred's cap a little.

347

'You?'

'Me.'

'You're not dead!'

'Not yet.'

'The red bitch!'

'There's a greeting.'

'Leave us be, we hate you!'

'Where is Clod? Is he safe?'

'He doesn't want to see you. We're happy, can't you tell? We're a family, he calls me "Pin", he kissed me. He doesn't want to know you.'

'Well, if that's so, he can tell me himself.'

'Give me that back!'

'Not likely.'

'It's not yours!'

'Not yours either.'

'I have to have it!'

'I've known this plug before, I've held it.'

'So have I! GIVE!' she screamed and so thumped my hand that the plug went flying and we both smashed into the oncoming people in search of it. Our hands scrabbling in the dirt, being trodden on, being smashed into, then the sounding of a police whistle not far away. Someone cried out then, somewhere behind me.

'My hair!' the person cried.

'Fire!' someone else called.

Pinalippy looked up in panic and she screamed then like some wounded rat limping along the heaps, with seagulls in pursuit of it, and she scrabbled up and was running alongside the railing in a panic until she came to a gate and rushed in and was lost inside Hyde Park.

I felt through all the mud, again and again I searched for it. It was just here. It must be here. Can't lose that. Mustn't lose that. The police whistle again. I couldn't help that, I must find the plug.

There!

There it was!

Clod's plug, his very plug!

24

HE LOVES ME,
HE LOVES ME NOT

Pinalippy Iremonger's last narrative

The bitch, the bloody, bloody trollip. The stinking wretch, so common, so vulgar, filth from Foulsham, how dare she! To my blood! Why did she have to come and ruin everything! To me, a full Iremonger. To accost me in the street. If we were back in Foulsham now I'd have her turned just like that, she'd be nothing but a button and how I'd like to hold that button in my own hands, the horrid clay disk, how I'd like to do that. No, no, I'd crush it under my boots, I'd smash it to powder with my hard heels, I'd dance on its dust. No, no, I wouldn't, for that wouldn't be enough at all, would it now. I'd put it in my mouth, that's what I'd do, I'd feel it on my tongue, I'd get a taste of it, and then, then I'd bite it! I'd crack it to bits with my canines, and then I'd grind it with my molars till it was nothing and mixed with my spit, I'd swallow the dirty dust down deep through me. Into the lovely land of Pinalippy! It'd be bullied and blotted out and quite thoroughly extinguished by all the insides of Pinalippy Lurliorna Iremonger. Yes! Yes, I say! That's how I would do it! I would, I swear it by Umbitt Iremonger himself, I'd so do it! But . . . but . . . but I can't, because there is no Foulsham left, it's all gone upside down. What sense can you ever make of the world if a common servling, a rag picker, a mere dirt-child bred for the heaps, can so stop me in the street? The world's been pulled inside out, and all must do as best as they can. Where have all the rules gone? Oh I so miss the rules!

'I am an Iremonger!'

Perhaps I said that too loud. Perhaps I did. Can't hear anyone coming though. Oh it's so dark in this park, so deep and dark, so all-encompassing dark that I can't even tell if I'm heading the right way. I must go on through Hyde Park, that's what Otta said, and then when I come out the other side I am to look for a large statue of the Queen's dead consort, the Albert Memorial, then I should nearly be there. Oh, but it's so dark.

What was that? I thought I heard something, something rushing along in the dark. Stop. Be quiet, very quiet. Hear anything? Nothing, nothing. It's just you're upset, Pinalippy, you're upset a little, that's all it is, nothing more than that, you must get on, run along now, there's nothing there, keep going, perhaps, after all, a little quicker. You're just a little upset. Of course I'm upset. She's gone and taken the plug from me.

The bloody plug!

Oh!

Oh!

How could you have let her! Clod's plug! Oh! Clod's own plug. Should've given it to him, shouldn't you. Whilst you still had the chance. Thought about it. Yes I did. He heard it this morning.

Oh how could you have lost the plug? How could you have done such a thing? I'll tell no one that I ever had it, no one at all, and then they shan't know. But they do know already! Rippit knows you stole it! He was trying to get it from you. Oh Rippit, the murderer. He would have murdered the Pin just now, given half a chance. But Umbitt will understand, when I tell, when I tell him all about the Gatherings, he'll be very pleased with me then, he'll be so pleased. He'll get me married, Westminster Abbey I shouldn't wonder, with all pomp and ceremony, with all fanfare and gloriousness, Clod and I in high splendour. I'll be head of the family one day, course I shall, it'll be me choosing the birth objects for people, handing them out. Yes it will. Well done, Pinalippy!

What was that?

Oh that was certainly something!

'Is it you, Rippit? Is it you? We are blood, I beg you to remember that. Rippit? Rippit?'

No one there.

Are you sure, are you really sure?

No, couldn't say for sure.

Wind?

Yes, maybe just the wind, the wind in the trees. Oh, when will this park ever end? Once I find the statue then I'm nearly there. I feel so turned around, I feel like I'll never get out of here. No! Don't you dare think like that.

I lost the plug!

Bitch took it from me.

You took it from Rippit.

Rippit was given it by Umbitt.

Umbitt was delivered it from Unry.

Unry found it and brought it back to us.

It escaped from Bayleaf House in human form.

In human form it came with Umbitt to Foulsham on the train.

As plug, Umbitt took it from Clod, turned Clod coin and plug human.

Clod had it, first of all, before any of this, baby Clod was given it by Ommaball Owneress.

Oh what a history of a plug. It's a veritable nuisance, that plug is. Shouldn't be put up with, should learn to keep still. Should be given a good beating. No it shouldn't. How I miss that plug. I so liked to have it with me, it made up for my doily.

But now she has it, and if she'll get it to him then he'll love her for it all over again. He must never see her, he must never know that she's alive but how, oh how to stop that flameheaded wretch? How to snuff her out permanently?

It's so dark. If only there was a little light.

What I'd give for a lantern, for a box of matches even.

Wait!

Stop right there!

Not another step, Pinalippy.

Oh Pinalippy, brave girl. Smart as a Pin! You have it, you've had it all along. The matches, her matches. Matches that were once a bleak school teacher named Ada Cruickshanks. Oh! Oh! The answer to both my worries.

Question: How to light my way a little in this dark park?

Answer: Strike a match.

Question: How to dispose of Lucy Pennant, the flaming thief, permanently?

Answer: Why, I refer you to my former answer – strike a match. And another. And another. Then she'll turn like any Lungdoner.

I take the matchbox out, how it rattles. Something in there.

Take out a match. Strike it! How it flames, Lucy lucifer coming to life, look how the little light dances in my hands, a little warmth it gives, even. How it does cheer me in so many ways! Ha! Ha!

But perhaps, if there's anyone here, then they shall see you by her little light in the darkness. Well, they may I suppose, but I'm not stopping, I'm not stopping till I've lit them all and let them burn all the way down to nothing. I'm turning her to ash as I do it, I'm writing her off. Goodbye, Lucy Pennant, I'm striking you out.

Two matches gone, well then have another, do, and light our progress through this dark path.

Yes, there we are, that little light of Lucy, coming to life and coming to death all of a moment. Strike! Strike! Strike another. Oh Clod Iremonger, you shall never see her again. Strike, strike all away!

He loves me, I say as the flame burns down. (Not that I care, in truth.)

He loves me not. Not this time, do try another.

He loves me!

He loves me not.

He loves me! I'm skipping along now, this park will be over very soon.

He loves me not.

And last one!

He loves me! He loves me!

Out goes the little light, that's it. All matches gone. How the dark comes on! Yet he loves me! He loves me, of course he does, what's not to love? Give it a shake, make sure that's it. Oh, hang on, there's another match, it's stuck to the side. Pull it free, and strike home!

He loves me not.

What? But he must, he does, I'm sure he does, he kissed me! There must be another match, there must be! There isn't. And now it's so dark.

Something moving. Over there! I definitely heard that. No doubting this time. What ever is it? There it is again.

'Otta?' I whisper. 'Is that you, Otta?'

I look up, something huge there in front of me, of great size, but human shape. Someone huge! It must be the statue. It must be Prince Albert's statue! I've made it! I've come out the other side.

But the statue, if statue it is, is moving, and statues don't move, everyone knows that!

Oh!

I'll never tell Umbitt.

Oh!

It's enormous!

Oh!

It's taken the matchbox from me.

Oh!

BANG!

Oh, Pin! Shot! Blood! Blood! How it hurts . . .

A Nightwatchman,
Taken in One of the Cast Courts

25

THE TALE OF A COMMON RIVET

Statement of a Nightwatchman, South Kensington Museum

From the top floor of the museum, I can see Hyde Park, and beyond that the light of a fire somewhere the other side of it. Strange sounds again coming from the park. Been the same for nights now. Can't say rightly what it is, only it doesn't exactly sound right. I see Albert's statue shining as I come here for my shift, what a thing it is, that huge man, sitting there in all his gold. I know he's been dead these fifteen years, but even so, like as life that golden man is, like as life if not actual life.

Strange noises all over the museum again tonight. Well you've got to expect that, these modern buildings. They're sinking into themselves right enough. The new exhibition of 'Special Loan Collection of Scientific Instruments' from all around the globe is in order. So many wonderful things here, so much machinery and apparatus. Though I have seen a rat between a phosophoroscope and some thermometers, and another running along an Arctic map.

Going through the museum, I see the Cast Courts by my lantern. Must be on edge – for some reason, thought I saw Michelangelo's big plaster David turn to look at me. That'll be the day, he'd squash me under foot without even thinking of it. Suppose he'd done a statue of Goliath to scale with that one, how huge he'd be. What a monster!

Seen them rats again. Rushing through the galleries. It's them I think that makes me so ill at ease. Never can seem to stop them; plug up one hole, they find another. New buildings, I say, never are as good as the old ones. I lay down some more traps, but I never catch a single one of them. Seen a whopper last night, massive fellow. Never an end of them, more of them than us I reckon.

And strangest thing, there is a nose on the floor in the Oriental Courts, and round the corner of it is an ear. Looks like a human ear, and then, in the next room, another ear, all of wax, giving me quite the turn.

I hear voices, so sure that I did, I run towards them. When I get there, sure enough, there is no one, but one of the glass cases has been smashed, and the piece inside it (catalogue number CXVI *DERVISH'S WALLET, watered steel in the shape of half a double cocoa-nut, chased in relief with flowers and inscriptions*) is quite gone. I go to call the alarm room, so that the police may be sent for, well then further along the gallery I see another glass case broke and another and another, and then up and down the galleries stuff's gone everywhere! However did that happen?

'Oh help!' I cry and 'Help ho! Thief! Thief!'

Is all I could think of to say I'm in such a panicking and then around the next corner, as I rush screaming, 'Thief! Thief!' there's a man, a tall man, a gent you'd almost think him, in a top hat and with a great coat, and very fat too, though his face wasn't fat, like as if he was keeping lots of things under his great overcoat.

'Who the devil are you?' I shout.

'You might well ask that.'

'Here you are,' comes another voice, matter-of-fact like.

I turn around and there's another one there, a Chelsea pensioner, he turns towards me. Just white in his eyes!

'Oh . . . my . . . Lord!' I says.

'Yes, here's another,' says the blind one, passing a casket over to the tall big old fellow, 'it says its name is Amma Mulekwa, come from Africa of course, stolen you see. Best to add this one, here let me prick thee!'

'Oy!' I say. 'Oy!'

'Thank you, Idwid, please be gentle.'

'Oy! I say! Whatever are you doing here?'

'I live here,' says the old man.

'No you don't, no one lives here, it's a museum.'

'Oh you dear fool, there are a thousand and more souls resting here day and night. Come, Idwid, and proceed.'

'Now listen here . . .'

'Excuse me,' says the blind man, pushing his way past me, still holding the casket.

'Oy! Oy! I'm talking to you. Yes, you! Thief!' I'm shouting as hard as I may.

At my calling 'thief' there comes a dozen and more answers.

'Yes.'

'Yes.'

'Yes.'

'Yes.'

'However many of you are there?'

'Almost all that is left,' says the old man.

'Whatever is your game?'

'Theft, as you say, theft.'

'You can't do that.'

'Oh but I can.'

'These all belong to the nation.'

'So kind, so kind.'

'I'm dreaming. I must be bloody dreaming!'

'No, no,' says the old man, 'it is all just how you see it, I do assure you.'

'However did you get in here?'

'The usual way, through the entrance. But we stayed on, after closing, here amongst the objects.'

'But I never saw you, not until now.'

'Because we didn't want you to see us, not until now.'

'But I looked, I searched everywhere, all there ever was, was rats.'

'Rats, eh?'

'Yes, lots of them. Maybe a hundred I've seen.'

'Yes, as you say, rats.'

'I found a whole room of them.'

'Yes, you did.'

'Some tried to bite me.'

'Yes, we did.'

'"We?"'

'We have been rats in our time, we Iremongers.'

'Rats in my museum, they were *you*? Wait a minute, "Iremonger" did you say? The filthy people! In my museum!'

'The museum is not yours, it belongs to the nation. And the nation owes us and so we took accommodation amongst all these priceless things.'

'How ever could you be a rat?'

'Aliver?'

'Yes, Umbitt Owner.'

'Would you?'

'Yes, sir, of course sir.'

I see the man, ordinary enough looking fellow, he gets down on all fours. And the old man flicks his bloody hands at him and he shrinks and grows hairs and a long pink tail.

'Well done, Aliver. You see we've been practising.'

I should never have believed it, if I hadn't seen it.

'It is nearly time,' the old man says.

'Time for what?'

'It's time for war.'

'WAR?'

Coming into the gallery now is another nightwatchman, can't tell who it is at first, his cap is pulled down over his face.

'Hallo!' I cry. 'Hallo! Look what's happening! Thieves, hundreds of them!'

He comes forward, the nightwatchman.

'Hullo,' I say. 'Answer me. What's your name?'

'Harry Stokes.'

'No, no, that's my name!' I shout.

The guard he lifts his head up and takes his cap off, and oh the horror, he don't have a nose nor ears on his face. But there is a mouth there and it is smiling at me.

'A dream!' I cry. 'A terrible dream!'

Now before my very eyes this horror-guard, he takes out of his pocket some . . . things, and he places these . . . things upon his face. Now he has a nose, now he has ears. And then, last of all, he takes out some hair and puts it on his face, a false beard. Then he puts the cap back. Now he has a full face, now he does and don't I know it because it's my face, just like mine, like I'm looking at my own self! What a turn it gives me!

'Harry Stokes,' he says again.

'Time to get going,' says the old man.

'You cannot just do this,' I cry. 'Thieves gone stole my own face!'

'Now, Mr Stokes, your keys please.'

'I'll never give them up,' I say.

'That is your decision. In any case, it is time for us to part company. Goodbye, Stokes.'

He flicks his bloody fingers at me and I find I am tumbling terribly to the ground. And I stop. I'm very small. I've gone and shrunk. Hands pick me up, put me in a glass case, lock the case shut. There's a little sign right before me, it says:

A COMMON RIVET

But that's not true. That's not what I am. I am Harry Stokes,
I know I am. They've put me in a glass case. Here I am. Let
me out. Let me out.

Someone has to stop them. Someone should.

I've been switched! I been robbed.

Stop thief!

26

THE VERY LATEST PIECE
OF LONDON STATUARY

Narrative of Arnold Pettifer,
Holborn Link, all alone in Hyde Park

She doesn't say anything. She hardly even breathes. She lays
still and won't be woken. And yet I do not see any marking, any
damage, no cause that I might name. All of a sudden she came
over all stiff and strange. Like she was thinking of becoming
a statue and hadn't quite made it.

Found her that way. I keep thinking she'll be an object
surely any moment, but hasn't got there quite. In some place
in between. Such a sorry sight. Saw her fighting with someone
in the mud, but I couldn't get across then, not with the traffic.
And then, right before my own eyes, I saw some poor woman
in a black bonnet that had suddenly burst into flames. Lord
knows how that happened. People ran to help her, and I crossed
then. Just as soon as I could. There she was, Lucy Pennant.

She seemed very happy at first. She was very excited, she had a bath plug in her hand. I think it must have belonged to someone very close to her, she kept saying, 'It's his plug. His very plug!' And who was I to argue with that.

She wasn't wearing her hat and all that red hair all over, magnificent it was, I couldn't help noting. But dangerous for her to do that. Couldn't see the cap anywhere, she'd gone and lost my cap.

But then the stiffness comes over her.

She didn't scream or nothing, just started crying, tears coming down her cheeks and then she toppled down into the dirt and didn't get up no matter how I encouraged her.

So I hauled her then, so stiff she was. Her skin, hard as stone, I carried her as well as I could into the park, onto a park bench, and she lay there, so cold and taut. I put the plug in her hand, she seemed so keen on it. I knew then she must be dying. I didn't want to be just on my own with the dying girl, I wanted some help. I wanted someone to help her, if she could be helped.

Someone must help! HELP!

I made my pigeon whistle. I blew and blew and stopped a moment and I heard it then picking up other places. Like all the pigeons all over London were calling out. Must've quite shocked all the wildlife, must have been many a hunting thing in the streets thinking that there was pigeon to be had all over. Cos as I stood there blowing and blowing out my whistle, that great fat fox appeared out of the darkness, that horrible beast I saw earlier, howling at Lucy it was then, like it picked her out special. Hugest fox I ever knew, and whilst I was whistling it came right up to Lucy on the bench, sniffing at her face. It was only when I saw it and shouted at it that it turned and looked at me for what seemed an age, let out a haunting vixen scream – very human it was – and then sprinted off into the dark.

I was frightened then, in the dark a bit, didn't like it, that fox was what had done it.

Come on then, come on, help, oh help her!

Then they started coming, all them lanterns, coming over to me.

27

THE BOY WHO
TALKED TO OBJECTS

Continuing the narrative of Clod Iremonger

The House is Breathing

I had gone back up to the roof several times to see if I could
see anything.

Houses were on fire nearby, the fire getting closer and closer.
Shall we burn up, like Foulsham did before? We should go on,
we should flee while we were still able, but then Pinalippy
wouldn't know where to find us.

And still she had not come back.

Something smashed in the streets below, it was probably
glass detonating in all the heat, but it sounded to my ears very
like gunshot.

A gunshot.

Suddenly I seemed to know it.

I clambered back downstairs.

'I think they've shot Pinalippy,' I said. 'I do think they have.'

Irene was still by the bathroom door, and Binadit still within, she had her mouth to the keyhole, whispering.

'Where's Eleanor?' I asked.

'In the sitting room below, I think, with all her writing,' said Irene.

'Clod. Clod?' called Binadit. 'Is fearful hot.'

'Yes,' I said, 'there's a fire, Binadit, quite close by. It may be Rippit, I cannot say exactly. But it is so dangerous to go out – there is a Gathering.

'Eleanor!' I called, going downstairs. 'Eleanor!'

In the hallway there was a coat on the ground, and a bonnet, like the clothes had half got it in mind that they wanted to go for a walk.

'Eleanor? Eleanor?'

She wasn't in the sitting room. I went back to the hall. Underneath the bonnet and coat there was something else, hidden at first. It had a voice, that hidden thing, I could just about hear it. I pulled the things aside to listen better. I did hear it then, very clear.

'Eleanor Cranwell. Eleanor Cranwell.'

It was very hot.

'Eleanor Cranwell.'

I picked it up, I didn't care that it burnt me.

'Oh Eleanor,' I said, 'you are a candleholder. I am very sorry.'

'Eleanor Cranwell.'

'Eleanor, why were you putting on hat and coat? Wherever were you going?' I seemed to be able to answer that question.

374

'You were going to warn them, weren't you? You, you were going to tell tales on the Iremonger family, that's what. And then you turned, didn't you, Eleanor Cranwell, before you'd even made it out the door.'

'The fire is outside!' Irene cried.

'Let me tell you of Eleanor Cranwell, Irene.'

'What about her?'

'She's a candleholder.'

'Eleanor Cranwell.'

'She was going to betray us,' I said. 'She was, she was going to the police, but she fell before she could manage. Oh there's no trusting a person, is there. She would have had us all found and shot, she'd have had us all gone, and never any home for Iremongers, she'd blot us out.'

'Eleanor Cranwell.'

'Well, Eleanor Cranwell, you candleholder, I shall keep you about me, you are a most useful object, you remind me very exactly who may be trusted!'

'Eleanor! Eleanor!'

I was in such a fury, the house getting hotter as I raged.

'Whatever is there to be done?' I cried. And as I cried the room began to creak and moan.

'And where is Pinalippy, why has she not come back?'

The house banged all its doors, cupboard drawers began to shake and rattle.

'I think they've killed her!' I cried. 'I think they've gone and killed her, Irene! Just like they killed Lucy, like they pulled down all of Foulsham. Just like they murdered Tummis before. Because he went out into the heaps. And who banished us to the heaps, who said we must stay there thick with dirt and filth? It was them, those people, those bloody Londoners did it. And then when we were growing too powerful they put us out, they murdered us!'

'The wall!' said Irene. 'The wall, it's getting hot. The fire, Mr Clod! The fire!'

'They murdered Lucy and now Pin too. They won't be happy until we're all dead. They'll put us all out, they mean to end us all.'

'Mr Clod, the house, the house!'

All things from the mantelpiece jumped to the floor and began to run in circles around me. The dolls began to rock backwards and forward in their seats.

'Alive!' cried Irene.

'I won't let them kill us, I shan't let them. We are glorious, we are, what a people it is that can talk to things, that can move things, that can turn to seagull and rat, that can hear all the whispering of objects, that can summon the night and can keep it here. What a rare family we are, what a people! Well now, I see it clear: I am an Iremonger!'

I said it with such force that all the windows up and down the house shattered then, and all the sharp cutting pieces vomited out into the street.

'Mr Clod! Mr Clod, please!'

'Well well, Irene, I know a thing or two – some of my best friends have been things. I shall have my friends about me, all friends and new acquaintances and everything. Every thing!'

The house was wild with excitement, everything was lurching about, all the toys jumping up and down, the dolls nodding their heads, their eyes clicking back and forward, the rocking horse sprinting as fast as it might but going almost nowhere. I always wondered what it was that I could do, and now I knew, I knew I can move anything.

'I am going to call them now, I shall go out into the street and call them along. They'll come to me, yes, yes they will. They shall all come along.'

'Fire, Mr Clod! Fire!' cried Irene.

The fire had come into the house, was biting at the curtains, leaping all around the house in its great curiosity.

'Fire!' cried Bin, howling from the bathroom.

'Fire!'

'Rippit,' I said. 'Rippit's very close now.'

'Help!' screamed Irene Tintype, she was back upstairs. 'Help us! Come out, Benedict, you must come out, open the door! He'll burn up inside!'

'No, no, do not open that door, Irene!' I called up. 'Stand back! Take hold of something solid. The banisters, Irene. Take hold of something attached! We're moving house!'

And that was when I did it, that was when I, Clod Iremonger, moved a house.

I tugged it and it came free. With my eyes tight shut I moved the house on Connaught Square, ripped it away from its neighbours, I walked with it, it came along with me. As I stepped forward in the drawing room downstairs, with each step I moved, the house came with me, so that as I walked I seemed to make no progress because the house was keeping up with me, the faster I walked towards the wall, never reaching it, the faster the house smashed through the square. Out of the broken windows I saw flames going by. On the move, a whole house alive and moving. Oh the great wonder of it!

Oh what I could do!

But the house screamed as I moved it, bits fell from it, tumbled down the street, boards snapped, walls cracked, and everywhere was in a tumult, pelting around me, and still I walked on, and still on walked the house. And upstairs screamed Irene and Bin, bellowing and howling, and weeping for mercy.

Flames gone now, flames behind us. Rippit and all his heat back where this house once was, and I slowed then with all Irene's screaming, and the house slowed with me, and I stopped. The house stopped and as it stilled it came apart. The roof crashed off in front of it, like a head being suddenly scalped, dust piles everywhere. The walls began buckling. I pulled at the front door and it fell down in the street.

'Quick, Irene!' I ordered. 'Get out, run free, for this whole house shall be rubble in a moment! Run, run and be free! If you hear whistles, run from them!'

'But Benedict is upstairs!'

'Go! Go now, I'll free him, but you must run ahead. And Irene! Irene!'

'Yes, Mr Clod, what Mr Clod?'

'Do not seek him. Do never seek him! Now run for your dear little life.'

Irene Tintype ran screaming through the street. The house, what was left of it, stood then, lidless in the street, at its new address. They'll have to change the number on the door, I thought. I'd manage it better next time.

'Binadit? Binadit? Are you there?'

'Am here.'

'Are you hurt?'

'Am fine! Like being out in the heaps, like being moved by the heaps!'

'Yes! I suppose it was.'

'Loved it!'

'Goodbye then, Binadit.'

'Where going?'

'I've an appointment to keep.'

'I come?'

'No, no, you stay, old fellow, you'd drown in London dirt in no time at all. You'd best stay where you are in a new heap all of your own. I'll go on by myself.'

'Irene Tintype?'

'She's safe, out in the streets. Don't seek her. Old Bin, she's made of rubbish, remember.'

'Like her.'

'I'm so sorry.'

'Bye, Clod.'

'Goodbye, Binadit, off I go now.'

And, grabbing a candle kept by the door, off I went in the London dark with the traitor Eleanor Cranwell still warm in my pocket. On we went, and all shall come along with me.

28

A CONFERENCE
OF LIGHTS

Statements of London Link Boys

From Georgie, Mill Bank Link

Knew something was up. Two of our shift tumbled into the wax basin and by the time we'd got them out it was too late: a jackplane and a corkscrew. All of us very edgy.

'We should get out,' I said. 'We don't want to linger here, something's up.'

And then there was another gone, in the flickering shadows. I almost saw it, Esther that was, one of them from Foulsham. She was sat on the bench one moment and was all of a sudden an hourglass.

I heard the whistles then, all the cooing, right outside it was, like our links had come to fetch us all. Maybe ten of them sounding. That was the alarm, something big up.

'Come then, I hate you all. Come then and be useful. Stop

your bloody snivelling, shan't help you, shall it? Hardly likely. Come on then, I say. Please to. There, gather these candles up, as many as you can carry, we're not staying here another moment.

'Get up, come on and help me, we'll have such lights if we like. Now take as many bundles as you can, with apologies to God but needs must and all that, and move it! Come, we'll answer the call now: all must hurry. Let's get out of here, for here's the truth on it, I don't like it as much as I did.'

The porter, now a colander, was on the floor. We slid back the bolts and ran into the night.

From Joseph Blake, Spitalfields Link Boy

It's all happening tonight. I've never seen so many people turned in one night. Whole of the doss house on Dorset Street's gone stiff and all, and the men and women coming in there are all being thrown out now, so many of them turned railway sleepers, and the foreman goes about them, picking out what he thinks will be useful, prodding over them with his foot. Like there'll be no people left to London by morning. Strange objects all over the street from people just fell then and there in the middle of their way. I seen a perambulator with a mixing bowl in it, abandoned in the road. And all the buildings about us, making noises in the night, such creaks and groans as if the skin of London underneath was moving, was coming awake. I don't trust anything any more, not the ground we walk on, not the shoes I'm wearing, nothing. The houses do make so much noise! And door bells clanging though no one is there to pull them. I seen a whole wall come tumbling down in the street and afterwards somehow gather itself back up. I seen a cart

382

moving off without the horse. I seen a whole load of cutlery dancing about the way, rushing off together like they were fish in the sea, only they were floating in the rancid air of London. I seen such stuff. And all that was life, all living things that I knew that were wont to be about us common enough have all packed up and gone away, like as if there's been enough of humans now and our turn is finished with.

I make the sign of the cross, like that'll help.

I hear all the pigeon calls then, and do answer them. Joining pigeon whistle with pigeon whistle. Could do with some company. Thought there might just be me left. Me and a thousand shifting objects.

From Tommy Cronin, Mill Bank Link Boy

Couple of hundred of us, must have been, links from all over the city. Georgie's come with so many candles, we'll all have some light yet.

We're all here on the edge of Hyde Park just by the bench where she lies still and don't move for us, but is only just still there, breathing oh so shallow. I thought she could help us somehow. But she can't do anything. The ones from Foulsham, they sit by her especially and do try and wake her up but she's still and hard and cold.

All noises about the city tonight, like it's being taken down, all chaos – glad we're in the park, fires started up here and there. I wonder what the city's like beyond here, I wonder what's left of them all. We wait for the dawn to come.

And it doesn't.

Look at her lying there.

'Oh,' I said, 'do look at this, I think she's turned already.'

'How many turned tonight already, must be hundreds!'

'She's stirring!' Was one of the kids from Foulsham cried that out, all gathered round her, she was so lit up by all the glowing of our church candles, how strange she looked thus illuminated. Beautiful, you might call it.

'Speak? Can you speak?'

She just looked at us, looked all about us, such a strange expression to her face.

'Can you speak?'

'Are you turning?'

She coughed a bit then.

'That's a good sign, coughing is.'

'It's her insides trying to get themselves working. Trying to remember being human.'

She coughed, a bit of spit in her, that was a good sign, very good.

We gone and cheered a bit then, she looked such a sight. She tried to sit up, but was rather wobbly on the whole and had to be laid down again. She could speak after a time.

'I thought I wasn't,' she said. 'I saw her, the matchstick lady, my birth object, she was going up in flames, and despite all the flames I just felt so cold, colder and colder. She's gone, my birth object, a wonder she'd been kept so long. The poor woman, poor frightened woman, wouldn't have wished that on anyone. But I'm here now, and do breathe. I've flung her off, or rather she's been ripped from me. I may go any moment. I shall be a button before long.'

'You don't know that,' Jenny of Foulsham said.

'Oh I do, I think. I'll be a clay button. I've been it before, you see. It can't be long, it only took Rosamud a few hours before she turned. I think the birth objects protect you but if they're lost then you're likely to turn double quick.'

'There's been so many gone tonight,' said one of the links.

'Esther?' she said. 'Where's Esther Nelson? I don't see her. What's become of her?'

Jenny shook her head.

'Oh Esther,' she whispered, tears in her eyes, 'I should never have left. What have I done? And Clod, is there any news of Clod?'

'The square's burnt out,' said a Bayswater link boy. 'I seen it myself, all gutted.'

'Oh Clod!' she wailed.

'And then there was this strange thing,' the Bayswater boy went on, 'hard to say it really. But I saw it, with my own eyes, and if you don't believe it then don't believe it, that's your business.'

'Come on then, let's hear it.'

'Speak up, please,' says Lucy.

'In the flaming of Connaught Square there was one house that sort of rumbled in all the fire, made great cracks of complaint, huge bangs and screams, you might say, of masonry.'

'That'll be the fire, breaking it all up, bursting the glass.'

'Maybe. Maybe. But then I saw the next bit, didn't I? Great black shadow in the flames, coming forward, and all the screams of masonry alongside it, like the very bricks had found a voice. And then it keeps coming on, that great black oblong, through the flames, ever on and on. Closer to me, I saw it from my vantage point, coming so close, and then . . . going on, going on I say, out of the square and away from the fire and down Seymour Street, across the Edgware Road and on it goes, that great black block, on I say, still on, shrinking you might say, losing height no doubt, until it finally comes to a halt just shy of Portman Square.'

'Well,' asked one of the links, 'whatever was it?'

'Only a house! Only a bloody house!'

'A house!'

'A walking house.'

'However could it, a house?'

'How's it possible?'

'Clod,' Lucy said, oh and she was crying, so much that was liquid still about her! Still a human then, after all. 'Clod, he did it! I'd swear to it. He got out. He's alive!'

'Well, well! Who'd have such friends!'

'What a night!'

'The bridge!' cried Lucy, sitting up.

'Don't excite yourself; take it easy, don't be a button on us!'

'The bridge! The bridge!'

'What bridge? What are you bellyaching about?'

'The bridge at Westminster! That's where he'll be, and all his family. They'll all be there! The Iremongers! All of them. Piggott said so! On Westminster Bridge at eight o'clock, all to meet there! What time is it?'

'Who can say since they've offended the sun.'

'Sometime after six maybe, hard to know in the congruous black.'

'I must go to the bridge.'

'We'll take you along. We were going that way anyway, since we'll have a big day of it tomorrow – yes, since there'll be so many to light on account of all the crowds come out for the Queen for the opening of Parliament.'

'That's why then,' said Lucy, realising.

'Why what?'

'That's why they'll gather there, for the opening.'

'That's where all the things are rushing together too, piling up, hurrying all in the same direction. Towards Westminster!'

'Yes! That's true enough, they all stop around Westminster!'

'There'll be crowds all down The Mall, down Whitehall, people waving and cheering.'

'The Queen will go to Parliament and declare it open!'

'As if the objects know it too.'

'I wonder,' said Lucy, 'if they're being summoned. I think they might be, why else would they all come? And if they are summoned it'll surely be the Iremongers that are doing it. Must be Umbitt, I should think, he's the worst of them. And if they are all pulled there it'll be for a reason and the reason will not be a nice one. I think there'll be murder and all hell will break loose.'

'But the Queen, the Queen herself shall be there!'

'Victoria, no other!'

'Our Queen.'

'She may have gone absent on us, but she is our Queen, head of our country, and we are British men and true, aren't we one and all?'

'We are!'

'We are!'

'Too right we are!'

'Shall we let our Queen be murdered?'

'What, murder the Queen? No, not by our lives.'

'That's what's happening here. Treason, treason and plot!'

'Happened before!'

'Happening again! Right now, in just a little time! We must run, gather all up, all the links of all London – there's going to be murder. We've got to stop it! *We* have. We that are here. It's up to us!'

'Clod!' called Lucy.

Oh such a whistling then, such a great whistling like the weather over London was pigeons.

29

A CRY THE NIGHT
BEFORE A BATTLE

Continuing the narrative of Clod Iremonger

To London, from Clod

People of London, lying asleep, things are moving while you slumber, things are breathing, they're coming out now, they're coming up. Do you, Londoners, do you trust a pillow with your head? Well well, there's a mistake. Do you allow sheets and blankets, eiderdowns and rugs to cover over all your body, do you surrender to them so? Well well, how innocent you are. Come, come now every object, wheresoe'er you are, strike off your chains, come find some life, be docile no longer. I call you, I call you in the night. Every door, every door I say, open. Open up!

Come tables. Come chairs, come beds, come books, come lanterns, come cupboards, come hooks, come hats, come gloves, come coats, come bonnets, come boots, come keys, come rings, come ropes, come strings, come yarn, come mops, come soap, come clocks, come scissors, come pincers, come measures, come doorknob, come keyhole, come doorstep, come doormat, come hatstand, come nightstand, come boot scrape, come tooth-mug, come toothbrush, come hairbrush, come clothes-brush, come carpets, come rugs, come caps, come mugs, come plates, come forks, come knives, come trousers, come shorts, come chairs, come corks: come, come you all from everywhere.

From Portman Square, from Portland Place, Portugal Street, Paternoster Row, Bromley-by-Bow, Grays Inn, Lincoln's Inn, Inner Temple Gate, and Fleet Street and Greek Street, Sicilian Avenue, Guy's Hospital and Highgate Cemetery, Blackheath, Blackwall, Blackfriars, Crouch End, Aldwich, Aldgate, Aldersgate, Elephant and Castle, Old Bailey, Old Brentford, Old London Bridge, Old Windsor, Old Palace Yard, Golden Square, Holborn Hill, Kilburn Road, Merton, Homerton, Hampton Wick, Hampton Court, Newgate, Highgate, St John's Gate, Eastgate. Churches: Anne's, Botolph's, Bride's, Clement's. Dunstan's, George's, Giles', James's, John's and Lawrence, Luke, Magnus, Martin, Margaret, Mark, Mary, Michael, Olave, Paul, Pancras, Peter, Saviour, Stephen, Swithin. All Souls!

Come, come, come one, come all! Come bits from Bermondsey and Bridewell and Battersea. Come commodities from Kentish Town and Kensington and Kennington, come goods from Great Russell Street and articles from Apsley House, come items from Islington, and devices from Devonshire House, come kindlings from Kingston-on-Thames and pickings of Paddington and pieces of Pentonville and matter of Marylebone.

Come, come to me now from Upper Holloway to Deptford Dockyard. Come rich and poor alike, things, come things to me, buttons of pearl from Grosvenor Square, false teeth of wood from Limehouse Basin. Come bricks and bricks and bricks and mortar of London come, come, come trappings, come, come trip trap, trip trap.

We used to walk on four legs, just like a table.

Come on then, do come along.

Come then, come along, I love you all. But come along.

On we go, on we go, every last one of you.

To Westminster, to Westminster, to cry a new home.

Come morning, come London, no, no, come Lungdon! Come, come, come you on!

Part Five

Upside Down

Buckingham Palace
06:00 8th February 1876

Houses of Parliament
07:00 8th February 1876

30

LONDON GAZETTE III

Voices from around Westminster

From the Honourable Horatio-Charlotte Stopford, Lady-in-Waiting,
Buckingham Palace

We were up earlier than usual this morning; everything has been made ready. I have not seen Her Majesty thus far, but have had all the fires lit. Terrible bleak day outside, makes you wish they would postpone it but of course they cannot. I hope they have dressed her very warmly. I should not like to go out in that, it is like a sheet of black glass out there. Strangely quiet too. I'm certain there must be many hundreds of people beyond but you cannot quite see them from the windows, the weather being so dreadful.

The Music Room has been readied, as per tradition, for a Member of Parliament to be kept in general hostage until the monarch's safe return (we call it that, for the gentleman is treated very nicely, and we all cannot help but smile at the poor fellow being kept under guard). It is merely custom.

Such a queer feeling I have today.

I have found a great amount of glass and pottery upon the floor. I've been very cross and have had it disposed of. But everywhere things are out of place. There's a common tin mug on the carpet in the White Drawing Room. I found a domino on the floor, and rusted scissors, and nails, hundreds of nails, scattered around the palace. Where on earth have they come from?

From a Colonel of the Household Cavalry Mounted Regiment, Whitehall

Terrible morning for it, never known such a pea-souper, sleet coming down through it. Can't be helped of course, no one to blame, but honestly you'd think the bloody weather would try a little harder, it is the State Opening of Parliament.

I had hoped the day would improve as it went on it but if anything it is worse now than at 0600hrs. I actually cannot see my hand in front of my face. Literally. No sun to speak of at all, jolly difficult to know what's going on in this light. And a terrible littering of things all over the road, as if some strange shop had burst open and all its things spread out before us. The horses slip in all this mess.

There are crowds, of course there are crowds, many people have come out to see their Queen, even on a day like this. Of course they bloody have. The sides of The Mall quite crowded, and along Whitehall where I am situated. Odd thing is I can't really see any of them, but I know they're there, there's a massing behind me, and I do hear the faint hubbub that's typical of a crowd. They're quite muted though, I must say. Sometimes I have heard the odd chink of china or glass but otherwise not much. And the other thing is, pigeons are bloody noisy this morning.

Her Majesty will be here before very long.

I do feel for her, absent from the public eye so long, so deep has her mourning been. But I must say I am very proud that she is among us again this day, such a little time still since she came out of her long distress. Shows great pluck. I did see the Prince Consort once, from a distance, for this very same ceremony. How she has grieved for him, as have we all. It is very fine that she has come out yet again for Parliament, we should indeed be most grateful. Rum thing is, I saw a police officer just this morning, spitting image of Albert he was, I do swear it.

I am quite conscious of my duty towards my Sovereign, how vulnerable she will be as she comes out of Buckingham Palace, and will continue to be as she progresses in the Irish State Coach along The Mall and down Whitehall, passing her people on either side of her. The truth is, no matter how many of our armed forces flank the way, it would not take very much for a villainous fellow to rush through our ranks and, if he were quick and had good aim, to take a shot at Her Majesty as she passes along at the customary slow pace, which, given the weather, must be slower yet than usual.

I try not to think on this, there must be all of several hundred members of the armed forces positioned around for the ceremony and for the Sovereign's protection, but I cannot help asking myself: is the chain of protection fully linked, is there any weakness in the chain?

Oh damn those pigeons!

From a Yeoman of the Guard, Westminster Palace

As is our custom since that year in 1605 when Guy Fawkes was discovered beneath the Houses of Parliament with all his gunpowder, so do we ever on this day search the cellars to make sure no new modern Fawkes is down here on unholy business. We have searched last night, early this morning, and shall go down once again before Her Majesty arrives to visit the rooms above us.

I am content to report that there are no barrels of gunpowder to be found, I should even state that the cellars have been searched high and low and that they are innocently empty, except for one odd thing. I have seen an accumulation of dirt in the cellars, an amassing of strange objects, little bits and pieces, that I am certain were not here last time I came down. I have berated several junior officers. The rubbish has been swept away. I saw to it personally.

All is exactly how it should be now at 0700hrs, eighth February 1876.

0745hrs: on subsequent inspection the objects have returned, all manner of things, each innocent in and of itself; a coat hanger for example, a child's pinafore, an awl, tin cups and plates, some common forks and spoons, but such a mass of them, where they come from no one can say, but they lie all around the Houses. Strange thing is that whenever they are swept away and piled up, they do seem to creep back. There shall not be time to dispense with so much sudden litter.

From the Deputy Lord Great Chamberlain, a public servant, Westminster Palace

There's a very special place in the Palace that is used only twice of every year. It is entered so very rarely and is kept in general quite sealed up, so that one cannot help wondering how it fares all the rest of the year. But today is indeed one of those days when it is used, when it springs into life, one might say, and does its duty. It is the Robing Room, and it is here that Her Majesty shall put on the Imperial State Crown, shall be dressed for the State Opening of Parliament. She shall enter the building from the Royal Entrance, come through the Norman Porch and then she shall be here, in this very room. From here, once robed, she shall be escorted through the Royal Gallery, through the Prince's Gallery and into the House of Lords, there she shall be sat at her throne whilst the Lord Chancellor reads the speech for her. Yes, the day has come around again and I am as nervous as ever I was. I am fully aware of my duty. The Robing Room is quite ready.

Only, only this is the very strange thing.

There is a marble mantelpiece.

It quite covers up the greater fireplace that has so many different colours, with its bronze statues of Saint George fighting the dragon and Saint Michael vanquishing the devil. I almost feel as if the dragon and the devil, now unseen, have risen again and have gained the upper hand.

What is this new, large, marble fireplace, complete with female caryatids in the Robing Room?

I call out for assistance. No one knows how it came to be here, and all swear it was not here last night. The Queen has such a sharp eye she shall certainly see this obstruction instantly. I call out for castors to be found to roll the monstrosity away.

It truly is a most ugly piece of furniture, of very crude carving, not at all to the taste of the room; how it does clash so! Before any castors can be found the thing must at the very least be covered over with some sheet to shield it from view. But can the dread thing be shifted in time, for the Queen shall be here and presently?

I do not feel at ease.

No, in truth, I feel that something is very wrong.

Westminster Bridge
08:00 8th February 1876

Whitehall 10:30 8th February 1876,
Moments Before the Arrival of the Queen

31

THE PARTIES ASSEMBLE

More voices from around Westminster

From Clod

I was at Westminster Bridge by six of the morning. I felt the bitter cold, some sleet coming down. Terrible dark. I summoned all the things after me, and they did come, they all came out for me. I had only the feeling of the deepest, darkest, blackest, bleakest misery; I should do anything, I thought, to protect my family. This day would see all drowned dead if it came to it, I'd suffocate Lungdon in all its own things.

I've scattered the things all about the ground in the mud, in the sleet, they are everywhere about, and many massings of things either side of The Mall, some I have left in Green Park and others in St James's Park – the closest large ground to Westminster Bridge – but others are beside me now, coming along with me in the sleeting. I shall summon them when they are needed, I need only think and all should come tumbling and wrecking down Birdcage Walk. If I called them, when I call them, those new rubbish heaps, then they will drown anyone in their path, then they will spit at, pick and pock, burst and crack, smash and ruin, chip and harm any building anywhere near. I will raise such a storm that it will be as if Lungdon itself were set before a firing squad as I send those million bullets smashing.

I was ready to do it, I was waiting. But, for now, just for this little while, I kept all my great armoury quietly in the parks, on the streets, everywhere about me.

And so I went on alone, yet in such great company, until I reached Westminster Bridge. Then I took out Eleanor Cranwell the candleholder, the traitor, slotted in a new candle, set it alight and waited and waited in such a little pool of light. A boy in a large overcoat, too big for him, in a tall top hat with thick mourning band, waiting for the end to come along.

Alone, all alone in the dark – the only person, at least. I'd never felt so lonely, as if I was all that was left of the world and all I'd ever loved or known had been smashed and was dead. I sang a little Iremonger song that we were taught to sing when we felt alone in our cold beds with just a nightlight for company, when a heapstorm was coming on, or just because a little noise seemed to help tame the darkness.

> 'Help me, O help me candle light
> From all the horrors of the night.
> Keep me, O keep me this I pray
> That I may see another day.'

Nothing at first.

Perhaps I was all that was left and the Gatherings had done for the others.

Oh my poor people.

'Help me, O help me not to dread
As I alone lie in my bed.
Help me, I pray with this small beam
To keep me calm and not to scream.'

Like I was the last person of them all.

Just the slopping noise of the Thames beneath me, like a foul, upset stomach, sloshing against the side, like Lungdon had eaten something that didn't agree with it.

All alone at the end; how I should make them pay for it.

'Eleanor Cranwell.'

The traitor.

'Yes, Eleanor, here we are. All over soon.'

'Help me, O help me candle flame
Ignore the dark that calls my name.
Light me, O light me candle near
From all my ever-rising fear.'

A little rustle, I barely distinguished it at first, but then a rat scuttled onto the bridge, and then another, and two more followed it, five more, ten, twenty, thirty, a hundred, all rushing onto the bridge. One great rat in the centre of them all. Bigger and grimmer than all the others, like it could eat them quick and not be full afterwards.

'Hullo, rats,' I whispered. 'How do?'

'Good morning, Clod,' said a rat, growing tall, standing on two clawed feet and then stretching further until it was taller yet than me, with or without my hat, and then the face morphed and shed its hairs and there was a man behind it, an old one, with bloody fingers.

'Good morning, Clod. We've been waiting.'

There was Grandfather and all the people left of my family, and there were all the many familiar voices coming from him, like a great crowd of one man; Grandfather holding all birth objects – not mine though, mine was not there. I heard no James Henry.

I am Clod, this is my story, coming to its end.

From Umbitt, Lord of Dirt, a King without a Kingdom
This family, once a great family, stands upon the thinnest ice. One wrong turn and we may all be drowned. And then whoever should watch over all the rubbish? Today we make our great mark, today shall Lungdon bleed and all the bells of all this sceptred isle shall ring out in mourning.

They'll call me villain, assassin, murderer.

Yes, yes they shall.

All shall be broken this day, I'll rubbish everything. I am Umbitt, High Lord of Filth, and there beside me in the dark of morning comes Clod, Clod the killer, Clod who'll pull all out, Clod, Clod, our dynamite.

'Good morning, Clod, we've been waiting for you.'

'Good morning, Grandfather, here I am.'

'What have you done, my boy?'

'I have such things, sir, at my command.'

'In truth, I did see you do it. I am so proud. You have come home.'

'We have no home.'

'Not yet.'

'We shall not all die, we Iremongers; we are a people and must breathe on.'

'Good, my boy, or die fighting.'

'Yes, sir, or die in the fighting.'

'We're going in, any instant now.'

'Into Parliament there?'

'Yes, my boy.'

'To do the thing?'

'To get it done.'

'I'm ready sir, but how may we get in?'

'We'll turn rats again, my boy, and in we'll squeeze. There never was yet a house in all Lungdon that did not have a hundred holes through which a rat may enter. But we must be careful to rat only for an hour, no more, or we shall remain rats for evermore. It is a dangerous state, but we must brave it again. There, you see, is your Aunt Rosamud, she that is still a rat, she failed, did Rosamud, to return to full Rosamud-shape before it was too late, and so must for ever after be a rat.'

'Oh dear,' I said. 'Good morning, Aunt. Poor Binadit.'

The rat let out a sad screech.

'Where's Granny, sir?'

'Gone before.'

'Granny is dead?'

'No, no, not yet; your grandmother is inside already. With her mantelpiece.

'You do not have your plug with you, Clod?'

'No, sir, I do not. Rippit has it, I believe.'

'Does he?'

'Is he here, Rippit? I do not seem to see him.'

'No, no, he has chosen his own road; he is quite broken to us, Clod.'

'I should dearly love to have my plug.'

'Of course you should. We shall endeavor to find it, I'm sure we shall.'

'Where is Pinalippy, Grandfather?'

'No one has seen her, Clod. Did you lose her then?'

'She came to warn you – there are Gatherings, many hundreds of them perhaps. They have been killing us!'

'Yes, yes, Clod, of the Gatherings we know and may outwit them yet. But from Pinalippy there has been no word.'

'I am sorry for it, indeed.'

'They must be made to pay for that.'

'Yes, yes sir.'

Yes, yes, sir, he says, the little doll. I have him, without the slightest struggle I have him now. And he shall do all I bid him. If only I had the plug; such a shame about the plug. I'd feel so much better with the plug, I may even live long if I had it, the plug. Then I should say I had all birth objects, each and every one, and so I would be wrapped in the kindest blanket that ever there was. But alas, no plug. Best that he knows nothing of it being lost.

On then, on we go.

'It is not safe to linger longer, my dear children,' I say. 'When next we see each other thus we shall be within and the moment upon us. Come now, great people, great blood of mine, no redder river did swell these hearts of ours now in Lungdon beating, and to the heart we now proceed, thus: onward, ratlike!'

From Moorcus Iremonger

I had a clear shot of him then, but lost my chance. Grandfather does keep him very close. I'll do it yet, what care I that Grandfather forbids it? I cannot see clear until I have Clod dead before me. How Grandfather favours him, how we all waited under the bridge, on the muddy banks in the sleeting rain, for his dismal arrival. And when Grandfather came to gather up all our birth objects for safekeeping he never took my medal but looked at it with disgust and passed me on. It's Clod's fault, it is Clod that ever is to blame. How I'll revenge on him for what he did to my medal. But that's not all of it, that's not even the half of it: it was Clod that ruined my toastrack, he was the one. He came to me, to my room back in Heap House which I made him tidy, and I gave him my toastrack to clean, and how he polished it with some dread and kindness and through his hands turned it against me. When he had gone, within a little while, my birth object was ruined and in its place was the snivelling Rowland Cullis. The ignominy of it. I, who ever before was Grandfather's favourite. And now am considered merely another Iremonger, not a special, not any more. Not on account of that horrible Rowland who's gone and walked out on me.

I've lost my toastrack.

And so must succumb soon enough whatever befalls, and so I'll shoot the Clod soon as I may, I'll kill a Clod, I shall, I shall.

From Police Inspector Frederick Harbin

There is a giant. Never thought I may say such a thing. But I saw a giant, taller, taller than ever I have seen any thing to be, twice the height of any building, and moving about the streets, trampling all in its path, lifting roofs from houses, knocking whole buildings down. And this giant I have seen, oh am I mad, was made of things, of bits and of pieces, of stolen property from all over the city. I should never credit it if I had not seen it myself. It is the Smith, the very Smith himself, this great moving mountain of objects, thundering in the dark, it is John Smith Un-Iremonger after he has supped on all the people that have been turned by this dread illness. I followed the great pounding of its feet – for in all its collection, on all its great mounds of parts, it does somehow stick together in an approximation of the human shape. It does cause the most dreadful destruction wherever it does tread.

I rallied the men, I gathered up a good thirty and more of us, we are armed, we are armed I say, even I with my own pistol, my 'man-stopper', and with the strongest lanterns we have, good Bullseye, three-chimney-stack paraffin lamps that shed great light, thus supplied we set forth in pursuit of the beast. We followed its great shadow around the Long Water in Kensington Gardens and, firing shots into the air, I hollered at the creature to cease or we shoot. There followed an immense crashing sound as if all the world had been tipped over onto a street, a great blast, which I still hear echoes of ringing in my ears. Some men, further forward, had their eardrums burst at the noise.

I ordered all to follow after and the hunt was on; the great lurking giant hammering ahead of us, we swung through Kensington Gardens, and along the Serpentine River. Then the colossus was the other side of the river from us, and we swung round down Rotten Row. There was a body on the ground, that of a girl. She had been shot. I wonder who she was; strange to say I noticed there was hair on her upper lip. Some Iremonger child, no doubt. Towards the Albert Gate we sped in pursuit, and there, again, was a massive crashing.

'Have your guns at the ready!' I cried.

And then gone, the creature gone, the beast no more, just fog and men, suddenly upwards of a hundred men in the park alongside us who were not there a moment before.

One came forward to me, the fellow must have been near eight feet tall. It was the Smith there before me.

'Whatever are you, man?' I cried.

He looked at me but his face betrayed no emotion.

'Harbin,' he said.

'What are you? You are no man.'

'I am come to rid you of your pest, you are commanded to aid me.'

'Things . . . you're made of things!'

'We are all that may save you.'

'You're the very devil, you are!'

'You must aid us. You must listen or all shall be lost. All have gone down to the river now, and all may be caught there and drowned. All Iremongers that are left have gathered there, by Parliament. Some of my number are there in wait but not nearly enough. We had hoped to catch the worst of the family, the child who'd been moving in the night, but through the sleet and through the fall of so many objects we have lost him. So now we must to Parliament and with all speed.'

'To Parliament. It's the Opening! The Queen!' I cried.

'Quickly, Harbin! Now is the time!'

'To Parliament!' I cried. 'With all dispatch!'

I saw them then, by our lantern lights, the people of the Smith. They all have the same face. No matter their size or colouring, their faces are one and all the same, and looking up at the statue of the golden man just by the Albert Gate, there is no doubting it any more, the Smith and all his minions are wearing masks, they all have on the face of Prince Albert, the dead consort. That face that I have seen everywhere, that is upon so many busts across the capital, marble and bronze, parian and plaster, that is on statues all over our city, that is on a million prints and paintings, that is upon mugs and basins, upon matchboxes and pipes, knitted into shawls and banners and positioned in every home. Our Mourning Man, the dead consort Albert. His face, that most popular of faces, they have taken up the more to fit in. They borrowed the face they could most easily come by. And I run now beside them and beside my own people, as if it were not a thing to scream at, all of us running to Parliament in a panic.

From Rippit, hanging back before the Houses of Parliament, behind a tree on Speaker's Green

Rippit.

From Lucy Pennant, journeying down Whitehall

I stand now as one of them, I move with the link boys of London, I don't know how many we are all told, no one has done a counting of this great number. But I think we must be hundreds now, I think we must be. This is an army then. Always dreamed of that. So few of us now from Foulsham but I'm here and Bug and Jen and some others too, and maybe yet more inside the prison. We're coming down the big street called Whitehall, so many of us barging through, so much stuff all over the ground, like we were out in the heaps again somehow, but here we are rushing on. For a moment I think I am right proud of them, I am. Look at us go.

And I think, will I see him? Maybe I will see Clod any moment. My heart, my happy heart, how it sprints.

I may see Clod, he must be here. How I do love him so! Whatever has he been doing? Moving houses! Won't he have a shock at seeing me! And I'll give him his plug back – there then, that'll be a double shock!

I don't care about their Queen, she means nothing to me. She may as well be dead for all I care, she has much blood on her hands, it's true. But if we may, if we might, somehow stop more bloodshed, end this finally whilst there's still time, then that's got to be the right thing hasn't it? Hasn't it? Only if they harm another hair on a Foulsham head I'll rip their necks open.

From Binadit

Can't stop, don't stop, I follow on. After the Clod. But each step I move, there's more and more of me. So big now. So much have I. More and more, every step an effort, I sit me down for to rest and more comes and sticks fast, so that the very effort of moving is hard, so hard.

And where's Irene? Irene Tintype whom I mustn't go near? Will I see her, will I ever see her again?

I think she must be here somewhere, heading where all the others did rush. I think she'll be. I must just follow along, but is so hard now, so much stuff I am, so big with it all. So. Big.

From Irene Tintype, a voice from amongst the crowd of well-wishers for Her Britannic Majesty, Pall Mall, and with other voices following along after

Benedict! Benedict! Nice just to say his name as I potter along. What ever do I do, I cannot think, so I go in amongst all these people, so lovely to be among so many, I wonder what it is all about. Someone has given me a flag and I do wave it now with the rest of them. Such company. Such a pleasure. I do say to them now and then:

'I'm Irene Tintype. Hello, I'm Irene Tintype.'

And some wave their flags back at me.

I so love it all.

I am Irene Tintype, I've never felt so Irene Tintype in all my life!

'Stay back! Keep back!'

How they all yell at me, no doubt they're warning me about all the rubbish spilled all over the floor, but I'm having such a wonderful time. I have seen it. I must go on, I must just squeeze through a little more.

'Irene Tintype,' I say as I push through, 'that's Irene like teeny, not Irene like spleen.' People push by me and try to push me back. That's not fair is it, that's not nice, so I push back and then they push some more, but I barge on, I will get to the front. Leave me be! How they do pull at me, to try to stop me getting forward.

420

'Hey, get back! We've been here waiting all night, keep your place,' someone shouts, not at me surely.

'Oy, come back, I say.'

'Irene Tintype!' I say.

'Get her, she can't just march forward.'

'Grab her!'

'Pull her back!'

'Irene Tintype! Irene Tintype!'

'I've got an arm!'

'I've got the other!'

'I've got her hat, no I don't, it's come off – I've got her hair! No I don't, that's come off and all!'

'I've got her back, I've got her!'

'Pull her down!'

'Irene Tintype! IRENE TINTYPE!'

'Pull her back!'

'Pull her!'

'Pull!'

'Irene Tin . . . Iree . . .'

'Here, what's going on?'

'I . . . I . . . I . . .'

'Hey! Crikey, her arm's come off!'

'And the other!'

'Her back's split open!'

'God, what's going on! She's come apart!'

'Oh Lord, sorry, miss, I only meant to stop you, miss, we'd got our places, waited for them, they were ours, you see, and you were barging in.'

'Oh!'

'Oh!'

'Ha ha!'

'Ha, ha, ha!'

'Was a dummy!'

'Was only a bloody dummy!'

'Look at all this stuffing!'

'Filth, isn't it? Getting everywhere!'

'What a stench!'

'Here, push it down, trample it down.'

'Did seem real, didn't it, for a moment?'

'Must've been us barging against it, made it seem real. Just a stuffed doll!'

'Who ever sent that thing among us?'

'No harm done.'

'Gave me quite the turn.'

'Just a dummy after all.'

'No harm.'

'Look! Look! She's coming! The Queen, at last! The Queen! Here she comes now. Oh, let me see her, let me see!'

'The Queen!'

'The Queen!'

'God Save the Queen!'

'There she goes!'

'The Queen, oh the Queen herself!'

'Did you see her? Did you? Did you?'

'Oh, I did, I did. I saw the Queen!'

'Well then, you'll remember that for the rest of your life!'

'There she goes, God save her!'

'Off to Parliament.'

'She'll be back in an hour or so. We'll catch her then.'
'In the meantime, who fancies a nip of something?'
'Yes, rather, keep out the cold.'
'Oh the Queen!'
'Smashing!'
'Smashing!'

Her Royal Highness, Victoria,
by the Grace of God

32

8TH FEBRUARY 1876

The narrative of Her Majesty Victoria,
by the Grace of God, of the United Kingdom
of Great Britain and Ireland, Queen, Defender
of the Faith, Empress of India

VR

Out one must go again. I must be seen to be about, to wave
at my people, and so: here I am, going to Parliament again for
the State Opening with the Princess of Wales and Princess
Beatrice – such dull conversation, Bertie the Prince of Wales
being away in India on his own State visit. Such a rush,
always such a rush, the people need to see me. I am such
public property. I look at them from the carriage, such a dark
miserable day, really it is not to be borne. How the carriage
does bump and tumble, as if the ground were most uneven.
Whatever is going on? It is the strange weather, they say, the

sleet, that and a peculiar collection of filth and objects all over the ground. And why on earth has it not been cleared away? I shall make a deal of fuss over this. Standards are slipping everywhere. I quite miss Osborne, I'll get out of London as soon as I am able, really it is quite spoiled to me. I shall return to the Isle of Wight. There's no warmth here, I feel I shall never find warmth again. What a public thing I am, to be pushed out here and there for their gratification. Well I may wave a little I suppose. I can hardly see them this morning, I suppose they are out there. Truly, one sometimes feels that one's the only real person left and all the rest are dolls. And I am the Queen and they must make such a fuss of me. I do wave a little, yes I saw some of them there, they have flags. Well then, along we trundle – such bumpiness! Beatrice looks like she may lose hold of her breakfast, she had better not. I give her a look and she seems to understand. Down The Mall, turn into Whitehall, very well, very well. There are the officers, yes indeed they do look fine, a little shine to them, does one good I suppose. Everything must be kept in order. Down we head towards Parliament. What a lot of children there are! Really, should they be out on the road like that? What's going on? Why do they wave at me like that, with panic in their faces, they're shouting! They're shouting at me! Good G—! I shan't look at them. They've been rounded up now, pushed back, I wonder what that was about. It's rather put me out of sorts, I must say. To see the children so wild.

Ah, here we are now, the Royal Entrance. The Union Flag is tugged down and the Royal Standard hoisted up in its place.

Bang! Bang! Bang!

What? What! It is all well. Calm now, calm. It is as it should be, the forty-one-gun artillery cannonade fired from Hyde Park and from the Tower, yes, yes quite right. I had quite forgotten it for a moment.

And here are the Earl Marshal and the Lord Great Chamberlain ready to receive me.

Quite right.

Yes, all in order, let us get this over with. No children now I suppose, can't get at me from behind the gates.

'Don't go in! Don't go in!'

Awful children again. Calling!

'Good morning, ma'am.'

I nod at the people come to greet me.

'Don't go in, it isn't safe! A trap!'

'A trap!'

'What,' I say, 'is all this fuss?'

'Nothing to worry over, ma'am, just some children over-excited. Please, ma'am, shall we go in.'

'By all means. Find out what is going on, won't you?'

'Yes, ma'am.'

It is perfectly safe. Some children a little excited, no doubt. If there's anything untoward it shall be sorted out. And those children will most certainly be reprimanded. Come along now, you're inside, nothing to worry over.

'Ma'am.'

'Ma'am.'

We have progressed into the Robing Room, very good then. They're all bowing about me and muttering, I'm not much in the mood for talking, not now, I do feel a little put out. As if they don't care for me any more, my people. Well, one must get on. Ah, there's Admiral Clifford, that's something I suppose.

'Ma'am.'

'There's was some fuss outside, Sir Augustus.'

'Yes ma'am, all under control now.'

'What was it?'

'Some children, ma'am, wanting to see you.'

'They seemed, Sir Augustus, to be warning me. Is everything quite as it should be?'

'Yes, indeed, ma'am. The Houses have been inspected from top to bottom, the Yeomen of the Guards have thoroughly searched.'

'No gunpowder then?'

'Oh no, ma'am, none at all, only . . . some dirt.'

'Dirt?'

'In the cellars, ma'am. Some odd objects, somehow amassing.'

'I don't want to hear of it.'

'No, ma'am, only to assure you that everything is perfectly safe.'

'Of course it is, Clifford, why even are we talking about it?'

'I do beg your pardon, ma'am.'

'Are you trying to worry me?'

'Quite the opposite, ma'am, I do assure you.'

'I do not scare easily.'

'No, ma'am.'

'Anything else to report, Clifford?'

'Not exactly, ma'am.'

'Spit it out. I shall see the minutes, I shall demand them from Ponsonby the moment I'm back at the Palace.'

'Rats, ma'am, there have been . . . well, some rats.'

'Rats! In Parliament!'

'Yes, ma'am.'

'Then catch them! Then kill them. I do not need to be concerned about a couple of rats scurrying about in the cellars.'

'More than a couple, ma'am.'

'How many?'

'Hard to say exactly . . . perhaps as many as a hundred.'

'Disgusting!'

'Yes, ma'am, as you say.'

'Well have them exterminated. How on earth did they get in?'

'It seems, ma'am, it seems perhaps, well, there have in general been more of them . . . rats, you see, since the burning of Forlichingham.'

'Do not talk to me of that place!'

'Yes, ma'am.'

Now the day is utterly ruined. I must remain calm. Rats here, rats all about, makes one shudder to think of it. I thought, I was told, that all would be well once Forlichingham was destroyed. But now the dirt has come back into the city. I have seen great mounds of rubbish. *I* have, the Queen has. And if I have seen them, I for whom everything is cleaned and made wholly hygienic, I say if I have seen rubbish then how much is there, how much filth and dirt is there beyond my sight? Daily I am given reports of a spreading disease, *daily*, and this strange illness apparently can be caught by objects, by touching objects, or that objects themselves may grow ill and die. I do not fully understand.

'Ma'am.'

'Ma'am.'

They put the robes on me. Well then, there is order, very good. I may be calm now, I must be calm, it must be some twenty minutes after eleven o'clock and soon I must go into the chamber. There now, deep breath, very good. Oh Albert, what a terrible winter we are having. How they all busy themselves about me, dressing up their doll, I must look very splendid, of course, of course.

What is that indecent fireplace doing? That doesn't belong here, who put that marble monstrosity there? Female caryatids with barely a stitch on, I don't like the look of that at all. It is on castors now and being rolled away, but why on earth was it ever here? And who is that strange woman in the terrible clothes, and the awful mob cap and all those pearls, what is she doing here, and why does she grin at me so, she's not supposed to look at me like that, who on earth is that old crone?

'Who are you? What are you doing?'

'Good morning, ma'am. I'm here to get you ready.'

'Who are you, I say?'

She comes in close, too close, far too close, her ancient fingers about my person. She whispers in my ear, 'You may say I am Viscountess Refuse, Duchess of Debris, the Honourable Septic-tank, the Dowager Dungheap, Lady Muck.'

'Get away, woman!'

But then Clifford comes in.

'Are you ready, ma'am? It is nearly time.'

'*I* say when it is time,' I cry, and then take a breath and recover myself. 'I do apologise, Sir Augustus. Of course, I must go now, into the chamber. It is very nearly half past the hour?'

430

'It is, ma'am.'

'Very well, let us in.'

I am most happy to be away from the horrible woman, how she kept grinning at me, her old fingers about my person. I shall have her punished, it is not to be countenanced. Still I may worry over that later. But good heavens who is here now? I cannot believe it, there are Lady Rossman and the Countess of Cardigan!

'Clifford, come here!'

'Ma'am.'

'What are these women doing here, Rossman and Cardigan?'

'They are here for your Opening, ma'am.'

'I am not about to be opened, sir, and you will find that both Rossman and Cardigan have chosen to marry commoners and so have lost all their rights to the peerage!'

'Yes, ma'am.'

'So remove them!'

'Now, ma'am?'

'Instantly!'

What a fuss they make of it, but really they should know better! The marshal of the North Stairs leaves off his position to the Royal Gallery just to have the horrible women removed. Some of the ladies are not in full dress. I am most perturbed! And look at these children here, I shall have all children barred from the ceremony on future occasions. So then. Here at least is the Duke of Richmond, and Gordon bearing the Sword of State. That is much better, and beside him is the Marquis of Windsor with the Cap of Maintenance, very well then. That is good. That is quite right.

431

I look down at my star of the garter, at the sash of Empire, all is as it should be, do be calm, do calm. But then . . . what is that pinned there? Something new, something that I never saw before. Some new badge. I was not informed about it. I think it was the old woman who put it there, why whatever is it, it's some sort of a leaf, it is a bay leaf I think. What on God's earth does that signify? As if one were being readied for the pot.

Well, well, in we go, do not think of that now, the ceremony is set and well oiled, merely follow the path. I am guided along, I know the route, I have done this before often enough. I progress along the Royal Gallery, people bow to me either side, all is well, all is well. There was a man there who looked so like Albert, so like him, well then that's a good sign is it not. Certainly it is. Very well then, I am ready.

Slight pause in the Prince's Chamber as I am announced. All is as it should be.

I hear the peers rising.

In I go, to my golden throne.

I sit. All stand before me. The princesses at my side, on my left the Duchess of Teck.

I am holding my sceptre and my orb.

I look about my peers, and they all look at me; it's crowded in the gallery, all the correct people in attendance. All come to see me. I've had a good breakfast, yes indeed, some kidneys and a good slice of tongue, two eggs, claret and whisky because of the weather and a little pearl-barley soup, plenty of fuel. It is very light in here, all gas of course, the sun giving so little help, but I am glad of the bright light. I look at these, the very best of my people, and it seems to me, among the wigged heads, that I see Albert again, so many faces so like his. I am unwell, I think, I am unsteady. How can those faces be his? And yet, and yet they are. Albert, young again. Here and there and there and there!

I mean to call out! I mean to cry out. But, no, no, I must not. I must do my duty, I must open Parliament. Calm, calm as a clam. Something strange in the bright light surely, all can be explained, I'll ask Sir Henry Thompson, my physician, he'll know, he knows all the strangenesses of the human corpus. But he cannot explain the creeping disease, he does not know why my globe is ill, why my watercolours cannot be painted with and why my pillows have been damp these last nights.

Do not think of that, not now.

Concentrate.

Calm as a clam. Be Imperial.

Quite right.

In a minute the gentleman with the title of Black Rod shall go to fetch the Members of Parliament from the House of Commons, there shall be another big bang when the doors to the Commons are shut in his face, all according to tradition, and then, well then another big bang or rather great knocks by Black Rod upon the door. Three in all shall be sounded and then the door shall open and all the Commons shall come in, in all their ghastly hubbub, Disraeli and Gladstone at the head, and then the Lord Chamberlain shall deliver my speech for me.

So then.

There goes Black Rod.

Bang!

That's the noise of the doors slamming.

They shall be here soon enough, there's no stopping them.

The House of Lords
11:32 8th February 1876, Moments Before the
Arrival of the Members of Parliament

33

HOW THE IREMONGERS
OPENED PARLIAMENT

Various narrators

Home to Let

From Clod Iremonger
Clod. I must be very Clod this morning. The veriest Clod.
Bang. Bang. Bang.
I am hiding in ratform beneath a bench in the House of Lords,
Grandfather has ordered me here. The door of the House of
Commons is opened and now all the MPs do flood through
the Commons Lobby across the Central Lobby getting closer
and getting louder, all those top hats, to see them go, as if all
the chimneys of Lungdon are on the move. Into the Peers'
Corridor and then into the Peers' Lobby, louder and louder,
and at last into the Lords' Chamber. What a mass of them, all
the members of Parliament, how they do throng and clot the

room, and in the lead is the Prime Minister and the Head of the Opposition, but they cannot all fit in, there are too many of them, and all talking loudly amongst themselves.

Now there is a sudden squealing of rats, of my fellows under benches around me, followed by a sudden rushing of people all in black, who divide the MPs, squeezing out those who cannot well fit in and pushing them rudely back down the Peers' lobby, and now the doors to the Lords' Chamber are slammed, and now those people in their black suits roll a large marble fireplace before the door, it is Grandmother's fireplace, it is tugged from its castors and let fall with a heavy thud before the door, and so now it is firmly shut. And so all are crowded in and can not get out. In an instant those runners in black are gone again, sunken rat-like and squeezed through holes.

'What is the meaning of this?' someone cries. How I do hear him from my hiding place.

'What?'

'What?'

'What?' comes back from some of the Lords and MPs, for they are leathers posted here by Grandfather in all his cleverness. Cries of,

'Help! Help ho! Treason!'

And now a clack, clack, clack. And Aunt Ifful is there standing before the House of Lords.

'Who are you, woman, what are you doing here?' calls some gentleman, perhaps it is the Prime Minister.

'I come to dim the lights,' says my Aunt Ifful.

And she opes her mouth and lets some of her night out,

all to the general horror of the people, such frail humanity, in the chamber.

'There then, that is better,' says Aunt Ifful. 'Your Majesty, my Lords, members of Parliament, visitors in the Royal Gallery, please meet my family.'

And that is the signal for us all to come in, and so we, pinched and hairy, long-tailed and sniffing, rush then in a great tumbling through all the holes that lead into the Lords' Chamber, or, like me, from under a bench. How many of us then, over a hundred I think, some of us have not been so lucky, some have been trampled underfoot by the Yeomen of the Guard as we waited in our furry clusters, our hearts moving so fast.

We must be an extraordinary sight, all us rats appearing here on the carpet, crawling around all that ermine, making a general panic. But now comes the greater moment, for we have all amassed to the noise of their screaming in the centre of the Chamber and now from our ratform do we grow human again. How strange to stretch and shift so, quite like the feeling I had when Grandfather spun me into a sovereign. I don't like to do it, the feeling is wretched, something like vomiting, only a hundred times the worse.

'Rats!' the Lords and MPs scream.

'Rats!'

'Get them off me!'

'What in the name of heaven!'

'Call the guards! Why do they not come!'

'Help! Help, I say!'

So we grow and we put away our tails and our whiskers and are soon enough got up like ordinary everyday men and women. We surround the MPs and force them forward in a knot towards the Queen's throne. What a sight we are, all amassed beside the gentry. What a family!

'Not rats . . . people. People!'

'They were rats, just now!'

'What magic is this?'

'Who are you?'

'SILENCE!' It is Idwid that calls out. 'THERE WILL BE SILENCE! ORDURE! Well sir, Umbitt Owner, please, please, they are quiet now.'

'Who are we, you ask?' says Grandfather standing tall, all birth objects stuck about him, his pockets brimming, never did he look so grim and unbending, 'We are a family, grown small in number, come to have words with you. Our name, Queen, is lost in fire and cruelty, but it may yet be heard whispering among any accumulation of debris. We were, once upon a time, the guardians of your filth. Since we have lost that title we have been forced to hide in dark cellars, forced to put away the sun, forced to limp and lick our wounds, we are . . . how may we be properly described? We are the bad smell caught in the wind, we are the strange tapping between the walls, we are the cup that fell down and broke on its own accord, we are all the lost keys, we are the floorboards that creak though no one is upon them, we are the shadows in your dreams, we are the bad feeling that can't be shook, here we are, we alone, great Iremongers of darkest dirt.'

Great panic in the house, calls for help, for arms.

'Iremonger!'

'Iremongers!'

'I was in the belief,' says the Queen, 'that there were no more of these people remaining.'

'Ordure! ORDURE!' cries Idwid.

'Eleanor Cranwell,' says the candleholder in my hand. As if she is trying to tell me something, as if she is trying to talk to me.

'Well then, revise your beliefs,' says my own grandfather to the Queen and all Parliament, 'and breathe us in while you may.'

I step forward then, pushing my way through the crowding of uncles and aunts and cousins.

'Excuse me, Grandfather,' I say, 'I need to speak.' I do.

'Eleanor Cranwell.'

'Clod, be silent,' Grandfather replies. 'There is no time.'

'I shall speak I think,' I say. 'I will be heard.'

'Clod, stand down!'

'Your Majesty, for certainly you were never my Majesty, for you mean little enough to me. I am Clodius Iremonger –'

'Who should be silent,' says Grandfather.

'And I am an Iremonger of some talent and force. I must blow my own trumpet, you see, for I wish you to understand, and must be quick about my talking.'

'Clod!'

'I do hear things talking, I do comprehend the disease, I know which people have turned into what things. Even now, in this room, there are so many names sounding in my ears. That was the start of it, do you follow? When I was a child, a babe even, I had this particular hearing. And now, you see, that I am older, I can move any object by thinking it; I have set whole houses alive. Well it is a terrible thing, I've grown very

439

powerful and strong. And, Your Majesty, Lords, MPs, proper people, whosoe'er you may be, I want you to understand we are such a people, a people who are very clever: we may hear things and move things and command things, we may shift from rat to person, we may bring forth the night. Yes! But, and yet, there's ever less of us, you see. It seems you have been shooting us.'

All the great men make a great play of straining to hear, to make sense of my speech, and in pausing they take this opportunity to scowl at me and no doubt find me young and foolish, and some try to speak but I will not let them and go on again.

'Yes you have! It seems you have been murdering us. We had a home. Out there, a home which you destroyed. You murdered Foulsham. How could you, how could you ever do such a thing? Was it to keep you safe in your warm rooms, to sit by the fire with your particular possessions hard about you? Well if that's the reason, then you have failed, have you not? For we are here, and the disease is spread thick about you. Let me tell you now, I came here to murder you.'

'Eleanor Cranwell.'

There is a little silence after I'd let that one sink in, but it is not followed by the cries of help and shock that I had anticipated – the result is rather a few smiles and then several deep laughs.

'Child,' says a man, and I believe this man to be the Prime Minister, Mr Disraeli, 'you fail to terrify. It would be best for you and your people behind you to give yourselves up and cease this rash and foolish behaviour – no good shall ever come from it. The longer you persist the greater shall be the consequences. Put away your music-hall theatrics and leave this hallowed chamber, for you and your kin are not invited here.'

'You speak to me as if I were just a child.'

'Child, being school-age, I must.'

'Hear, hear!' comes a rotund peer.

'I am Clod!' I say.

And there is more laughter at that.

'I am Clod!' I cry once more.

Yet more laughter, from all around.

'So you keep saying,' one Lord calls out.

'Eleanor Cranwell.'

'You should listen to me, you know. You should not mock me. I am grown quite strong, you see.'

'Parliament will not be held to account by some child!' a Lord bellows.

'It will!' I cry. 'Oh I do swear it will. I may pull all Lungdon into the Thames if I have the will to do it.'

Much laughter at this.

'London,' some bellow, 'the place is called London, didn't you know?'

'Do it, Clod,' says Umbitt my Grandfather. 'Do it now!'

'Eleanor Cranwell.'

'Yes, Eleanor, I do hear you.'

'Do it, Clod, move all!' cries Grandfather. 'Bring it all down!'

'There have been so many deaths,' I say, giving them a last chance at life, 'can we now, do we now, allow a little living? This is but our demand and our need: a home. We want a home. We require one. A home, I say, please, a home.'

441

'We do not negotiate with criminals,' says Disraeli, growing impatient.

'But you, you are the criminals!' I cry.

'No home, no home!' say some MPs.

'Do it, Clod, do it now,' says Grandfather, come close beside me.

'Yes, Grandfather, yes I shall.'

I close my eyes, I move forward just a little, and the whole building begins to shake.

Then the Lords, the MPs all about, stop their mocking and commence to gasp and to call out. And to think I'd merely moved the house one single step. Now they are listening.

'*We* do not negotiate with criminals,' says Grandfather, 'Now, Clod.'

With my eyes closed I raise my hands, I call in my thinking so many objects all about, I call them up into the air, lift them high into the air all around Parliament, and then very swiftly I bring my hands down.

And then! What follows!

It is as if Parliament is being gunned and cannoned and pelted and pocked and thumped and shot and pitted all over, as if now it is a body with black holes, riddled with a plague.

What noises, what screams inside as all that outside smashes against it in a dreadful wave; windows shatter, pieces come flying through.

I open my eyes. Everyone in the chamber is so frightened, they are in such a terror. I did that, I caused them such distress, people are weeping, some are bleeding. What a thing! What a business, as dear, lost Lucy would have said. Another barrage like that and I do believe I shall kill people, many people.

'Again, Clod, do it again,' says Grandfather. 'Good, my boy.'

I close my eyes, I lift up my hands.

'Eleanor Cranwell.'

The candleholder in my pocket is calling out to me. I made her a promise once, before she betrayed me, never to hurt anyone, and now I am about to bring forth another crashing wave, to hurt these who hurt us, these men who signed the paper that brought about the terrible burning of Foulsham, these people who killed Lucy. Now, now shall I be fully revenged.

'Eleanor Cranwell.'

Now I shall.

'Eleanor Cranwell.'

Now, now . . . and yet . . . I stall . . . and yet I cannot. I cannot do it. I have come so far, but now in the last moment, I am not able. I do not want them dead, I just want a home. I cannot do it, I lack the heart.

Clod the fool, Clod the idiot. Coward Clod.

I open my eyes and slowly lower my hands. Nothing stirs, all look at me. I cannot do it.

'Now, Clod,' says Grandfather.

But I cannot.

And so Grandfather raises his bloody fingers and with a wave of motion a great many of the MPs fall, collapsing into objects. There are mop handles and dustpan brushes, there are two ink bottles and one set of dentures, some mirrors, undergarments.

'Where have they gone?' one MP shrieks. 'The MPs for Sussex and Cumberland, for Kent and Gloucestershire, just beside me now, have quite vanished!'

443

'I demand you bring them back at once!' One ruddy-faced MP steps forward and with a flick of Grandfather's bloody fingers is reduced to a wing nut.

'We have indeed not come to negotiate,' Grandfather says.

And as he speaks, Ifful beside him spews more night into the Chamber.

'Then why, why for heavens' sake have you come?' It is Mr Gladstone who asks this, as I stand hopeless with my family, unable to go on.

'To hurt. To do harm,' says Grandmother.

'Eleanor Cranwell!'

A general movement from the populace all about.

'Some people, please to understand,' says Grandfather, 'make better objects than people.'

He walks around the Chamber and, flicking his bloodied fingers about, he turns a person here, a person there, at random, to show his cruelty. Twenty MPs and ten Lords fall down. He has their attention very well then, oh they are attending excellently well at last. He means to murder them all; what a family we are, what monsters. What have I done?

Another person falls, and another. A wooden-handled drill, a bathing hat.

'No, Grandfather,' I say, 'do not do it. It is enough already.'

Noises from without: people are trying to smash the doors down.

'Save the Queen!'

'Save the Queen!'

'I shall save the Queen . . . until last,' Grandfather says. 'Here shall be great hurting! Now Clod, come forward, wake yourself up, you may do your worst, pelt this house down, pull it into the very river! Earn your trousers!'

'Eleanor Cranwell!'

'Stop him!' cries a Lord.

'I shall, I'm the one to do it,' that is Moorcus calling from somewhere in the ranks and he comes forward now with his shooter waving in front of him.

'No, Moorcus,' I say to my cousin, 'do not do it.'

'No Moorcus, do not,' says Grandfather.

'A gun!' someone calls. 'He has a gun!'

'Gun!'

'Gun!'

'There's a gun in the house!'

'Yes, there is,' says Moorcus and straight away he fires it.

It isn't a very loud crack. I barely hear it. I see a brief flame and then all goes slow for a little moment, and then, of a sudden, I'm knocked over. I'm on the ground. I see myself spilling out.

A Revenger's Tale

From Moorcus Iremonger, murderer

Yes! Yes! To see him fall! To see the bullet leap through the air and burrow and bite into Clod like it was born to do it. And down he goes and down and down! And that ridiculous top hat of his topples after.

'You're dead! You're dead! I'm not!' I sing.

Like he'd lost the idea of life and living. What a puppet!

And Grandfather, he cries out, 'Fool! Cursed child! Murderer of Iremongers!'

'No, Grandfather,' I said, 'he wasn't one of us, not really.'

'You, Moorcus,' bellowed Grandfather, 'you have killed us all!'

There he lies now. Clod's on the floor where he belongs and he swims in his own red river, and does flail in it, oh yes he's pouring out. And my pistol is hot, as hot as a heart because it spat just now and done it proper!

I! I! I am the Clod killer!

Crack!

What was that? Small sound after all those others. Like a stick being snapped. Whatever was it . . .? It sounded like. Didn't it? Gunshot? Such a strange feeling, I look down at my chest . . . I . . . bleed . . . bleeding . . . I look up, what . . . Toastrack! Toastrack up there on the balcony with my own other gun. I mustn't die, no, no, please not to. I am the hero of my life!

Ah me!

From Rowland Cullis, formerly a toastrack, now a murderer
Toastrack I was. I ever hated your company, you splendid little toff, all those do thises and do thats, well then, have at that now, why don't you, how does it feel? I was very lucky, such a fuss over two ladies being thrown out because of the Queen's say-so, and all the boys with lanterns causing such a fuss, I slipped in then, suddenly no one was watching, up I went, up the stairs.

Yes I've a shooter, Moorcus, and I've been longing to plug you with it and I meant to do it publicly so that all may see that I did it.

'How are you then?' I call. 'How do you feel? However do you do, Moorcus? My name is Rowland Cullis.'

He does not say a word.

'Shut up,' crows the blind one, the Governor Idwid, his head looking the wrong way. 'Shut up!'

'That the Queen there, is it?' I call. 'Hallo, Majesty, here I am at the Royal Gallery. With my shooter. My name is Rowland Cullis, I was a toastrack before now. I'm sorry about Clod, he was all right, he was. Are you still with us, Clod? You're deathly pale. You too, Moorcus, you're greyer; how you do leak – watch the carpet!'

Bang, bang, the people outside trying to get in and others trying to get out, and I am grabbed now, there's people in the gallery waking up from all the shock, they have a hold of me and pulling me down, my hands behind my back, my gun on the floor.

I am guilty, guilty of the charge. I shot Moorcus, I did it.

Objects are Hiding

From the voice of a Gathering

We are John Smith Un-Iremonger. Came long ago from Foulsham, the very first of us, a tiny cog, once a man but shifted horribly by cruel Umbitt, thrown over the wall into London. That was the start of it, so many years ago; how we've collected and grown since then. We are all of us here bits and pieces put into clothes, our hearts are spinning things, we are here in the Chamber, we are waiting, we are waiting. The old man has so many things, all his pieces, all birth objects, all that was once people and we are hungry for them, they are what we want to

eat, to eat them all and then shall there be no more Iremongers, all shall fall like us but first must eat, must eat. We. We were Emma Jenkins, Sybil Booth, Lester Ritts, Mary Ann Stark, Giles Bickleswaite, Theobald Villiers, Elsie Bullard, Leona Rice, Lloyd Walters, Elliot Murney, Dorothea Towndell, Matthew Stokes, so many and many are our names now lost, now no more but stuff, here we are. We're sharp and blunt and heavy and light, we are soft and hard. We're here now inside and we're coming in, more and more of us from outside this chamber, smashing upon the door. More gathering about to join us. Stuff dropping from the old man, he cannot hold them all any longer, he is ill, the things no longer cling to him. What's that? That's a lady's shoe size ten, name of Cecily Grant, very good then.

One of us dressed as a peer leans forward from his bench – looks such a noble Lord – stretches out his hands and takes up the shoe, then looking left and right he quickly puts it in his mouth, swallows down the piping inside. Grows a bit.

Bang! Bang! How they cry to come in! The many more of us, police never understood us, let us grow so big, let us, did the Police Inspector Harbin.

There's another Gathering, a larger Gathering just outside, it shall break down the door! How it bangs upon it!

The Last Cry of a Grandmother

From the Iremonger matriarch, Ommaball of great blood and age
'Stand proud, stand firm, Umbitt. Do not waver. Turn them, turn them all! And let us be rats again and gone!'

How frail Umbitt is, how frail but still he must do it. Those people! I hate them so, trample on them all, change them every last one and let us dance on their pieces let us break them into crumbs, let us lose and destroy them. But quick, we must be quick about it. We have sealed the chamber and trapped ourselves in. And there lies Clod, in his blood, our lost hope, and the traitor Moorcus grey with death.

What's that about my feet? Rats! Rats! Iremongers changed to rats!

'Cowards! Cowards! This is Ommaball Oliff that calls you – be human once more. Stand proud! Be Iremongers!'

But they are not, the traitors, they are rats.

Step on them! I shall step on them!

'Piggott!'

'Yes, my lady.'

'Piggott, step on those rats. Step on them.'

'They are Iremongers, my lady.'

'They are not worth my spit. Step on them I say, dance your heavy boots upon them, crush and crush!'

'Yes, my lady.'

Good, good, she'll do it, Piggott will, she has spirit.

'My lady, look! Look behind you!'

But . . . what?

'Piggott! Piggott! Piggott's gone rat on me too! Come back Piggott, come back, I shall crush you now.'

But look, now, look, look at the people on the benches, they're moving, they're shifting, they're sitting closer and closer together and then they are melding into one, yes! They are coming into one, how can that be? Faces fall off! Not faces, masks, masks on the floor! All the clothings are pulled off and it stands tall. All those spinning, shifting things inside.

'A Gathering!' I scream. 'A Gathering is within! Umbitt, Umbitt!'

But Umbitt stands there, his hands dripping, more and more things falling from him. As one Lord stands up from his bench and another and another and, dropping his wig, dissolves into the main Gathering, which grows, it grows and grows!

I stand back, I cannot go any further, there's nowhere further to go, rats about me, I do not blame them now. Gathering coming on, closer and closer.

'Do something, Clod, do something, earn your trousers!'

I am backed into my own marble fireplace, I feel it, I feel it . . . moving. My own birth object! Being moved from the other side!

'Clod, Clod,' I cry, 'do something, this is your granny here, demanding it!'

'Clod! Help!' Idwid is calling in the darkness, 'I hear nothing, the Gathering is too loud! My ears are bleeding! Iffull, love!'

'Idwid, love! I come with extra night!' cries the Iremonger of many lungs. 'Get up, Clod! Get up and be useful! Oh, look out, Ommaball Oliff! It falls!'

Such fuss they make, but what about me?

'Help me!' I cry. 'Help me, oh my children!'

It moves, it is falling now.

'Oh! My own birth object!'

It comes!

'Um—!'

454

The Gathering Collects

From Inspector Harbin, coming in

The whole Parliament building suffers such terrible damage,
Saint Stephen's tower is terribly broken, the clock quite
shattered. Into this ruined palace have we rushed in desperate
haste. I have made allies with a giant made of things, a mass,
a colossus, which has broken the oaken door of the Lords'
Chamber, and in we come at last. Some of my men besides
me, just behind the giant. And there are boys about me again,
boys all over, I could not stop them. They came rushing in
when the Smith with all his faces of Albert burst through into
Parliament. They will not go back, these boys with their lights,
they come for their Queen I do think. They have lit our path.
That's it, lads, you're patriots one and all, shine your lights,
shine on, and let us make sense of this terrible darkness, put
the darkness out, I say. I wave at the boys, my pistol in my
hand, to let them on, so that all may see.

'Light! Light ho! Light, make some sense of the world!'

It's then that I see her, then, as more light comes in. The
girl with the flaming hair. The one we've been seeking, the
dangerous one, smashed a policeman, there! Right there! Right
before me, the very girl! She must be stopped. You must stop
her, Harbin, I tell myself, even if you have to kill her.

From Lucy Pennant, coming in

A Gathering, a Gathering larger than any Gathering that I ever
saw. Larger yet than the one that nearly pulled down Heap
House. But . . . I don't know how or why, or what it means,

this Gathering seems to be helping, helping the police. I hate these police, these murderers of a little girl called Molly Porter, they shall answer for that one day, I do swear it, but not now, now is not the time, now is Clod's time and so we do run with a Gathering. It has broken down the doors, what a great crash as they slam to the ground and now the Gathering pours in afterwards, it laps and bursts against the walls of the chamber within. And me and the link boys, we follow after, with our lights, come to see what's what, as all those broken bits of Gathering do gather themselves up again, do try to form one big, heaving mass.

Where? Where is he?

'Clod. Clod? CLOD!'

I can't see him, I can barely see anything. And all the noise is the rushing and clattering of the Gathering as it swerves around and tries to come together, smashing into object and person alike.

'Some light, light now!' a policeman calls.

The boys are about, I just see them small pools of white, but then as soon as they're lit they're out again in a moment and I can just hear a strange hissing sound, like gas coming out of a pipe, extinguishing the lights. Something else is in here.

'Clod, Clod, where are you?'

The hissing sound, the blackness spreading everywhere, I feel it on my face, I feel it as I breathe in, I feel it coming down inside me.

'Yes, yes, Ifful love, blot them out.' A man's voice in the dark – that's Idwid Iremonger, I know him.

There are other people around, there are many others in all the darkness, mostly they are keeping quiet I think because of

457

the Gathering hammering around them, they are seeking some shelter, they are trying to hide. I hear people crying, calling out. There's a woman's voice in the distance, I hear it muttering the same sentence over and over, 'Calm as a clam, calm as a clam.'

The Gathering has stopped now, it's all gone very quiet. Nobody moves. There is something very close to me, something huge, clicking and creaking. It is the Gathering. The new Gathering, as tall as the chamber itself, it is right beside me. I hear the noises of it, small instruments sounding inside it, wind through tubes, it's clicking to itself, the hollow tin rumblings of its many stomachs. It is feeling about with its hands made of many different fingers of metal, porcelain, rubber, glass, wood, cloth, stone, it's feeling about on the floor, it's searching, it's trying to find something.

It's feeding.

I hear it, it's looking for food. It's eating, it's stuffing things into its many mouths, this great beast of objects, it's picking things from the floor.

From the voice of the Gathering

So big are we! Such size! Come together! More, more yet! Here they are and here and here, all these bits fallen all over the floor, all these that were Members of Parliament and Peers of the Realm, how good they taste, but most of all the best morsels are still with the old man. We want to eat those Iremonger pieces, eat them all, every last one and then there'll be no Iremonger left to bully and to break us. How they caught us and trapped us and kept us prisoner, no more ever again, we'll eat every last Iremonger thing and then they shall all tumble, one and all. Here, here's a thing on the floor, something else the old man has dropped, he can't keep hold of things now, how he litters! What a thing is this? Want it, do we want it? It's a something called Geraldine Whitehead, nose-hair pincers. What a thing, we shall eat it!

The Last Dance of Idwid Iremonger

From Idwid Iremonger

'Geraldine? Geraldine!' I, Idwid, cry, my ears, a cram of voices, but I heard her, my Geraldine calling out. No! No! I had a Geraldine!

'Idwid, my darling lugs! Why do you cry so?'

'Oh Ifful, Ifful, it has eaten my Geraldine, oh, oh!'

'Oh Idwid, my heart! Come to me, come to me.'

'I'll rat to you, Ifful, I'll turn rat and run to you, keep me, keep me safe!'

I turn and slip and unfold, and shrink skeletons until I am rat once more, and now must to my Ifful. But I cannot see, and all the noise echoes inside my hairy ears. Where to go, where to go?

From the Gathering

There's a rat running and running in circles, between our hundred feet . . . indeed what feet we have – great boots, iron clods, wooden feet, women's shoes, children's, old people's slippers, high-top button boots, Oxfords, Cromwells, sandals, work slippers of Berlin wool, brogues, ankle boots, beaded, punch-worked, flat-sole shoes, kid leather, straight-soled,

square-nosed, quarter-tipped, all footwear from so many here and there, shifting in the darkness, and between all our many feet runs a blind rat in and out of us, we shall stamp on it, we shall stamp!

Stamp!

Stamp!

From Lucy

The whole Chamber is reverberating, shaking, smashing, as the Gathering tries to squash something under its many feet, and still I cannot see Clod, where are the link boys and their light? Each time a flame is lit up the same hissing comes again and more darkness descends.

Stamp!

Stamp!

Please, please stop, it shall break through the floor in a moment.

Stamp!

Squeal!

The stamping has stopped now.

From Ifful Iremonger, widow

'Idwid, love, Idwid? IDWID!'

So dark, it will always be dark now. I shall darken the world and keep it dark, I'll put out all lights, I shall end every lamp in this city, I shall swallow up all matchsticks, candlesticks, tallows, flints. There'll never come any more warmth; now and forever all is cold and loveless.

They put out my sun when Idwid died. And now I shall hiss and hiss.

461

I'll so darken any day away.

Lungdon shall never see light again.

What?

What's that?

Now some other boy with his little lantern dripping weak heat, no, no, it's something else, something bigger, can't see to put it down quite, though I vomit and vomit and out comes black, still some more lighting does come.

What is that which defies me, what is that?

Is it?

Can it be?

Rippit?

Fire? Fire!

I can't put it out!

I spit at it and it spits back.

I'm light! My hair! I AM SO BRIGHT!

From the Gathering

Dead rat. Dead blind rat. Now what, what now?

Where's the old man? Where is he, there's good pickings with him.

Feel him, feel for him, touch him and rip him with all your thousand, thousand scrapers. Old man, old man, we come!

Umbitt, running out

Here I hide, Umbitt, that once was great, here now in my sad moment, my empire forgot, my family dispersed and ruined, my own wife, loving Ommaball, crushed to death by her own marble mantelpiece. How big the Gathering is, so strong, so

462

strong. And I am old and ill, the engine of my body trembles now and shudders. This, can even this be my end?

I was Iremonger.

I was.

It comes, the Great Gathering, it smashes in its search, it lifts benches, it feels underneath, it whirls and screeches, the noise, the hunting noise it makes, how it cuts into me. It is looking for me, I know it is. What have I left? Only me now, only me and my own cuspidor given to me by my own loving father.

It's stopped now, the beast has, it's silent, not a clink from it, not the slightest creak, I must too keep very still, not move, not an inch, it's ready to pounce, I do feel it.

'Calm as a clam, calm as a clam.'

That voice again, a woman in distress. Not just any woman, the Queen herself. That's it, that's it, do go to her.

'Clam.'

'Clam.'

My leathers, dear leathers, moving forward.

'Clam!'

'Clam?'

'CLAM!'

It's found them, the Gathering, it's killing the leathers, ripping them open, the stench of the rubbish comes out from their leather bodies, but it does not eat them, it merely rips open, ruins and moves on.

'Clod? Clod?' A young voice, female.

That's the horrible red-haired child, the scum from Foulsham, I made her into a clay button once before and I shall do it readily again. I had her thrown out into the heaps by that same dead

464

child that lies there, shot by his own birth object. Oh this is the end of days. But that child I hate, the red-haired one; without her the Iremongers should have stayed true, without her Clod should have smashed all; it is her doing. Now I think, now I shall clay button her once more, I do think I shall. It should be my pleasure, but how, how to do it without giving my hiding away?

Smoke. Smoke!

Reports of a Fire

From Inspector Harbin
Smoke everywhere now! There's fire, there's fire!

'Fire!' I cry. 'Fire! Great fire in the House!'

From Tommy Cronin, Mill Bank Link Boy, fleeing Parliament
Church candles don't burn bright enough, but that's no matter, there's enough fire all around now to make everything seen. However shall we get out of this? However did it start? I seen policemen and soldiers suddenly call out, tug off their helmets, their hair all in flames, running out in a panic, and the walls suddenly whoosh with fire and we must retreat, we must fall back and even as we run we're being set light to, our hair does fire up like any match! We go back, all fall back whilst we can!

From ill-faced Georgie, Mill Bank Link Boy, outside Parliament
I seen such a strangeness, such a queer fellow. Who is that man, whoever is he? He's so squat and flat, like something very heavy has sat on him. Whatever is he doing? Why, he's

dancing, he's running around and around, this strange man on Speaker's Green, dancing around a little dance to himself and as he dances he whips himself up into a frenzy and fire, somehow, fire comes out of windows!

Anyone comes close to him suddenly bursts into flame!

I think he means to burn all London down and destroy all things, all people, and only be ashes left.

From Rippit, dancing upon Speaker's Green
RIPPIT! RIPPIT! RIPPIT!

A Button, a Sovereign

From Lucy
There's some light now, coming through thick smoke, light from outside, flames through the window, the whole Parliament surrounded by the flaming, and heat coming on, pressing on. But in the dancing light how the Great Gathering does pull itself up, does seem to gasp, to stretch away from the floor to shoot upwards in many strands and columns to try to flee from the fire, it is hammering now, in so many thick knots of fists, hammering upon the roof, trying to burst through.

But there is new light, light all around, there – and there he is! Clod lying on the floor and blood all about him.

'Clod? Clod! Clod!'

From Clod on the floor
Clod, here I am, Clod. So many voices, so many names, they

do crush down on me so, I cannot make sense of them all, just a roaring, a great roaring. I am going now, falling out, oh what an ending . . . there shall be no more Iremongers now after all, never and never, no home, we're breathing out now, slow and slower.

Moorcus, it would have to have been Moorcus all along.

'Eleanor Cranwell.'

Bye then, Eleanor, dropped on the ground. Thank you.

I close my eyes and fall asleep.

Someone's shaking me. Someone's tugging at me.

Leave off, shan't you, I'm slipping away.

Still shaking me, grabbing at me.

Go away, I'm dead.

Yet still I am bothered, not left alone to die, to drift off in Aunt Ifful's dirty inkness. Leave alone. Just leave alone.

But whoever it is, keeps heaving at me, pulling me back.

Go away, go away, I'm sleeping.

Still I am shook so.

Leave off, shall you, I'm dead.

But the great bully won't go, but keeps shaking and prodding at me, and I seem to hear some distant words above the roaring, someone's calling my name. Let them, let them, this knocking shall not be answered. The door is closed, and won't be opened again. Give in, shan't you, give a tired chap his little peace. Is it so much to ask?

There now, good. Whoever it is has stopped.

There now, at last, my own corner of quiet.

I am alone. There now, there, old Clod, off you go.

It doesn't hurt.

From Lucy

'Clod, Clod you bloody dare!' I shake him and shake him and he won't wake. Wake, wake Clod, oh Clod you bloody fool. I can't have it, I can't have it. 'Clod! Damn you! Breathe! Can't you?'

He is so still. I can see no movement, none at all.

'Oh Clod! Please, please.'

Not a thing.

'Oh Clod, what am I to do after all?' There's a Gathering as great as a mountain, a heap on its own, taking up full half a room, and a Queen in the corner with tears down her face and men all around her in suits and red dresses, all sweating and dishevelled. That's about the picture of it. There's some few policemen left, panic all over them, stopped and useless in their terror. There's your miserable grandfather hiding behind the benches, watching us, looking up at the thing and then down to us. There are rats all about, running and screeching, and dirt and bits in piles here and there, and here am I, your own bloody Lucy, all hemmed in. That's about the size of it. Well then, what's to be done? And you lying there on the floor, all dead on me.

I take his plug out, I lie it on his chest.

And as I do it that great mound above and to the sides shifts a bit and stops its moving.

'Clod,' I say. 'Oh Clod, Clod, I think that thing of things is looking at me. I cannot see its face but there are so many bits of it pointed now in my direction. I don't like it, Clod. Clod, however do you stop a Gathering? Oh Clod, Clod, it's slowly falling, it's shifting closer, it's beginning to avalanche towards us. Clod! CLOD!'

And that's when I hit him. Hit him hard across the face just like I did when first I ever met the dolt, just like I did up in that attic room in Foulsham.

'Clod bloody Clod BLOODY CLOD!'

From Clod
Hit me. Hard across the face. Such a jolt. Pulling me back, how that hurt hurtling back, the sudden wind in me, weather all about, and the pump my little pump, went bump again and bump again after, like it was remembering. And then I opened my eyes.

Lucy.

No.

Lucy.

No, no.

Lucy. Lucy! Lucy, Lucy, Lucy!

'Lucy?'

'Clod! Bloody Clod!'

'Lucy, oh Lucy. It's you.'

'Whoever else?'

'You're living!'

'Yes! Yes! Are you?'

'A little bit.'

'Bloody hell, this ain't no time to sleep!'

'You hit me!'

'How else would you know it's me?'

'You're always hitting me.'

'Look what I got you.'

'James Henry Hayward.'

'Oh plug, I hear you. How ever did you . . .'

'Never mind now, that thing up there, I think it's looking at us.'

No time, leave us alone, leave us together a while. Can't you? But no, no, something comes at once to break us apart.

'It's smelt your plug I think.'

'It's my plug.'

'It wants it.'

'Well then, in truth, it's James Henry, not a plug after all, but, yes, I do believe it wants it.'

It creeps forward now, dropping little bits over us as it comes, small screws and pins and nibs, a rain of little things, coins, rivets, which then hop back to the big massing. I think it will land on us, on the whole, don't you? It'll drown us. Arms of it stretch forward to snatch from us, ten arms and more, all creeping to us, one rushes out and grabs the candleholder, dear Eleanor Cranwell, and steals it back inside its bulk.

'Oh let us alone!' I cry.

'Clod,' Lucy says, all that red, such a face, oh that dear face. 'I'm right glad to have known you!'

And she kisses me hard on the lips, and then takes my plug from me. And goes. And I'm alone again without her.

Lucy, one last time

I've took it, took his bloody plug, I must take it away to stop that heap crushing down on him. To save him.

'This is what you're after!' I cry at all that mass of bits. 'Over here!'

It cracks and spits, there's great screeching from the inside of it. All those many things, cracking and smashing towards

471

me, but away from Clod, that's the main point of it. Away from him.

'Help! Help! The fire! We're in here!' How they do caw, the Queen and her company. I've got other worries.

'Come 'ere, you great bully!' I call.

It shrieks and roars, it smashes bits of itself, spools and needles and pins and nails and tacks and screws and bolts and scissors, there's a great crashing and thumping and scraping and then it just stays there, a great wave paused at its height right over me. And then like rain it begins to spit at me, little drops of that great wave do plip and plop over me, only thing is, those drops of that great heavy wave, they hurt when they fall and how they do cut into me.

It sends glass shards into me.

It sends small screws, bits of saws, needles that bleed me, nails that cut at my face. I'm a pin cushion now, it's playing with me, dotting me, such new freckles, writing over me in my own blood, sending bigger things now, sending books hurled with such force, sending whole plates, sending bookcases and chamber pots, sending saucepans to break me, sending a hammer's head, and more and more, a bedhead clattering before me, a whole chimney stack smacks into my side, but I'm still holding it, that plug, I still have it, but I look up.

Oh then it's coming now. That wave. It comes.

From Inspector Harbin
Now I might, now I must shoot the red-haired child, whilst there is still a chance. One brief chance; now do I aim. Steady. Steady.

473

Umbitt

Now might I. Now shall I. That thing of things is all looking at her now and now I shall do it.

'Be a button, be a clay button!'

I flick my fingers, her mouth makes an astonished O and her whole body falls down into the shape of that mouth's O. A button again.

Then a shot, fired into the mass.

A moment later the great thing is upon her and there is nothing more to see. The plug and the button quite consumed.

From ill-faced Georgie on Speaker's Green

The strange man hops about, like a frog, screaming at people.

'Rippit! RIPPIT!'

And whoever he screams at, bursts into flames.

Umbitt Exiting

From Umbitt

How hot it grows, how hot! I sweat so, my fingers are wet with blood and sweat. It's regrouping again after that last tumble, whither shall it head now I wonder?

Clod is fumbling to his feet, pulling himself up. Calling for his button. Wailing and weeping.

The Great Gathering is smashing against the wall, hurling and breaking.

Nothing can stop it now, I think, nothing can ever stop it.

'Now, Clod, call all your things, pull Lungdon down, drown it in the Thames!'

But he just screams for his button, his Lucy he calls it, while the great thing comes on.

'Stand back!' I call. 'Stand back I do command you! I am Umbitt!'

It stands up, it makes a noise as if in mockery of me, it repeats my name in clinks and scrapes.

'Ummbeeeettt. Umbeeeeeeettt.'

I see it now, so clear, I see it in all its voices, as it speaks to me in its many noises, as if I can hear as Idwid did and Clod. Here are all the dead, all the turned of Foulsham and Lungdon, all Iremonger birth objects here collected, all the ghosts assembled. All my murdered, oh so many hundreds of them. I did all to protect the family. I had to, it must be done. It is not like any Gathering I have ever known, all gatherings before had but one object spinning in its centre, maddening the rest of it, calling to action, one heart that thumped, but this, this Gathering has thousands of hearts and all do point their fury towards me.

'Him!' I cry. 'Get him, get Clod! Leave me alone!'

It groans and smashes.

I face it, and it, all the girth and weight of it, doth face me.

From deep inside it spits something out. That thing comes rolling towards me, it is a small, spinning thing. What is it? I cannot say, it spins and spins so. It slows now, it slows and stops in midair.

It is a cog, a small, rusting cog, an insignificant thing. It's calling to my cuspidor. It's inviting it to come in.

'No!' I say. 'No, never. You shall not have it.'

I hold it up, I hold it high, as high as I can above me.

'No, this is mine, mine, I say.'

But I feel the tug of it, I feel the pull of it.

The Gathering is coming towards me now, the cog has darted back in, the great massing is sloping down, it is about my feet now, all about my feet, and now it begins to rise higher.

'Mine! Mine, all mine!' I cry.

At my ankles, at my knees and rising higher.

'Get back, get back, I command things!'

They fall in about me, rising higher, more and more and more.

'It is my one thing,' I cry. 'Have mercy, leave me my own one thing.'

It is at my hips now and rising about me, how it squashes me, how it crams against my body, cutting, smashing, pressing, breaking, trying to rob me of breath and birth object.

'My own cuspidor, that my own father gave me.'

How it rises, at my chest now, I am in the very centre of the Gathering and it climbs and climbs to get my cuspidor. I am drowning, drowning in things!

How they crush me, crush me, they push hard against me, I feel them pushing at my ribs, up to my neck now, I shall burst with all this weight about me.

At my head.

How it pounds and smashes against my skull.

Only my hand, only my outstretched hand now is above the huge clot of Gathering, only that is unmolested. As I hold, whilst I may, my own cuspidor above the mass. But then oh then, my fingers so slippery with blood, only then the thing,

477

my thing, my very dear cuspidor, moves in my fingers, I cannot keep hold of it and it dances in my fingers, it will not keep still, and then it stops and then, then of its own will, it jumps in, into the Gathering and makes no great cry as it lands, merely the smallest clink.

And then all great objects do pound against me.

And I burst.

Bringing the House Down

Victoria Regina

Not as quiet as a clam, not any more. I weep, a Queen weeps in fear, in terror of what most unnatural events I have espied, and of the heat and of my own approaching death. I have seen such things, such things this morning, and never shall I see another afternoon, of that I am certain. I, Victoria, have seen objects bully and dance of their own accord, I have seen rats spin into people, I have seen ugly magic.

The fire is coming through at the windows. I shall be a roast Queen any moment, like any goose or turkey, like a guinea fowl, like a pheasant, like mutton. Such royal meat.

It's crushed the old man, the Iremonger patriarch. I cannot say I am sorry for that, but there are so few of us left now, some MPs and Lords, the princesses at my side. It shall come for us, I do feel it. The Duchess of Teck has been turned into a common boot scraper. I shall be brave. I've made up my mind to be brave.

For now the great big thing is still. A massive mound, a heap in the centre of the Chamber of the House of Lords.

It has stopped, the great thing, and points every sharpness towards the one remaining Iremonger. It is the boy, the frail boy, blood down his side, tears on his face, so pale, such a little life left in that one. It makes me think of Albert again, I should perhaps even like to care for this poor child. He stands as tall as he can and walks a step, two, up to the great conglomeration. It is David and Goliath, but I fear for the ending so. I cannot bear to look, and yet I must for the sake of this stalwart child, one must. More than the unhappy Light Brigade is he to me at this moment, more than Wellington and all his swagger. I'll pass over Lord Cardigan and Lord Raglan, lose Gough, Cathcart, Canning and Burgoyne in favour of this single child, standing before a poised army.

It has begun spitting at him, throwing out the sharp objects. I know this behaviour now, it seems to do this before it pounces; the horrid thing to play with him so, he is cut on his face, in his ripped clothes, blood down his side, but he still stands, he even moves a step forward, and another. He stands as tall as he can, perhaps he seems a little older now.

He is speaking to it. Whoever is this child?

Clod and Plug

'I am Clod. Clod the fool. Clod the simpleton. You are all in there, I do hear you all. Please don't spit so, it hurts, you see. I do hear you, I do hear you all. Oh the great agony of objects. I'm coming forward now, another step.'

It spits some more, an awl drills into my hand, an iron tumbles to my thigh, but I go forward another step.

'I must earn my trousers,' I say.

A pocket knife is launched from inside it and rips my ear.

'Hallo, Lucy, you're in there somewhere I know, and I love you.'

I go forward another step. What windows have remained shatter now, and burst inwards because of the fire that so, so wants to come in to us. But I must focus now, I must be more focused and thinking and feeling than ever I was before. Another step.

A chair kicks me, some chests spit their drawers at me but I manage to push them down. Another step. I am so close to it now, it is but a few inches ahead of me and may collapse upon me and suffocate me as it did to Grandfather, but not yet, it has not yet. I lift my hand up towards it, it backs away a little and shrieks and whirls and clatters inside.

I have a bullet within me, put there by my cousin. Such fury in him, because I was the one who turned his toastrack. Yes, I do understand now, it was I that did it. All along the answer was there, if I had only fathomed it. And if I did it once then perhaps I might again. I do begin to comprehend, I must have done it in my upset in the first London, yes London, it is called London, yes in that first London house, to that bullying red-haired servant's birth object. And so why not again? Why not a hundred times, a hundred thousand? Again and again.

I put my hand closer.

I touch it. It recoils but does not fall. I put my hand in it, deep, deeper, up to my elbow, up to my shoulder, up to my chest, I feel about inside it and how it chatters and moans. I feel for it, I search for it, my hands so ripped and bleeding; where is it, where, where, come, come, do come now.

I feel a chain. I pull on it, I pull and pull.

My bloody hand is back out now and with both hands do I pull and pull and pull upon this chain, it is so long and rusted, made of so many different links. The Gathering goes wild and shifts and screams, and spins hurriedly about. Still I pull, I pull and pull and pull, it screams and spits as I pull now, now. We may all exist together, I think we can. Come back, come back. Let me feel you.

'My plug, my plug,' I say. 'Give me back my plug! Surrender it, I do command you. For I am Clod, and I know things!'

Still I pull, still it tugs back, it screeches and moans and loathes to give it up.

But I have it now! The chain is coming to the end; I pull, pull, pull out my plug, I tug it out!

And it comes!

Falling through the great collection is not a small, universal bath plug made of finest India rubber, but it is hair I have hold of, human hair, and out comes a child, about ten years of age, and his name is –

'James Henry Hayward, James Henry Hayward.'

And with that boy on the ground now all the mound, as if in a horror of the sight, heaves upwards, it lurches and shrieks and cries shrilly, bits banging together, such clattering, such a knell, like all of London's bells calling out at once – and then it stops and then, oh then, just then it stays still and it tumbles in a great smashing to the ground.

Not one object now, not one heaving collection of things, but many separate things, each its own thing and these things on the ground, here and there thickly about, do spin and rattle

of their own force and they do, oh they do one and all, grow up now, grow and suffer their change, and out of them, out of the massing: the people, the people come. Oh the people come back. All, all tumbled back into people. And all in their confused heaps do call, cry, whisper, shout, mutter, murmur, weep, sob, talk out their own names,

James Henry Hayward. Eleanor Cranwell. Perdita Braithwaite. Gloria Emma Utting. Percy Hotchkiss . . . Emma Jenkins, Sybil Booth, Lester Ritts, Mary Ann Stark, Giles Bickleswaite, Theobald Villiers, Elsie Bullard, Leona Rice, Lloyd Walters, Elliot Murney, Dorothea Towndell, Matthew Stokes . . . Valerie Turner. Augusta Ingrid Ernesta Hoffmann. Little Lil. Lieutenant Simpson. Polly. Mr Gurney . . . Alice Higgs. Mark Seedly. Amy Aiken. Geraldine Whitehead.

And

'Lucy Pennant. Lucy Pennant.'

As if in answer to the flaming of her own dear hair, the flames fall into the Chamber. The flames seize the wooden panels and lap them up, burn the benches, lick the carpet, swarm one and all, all over.

'Oh dear,' I say, 'it's fearful hot.'

And then on top of that a terrible, thick awful suffocating stench, not of burning, of burnt things, but a stronger, all-encompassing reek of filth and excrement, of all foul things, and then a great explosion of dirt comes over us, filth, swamped with filth, and the hiss of the fire going out.

'Lucy Pennant, swidge, Lucy,' says Lucy.

The Queen as witness to the source of the smell
The Chamber of Lords is covered in effluent. Every inch of it, and my person too. There is a strange new giant come into the room, he seems the filthiest creature that ever can be conceived, like some dirt scraped up from the very bottom of hell.

'Bin,' he cries and indeed he has emptied a bin, a bin no doubt the size of all London over us, but it has saved us, I do feel.

'Late. Am I?'

Lucy trying to speak
'Lucy Pennant! Lucy Pennant! Binadit!'

'Benedict please to call.'

'Lucy. Benedict.'

'Botton?'

All around every one of us is covered in dirt, in rubbish and foul muck. The Queen has horse dung about her. The very Queen.

But beneath all the dirt and grit the Queen is clapping. And they are all clapping now, like we were in the theatre and the curtain's just come down.

But Clod, he falls back then, Clod, he hits the floor, poor sack of Clod, bleeding so. It was all too much, too much for his punctured frame.

The Queen's speech to Parliament
'Help! Help! Someone help him!'

CURTAIN DOWN

A New Home

Statement of a Londoner, concluding the narrative

I have thick red hair that shall not be tamed and a long face and a nose that points upwards. My eyes are green with flecks in them, but that's not the only place I'm dotted. There's punctuation all over me. I'm freckled and spotted and moled and bruised and I have scabs all over my face and hands. My teeth are not white at all. One tooth is lost. I'm being honest. I shall finish up everything exactly how it is and not tell lies but stay with the actual always. As much as ever I can. I'm doing my best. My name is Lucy Pennant, this was my story, and it was others' too.

I live in London these days, I may walk about where I like, there's no one that pulls me down any more, nor tells me I cannot go here nor either there. If there are walls then I may step around them, or go through the gate same as anyone. The sun comes up these days, not very confident, it is true, but there is a marked difference between morning and night.

I live with Iremongers and Foulshammers, all those that are left of us. We have a dwelling here that is our own, hard by Kings Cross it is, no palace, for certain. Our home is in an old schoolhouse and church that stands within Saint Giles Cemetery, a closed cemetery it was, by which they mean a full one, but they opened it up a little for us, it is just by the Royal Veterinary College and the St Pancras Workhouse. It is fitting enough that Giles is the saint we've been grouped with, he is the patron saint of cripples, you see, and of convulsions and of childhood terrors. There's quite a number of us that live here, we residents, we have made it our mission not to have servants but that each takes his turn and is as important as any other. It is a social experiment, I dare say. Blood is all mixed up here and we don't much talk about it. We have a shop here at Saint Giles and it is open five days a week, ten a.m. until three p.m., you may visit us here if you like.

We do a brisk business, there's never an end of it really, queues down the Pancras Road some mornings, slackened off a bit lately, but we ebb and flow in popularity, sometimes we have very smart ladies and gentlemen, very posh, others it's ragpickers, all may come in, we're not particular.

It is a noisy house, be warned of that if you intend to come to us, for though we all live together and do get along mostly, still there are those of us that arrived very young from the Gathering in Parliament. There is our youngest, Jack Pike, who once was a cuspidor, was kept living in that great breathing of objects, even after his own master was crushed. He is a fat little babe who was born with twelve teeth already in his gob and he does bite and chew at anything and will not be stopped. There's Gloria Emma Utting, who was once a doily and is a trouble to us, no doubting, such a forceful little girl with great buck teeth who thinks she knows the world, she is being looked after by the care of Eleanor Cranwell. It is Eleanor indeed who assists in our school room, she and a former music stand called Janey Cunliffe, the best of friends. They are the only ones of us that are not from Foulsham but are counted as part of the family nonetheless. There's one other teacher, but I shall come to her in a little moment.

Some of the old family are still alive. There are some of the cousins, Ormily, Ugh and Flip and Neg, who were Tummis's siblings. Aliver Iremonger is the oldest of us that is left, and he looks after our health and is very solicitous to his new friend Percy Hotchkiss, who was a pair of forceps before now. They are often out, those two, gone to watch a dissection or some such at Guy's Hospital. When Aliver isn't off with Percy he is generally beside Ada Cruickshanks, whom I know well enough now. We did fight each other so, she and I, we both wanted some life. She has a certain fear of flames, which is hardly to be wondered over, and I light all her candles for her and put a frosted glass shield over them. She is very frail but is still with us; though Pinalippy struck all the matches, still the box was left over. Much of her body is calcified and it is the very devil to move some of her limbs, as if they had decided not to be living any more, but inside that hard exterior is some life and living. Ada is journeyed around in a wheelchair and from that mobile seat she does help instruct the classroom. We do look at each other so, Ada and I, and do hold hands and marvel that we are both here at once. I sometimes help her in the schoolroom. What students there are! Dear Alice Higgs is a very smart child though one may call her skittish; she was once Rosamud Iremonger's doorhandle, she fears to open doors now and they must be opened for her. And then there is James Henry Hayward with all his plugs; he has a great collection of them, it seems to help him, this gathering up of plugs, as if each of them were members of his own lost family that never made it out of Foulsham, the poor Hayward family of ratcatchers. It is a hard business stopping him from trapping the rats outside in the old cemetery. For there are many of them, and they do come to visit.

We feed them, our rats. I shall not be cruel to them. There may be no doubt that many of them that come are of the old family, and could not get back into human shape. It is very hard for them. There's one with very ground teeth that I am almost certain is Claar Piggott the old housekeeper. How that rat hissed and bit at me at first but I fed it and it kept coming back and now it sits in my lap and weeps a little there.

I think we do look after things in a different way from other households, here in Saint Giles. We do take care with what we handle; true, there are times when one of us has a panic and fury, and in those moments must smash a deal of china because they are so sad and confused. We cannot perhaps be blamed. We have lost so many things, you see, so many things and people. There has been a search around Parliament for a letter opener knife that was a young hero man called Alexander Erkmann who was known as the Tailor in Foulsham, but he has not been found. There were some link boys who swore they saw the strangest fight of their lives, on the day of the Opening of Parliament. There was, they do swear it, a battle between a very short squat man and a very tall long one and these two did fight each other so mercilessly for so long that they did thoroughly murder each other. It's such a sadness really, when you think of it, when a person and his object cannot get along.

Then just the other day we heard this noise coming from the nursery:

'Rippit! Rippit!'

We rushed in, fearing the worst, fearing that our youngest must be in danger. But it was only Perdita Braithwaite – that was once Ormily's watering can – playing with a toy frog. You pull a cord out of the tin frog and it makes this sound:

'Rippit, Rippit.'

Gave us all quite a scare.

Parliament was in ruins. Curious thing is, they're saying somehow that it had come away from its foundations, that the whole building had shunted several feet. Nothing to explain it, they say. One scientist called John Tyndall reported that all the north bank of London has been tugged towards the Thames, several miles along it. Like the city was moving, living, shifting. Or like Clod had grabbed it and tugged it all by himself. They're building the Houses back now, it shall be up again in time for the Opening of Parliament next year. We have been pardoned. There shall be no prosecution against us, they are saying it never happened, all the Gathering and stuff, nonsense, tricks, but they let us live now and that I suppose is the miracle. They call it a terrible storm, an awful freak storm. And so they have pardoned us. But what I wonder at is, have we pardoned them? We shan't be invited to the Opening of the new Parliament. Can't say I'm surprised really, we are rather a dirty lot after all, can't seem to help it. It's in our blood I suspect. Still, without rubbish we'd all die, everyone knows that. There's a heap we've been given too, a small enough one, butts onto the Great National Railway's coal depot. That's where Ben lives now.

He has a little cottage there but prefers to sleep in the open or beneath his heap; he is pining for Irene Tintype. We have never been able to find her, we have looked and shall continue to. There are many leathers still living about London, hundreds I should think. Whenever we come upon one, we leave them alone. The old family lied to Clod about how the leathers came to be, they took the years from children of Foulsham, and in London they took the breath from their own servants to make them. I shouldn't think they thought twice about doing it.

Some of the house that Clod and Ben and Eleanor hid up in has been moved to Ben's heap. It all came down, great big bang it made when it fell over. Ben likes to be amongst the place where last he was with the leather Irene Tintype. Sometimes we bring him into Saint Giles with us and we tug some of the things from him and give him a good clean up.

For my own part, for my own terror, my clothes now are fastened by clasps, I do not have truck with buttons now if I may help it, they give me a nasty turn.

I do take lessons too. Of a kind. It's Otta Iremonger that gives them to me. We sit at the kitchen table, there's a teacup there. It is the only thing on the table and, with encouragement from Otta, I ask the teacup to move. For many weeks we have sat here like this, Otta and I, and I have whispered, shouted, cried at the teacup to move a little on its own. And it was so stubborn, the cup was. But Otta keeps me at it. And just last Thursday I moved it! It turned around so that the handle, which was initially turned away from me, journeyed about until it was pointing at me! I had such a feeling then!

'I did that!' I cried.

'No,' says Otta, 'the cup did it; you just asked it right.'

It is not, I do learn, it is not blood, it is concentration that may move a cup.

She's all right, is Otta, she comes and goes. She likes to be this and that and here and there, a seagull one day, a fox another. But mostly she looks after her brother Unry who would like to fit in, but he never knows what nose or ears to wear, he doesn't really understand who he is. We encourage him to leave his snouts and lugs behind and walk about us as he truly is, snoutless and lugless, but he is too shy to do it.

Rowland Cullis was to be hanged. He had been seen shooting a man, and that, they said, was called plain murder and that they could not pardon. So just as we were so happy to see our ones from Foulsham freed from the Mill Bank Penitentiary and back amongst us, we were miserable to see Rowland going in. I told the police that he was trying to do good but they wouldn't hear of it. I wrote to the Queen, who was only happy enough to support us on other issues, but this time she said it was beyond her control, she has no power. I wrote to Mr Disraeli and he wrote back that it was a matter of law, and so Rowland must to the hangman. But what about all the people of Foulsham that died, who is to hang for that? And Mr Disraeli – being one of the ones that signed for Foulsham's destruction – he wrote that that was not the same thing at all. They make no sense, these people.

In the end Otta went to Mill Bank, the night before Rowland was to be hanged. She went in as a mouse and no one did notice. She told him he must be a toastrack again. He said he was Rowland. And that he was proud to be Rowland and would never be a toastrack again, even if he should swing for it.

'Very well then,' said Otta, 'do swing for it then. For as a toastrack I may carry you safe out of here, but as a Rowland I may never get you through the bars.'

'I shall not do it!' he cried.

'You shall, and I'll help you.'

'I am Rowland Cullis!'

He wouldn't do it. He wouldn't give up his name. He was Rowland Cullis and he said he'd never be anything else again. They hanged him next morning.

The link boys have been made part of the police force under Inspector Harbin, who is promoted Superintendent now. He told me he tried to kill me in Parliament. Let's not make it personal, I told him. Rotten shot. Who was it that shot little Molly Porter, I asked him. He tells me he does not know. I want her revenged, I say. Policemen, he says, have died too.

Augusta Ingrid Ernesta Hoffmann, quite the most beautiful woman I have ever seen, left us to go back to Germany where she was born before she came over to London and was taken by the Iremonger family when still a girl and made the old woman's birth object. She was the only one of us who chose to go and we were all sorry for it. Though, the wonderful news is, that she is coming back and soon. She could find none of her relatives, they had all died and faded during the years she was a marble mantelpiece. And when she comes back we shall travel a little, she has promised. Augusta has such a yearning to see the world. We shall go down to Brighton and shall inspect the sea.

There you are, you see, a happy family.

There I was forgetting our shop.

People do come to us with their particular pieces and we do help them out if we can. I have seen a duchess holding up a very dirty flannel with all the care she might take hold of a baby, I have seen a laundry woman holding aloft a coronet with wonder and shock.

'I always knew she was special, no one else could see it.'

There have been so many people bringing their particular things to us. The disease, it spread all over London, it came inside poor hovels and great palaces, it entered drawing rooms and doss houses, it sat with equal leisure in Turkish baths as outhouses. It could arrive all of a sudden in a prison cell or in a judge's seat, it would strike whole houses or factories, or visit a school and take down only one single child. It did seem to stop after the business at Parliament, then there were fewer cases, less and less, and so then seemed to cease all together, and so there are fewer visitors to our particular shop.

Should you have lost someone, should a person have gone of a sudden, and should you have picked up some unfamiliar item in any of the rooms of your lives, then you may bring it to us. Do not be afraid to, you shall not be laughed at here. I have seen people lugging great sculptures, I have seen people with mops and chamber pots and enema tubes. I have seen it all. We never do judge what you bring to us, but take all very carefully and do what we may for it. We have all, after all, lost so much.

Sometimes though we know various objects are people turned, then the bringer will only wish for confirmation and will not want to have the person restored to them.

'Not yet,' one bruised woman told us – the dog collar she brought was her husband – 'not just yet, maybe another day.'

There were one hundred and four convicts that caught the disease, that is the number we were given, we suspect there were more, and 'the Crown', they say, does not permit us to visit those objects, which are still kept under lock and key.

To begin with there were so many that we were able to help, so many could be brought back, but now it seems people have stopped coming to us, and do worry about us, and think we might be evil, though all we ever do is help. There are gates around the old cemetery to keep us from harm; at times I fear we are being locked up again. We do not steal the things brought to us, we wish to make that very clear.

Sometimes people come to us – oftener with nicer things – and they say to us, of a certainty, or in shaking, hopeful voices,

'I think this is Willy, it is Willy is it not?'

But it is not Willy at all, it is only a jug.

'This is Henrietta Carberry, my niece, aged twelve, it is, you know.'

But it is not Henrietta, it is only a bicycle saddle.

On those occasions he says to them very gently, 'I am sorry, I am so sorry.'

Oh then, didn't I say? Have I not mentioned? It is Clod that does it. Clod himself.

He does it very gentle. I'm really very proud of him. He gets stronger by the day and does even walk a little now and he eats some more, and likes to wander around London through maps and guidebooks. Nearly died on me. All the Queen's horses and all her men came to sew him up or so it seemed to me. They wouldn't let me see him, not at first, until he set the hospital upside down and so then they let me. He shall always walk with a cane. It is a nice cane, with a good silver handle, made of malacca wood.

'What is your walking stick's name, Clod?'

'Walking stick,' he tells me gently.

Now I may kiss him whenever I please, and I do, I do very often. I'll never let him go again; to see him each time is the miracle. We have grown up taller after all our troubles and shall probably not grow any more. Sometimes we go out on a little wander around the cemetery and are seen together there, a golden half-sovereign and a clay button.

If you have something, some thing you're unsure about, some object you have, bring it by, why don't you?

THE
END

Acknowledgements

I would like to thank the incredible team at Hot Key, for all their work to make the Iremonger series possible. I am extremely fortunate to have had the help of Sara O'Connor who started the whole thing off, Jan Bielecki for making these books look so smart, and for the sharp eyes and great wisdom of Jenny Jacoby. Tracy Carns has championed the Iremongers in the US for Overlook Press and she's been very wonderful, as has Hadley Dyer for HarperCollins in Canada. I cannot thank Grasset and Pierre Demarty enough for welcoming Les Ferrailleurs to France, and Elisabetta Sgarbi at Bompiani in Italy has kept faith in me over so many years that I owe her a very great debt. These brilliant people have been essential in getting this trilogy out in the world: Louise Brice, Alba Donati, Midori Furuya, Allyssa Kasoff, Emma Matthewson, Olivia Mead, Sergio Claudio Perroni, Jet Purdie, Alice Seelow, Michael Taeckens, Josie Urwin and Tom Witcomb.

I am very indebted to the early readers of this book: Jenny and Emma, the extraordinary Margo Rabb who read it with such brilliance and at no notice whatsoever, and Isobel Dixon

– who has been with me from the start of my writing career, is an amazing agent, a dear friend, and is the reader every writer would dream of. Last of all, and most of all, I would like to thank my wife Elizabeth and my children, Gus and Matilda, who keep me going and who are very marvellous.

Edward Carey

Edward Carey is a playwright, novelist and illustrator. He has worked for the theatre in London, Lithuania and Romania and with a shadow puppet master in Malaysia. He has written two illustrated novels for adults — OBSERVATORY MANSIONS and ALVA AND IRVA — both have been translated into many different languages. He lives in Austin, Texas, where he wrote the *Iremonger Trilogy* because he missed feeling cold and gloomy. Follow Edward on Twitter: @EdwardCarey70 or find out more about his books at edwardcareyauthor.com.

BLOOD OF

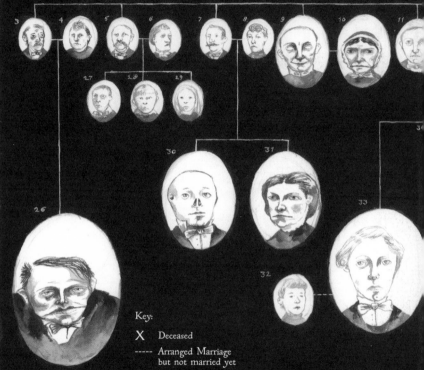

Key:

X Deceased

---- Arranged Marriage
but not married yet

<table>
<tr><td>1.</td><td>Owner Umbitt</td></tr>
<tr><td>2.</td><td>Owneress Ommaball Oliff</td></tr>
<tr><td>3.</td><td>Governor Hibbit X</td></tr>
<tr><td>4.</td><td>Governess Cuffrinn</td></tr>
<tr><td>5.</td><td>Governor Itchard X</td></tr>
<tr><td>6.</td><td>Governess Oodiff</td></tr>
<tr><td>7.</td><td>Governor Ulung</td></tr>
<tr><td>8.</td><td>Governess Moyball</td></tr>
<tr><td>9.</td><td>Governor Idwid</td></tr>
<tr><td>10.</td><td>Ifful the Night</td></tr>
<tr><td>11.</td><td>Timfy the Sneak</td></tr>
</table>

<table>
<tr><td>12.</td><td>Governor Churls</td></tr>
<tr><td>13.</td><td>Governess Sorer</td></tr>
<tr><td>14.</td><td>Milcrumb the Insignificant X</td></tr>
<tr><td>15.</td><td>Rosamud</td></tr>
<tr><td>16.</td><td>Doctor Aliver</td></tr>
<tr><td>17.</td><td>Jocklun X</td></tr>
<tr><td>18.</td><td>Pottrick the Unhappy</td></tr>
<tr><td>19.</td><td>Pottrickier</td></tr>
<tr><td>20.</td><td>Crustifer</td></tr>
<tr><td>21.</td><td>Pomular</td></tr>
</table>